The Soul of

JUSTICE

SEVEN VIRTUES RANCH ROMANCE BOOK 5

BECKY DOUGHTY

BraveHearts
Press

The Soul of Justice: Seven Virtues Ranch Romance Book 5
Copyright © 2020 by Becky Doughty

Published by BraveHearts Press

For author information: BeckyDoughty.com

978-1953347282

JUSTICE

"Justice cannot be for one side alone,
but must be for both."

Eleanor Roosevelt

ONE

"WHAT DO YOU THINK?" Courage asked, her voice quiet, but full of hope. She sat on her bed with her back against her headboard, her broken leg propped up on a stack of clean laundry she'd just folded. "We could really make this work. With your head for business and my attention to details when it comes to the daily grind of things?"

"Coupled with our mad skills, of course," Justice teased, not wanting to burst her twin's bubble. It was obvious that Courage had given the idea a lot of thought, but it felt totally out of the blue for Justice. And with everything else on her shoulders right now, she wasn't sure she could take on even the thought of one more monumental change. Between the minefield that her relationship with Brandon had become, the looming rodeo circuit road trip she and Brandon would have to somehow endure since Courage wouldn't be with them to act as buffer or mediator, and the fact that The Twisted Sisters act was going to be one, single, solitary sister for the foreseeable future, Justice wondered how she found the wherewithal to get out of bed each morning.

At this point, she'd be happy if Brandon would just agree to a truce. Forgiveness and anything else he might someday be able to stomach could come later. Whatever it took for him to be able to share a truck cab with her for several hours a day; they didn't even have to talk. In fact, she'd sleep while he drove, and vice versa. But there was no way she could endure hundreds of miles with him side-eyeing her with judgment and distaste, or worse, his eyes going glassy with such intense emotional pain, she thought her heart would break in two and stop beating altogether.

How many times would he ask her to explain herself? "I don't get it. Why *him*? Of all people, Justice, why Tanner Ogdon?" Then he'd shake his head and turn away.

He wasn't looking for answers. He was just taking yet another opportunity to wave her dirty laundry in her face. To guilt her into feeling worse than she already did. To shame her into thinking that she was no longer worthy of being treated with dignity. At least not by him.

"Yes, coupled with our mad skills, sister of mine," Courage agreed with a chuckle. "And you know if we start putting the word out now for students, by the time we open, we'd already have a growing clientele."

She was right—a trick riding academy run by The Twisted Sisters? Folks would come out of the wood work for them. Their email inbox was constantly flooded with requests for private lessons for young girls and boys chasing the glitz and glamour of performing gymnastics on horseback. Programs all over the country sought them out for special demonstrations and guest lectures on trick riding. They'd been interviewed on PBS and some of the regional television sports networks, and in the rodeo circle, they were a household name. But between family, college, their jobs at Schooners, and the myriad of shows they performed all year long, they rarely had time to take on anything extra.

Sure, they'd talked about the possibility of giving lessons one day... when they retired.

For Justice, that had been a rather far-fetched 'one day,' though.

With Courage incapacitated after her near-fatal fall a month earlier, Justice was having to carry the torch alone this summer. They'd already committed to some of the bigger rodeos along the circuit, plus a few others that were personal favorites. Now it rested on her shoulders to represent them out there, all on her own. She wore a brave face about it all, especially in front of Courage, but she was pretty sure her twin saw right through the facade and wasn't fooled one bit.

Justice was trying to keep her head up, but it was exhausting. Especially since Brandon was being so cruel to her. He'd asked for honesty, and she'd given it to him. Now he was punishing her for it.

"Daddy plans to break ground on his new log cabin this fall. He told Joe and me he's going to take his time on the build, but he hopes to move into by Christmas next year, so we have lots of time to do our research, work out the details, and get things up and running. It'll coincide perfectly with Cord's plans for the Whispering Hills Rodeo grand opening. We could plan our own at the same time and capitalize on all those starry-eyed kids who come to see the shows."

"Now whose got a head for business?" Justice wasn't going to give her sister an answer, not tonight, no matter how much Courage wanted one. A riding academy definitely sounded plausible, at least from a distance. A trick riding academy. Right there at Seven Virtues Ranch.

And why not? Faith, now married to Cord Overman, still ran her eighty head of Dexters on Seven Virtues pasture, but it wasn't like she didn't have options. In fact, Justice believed the only reason her oldest sister hadn't already transferred the herd over to Whispering Hills was due to their father. The cows gave Faith an excuse to check on Daddy while all the other sisters were out and about doing their busy lives. In turn, monitoring the herd gave him something to keep him busy during the long hours he spent alone at the ranch.

In other words, Faith was keeping the old man occupied.

Jedediah Goodacre knew it, too, and that was one of the main reasons he'd gone and purchased his own property just across the road this last year. To get out from under Faith's sometimes claustrophobic nurturing.

Which meant he'd be handing over the operation of the ranch to his daughters at some point in the near future. Maybe the deed, too.

Faith might want it, or at least a part of it, but she didn't need it. She was now part-owner—by marriage—of the vast Whispering Hills Ranch next door, and she and Cord, along with their kids and dogs lived in the gorgeous new home Cord had built for them last year. Faith didn't need Seven Virtues Ranch; there was acreage to spare at the Overman's place.

Hope? Nope. She was the proud new owner of the Plumwood Hollow Veterinarian Hospital, the savior of the animal kingdom, and married, somewhat ironically, to Plumwood Hollow's big, brawny butcher, Levi Cordova. They had a sprawling place of their own only ten minutes' drive from the hospital, and Hope worried that distance was too far. There was no way she'd even consider moving all the way out to the ranch.

Charity was good with the cows, but that was because of her gentle nature, not due to any passion for ranching like Faith had. She had picked up and moved next door to Whispering Hills, too, having fallen head over heels with Frank Overman after he'd come home to heal from a mission gone awry in the Middle East. Together, they were converting the original ranch house where he'd grown up into a bed and breakfast. In the meantime, Charity, who was truly a "hostess with the mostest," ran her growing catering business out of the state-of-the-art kitchen that Cord had upgraded for her when he hired her on to be the ranch cook.

Abby already had plans for getting the heck out of Dodge in a few weeks. She'd been scoped out by a bigwig Nashville musician who took up-and-coming no names under his wing with the goal of turning them into superstars. He'd seen her play at The Smokehouse several months ago, and she'd been invited to join him and his entourage on the road for his summer tour. Once they got back to town, he'd help her produce her first full album. It sounded a little too good to be true to Justice, but she'd taken a good look at the paperwork Abby brought home, and she couldn't find anything shady about it.

"Still don't like it," she'd told her father after handing it back to him. "The entertainment business is rife with one bad deal after another, Daddy, and her agent isn't big time. This may be only the first of many contracts she'll have to sign, and who knows what verbiage will get slipped in and out of them. She needs a real agent."

She'd told her youngest sister the same thing.

Regardless, Abby wasn't a rancher. She wasn't a real cowgirl, either, but she sure looked like one on stage. Yes, she rode a horse. She even owned one, although Jasmine, Faith and Cord's teenybopper, had pretty much taken over the care and feeding of Loki. Justice thought her niece was secretly hoping Abby would hand over Loki's reins to her, quite literally, when she moved away.

No, Abby wouldn't have any use for Seven Virtues, other than to have a roof over her head and a table to eat at when she came through town to visit family and friends. Abby was headed for Nashville, and it looked like she aimed for the move to be a permanent one.

Then there was Prudence. Dear, sweet, and a little otherworldly Prudence. Who knew what went on in that head of hers? She wasn't a rancher, either, not by a long shot, although she did have an enormous Andalusian she'd rescued. The huge beast followed her around like a puppy dog. That said, of all of the sisters, Prudence seemed by far, the least interested in ranching, and yet, almost three years after graduating from high school, she'd made no plans to move on. She worked part time downtown and had her own line of botanical body products she sold online, but other than using the horse and chicken manure to fertilize her herb and flower gardens, she didn't seem to have any use for the place. In fact, Prudence was worse than a kid when it came to doing her share of the chores around the place. She constantly had to be reminded to complete one task before waltzing off to do something else, her head full of poetry and pretty smells. Flighty as a feather, a flibbertigibbet, a regular Maria Von Trapp, they all called her. Prudence took it as a compliment.

Justice and Courage, however, were a different story. They had their own arena and barn at Seven Virtues where they trained and stabled their beautiful boys, Flash and Fire, Irish Sport horses who'd never known anything but a life of trick riding. They even had a separate pasture fenced off for their stallions since they'd opted not to turn them into geldings. There were a few too many lovely mares in the Goodacre's big barn to let the boys mingle without causing a raucous. The twins already had a huge stake in the ranch, and although their father would likely will the property in equal parts to all of his daughters, until he did so, it made good sense for Justice and her sister to continue using it for their needs.

Of course, Prudence could stay as long as she wanted, or needed, whichever the case may be. She could garden to her heart's delight for all Justice cared. And maybe she could help with keeping helicopter moms busy while the twins worked with the students.

It was a good idea, really. It made sense, especially if Courage was seriously considering retiring from the show itself.

The girls had talked a lot about the future of The Twisted Sisters since Courage's fall, and although Courage wasn't coming right out and saying so, Justice was pretty sure she was ready to get off the road for good. Courage was in love with a man who had roots deep in the soil of Plumwood Hollow, and it seemed certain there'd be a wedding soon, maybe even before the end of the year, if Joe Lynxwilder would just pop the question already. An academy would be a great way for Courage to stay plugged into the industry without having to leave home to perform. Her sister was really good at engaging with the crowds that came up after their shows to talk to them, and Justice could easily see her working with the younger kids who still had stars in their eyes about pretty costumes and prancing ponies.

She wasn't so sure about herself, though. She supposed she could handle the older students, those who were committed for the long haul, who were serious enough about the sport to be able to take constructive criticism without bursting into tears. But would that be enough of a contribution? In all honesty, it seemed like a much better fit for Courage.

Realistically, riding solo might just be a much better fit for Justice.

Except there was her career in law to consider. If honesty was the word of the day, there were times she asked herself why she was striving so hard in that direction. She loved certain aspects of the law, but others she hated. If she could figure out how to make enough money to pay off her school loans just doing contract law, she'd be happy. But in this small town, she'd be lucky to find enough of any kind of attorney work to pay off her school loans. Maybe the riding school could provide a better future for her.

"Give me some time to consider all of this, okay? Have you talked to Dad about it yet?"

Courage shook her head. "No. Just you. And Joe. Oh. And Sarah, too," she added a little sheepishly.

Justice was going to have to get used to Joe—and most likely the man's mother, too—being a member of their inner circle. Courage aimed to marry the man, and although the thought still sent a tiny frisson of envy up Justice's spine, she was happy for her twin.

Yes, she was envious. Not of Joe in particular, although the handsome farmer did give off some pretty powerful strong and silent hero vibes that made folks want to lean into him. There'd been a time Justice thought maybe she'd lean into him, herself, this last year, especially with things so awful between her and Brandon.

"Why don't you talk to Dad about it while I'm gone, and I'll do some thinking during that same time." Justice sat on the edge of her own bed and studied her sister, a well of gratitude bubbling up inside her as she eyed Courage's elevated foot. Her injuries could have been so much worse, Justice was well aware, had it not been for the lightning quick efficiency of Brandon Stillwater and his crew. Because of them, she still had her sister. They still had each other.

The house was quiet with Abby in school and Prudence and Dad out in the gardens. They had the place to themselves for the time being. "It's a good idea, you know. A great idea." She tried to smile brightly, but the effort was wasted on Courage.

"Tell me what you really think," Courage said. "There's smoke coming out of your ears, the cogs are spinning so fast in that head of yours."

Justice shrugged. "Well, I think it's the right thing, the right fit for you, anyway. But it might not be the best idea for me. I love the adrenaline rush of performing; you know that. And you and I work well together, but we're sisters. Twins. Two halves of a whole. I don't know that I'd be good working with other people." She let out a rueful snort. "Especially other people's kids."

"Of course you would" Courage interjected. "You're great with the customers at Schooners, with the families who come in."

"Ah, but I'm feeding them, not teaching them to hang upside down from a pommel." Justice countered. "Big difference. They order what they want at Schooners. They'd have to follow my orders and do what I want if I took them on as students. Like I said. Big difference."

Courage didn't argue, and for that, Justice was grateful. Her sister knew her better than anyone else in the world. Which meant that Courage knew she wasn't just trying to put her off or take the easy way out by simply shooting down the idea. Justice really did need time to process everything.

"Well, I'm relieved. I was half afraid you'd just say 'no' outright," Courage said with a gentle smile. Everything about Courage was gentle these days. "So yes, take the idea on the road and mull it over. Maybe stick a bug in a few people's ears and see what kind of responses you get."

Justice nodded slowly. "Yeah, maybe I'll do that."

After a prolonged silence, Courage spoke again. "Do you want to talk about you and Brandon now?"

TWO

"There is no me and Brandon," Justice said, flopping back on her bed, then rolling to her side and tucking her pillow under her head.

"There will always be a you and Brandon," Courage insisted, but her brow furrowed with concern in spite of her flippant response.

Justice blinked hard. Her eyes stung with unshed tears and her throat constricted so that she couldn't speak.

"Sure, Brandon can come across as a big flirt," Courage said, her voice subdued under the sudden gravity of their conversation. "But you know as well as I do that it's all for show. It makes him bigger than life out there in the arena, right? He's handsome and fearless, and that smile—."

"I know," Justice grumbled, cutting her off, not wanting to think about Brandon's smile. She scowled through her tears. "I know, okay? He's beautiful in every way. What woman out there wouldn't drool over him?"

"I wouldn't," Courage declared, shaking her head slowly, almost indifferently.

"Yeah, well, that's probably a good thing, since Joe might take issue with you drooling over some other man."

"Joe." She murmured his name like a caress, and sighed, a faint blush creeping up her neck. Then she lifted her chin and narrowed her eyes at Justice. "Don't distract me. And you're missing the point," she said, bringing the conversation back around to the topic at hand. "In here?" She patted her chest over her heart. "In here, Brandon's a true-blue boy next door in every way."

"Literally," Justice muttered, glaring up at the planked ceiling, her eyes following the familiar patterns in the wood grain overhead. Brandon was a paramedic who also worked with the horses over at Whispering Hills Ranch. He'd moved into one of their newly-built cowboy cabins right before Thanksgiving last year. A move that had made him much harder to avoid.

"Yes, literally. The boy next door who's in love with you. And," Courage added, holding up a finger to waylay any rebuttal Justice might offer. "Whether you're willing to admit it or not, you're the girl next door who's in love with him."

When Justice didn't deny or agree with her, she continued, albeit a little hesitantly.

"Look. Don't hate me, okay? I love you—I love you both. You know that, right? And I'm not going to take sides because I don't know enough of the details. Nor do I need to know them all to know that you two are both miserable. And you're making everyone else miserable, too." Courage had recovered enough from her life-threatening injuries to be able to come home to the ranch, and over the last two weeks, the twins had spent long hours talking about the roller coaster ride they were both on. In a sense, they were catching up on lost time. Trouble had been brewing between the sisters for months, but Courage's fall had helped put things into perspective.

Today, the subject of Brandon had come up yet again, and Justice was on the verge of telling Courage everything. It was tearing her up to keep it inside when the two of them had shared all the ups and downs of life for the last quarter of a century. But part of her felt like she owed Brandon at least a modicum of the dignity she'd taken from him. If keeping their struggles under wraps until he'd had a chance to deal with things helped in any way, then that's what she'd do.

Then again, Brandon of all people knew that there were no secrets between the twins, so why would he assume Justice hadn't already disclosed all to Courage? Wasn't his withdrawal from both their lives evidence that he thought Courage knew—perhaps had known all along—about what had gone down? So was Justice's discretion really out of respect for Brandon?

Or was it self-preservation that had her so reticent to admit her shameful failure to her sister? Could she bear to see disappointment and judgment transform Courage's gentle features the way they had Brandon's?

She should just spill the beans and get it over with.

"I could never hate you, Courage, no matter what you say to me," Justice said, not looking at her sister. "In spite of the way I act sometimes, I hope you know that I love you, even when I'm angry at you."

Would Courage say the same after Justice told all? Oh, she had no doubt her twin *loved* her unconditionally, but Justice also knew that you could love a person and still judge them through the lenses of your own perceptions and standards. And Courage's standards were right up there with the heavenly beings.

Up until last year, Justice's standards had been practically above reproach as well. No shades of gray. No muddied water. No second guessing. No indecision or wishy-washy sentiments. And no regrets.

Up until last year. Last summer. Last July.

Up until the last weekend at Greeley Stampede.

"Say what you need to say," Justice prompted, not sure which of them she was ordering to speak.

Courage sighed. "Okay. It's just that—well, you're the one who changed the rules without telling everyone, and then you got mad when no one knew how the game was being played. Now that you've finally filled Brandon in on things, you're upset because he's not responding the way you want him to."

"You're not telling me anything I don't know." The words came out petulant, and Justice closed her eyes, hating how she sounded.

"Well, I wish you'd tell me something I don't know," Courage shot back, a note of frustration tingeing her words. "I'm kinda tired of this game, or whatever it is you're playing, Justice. Mainly because I don't know the rules, either." She lifted both hands in the air in a gesture of helplessness. "I want to help, but I don't know how."

Justice opened her mouth to defend her decision to stay mum, but Courage held up a hand before she could speak.

"And please don't tell me there's nothing I can do to help. That's just your stubborn pride talking. You're not an island, you know. You always think you can manage everything life throws at you on your own, without help. But there isn't a single one of us who can get through life without needing anyone, not even you."

Justice pressed her lips together in a grim line and glanced over at Courage who had paused in her reprimand. There were tears in her sister's eyes when she managed to speak again.

"The thought of sending you two off on the road together, knowing how rough things are between you right now? It's tearing me up."

Justice shoved her pillow away with her elbow, propping her head on her hand instead. "I know," she murmured, fighting back her own welling emotions. She would not cry. She'd already shed more tears in the last month than she had in the last five years combined, she was quite certain. "I really am sorry."

Courage was silent for a few more moments. Then she slid forward on her bed, lowering her braced leg to the floor with a quiet grunt. It wasn't the ankle that bothered her, she insisted, but her broken ribs and the subsequent collapsed lung she was still recovering from. Even taking a deep breath made her wince.

Finally, she said, "Look, I know I said I wouldn't press you for information, but this has gone too far, Justice. Brandon will hardly look me in the eye these days, and that's on the rare occasion I happen to see him, like at church or if I go over to Whispering Hills to visit Faith and Charity and the gang. He hasn't even bothered to come by here to see me since I've been home, and that's not like him. A year ago, he would have been here every day, bringing me goofy get well gifts and cheap chocolate. Or just making fun of me for being such a klutz."

"I know," Justice said again, feeling small. "I think he thinks you knew what happened and kept everything from him, too." She grimaced and flopped back on her pillow again. "I'm so sorry I've put you right in the middle of things. My intention was just the opposite—by not telling you, I was hoping to keep you free of it all." She swiped at her eyes with the heels of her palms. "Everything is backfiring, Courage. I'm such an idiot. I've made such a mess of things."

"Then let me help you clean it up. Let me help you figure out how to set things right again. I can't stand by and do nothing, Justice. I just can't." Courage leaned forward to adjust the straps on the brace she wore, then gingerly pushed to her feet. With a hand for balance on the edge of the long dresser between the two beds, she crossed the room to lower herself to sit on the edge of Justice's bed. "Please talk to me."

Two hot tears tracked slowly from the corners of her eyes to run into the hair at her temples, but Justice didn't bother wiping them away. Could she let the words flow out of her uninterrupted as well?

"I hurt him so bad, and I don't think things will ever be okay between us again." Her words came out barely above a whisper, but she choked back the lump of shame that lodged in the back of her throat. "The irony is that now that I finally realize how much I care about him, I also know I have to let him go if that's what he really wants from me."

"What do you really want from him?" Courage asked.

"Nothing. Everything. I want him to forgive me. I want him to love me again. I want him to look at me the way he used to—before—before—." She broke off, a small, anguished sound escaping before she swallowed hard and closed her mouth.

"Then you need to fight for him, Justice. Don't give up on him. Don't let him run." Courage bumped her in the hip. "Scoot over," she said, then twisted carefully to bring her foot up on the bed before stretching out beside Justice. "And he *does* love you, remember?"

"That may not be enough anymore."

"Of course it is," Courage countered gently. She reached for Justice's hand and squeezed. "You're just going to have to remind him that love is worth fighting for. That you both are worth fighting for."

"But... I'm not so sure I am." Justice took a deep breath and blew it out, steeling herself for what came next. "I cheated on him, Courage. I betrayed him in the worst way imaginable."

The silence that followed her admission sounded cacophonous in her ears, and she closed her eyes so she wouldn't have to see the look on Courage's face.

"Are you talking about this thing with Joe? I'm pretty sure Brandon already knew about you pursuing Joe. I mean, you didn't try to hide it."

Justice cringed inwardly at the still fresh mortification that rose inside her over her past behavior toward the man Courage was now in a very serious relationship with. "This isn't about Joe."

"People make mistakes," Courage said after a brief pause. She sounded so kind, so sincere. "Even you. Maybe you need to start with forgiving yourself."

But until Brandon forgave her, how could she?

"It wasn't a mistake, though. I did it on purpose. I went out of my way to make it happen."

"Make what happen?" Courage's voice was still gentle, but there was a hollowness to it that echoed with sadness. "What happened, sissy?"

The childhood nickname broke Justice's resolve. The floodgates opened as everything she'd kept bottled up for almost a year spilled out.

THREE

They'd promised each other they'd wait. They'd keep it sacred. They'd save themselves for marriage. Neither of them came right out and said it, but the unspoken part of their vow—they'd save themselves for each other—was whispered by the leaves that danced and swayed around them. Beneath the canopy of the enormous weeping willow that stood sentry beside the pond at Reed Park, they'd pricked each other's palms with his pocket knife, and had made everything official with a blood oath. It was a wonder neither of them had succumbed to tetanus or some other terrible infection, considering all manner of things he'd used his trusty blade on before their little love ritual.

"You could strike her down with something now," Brandon muttered with a quick glance heavenward. He shook off the stab of shame that followed his bitter words.

How could she?

He simply couldn't get over it. He didn't want to get over it. He wanted to wallow in anger and bitterness. He wanted to rage at her until she somehow managed to undo what she'd done.

Except that there was no undoing it. There was no going back to before.

Brandon and the twins had been friends for as far back as he could remember. Then again, he had no desire to remember anything that happened before the girls swept into his world and knocked him on his backside. The Goodacre family with their bevy of oddly-named daughters had moved to Plumwood Hollow the summer before he and the twins started first grade. For reasons he couldn't understand back then, he'd teased them ferociously, incessantly. About their names, about being twins but looking nothing alike, about their weird clothes and Texas drawls. Because on the contrary, he'd found the sound of the two girls murmuring back and forth while ignoring him to be the most beautiful music in all the world, even at the tender age of six. So he did everything he could to keep them riled up just to keep them talking. He'd found them fascinating, mysterious, and something he could pin his focus on in a world that had spun out of control.

Shortly after school started, Faith, the oldest Goodacre sister, had invited him to walk home with them. They'd crossed paths a few times en route to and from school, and one day, while he paced them from about ten feet behind, he'd started singing a song he'd made up about twins being clowns and belonging in the circus. He'd worked on it all day and thought he'd been so clever, but when Faith stopped in her tracks and turned around to face him, his mind went completely blank. He froze, his mouth open mid-taunt. Faith planted a hand on her hip and glared down her long nose at him, and when his brain did start firing off intelligible commands, the first thought that came to him was, *Don't pee your pants in front of them.*

To his astonishment, Faith had nodded slowly and said, "Good song. You might be right about the whole circus thing. Have you seen Courage and Justice ride horses? They're learning to be trick riders." She'd turned to glance at the twins who stood just behind her, holding hands and studying him. "You two need to remember about the circus thing. It would be a good back up plan if the rodeo doesn't work out for you."

The twins didn't glare at him; they didn't seem mad at all. More curious than anything, they studied him like he was some strange species they were trying to figure out.

"You walk to and from school by yourself every day?" Faith had asked.

Brandon had nodded, and she'd nodded back, her eyes narrowing as she seemed to consider his response.

"Right," she'd said after a few moments of silence while he grew more and more self-conscious. "So listen, kid," Faith had continued, beckoning for him to come closer. "Since we're heading the same way at about the same time every day, how about we join forces and cover each others' backs? Safety in numbers and all that, you know? What do you say?"

He'd had no clue what she meant by that, but he'd nodded slowly, speechless over the remarkable turn of events.

"Great. One more thing," Faith said as he approached cautiously. She waved a hand in the twins' direction. "As you probably already know, I can't go to first grade with you guys, right? Well, since we're all looking out for each other now, I really need someone who can be my eyes and ears. Someone who can watch out for first grade bullies being mean to my sisters. I've heard there's this kid in their class who likes to pick on them. They say he doesn't even believe they're twins." She'd rolled her eyes and shook her head. "Crazy, right?"

"Crazy." Nodding, Brandon had agreed whole-heartedly, relief flooding over him that she didn't know he was the culprit. "And pretty stupid, too," he'd added, trying to sound appalled. He waved nervously at Courage and Justice, who both continued watching him, their expressions a little less curious, perhaps more resigned. "Hi," he'd said, the word coming out sounding like a question.

"Well, maybe not stupid," Faith had hedged. "I mean, he probably just thinks they're cute and is trying to get their attention. You know how boys can be."

Brandon had blushed hotly and shrugged, smart enough even back then to know that if he denied the accusation, he'd give himself away.

"So you watch out for them, okay? Let me know if anyone is picking on them." She lifted a fist and shook it threateningly.

"You should see what she did to the last guy who teased us." It was Justice, speaking directly to him for the first time, her voice serious, her brown eyes boring into his. Then she'd turned away from him, looped her arm through Courage's, and they'd all started off down the sidewalk together, with Faith asking all of them random questions about what it was like to be in first grade.

Years later, when he and the twins were young teenagers, Faith had retold the story over a Sunday Goodacre family dinner, and Brandon had finally seen it for what it was. How had he missed it? Not an invitation at all. Reverse psychology, Faith had called it. He'd been blindsided. He'd been duped. He'd been beguiled by the smooth-talking Goodacre sisters. And they'd sworn never to let him forget it.

Forget it? Not in a million years. It was the best thing that had happened to him up until that point in his short little life. He had been given a purpose. An important job to do: Defend the Goodacre twins. He was needed, valued, and trusted. Wanted.

Over the weeks that followed, it became apparent that the twins had made some kind executive decision about him, and when Justice handed him a hand-written invitation to their birthday party, he'd felt like he was standing at heaven's gate.

Until he remembered he'd have to come up with not one, but two birthday presents. For girls. He had no idea what girls wanted for their birthday. He'd reluctantly agreed to go, then made himself sick over the next several days as he racked his brains for something that he could present to the twins without embarrassing himself.

It was, in fact, Faith, who steered him in the right direction, and he'd fallen a little in love with the glorious and so grown up twelve-year-old that day.

"You look like you might have some Native American in you," she'd said, dropping to sit cross-legged on the ground beside him. School had just let out, and he'd raced ahead of the twins to get outside, the panic building inside him as the party loomed large and foreboding on the horizon. Three more days until Saturday, and if he couldn't come up with a gift idea, he'd have to come up with an excuse for bailing. He simply couldn't go empty-handed.

"My grandma is part Shawnee."

"Then so are you, right?" Faith had elbowed him in the side.

He'd answered with a shrug, unable to focus on anything except the whole gift thing. He turned his gaze to the doors of the school that stood open as kids streamed out into the sunny afternoon. The twins would appear any moment, he was certain, and surely, that afternoon they'd finally figure out that he was, indeed, nothing but a stupid kid.

"Did you make that?" Faith had interrupted his thoughts yet again with her question, pointing at the beaded cuff his mom had tied around his wrist before she left.

"No," he'd muttered, glancing down at the narrow band with its simple diamond pattern. "My mom did. She made tons of them." She'd made them whenever she was sad, or lonely, or worried. Mostly when she was sad. "But sometimes I helped her," he added, hoping to see the light of approval in Faith's eyes.

"Lots of them, hm?" Faith leaned in close to study the way the balled up beads on one end of the strap inserted into a loop on the other end to hold the piece in place. "Do you think she'd sell me one? It's really cool."

"She can't—" At a sudden thought, Brandon had snapped his gaze up to hers so quickly, he heard a tiny pop in the back of his neck. "Um, do you think Justice and Courage think it's cool, too?"

Faith nodded sagely. "I'm sure they do. Justice was talking about yours last night at dinner. That's why I—."

He'd cut her off by jumping to his feet and punching the air like a boxer he'd seen on television. Without explanation, he'd darted off across the lawn toward the front steps, then shouted over his shoulder at her, "I'll go find the twins!"

He never sold Faith any of his mother's beaded bracelets—for some reason, he felt weird about making money off his mom's misery. But he'd chosen a really cool leather one decorated in tiny turquoise, red, and amber beads, squeezed it into an empty matchbox, tied a piece of red yarn around it, and stuck it under the tree with Faith's name on it that Christmas. She never came right out and acknowledged him for it, but every time she wore it when he was around, she made a point to exclaim over how beautiful it was, and how special it was to her.

Of course, that had been months after he'd gifted the twins with carefully selected unique bracelets for their birthday. They'd both hugged him fiercely and made him help put them on.

And he'd been the only kid from school at their birthday party. The rest had been family, including their mom who was very sick, and their tiny new baby sister, Abby, who had just been born a few weeks before.

Mrs. Goodacre had died right after Christmas that same year. Brandon had ached for the whole grieving family, but especially for the wide-eyed and frightened twins. For the first time since he'd known them, they had very little to say, even to each other. They wandered through each day, holding hands as if their lives depended on it, but barely speaking, even when spoken to.

"Maybe your mom and my mom are friends in heaven," Brandon murmured one day after school while they waited for someone to pick them up. Faith had stopped walking them home from school. She was too busy taking care of the tiny baby Abby to spend time with them anymore. She even started doing her schoolwork at home the rest of that year. Instead, it was Charity and Hope who met them outside the school by the bike rack, and although they were nice enough, they weren't Faith.

Then that summer, Brandon's father got out of jail and moved into a trailer park on the east side of town. He'd dreaded the thought of living alone with the man who was practically a stranger to him, so when his father claimed he wasn't in any position to take on a kid at that point, Brandon had practically sagged in shameful relief.

"I need a stable job and a decent truck first, so I can feed you and get you to school and back," the man had explained. "Once things settle down a little for me, I'll come get you." To Brandon, that was more of a threat than a promise, and he found himself secretly praying that his dad wouldn't ever be able to find a job.

He stayed on with his grandparents—his mom's parents—always on his best behavior lest they find a reason to make him go live with his dad in the opposite direction from Seven Virtues Ranch.

It was about that time that he realized he and his father didn't share last names. He was Brandon Stillwater, like his mother and his grandparents, while his father, Stuart, bore the last name Thompson.

"They never married," Grandma Stillwater said stoically. "He never gave her his name so she could give it to you."

"I don't want his name," Brandon had insisted. "I'm a Stillwater. Like you. Like my ma."

"That you are, boy," Grandpa had said from across the room. "And don't you forget it."

Over the next several years, his father moved one woman after another into, then out of, the trailer with him. He never married any of them, either, nor did he give them his name to pass on to their children. Brandon thought it was a good probability that he had a sibling or two out in the world somewhere.

In spite of all the girlfriends who came and went, Stuart Thompson never did ask his son to move in. Brandon couldn't decide if he should hate the man or be grateful that his father didn't want him around.

When he and the twins were twelve, Faith had a baby. She wasn't married either, and although Jasmine was deeply loved and cared for by everyone in the Goodacre family and in the town, too, Brandon sometimes saw the same haunted look in Faith's eyes that he'd seen in his mother's. Not nearly as bad—he was never afraid she'd do anything to harm herself or her baby—but he recognized the sadness and the loneliness there.

It was that summer that Brandon and Justice had stepped through the curtained branches to stand, hand in hand, in that sacred circle under the willow. It was that summer that they'd promised each other to wait.

Wait for love. Wait for marriage. Wait for each other.

He'd done—was still doing—exactly as he'd promised.

Justice had done the opposite.

No love. No marriage. No waiting for him.

How could he bear it?

FOUR

"Remember how Brandon and I kind of did the 'let's be friends' thing last summer? I thought we both agreed that we needed a break, that we needed to get out there and figure out who we were on our own before we could really figure out who we were together."

"I remember," Courage said, a half smile pulling at her lips. But it was a sad smile, Justice thought. "I remember thinking you two were only fooling each other with that notion, too."

"Yeah, well," Justice shrugged a shoulder. Shooting for brevity to make the telling of things easier, she said, "I think I might have been the only one fooled, and only long enough to make a right mess of things."

"Hm. I take it the whole thing was your idea?"

"Isn't it always?" Justice asked, shaking her head with frustration. "I don't know why I'm always looking for something more, something just around the corner, something I'm missing out on, you know? I like Brandon—no, I love Brandon—" She broke off and closed her eyes, surprising herself at her own admission. It wasn't like she didn't already know it, which meant Courage already knew it, too. But saying it out loud made it irrefutable somehow. Like she couldn't change her mind or take it back. Courage said nothing, so Justice continued. "I think I do, anyway."

Now her twin did speak. "You do."

Justice raised a brow at her, but didn't argue. "And I guess I've always just assumed we'd end up together one day, you know?"

"Hm."

"I think everyone in this stupid town assumes it, too."

"Yep," Courage agreed.

"And I think that's the problem. I'm afraid of doing something because it's what's expected of me. I'm afraid I'll lose who I am in the person everyone else already believes I am. What if I'm not marriage material? You know I'm not a team player."

"Unless you set your mind to it and really love that person," Courage countered. "Then you're an awesome team player. Look how far The Twisted Sisters has come. We couldn't have done all we have if you weren't a team player."

"That's not a marriage," Justice said. "You can't walk away from me. I'm your twin sister."

Courage opened her mouth like she wanted to say something, then shut it again. Without a word, she stood and hobbled gingerly, slowly, out of their bedroom, pulling the door firmly closed behind her.

Justice frowned at her sister's odd behavior, and after waiting for several long minutes for her to return, she finally got up to check on her. "Courage?" she called down the hall, wondering which direction she'd headed. There was no response, so she headed toward the kitchen where she found her sitting at the dining room table, her eyes closed, her bad leg propped up on one of the chairs beside her, an open package of Oreos in front of her. "What are you doing?" Justice asked, chagrin making her words a little harsh.

"Proving I can walk away from you any time, even with this bum leg."

Justice scowled at her. "You know, I'm trying to tell you some deep stuff and you're making light of it."

"No, I'm not." Courage stopped her with a quick shake of her head. "I'm proving a point. It doesn't matter if I'm your sister, your dog, or your husband. Which would be weird, by the way. Dog or husband, at least."

"Your point?" Justice said, the two words laced with sarcasm. Lately her sister came across as being just a tad bit dingy and easily distracted, and Justice wasn't sure whether to blame the pain meds she was still on or the love bubble she inhabited.

"Yes. My point." Courage sealed the flap on the cookie package and pushed it toward the middle of the table. "If you're going to be in a relationship, sister of mine, be in that relationship," she said, enunciating the last few words slowly. "Stop looking for reasons why you can't be in it, or shouldn't be in it, or even worse, why the other person shouldn't be in. Be. In. It. Fully. Just like you are with me and The Twisted Sisters. Just like you are with Fire." She lowered her leg to the floor and continued. "I may not be around forever. I may not ride with you forever. When I get married, we certainly won't be sharing this room together anymore. Talk about weird." She grinned, bringing a hand up to cover her mouth like a mischievous little girl. "And one day, Fire is going to have to hand over his glitter butt swag to another steed."

Now it was Justice's turn to chuckle. She shook her head, no longer put out, and she did get her sister's point, but she still wasn't sold on the idea that relationships were as simple as Courage made them sound. At least not where Brandon was concerned. Besides, maybe once she finally got through telling the whole story, Courage's advice might be different. "You want to take those cookies outside to the porch? It's nice out there." Besides, they'd be able to see company coming. The porch was at the back of the house facing the barns and pasture, but the long driveway curved wide around the house and vegetable garden, preventing anyone from approaching unnoticed.

As if reading her mind, Courage said, "And we can watch for Brandon out there. He's coming by this afternoon to hitch up the trailer, isn't he?" Without waiting for a response, Courage rose, grabbed the bag of cookies from the table, and hobbled through the screen door.

Justice followed a few moments later, milk in two tumblers wide enough to dunk the Oreos in.

"So being 'just friends' didn't exactly work out the way I planned it," Justice began again once they were comfortable on the bench swing that hung at one end of the porch. An enormous magnolia tree shaded much of that corner of the house, and although Jed had threatened to cut it down on more than one occasion, insisting it was too close to the foundation, he never did. The fact that he and his wife planted the tree the day after he carried Caroline over the threshold of the house he'd built for her and their daughters might have had something to do with his reticence, too. This time of year, it was lush and in full bloom, the sweet magnolia fragrance filling the air.

"If you'd asked for my advice back then..." Courage teased, leaning away a little when Justice threatened to elbow her in the side.

"You think that just because you're still recovering that you can get away with this smack talk, sissy-poo. Well, I'll have you know that I'm keeping score up here." Justice tapped her temple. "Just you wait. When you get a clean bill of health, I'm taking you down."

Courage grinned, happiness making her glow. "You'll have to go through a big, strong, farm boy to get to me." She sighed dreamily.

"Not a problem," Justice quipped. "I can take him down, too. Piece of cake." She snapped her fingers in the air three times. "But anyway." She drew the word out in long syllables. "This conversation is about me, remember? My lack of a love life. Not your sickly sweet gushing gooey gross sparkly rainbows and unicorns life."

"Right, right. Sorry." Courage turned to glance over her shoulder. "Go back and play on your rainbow a little longer, Moonbeam. We'll ride together when this is over." Then to Justice, she explained with a dip of her head, "My unicorn, Moonbeam."

"I give up," Justice said, rolling her eyes and crossing her arms on her chest and clamping her lips together.

Courage stuck out her bottom lip and blinked puppy dog eyes at her.

Justice just shook her head. "Nope. Too late. I'm not going to share my sad tale of misery and woe with you after all. You're too happy to be able to handle it."

"I'm not. I promise I won't let Moonbeam interrupt us again, okay?" Courage said, but in spite of her words, Justice could tell her sister was serious. "I mean it. I want to know. I do."

Justice rolled her eyes again. "Fine. But now you get the abbreviated version because you've wasted so much of my time."

Courage just batted her lashes again in apologetic anticipation.

Justice realized that the silly banter had alleviated some her nerves. Her hands weren't sweating the way they'd been when she'd asked Courage if they could talk. It shouldn't have been a surprise when Courage nodded and informed her that she had something she wanted to talk to Justice about, too. They often shared the same intentions, if not for the exact same reasons. Now that Courage had gotten her request out of the way—a trick riding academy with lessons, camps, and even tournaments of their own one day—and it was Justice's turn, she felt she could actually do this without throwing up.

And maybe, just maybe, Courage wouldn't look at her with the same expression of disgust and rejection that Brandon wore these days.

The words came out in a rush, jumbled and not even close to the way she'd wanted to tell the story, but out they came anyway. "Being friends didn't work. Brandon got upset because he felt rejected and assumed that I wanted to see other guys—which wasn't the case at all. Not exactly, anyway. So he started acting like a hormonal teenage boy and flirting with everything in a ponytail—which is saying a lot since it was the rodeo and all. There are a lot of ponies out there with tails, you know. And a lot of cowgirls with ponytails. Even some cowboys with them, too."

"I think you're getting off track," Courage murmured.

"Right. So he started flirting like crazy, remember?"

Courage nodded. "I remember. You did, too, if I recall."

"Right. But I did because he was. And then that last day we were in Greeley, he brought that girl, Sandy—remember her? The barrel racer he was talking to at lunch? The one who looked like a cross between Miley Cyrus and Katy Perry? Anyway, he brought her back to our camper."

"He did?" Courage shot her a shocked look. "Like, into the trailer with him?"

Justice nodded. "Yeah. I mean, he only showed her around inside, then they went right back out to sit in the hammocks. But still, it felt so in my face, you know? Especially after enduring his whole Casanova act all month long."

"He broke the rules, Justice," Courage said, shaking her head. "No dates in the camper, period. No exceptions. Why didn't you say anything to me? He shouldn't have gotten off the hook about that."

"He claims he didn't invite her, that she just followed him."

"Oh right." Courage rolled her eyes. "So she forced her way past big strong Brandon into the camper and forced him to give her the tour and forced him to get into a hammock with her?" Courage frowned.

"They didn't share a hammock."

"Semantics," Courage grunted, obviously disgusted over the whole situation. It didn't help that it was public knowledge that Sandy had a major thing for Brandon, either.

Justice grimaced. "It was even worse. She got into mine and he didn't tell her to get out. Just grinned over at me like nothing was amiss."

Courage sent her a narrow eyed look. "You should have told me. I would have let him have it. Where was I?"

"You were out with One Hit Wonder Warren Weirsby that night, remember? He had you all starry-eyed."

"I wasn't starry-eyed, and don't call him that," Courage said with a snort. "He was a nice guy. He made some good money at Greeley and wanted to share the love. I just happened to be the cowgirl who'd caught his eye that day, that's all."

"And just how much love did you two share?"

"Hey, now." Courage turned and scowled at Justice, their heads so close that they both went a little cross-eyed looking at each other. "You're the wanton woman we're talking about, not me, remember?"

Justice stuck her tongue out at her, then lowered her gaze to the beaded bracelet she held. Courage's had broken a few years ago, the beads scattering in the barn, and Justice had taken hers off, unwilling to risk the same tragic ending for hers. She kept it looped around one of the decorative iron swirls on her headboard, and every night, she kissed her fingertips, then brushed them against the beads. But while Courage had been laying out her trick riding academy idea earlier in their room, Justice had taken the bracelet down and toyed with it while they'd been talking. In her concern over Courage's disappearance, she'd inadvertently brought it with her to find her sister. Now she smoothed the strip flat on her thigh, running a nail along the edge of it, noting the frayed edges of the fabric backing. Finally looking back up at Courage, she said, "Warren was a nice guy, I admit. And cute, too. It was a bummer he never came back."

"I don't know," Courage said, eyes on the bracelet, too. "Maybe he did it right, leaving while he was hot. And yes," she said with a silly smile. "He was definitely hot." She reached over and traced a fingertip along the tiny green beads that made a zigzag border on the colorful cuff. "I still haven't told Brandon mine broke," she murmured. "I think it would break his heart. His mother made these, remember?"

"Yeah, but you should tell him. He still has a bunch of them. I know he'd give you another one."

"I don't want another one. I want the original. He was such a weird kid, wasn't he?" Courage giggled softly. "I'll never forget the look on his face when you said that thing about Faith beating up the last guy who picked on us. You were such a cold hearted liar."

"No, no, no," Justice contradicted, shaking her finger back and forth in front of her. "I did not lie. I never said Faith beat anyone up. I said he should see what she did to the last guy who teased us. Can I help it if Brandon assumed the worst?"

"But where did that come from? I mean, we were like—I don't know—three? How could you have been that smart? That mean?"

"I call it streetwise, not mean," Justice said with a cheeky grin. "Who are you calling mean anyway? He made fun of us every day for more than a month." She tapped Courage in the middle of the forehead. "And we were six, not three. We were in first grade, remember? I can't speak for you, but I was incredibly intelligent back then."

"Ha. Back then, maybe. Not so much anymore."

"Now look who's being mean," Justice said, batting her sister's hand away from her bracelet. "People make mistakes, remember?"

Courage turned and planted a quick kiss on Justice's shoulder. "I'm sorry. You're right. That was mean. And I'm also sorry I didn't realize how much you were hurting that weekend. I was pretty caught up in my own euphoria, it's true, and I just thought you and Brandon were having one of your dumb squabbles."

"It might have started out as a dumb squabble, but it turned into a raging squall before the night was out. He'd made me so mad. We'd been bickering over stupid stuff for days, remember? The whole stinking summer, in fact, but especially that last week. Things were just way out of control, and the trailer felt like it had gotten smaller and smaller with each passing day. I mean, the over the top flirting and partying? In the arena, sure. That's his act, like you said. But not behind the scenes or after hours. That wasn't what I expected 'being friends' to mean, you know?" She formed air quotes around *being friends*. "And then that girl showed up, acting like she owned the place, and he never said a word, almost like he was daring me to even try to interfere."

"You still should have called him on it."

"But really, what could we have done about it? It was our last night there, and then we were heading home. And it was his truck pulling our rig, so it's not like we were going to kick him to the curb or anything." Justice was a little surprised to find that the longer she talked, the less vulnerable she felt. She'd expected it to be the other way around, but Courage had been right. She needed to unload her burden, and knowing that she could trust her sister with it felt almost liberating.

"I can't believe you never told me any of this," Courage reiterated. "You've been carrying this stuff around all this time."

"Yeah, well, I got my revenge," Justice said with a rueful huff. "Only, it's backfired big time."

Courage took her hand and held it, and that was all the nudge Justice needed to go on.

"So when Cheryl, Trish, and Saralene passed by, rounding up cowgirls for one last ladies night on the town, I jumped at the chance to get far, far away from him. Only suddenly, he had something to say about it. When I ducked inside the camper to get ready, Brandon followed me, all worked up, yanking the door closed behind him. Presumably so we could talk without an audience."

"What about Sandy? Did she just hang out in the hammock, waiting for him?"

Justice shrugged. "I guess so. She was still there when I left."

"So what happened?"

"He tried to stop me. Told me I shouldn't go. When I tried to push past him to get to the bathroom, he blocked the door and said that I *couldn't* go, that he wouldn't let me."

Courage looked appalled. "He blocked your way? Seriously? What did he want you to do? Stay there with him and Sandy?" She frowned and shook her head, then got a hopeful look in her eye. "Do you think he was wanting to work on things with you since I wasn't going to be hanging around for the evening?"

Justice sighed and shook her head. "I can't imagine. Even if Sandy hadn't been there, he and I got so mad so quickly, that no talking would have taken place, it's safe to say. At that point, neither one of us wanted to spend a minute more with each other. I accused him of bullying me and trying to control me like he owned me, telling me who I could and couldn't spend time with, and he asked me why I would even want to be associated with amoral and trashy women like Cheryl and her friends. I asked him how he knew they were trashy, and he rolled his eyes and insisted that everyone knew that about them." She shifted in her seat and tucked a leg up under the other, turning slightly toward Courage. Her voice grew husky with misery as she continued. "But he wouldn't look me in the eye, Courage. Something about the way he said it, especially after all the other stuff that had gone down between us all week, well, it just didn't sit right with me."

"Wait." Courage turned toward her now, moving slowly, carefully. "Are you saying Brandon and Cheryl...?" She left the sentence hanging, but then added, "He wouldn't. Please tell me he didn't."

Justice shook her head. "No, of course he didn't. At least he denied it when I finally came clean about myself a few weeks ago. But that night, when I asked him point blank if he'd sampled some of what she was offering, he never answered me. Instead, he just got super ticked off at me for thinking the worst about him, but he never came right out and denied it. I was sure he was doing that whole deflecting thing, you know, where they get angry at you for asking so that they don't actually have to answer your question."

Courage didn't say anything, so Justice continued. "So I accused him of not wanting me to go out with Cheryl because he was afraid of what she'd tell me, then I stormed off, not waiting to hear his response."

"I can totally see why you'd think that," Courage said, her brow furrowed in contemplation. "He can be really defensive sometimes, especially when you challenge his honor."

"I know," Justice acknowledged. "When he told me I couldn't go out with those girls while that Sandy woman lay sprawled in my hammock waiting for him, it just sent me over the edge." She lay the bead bracelet over the back of her wrist, then held the ends together and stared down at it, the feel of it against her skin a familiar comfort, even after not wearing it for so long. She sighed again, this time even deeper, her breath catching a little on the way out. "Like an idiot, I got all dolled up and hit the bar scene with the rodeo girls. Let's just say we drank. A lot. And later that night, when I asked Cheryl if she'd ever hooked up with Brandon, and she regaled me with the details of when and where and how much of a good time they'd had together, I saw red."

It was Courage's turn to sigh. "Let me guess. It was all lies."

"According to Brandon it was."

"And you believe him?" Courage asked.

Justice let out a rueful laugh. "I do. I mean, at this point, why would he lie? Besides, which of them would you believe, Cheryl or Brandon?"

"Right."

"Right," Justice echoed. "But that's the problem. I wasn't in my right mind that night. And then we came across—stumbled across is probably more like it—Tanner Ogden and his buddies, and we kind of got sucked right into that melee."

Courage's expression was still gentle, but something in her eyes said she had a good idea what was coming. Justice licked her lips and turned her gaze toward the pasture that stretched out for several acres before the line of trees broke the property up into sections. Sunlight glinted off the surface of one of the ponds that disappeared behind a finger of woods. At that moment, she, too, wanted to disappear around the bend and never return.

She took a deep, fortifying breath. "Long, terrible story short, I ended up with Tanner. In his hotel room. I—I slept with him."

There. It was out. And the moment the words left her mouth, a lump the size of a grapefruit lodged in her throat, making it difficult to swallow and almost impossible to breathe. She pressed her fist to her chest where it felt like an anvil sat, pressing down on her rib cage. She opened her mouth to speak, but nothing came out.

Courage slid a little closer and rested her head on Justice's shoulder. "Oh, sissy," she whispered, then she laced their fingers together.

That loosed the floodgates, of tears and of even more words. "I hated myself," she ground out. "I was so sickened by what I'd done, by the fact that I gave myself—my virginity—to someone like Tanner. I mean, I was way out of control, but I still made the decision. He didn't force me or manipulate me, and honestly, I think he was so drunk, he may not remember much about it, either. But it happened, and I have wanted to die ever since. Not just because of what I'd done to myself, but also because of what I'd done to Brandon."

She felt her sister take sigh, but a moment later, Courage lifted her head. "But what exactly have you done to Brandon?" she asked with a whisper.

Justice thought it was obvious, but she whispered back, "I was saving myself until marriage. Marriage to Brandon. I was saving myself for him. We promised each other—" She broke off as her tears fell in earnest now. "And now—" she shuddered slightly, her voice cracking. "Now that I've told him, he can hardly look at me. He won't speak to me unless he absolutely can't avoid it, and then it's one word responses or cruel jabs about my character."

Courage remained silent for several moments, giving Justice the time she needed to get her tears in check. She wasn't a big crier; when she did uncork, it never lasted long. If it weren't for the actual tears overflowing from her eyes, there'd be no other indication of her emotional state. No bright pink nose, no red-rimmed eyes, no blotchy chest. Just tears. And then they'd be gone and she'd be back to her normal stoic self.

At least, that's how it usually was. Lately, though, she'd gone from one crying jag to another.

"You know, I think this road trip might be good for you," Courage finally said. "Sure, it would be grand if you could just apologize and everything would go back to the way it was. But we know it doesn't work that way." She sat a little straighter and took a slow, deep breath, grimacing slightly as she filled her lungs, then let it out. "I know without a doubt that Brandon loves you. Maybe even more than you love him. That's why this is killing him. And that's why he's trying to hurt you."

"Trying? He *is* hurting me. Badly. Every time he looks at me, there's so much hate and disgust there. And I know I deserve it, so I can't be angry at him. But that doesn't mean it doesn't hurt."

"No." Courage shook her head and took Justice's other hand, too. Fervently, she repeated, "No. You don't deserve it, Justice. You've apologized to him, and you've repented to God, right?"

"Yes. A thousand times," she said through a tight throat. "Which is mortifying. I mean, to think that God was watching when it happened?"

"You know, I don't think he's up there staring at a bunch of monitors, like some pervy security guard," Courage chided. "Just because he knows something is happening doesn't mean he's watching it play out *while* it's happening. I'm sure he's capable of turning away." She let go of Justice's hands and poked her in the thigh with her finger. "Besides, he's already forgotten about it. Already thrown the very idea of it into the depths of the deepest sea."

"I know," Justice said in a small voice. Her fingers trembled as she dabbed at her eyes with the lapel of her flannel shirt. "I think the deepest part of the sea must be like one of those coin funnels, and that our sins roll and roll and roll around until they disappear into a hole that opens straight into the very core of the earth where nothing can survive."

Courage nodded. "Yeah. At 10,000 degrees Fahrenheit, it would be all 'Burn, baby, burn.' Then poof! You're forgiven and it's forgotten."

"Poof. Yes." Justice nodded with a soppy grin. "10,000 degrees, hm? You *would* know the temperature of the earth's core, Miss Agriculture."

Courage smiled at that, but didn't let it distract her from her next point. "So if God can forgive and forget, maybe you can, too."

"I'm trying."

"Are you, though? I mean, if you can't forgive yourself, then how can you expect Brandon to forgive you?" Courage rolled her shoulders and pressed a hand to her side, then took a few deep breaths in through her nose and out through her mouth. Every so often, she'd start breathing too shallow and end up feeling lightheaded with a catch in her side. "And who's to say that you're the only one who needs forgiveness? I mean, Brandon did bring Sandy—Sandy? Really, Brandon?—back to our camper."

"She followed him," Justice said in his defense.

Courage made a dismissive sound. "So he said. But he also invited her in, knowing full well how it would look to you. She isn't the kind of girl a guy like Brandon typically brings home to meet the family, if you know what I mean."

"I know exactly what you mean." According to Brandon, once Justice was gone, he and Sandy hadn't stuck around the camper, though. He'd walked her back to her group of friends and left her there, then returned to the trailer, hoping Justice would see the light and come back, too.

"So why are you defending him?"

"Because I want to believe the best about him."

"You mean, because you love him."

Justice leaned her head on the back of the swing and let out a long, "Uuuh!" of frustration.

"Like I said, this trip might be good for both of you. I hate to think that God knocked me off Flash just to keep me from going with you this summer, but if that's the only way to get you two together for more than just a thirty-second glaring contest, then I'd gladly fall off my horse again." She grinned and nudged Justice's leg once more. "And look what I got out of the deal. Sweet, sweet, sugar daddy, farm boy, forever love."

"You disgust me."

"You're just jealous."

Justice paused and put a finger to her chin as if contemplating the notion. "Well, he is pretty hot. Those farm boy arms. Those sun crinkles at the corners of his eyes. And those blue, blue eyes."

"Hey. That's my man you're gushing about." Courage squeezed Justice's knee in just the right spot, making her squawk. She grabbed Courage's wrist, holding it up to study her fingers.

"I don't see a ring yet, sister of mine," she teased, but then stiffened, her eyes darting to the driveway where Brandon's truck was just pulling around the corner toward them. She dropped Courage's hand and looked wide-eyed at her. "Can you tell I've been crying?"

"As usual, no," Courage assured her. "Want me to stick around?"

Justice considered it for a moment, then said, "No. I'm good."

"All right, then. I'm going to be inside lying down. I'll have my phone with me. Call if you need me."

Justice helped Courage up off the swing, then gave her a quick—and gentle—hug. "Thank you," she whispered. Her sister hadn't turned on her, and she didn't look at her as soiled goods, trash, or worse. If Courage could see past the mess Justice had made of things, then maybe—oh, God, please, please, please—then maybe Justice could find the courage to hope for and fight for the day when Brandon could see past the mess, too.

FIVE

Brandon drove slowly past the long covered porch at the back of the Goodacre's ranch house. He nodded a greeting when he saw the twins standing by the bench swing at the corner of the porch, but he didn't stop. Justice would join him at the barn, but he was in no mood to play nice today, not even with Courage. Besides, he was certain she knew enough about what was going on that she'd understand his reticence.

And just how long had she known about all of this? Surely, she would have given him some kind of heads up, wouldn't she?

He pulled his truck up to the far side of the small barn where Flash and Fire were kept stalled. The twins had busted their backsides to save enough money to buy a used Exiss 3-horse trailer with decent living quarters. Their dad's big old Chevy could pull the thing, but during rodeo season, Brandon joined forces with the sisters and contributed his truck as his share. They split the travel and campsite costs equally between the three of them. This summer, things would be a little tighter since Courage wasn't able to join them. Sure, they'd have fewer expenses with only Justice and him and the two horses, but it would cost the same for the campsites and fuel. With tensions already high, the crack down on expenditures would be one more thing they'd be at each others' throats about.

Today, they were hooking the trailer up to his truck and doing one last inspection of all its components. If everything was good to go, they planned to load everything up, too. Last year, with some of their winnings, they'd gone in together on a large hay rack that sat on top of the trailer, and with only two horses going, they might actually have enough bales to get them through at least a month before having to stock up again. They also had the third horse stall available for storage and supplies—yet another benefit of having one less animal on board.

Brandon had gassed the truck up on his way over, done a thorough once-over of it—tire pressure, fluids, oil change, wipers, brake lights—and Justice was supposed to have filled the trailer's propane tanks and charged the batteries, as the trailer's hydraulics wouldn't run without juice and they'd need the hydraulics to get the gooseneck into place in the bed of his truck.

He almost hoped she'd forgotten to do so. Then he could be angry at her for something besides Tanner Ogden.

Tanner Ogden.

The name alone triggered rage that boiled up inside of Brandon like lava, hissing and spitting, burning him up from the inside out. He wanted to kill Tanner. He wanted to do all kinds of things to the guy first, *then* kill him.

He wanted to hate Justice.

He tried to hate Justice.

"I do hate Justice," he muttered aloud as he rolled down his window and leaned out to make sure he was lining his back end up as he reversed his truck into place in front of the trailer.

He watched her come down the steps from the back porch and hurry up the gravel drive toward him. He hated watching her, hated how just the sight of her made his blood sing and his pulse race. These days, he wasn't sure if it was from rage or betrayal or lust or love— No, not love. Not anymore. But he couldn't deny that she did, indeed, elicit an intense response from him.

Justice was, in so many ways, the polar opposite of her twin sister. Where Courage was the blonde-haired, brown-eyed girl from next door, soft-spoken and easy-going with a ready smile, Justice—with her dark hair and smoky makeup, jeans that were so tight he sometimes wondered what magic she worked to get into them—was edgy and tough, driven, and assertive. She took life by the throat and didn't let go until she got what she wanted. The shorter of the twins, the top of Justice's head hit right at his jawline—he knew because she'd tucked her face against his neck a hundred million times in the years they'd known each other.

The sisters' differences often made them seem two parts of a whole, but for those who knew them, it simply wasn't so. Sure, when they were together, they automatically slipped into comfortable roles with each other, letting one's strengths fill in for the other's weaknesses, communicating with almost imperceptible signals and expressions. Together, they seemed more comfortable in their own skins, but then, wasn't that common with twins, whether identical or not? Justice and Courage were definitely not identical.

"Hey, Brandon," Justice greeted him as she approached his driver's side window. "Batteries are charged and ready to go. Propane's topped off and loaded, too. I haven't filled the water tanks yet. I figured I'd do that once we're hitched up."

"Fine," he said, then rolled his window up, practically in her face. He didn't miss the discouragement that passed over her features, and it twisted his gut. But she deserved it. She deserved to feel some of the pain he endured daily since she'd told him about Tanner Ogden.

No, since even before she slept with Tanner Ogden, truth be told. He'd been in pain since that day almost a year ago when she'd told him they should take a break and figure out what they both really wanted out of life, to make sure they weren't just settling because they were comfortable with each other. And then she'd touted it like the idea had been both of theirs, as though he was in full agreement with the ridiculous idea.

There hadn't been a day in his life when he'd ever wanted a break from Justice Goodacre. He had no doubts, whatsoever, about what he wanted, at least not where she was concerned. He wanted Justice Goodacre, and he wanted to provide for her in a way that would show her how much he loved her. Not once since meeting her had he even entertained the notion that he was settling when it came to loving her. And never, in a million years, would he have come up with the suggestion that they take a break. In fact, if he had things his way, they'd be married already. Maybe with a couple of kids underfoot. Twin little girls as pretty as their mama.

But that was before he found out exactly what had gone down that last week in Greeley last summer. Before he finally learned what had turned her against him. Before he discovered that her words, her request that they give each other a little breathing room, was really a request for something far more intimate than breathing.

His grip tightened on the steering wheel as his mind conjured up visions of the pretty boy Tanner with his million-dollar hairstyle, the shiny new gear he brought with him to every rodeo, the handfuls of bills he whipped out at the bars to keep the drinks coming for anyone sidling up to his party. And Justice had been one of those partiers sidling up to him. And then she sidled right on back to his hotel room with him.

That was a picture he couldn't bear to linger on. He grunted angrily and shoved open his truck door with a whole lot more effort than he needed. The traitorous thing swung back closed before he could stop it. At least he hadn't been half out of his seat and gotten an arm or leg caught in it.

He secretly wished Justice had still been standing there so he could have accidentally knocked her on her backside.

"What the heck, man?" Brandon muttered under his breath, appalled at his own violent thoughts. He was a healer, a First Responder. He cleaned up after people who acted on thoughts like his. He had to get it together, and quick. If everything checked out, they'd be on the road tomorrow morning, just the two of them, for more than two months. If he didn't curtail his thoughts, one of them would be dead—or both of them since he was pretty sure Justice wouldn't let him take her down without a fight—by the time they got back to Plumwood Hollow. And then there'd be a whole lot of explaining to do. He hated the thought of everyone in town whispering about them behind their hands. It was bad enough that he knew what Justice had done. That Courage probably knew, too.

Crap. Did that mean Joe Lynxwilder knew, as well? And what about the rest of the Goodacre sisters? They were a tight knit bunch, and it wouldn't surprise him one iota if Justice had told her sisters all about last summer.

He couldn't bear the thought of all those people knowing how she'd passed him over for that frat boy party animal Tanner Ogden. How they were all feeling sorry for poor Brandon Stillwater, the scrapper from the wrong side of the tracks. "Couldn't keep a dad, couldn't keep a mom," he quipped dryly. "And yet the poor, misguided thing thought he could hang onto a woman?" He shook his head and tsked the way he imagined the local gossips would.

Maybe it was good he was leaving town for awhile. Granted, he was taking the bane of his existence with him, but at least he wouldn't have to endure the knowing looks of everyone around him.

Until, of course, he and Tanner Ogden crossed paths somewhere between Colorado and Texas. Because surely, they would.

"Brandon?" Her muffled voice came to him through the closed window on the passenger side. She stood about a foot away, misery etched into the lines and shadows on her face. How much of his display of temper had she seen? And why did he let himself get so riled up at just the sight of her? He needed to be cold. Hard. Unaffected. Aloof and distant. All those anti-relationship words. Instead, he turned into a hot mess every time he so much as thought of her.

He rolled down the window and glared out at her. "What?"

"Should I drop the tailgate or do you want to check out the hitch first?"

He paused just long enough to make her shuffle her feet. *Squirm, baby. That's right.* "I've got this," he finally said. "Why don't you go do something else?"

"I can help," she said. "It's so much easier with two—"

"I can manage." He cut her off. Although, she was right. Logistically, it was easier with two people. But working with Justice would make any task ten times harder, so that kind of negated the two people perks.

Justice hesitated, her arms crossed, her bottom lip caught between her teeth in consternation. "Look, Brandon," she began, and he could hear the tightness in her voice. "This is hard enough as it is without us going out of our way to make it worse. Can we at least try to be civil? Do this kind of stuff the way we always do? As a team? We don't have to talk—we both know the drill."

"But we're not a team, are we?" Brandon returned, keeping his voice droll. "Right now, we're two people stuck in the same caravan because we happen to be heading in the same direction. You do your thing and I'll do mine, and maybe we'll both survive this ordeal." He started to roll the window up, then stopped it at half mast so he could add, "And I'm not the one who made this 'hard enough' in the first place, so don't go pointing fingers at me." He made air quotes around the words *hard enough*. "I can take care of the trailer hitch myself."

Well. Good job with the whole unaffected thing. Aloof and distant. You did good, boy.

By the time he was out of the truck, Justine had disappeared, presumably into the barn since the horses were making welcoming noises.

He did manage to get the trailer mounted in his truck bed, as well as the safety chains, cables, and electrical hooked up, but it had taken him far longer than it would have if he'd accepted Justice's help. While he'd been busy with that, she'd wheeled out a dozen bales of hay and had several of them stacked near the ladder on the side of the trailer. One more thing they always did together, loading the hay rack, and this job also worked best with two people. Fortunately, they didn't even have to stand on the same side of the vehicle to get it done.

They loaded the hay bales to the rack on top of the trailer the old-fashioned way—with ropes, a pulley, hay hooks, and manual labor. Brandon worked the pulley system to get the hay up the ladder while Justice waited up top to set the bales in place. They made quick work of it, Justice keeping up with him without a single complaint, no matter how fast he worked, much to his chagrin.

And she wouldn't stop watching him. Every time he glanced her way, her eyes were already on him, studying him, something raw and unsettling in their brown depths. It was driving him crazy.

"Can you hand me up the hose so I can fill this tank while I'm up here?" she asked, just as he was turning away. He wanted to pretend he hadn't heard her, to make her manage it all on her own, but his pettiness was starting to bother even him.

While she filled the tank, he loaded several more hay bales into the third stall, not making any effort to keep from jostling the trailer with her perched on top of it. He didn't want her to fall off, not really, but he enjoyed—far too much, he begrudgingly admitted—the mental image of her having to hang on for dear life. "You're such a child," he muttered to himself, stacking the last bale in place and lashing the pile down with cargo straps. There was still plenty of room in the stall for more gear—maybe he should keep his clothes and personal belongings back there. He could commandeer this third stall as his own living quarters and not have to go inside the front part of the trailer at all. He could change back here and use water from the tank she was filling to hose himself off with. He didn't need to use her shower, to smell her shampoo, to see her makeup and other girlie personal items strewn around. And if an unsuspecting Justice happened upon him in his boxers, so be it. She'd get a good gander at what she was missing. What she'd never have.

Brandon knew he was easy to look at with his smooth Shawnee skin and the lean muscles that rippled underneath. Sea blue eyes were a bit of a surprise to folks the first time they met him, but with his dark lashes and brows, and his thick, straight black hair passed down to him from his mother's heritage, there was no denying his indigenous roots. Tall and lithe, quick on his feet both physically and mentally, he usually brought a calming presence to whatever situation he was in, an ability that worked exceptionally well for him as a First Responder.

This current situation, however, was proving to be an exception. Peace and calm felt a million miles away. Having his own personal space in the trailer had to help, right?

SIX

The usual excitement that rallied around the ranch each summer was still there, in spite of the obvious tension pinging between Justice and Brandon. They loaded up the horses, made room for a cooler packed with gourmet road trip food made with love by Charity, and hugged the whole family a second or third time. More than one of her sisters whispered encouraging words in her ear.

As if that weren't her own most pressing desire. Justice caught Faith murmuring close to Brandon's ear, and she wondered if her big sister had given him the same message as well. But Brandon shook his head, and responded with, "I don't think so," snuffing out the little spark of hope Justice had been nurturing. She'd been praying for weeks for this first day in particular, that once they were on the road, perhaps after a few miles, they'd form a tentative bridge between them, connecting over the excitement and anticipation of the upcoming events.

But Brandon continued to speak to her in short, clipped sentences, only when it was absolutely necessary, and it hadn't escaped her notice that he avoided being anywhere near her proximity. They'd had a big breakfast together with the whole Goodacre clan, including Faith and Cord and their two children, Jasmine and Elijah, Charity and Frank, and even Hope and Levi, and their daughter, Yvette. Joe was there, too, especially attentive to Courage. Both girls were far more emotional than they'd expected that morning. There was the unresolved situation with Brandon, sure, but it was suddenly real that Justice was going on the road alone, and Courage was staying behind after so many years of riding together. For more than two months. They'd never been apart for that long before. They stuck close to each other's sides until the last moment, their hands touching, shoulders nudging, arms draped around each other's waists.

After breakfast, everyone huddled close around Brandon and Justice—it was impossible to avoid each other with them boxed in by the gang—and Jed led the family in a prayer of blessing over the trip, asking for God's provision, protection, and peace.

Finally, Brandon climbed into the driver's seat and buckled in. It was time to go. He rolled down his window to say a few last words to Cord, right before Justice climbed into the passenger seat, her father drew her close. "My beautiful girl," he murmured against her hair. "I'm praying for your broken heart, that the good Lord will soothe your spirit, that he will lift you up, even when the way seems overwhelming. Remember that you are his child, and that he has your hand, and though you stumble, he will not allow you to fall headlong. We men are fools, and we fail each other again and again. The Almighty will never fail you, of that, I can assure you. A word of advice?" It was a question, but he didn't let her pull away, just kept holding her tightly.

Justice nodded against his chest, slipped her arms around his waist, and held on. Whatever he had to say might be hard to hear.

"Give the boy some breathing room. It usually takes a man a little longer to know that it's okay to be broken. Sometimes all you can do is be the safe place he can come back to after he's fought his own demons. Believe me, I speak from experience." Then he took her by the shoulders and held her away from him so he could look her in the eye. "Wait for the Lord. He's got a plan for you both." He lifted a gnarled hand and brushed a tear from her cheek. "He's got the perfect time and place already prepared for when he'll fill you in on it. And knowing him, he won't reveal the whole thing at one time, no matter how hard you push or how loud you rail at him, child. Waiting is the hardest task you'll ever have to do, I can assure you."

Justice sniffed and let out a bitter laugh. "I'm a doer, not a waiter, Dad."

"I know. So am I. But if this old man can figure out how to wait, then so can you." He hugged her again quickly, then opened her door for her. "Up you go." He looked past her to Brandon and said, "Son, you have in your care one of my most precious possessions."

"Yes sir," Brandon replied with a nod.

Jed always said the same thing to Brandon right before they rolled out, but this time, he added, "You two take care of each other, you hear?" then he closed Justice's door firmly, patted the hand she held out to him through her open window. Behind him, Courage stood tucked against Joe's side, a tissue held to her nose, surrounded by the rest of the Goodacre sisters and their respective families.

"Go show them who's rodeo queen!" Abby, Jasmine, and Yvette hollered. "We love you!"

Prudence moved up to stand next to Jed, one arm linked with his, one hand pressed to her chest.

"Ready?" Brandon asked. With the windows rolled down, they were still on public display, so she put on a brave smile and nodded. As they pulled away, she leaned out her window and waved and blew kisses until they turned down the driveway and out of sight of the back porch where everyone had gathered. She continued hanging out the window, waiting, watching, and sure enough, around the bend appeared her two young nieces, Jasmine and Yvette, Faith's dog darting after them, as they ran behind the dust cloud the trailer left in its wake. They waved frantically with both hands, jumping up and down and hollering silly things until Brandon pulled their rig out onto the road.

Then Justice rolled up her window and took a deep, fortifying breath before turning to look at Brandon.

"Radio or audiobook?" he asked. In other words, no talking.

"Um, audiobook, I guess. What do you have?" Justice had several downloaded to her phone as well, but she wanted to give him first dibs.

"You choose," he said, not looking at her.

Okay. Brandon liked thrillers, crime mysteries, and rugged tales of the Wild West, and usually, they were fine with her, too. But in her fragile emotional state, she thought something a little less stimulating might be a better option. "Um, Hope gave me a copy of *All Creatures Great and Small* by James Herriot. Do you want to try that?" It wasn't romance, something neither of them could stomach right now, and it wasn't about heartbreak or the loss of a loved one, or violence. No, the story of the young vet in the Yorkshire Dales was gentle, humorous, and soothing to the spirit, and the narrator's lovely British storyteller voice made the audiobook a welcome respite from the tension between them. Just what she needed, and maybe just what Brandon needed, too.

"Whatever. You choose," he repeated. His tone was flippant, but at least he wasn't ignoring her.

She connected her phone to the speaker system, then pulled up her audiobook app. A few moments later, the rich voice of Jim Dale filled the close quarters of the truck cab. *Give the boy some breathing room,* she heard her father say in her head. If that's what Brandon needed, if breathing room helped him come to grips with his broken heart, then she'd give it to him, and if Justice could figure out how to be the safe place he came back to, then that's what she'd do and be.

Their first stop had them pulling in right before noon with more than enough time to unload the horses and get them warmed up before they had to get registered and on the roster for the afternoon's events. Brandon was paired with a guy he'd roped with on several occasions, and that seemed to brighten his spirits considerably.

Justice, however, felt Courage's absence like a missing limb. In the past, they'd been able to tag team everything. Courage would take care of and prep the horses—"glitter them up," she called it—while Justice ran around doing paperwork and making necessary connections. Justice would stable and tend the horses afterward while Courage made sweet talk with their adoring fans. Now it was all on Justice's shoulders, and she couldn't very well ask for Brandon's help.

By the end of the day, she was deflated. She'd smeared The Twisted Sister tornado design on Fire's rump so it looked more like a child's scribble, she hadn't left herself enough time to do her makeup the way she liked it and ended up looking, she thought, rather clownish. Fire was fidgety and kept tossing his head and chomping at his bit as though something was wrong with his head gear, but she knew he was just wondering where Flash was. Justice couldn't blame him. On top of the pre-show frustrations, they'd had a terrible run. She'd practiced alone over and over back home, but in the arena live, she found that she counted on visualizing and listening for subtle cues from Courage throughout every moment of their show. It wasn't the same without her twin riding with her, and the performance felt flat to her, the response from the audience trite and a bit bored.

Again, she didn't blame them. It was quickly becoming crystal clear to her that they were best as a team, that The Twisted Sisters was great *because* there were two of them playing off each other, working together, and riding together.

The thought weighed her down even more than the lousy performance, and she headed back to the trailer as soon as she could get away. She was sitting in a camp chair under the awning, a cup of coffee in hand, wondering why on earth she ever thought she could do this thing alone, when Brandon and his beautiful gelding came into view.

Swaggering. That's what he was doing. Shoulders back, and wearing a self-satisfied grin. And she had to admit, the swagger looked good on him. He wore a sky blue pearl button shirt tucked into his low-slung black jeans that were bunched just right over his black snake skin boots. The belt he wore sported his lucky buckle—a beautiful piece of silver artwork that he'd bought with his first winnings almost ten years earlier. His hat was tipped forward slightly so she couldn't see his eyes until he got closer, but that meant he couldn't see hers, either, so she let her gaze linger on the man and his horse a little longer.

With a quick nod in her direction, he commandeered Tank up into the trailer, prepped him for the next stretch of road, then joined her under the awning, popping open another camp chair for himself. He hadn't stopped grinning, and Justice couldn't tell if he was warming up to her, finally, or gloating. She kinda thought it was the latter.

"Whew!" he said, reaching over and snatching a water bottle from the cooler of drinks nearby. "Nice way to start the season. Sitting way out front today. How about you?"

Yep. Gloating. Justice wanted to snap at him. He'd watched her show. He'd been standing with a group of regulars at the far end of the arena from her start gate, but she'd seen him there.

She bit back the retort and opted for honesty, instead. He was here, wasn't he? Even if he was thumbing his nose at her, he was here with her.

Alone, even. Maybe even checking up on her, albeit in a rather unkind way. "I really miss Courage," she managed to say, then pushed to her feet and stepped over to the open window of Fire's trailer stall so Brandon wouldn't see her face crumple. Her horse stuck his head out and whuffled against her hand. "We're ready to go whenever you are," she said over her shoulder. They had to be at their next stop in time to set up camp for the night. The events started early the next morning, and Justice was already on the docket. She had a lot of thinking to do between now and then. She had to figure out how to make her prep time run more smoothly, now that she was doing everything solo.

They hadn't discussed sleeping arrangements before they left, but Justice wasn't too worried about it. When it was the three of them, Brandon typically slept wherever he felt the most comfortable, depending on the restrictions of each campsite, the weather, and the condition his body was in. By the end of the circuit, after being battered and roughened up by the games, he appreciated the comfort of the foldout sofa bed in the trailer. But he usually started out sleeping in his hammock strung across the trailer door. "Standing guard over Jed Goodacre's precious treasures," he'd say to anyone who asked. Sometimes, if the bugs were especially bad, he'd move the hammock inside, but for some reason, mosquitoes didn't get to him the way they went after the girls. And if it rained halfway through the night, rather than waking Justice and Courage, he'd find refuge in the passenger seat of his truck; it leaned back into a comfortable reclining position. Considering how things were with them right now, Justice had no doubt she wouldn't be seeing his big, slumbering body sprawled on their foldout sofa this season. So far, he'd barely set foot inside the living quarters at all, other than to use the facilities. He even kept his bags and gear in the extra stall next to the bathroom door, rather than in one of the closets inside the way he usually did.

Which meant Justice didn't just have twice as much room without Courage; she had three times as much without Brandon's things. She should be thrilled with the extra space, but it only made her feel lonely.

SEVEN

Three more stops, three more lousy shows for Justice, and three more winning runs for Brandon.

He was far more jovial than he'd been in quite some time, and Justice was glad for him. He deserved validation for his hard won skill, and she hoped he'd do really well this season.

After her response to his question that first day, he no longer boasted quite so openly, but he didn't offer her his assistance the way he did in the past. He was never one to stand by when there was something he could do to help. He'd painted glitter tornadoes, held makeup mirrors, braided their hair. He'd even stitched Courage back into her costume when she'd caught her side seam on a gate latch and ripped it open minutes before a performance.

No, the moment they arrived on site, he went off about his business and left Justice to her own devices. The fact that he was trying so hard to keep his distance, the fact that it went against his very nature, told her that he might be just as miserable as she was, in spite of his current rank. At the end of the day, when all she wanted to do was crawl into bed and forget about the day's happenings, she found sleep slow in coming as she listened to him settle into the hammock hanging outside the trailer door. And if she wasn't mistaken, sleep wasn't coming to him any easier.

In Stockton, Brandon's performances started slipping. Behind the scenes, his celebratory facade did, too. Although he still stayed clear of her as much as he was able during the events, he ended up back at the trailer earlier than usual, sullen and brooding, all but ignoring her.

Back to how things were before we left, she thought. Justice was finally beginning to find her stride—she was now managing to have both her and her horse made up, in costume, and at the starting gate at the right time—although she acknowledged with growing clarity that The Twisted Sisters would never be a solo act. Every time she heard their opening guitar riff, something in her shriveled up just a tiny bit more.

In Almington, Brandon made up for lost time in his first two runs, but on the third, the steer somehow wrestled free of him, lurched to his feet and stepped directly on Brandon's left wrist. Justice had seen the whole thing, but by the time she made it down from the bleachers to find him, someone else had already stabled his horse and Brandon was off to get his injuries treated. No one could tell her what his prognosis was, but she felt abandoned by him in his time of need. This wasn't how they did things. As silly as it might seem, this felt like proof that things were truly broken beyond repair. He was making a statement to her that he didn't need her. Not even when he was injured.

He returned to the trailer that evening, his wrist in a bulky brace, having refused a cast, and with orders to keep his arm immobile for at least two weeks. Justice had set up the camp chairs already, and without greeting her, he dropped into one of them, nearly toppling backwards, and let out an uncharacteristic expletive.

Justice felt his pain deeply, but didn't say anything.

"Two weeks," he growled a few moments later, talking more to himself than to her. "Two weeks! And even then, they won't clear me to enter without a doctor's permission. I'm pretty much out of the running at this point." He had a hairline fracture that would heal fine if he took the right precautions. "So how was your day?" he asked, still not looking at her. "It had to be a heck of a lot better than mine."

"I made it to the starting gate on time," she said quietly. "But I lost another sponsor." This was the second one, and one of the bigger ones who'd just signed them on last year. The representative had approached her after her program and asked point blank if Courage would be returning. When Justice told her, truthfully, that she wasn't sure, the woman explained that they'd signed them on as a team, not as a solo act. *Tell me something I don't know!* Justice had wanted to yell at her retreating back.

"Huh," Brandon grunted in reply.

She waited, wondering if he actually wanted to talk, or if he'd intended the question to be rhetorical. And now they were back to one word—or a single grunt—responses. Finally, when she thought that was all she'd get out of him, she started to rise. She had sandwich supplies inside; maybe she'd offer to fix him one. But she paused when he cleared his throat.

"Um, thanks for looking after Tank. Roger said you took over after I left." He tipped his head toward the trailer where both horses were already loaded up for the night. They'd planned to drive tonight, so she'd boarded the gelding while she waited for Brandon's return.

"You're welcome," she said. She wanted to tell him that she would have looked after him, too, if he'd waited for her, but she kept her words few. *Breathing room,* she heard her father say. He repeated himself in her mind on an ongoing basis, it seemed. "Would you like a sandwich? I have roast beef and Swiss cheese and some of Charity's ciabatta rolls."

Brandon finally—*finally*—looked up at her, his still water blue eyes full of the misery he'd been trying so hard to mask since pulling out of the Seven Virtues Ranch driveway. "I could eat," he said, studying her face. "I don't know how much help I'll be in the kitchen, though." One side of his mouth hitched up just the tiniest bit, almost tentatively.

It was a running joke with them; the trailer kitchen was nothing more than a sink, a two-burner stove, and a counter that measured a foot squared. They extended the space with the stove cover, but even then, having more than one person cooking was all but impossible.

Unless they really, really liked each other, of course. The thought of sharing the tight quarters with Brandon made her stomach flip flop.

It felt like a breakthrough, him tossing it out there like that. A white flag of sorts. Justice wanted to weep with relief, but she kept it together long enough to say, "Ha ha. You're off the hook, just this once. I'll do the cooking tonight." Then she hurried into the trailer, closing the door behind her, and leaned heavily against it. She was almost afraid to hope, but she couldn't deny that maybe, just maybe, this was one small step in the right direction. They might not ever be able to go back to the way things were, but maybe they could move forward toward something else. Something new.

"I'm going to make the best sandwich the world has ever known," she said to herself as she began collecting ingredients, making sure to grab Brandon's favorite fixings.

Several minutes later, she handed him a plate with what might be mistaken for a Dagwood. Stuffed with meat and cheese, fire-roasted red peppers, Dijon mustard, mayonnaise, pickles, lettuce, and his favorite, sliced Greek olives, the sandwich was enormous. She had no idea how he was going to fit his mouth around the thing, but she didn't care. She'd poured all the remorse and longing she felt into each layer, and she thought it apropos that it might be a little more than he could chew.

"Wow," he said, his eyes growing wide at the sight. He'd removed his hat and it now rested on top of the cooler next to a bottle of water. Neither of them were soda drinkers, except on rare occasions, and by the time they made it back to Plumwood Hollow, they usually had a large trash bag full of empty bottles to take to the recycling plant. "This looks amazing." He glanced up. "Where's yours?"

She tipped her head toward the trailer. "Inside. I'll grab it. Didn't want to try to juggle them both. You know me and carrying things while walking. Neither of us would eat."

He grinned at that, although it was fleeting. "Right. I'll wait."

She returned with her own plate, a bag of her favorite salt and vinegar kettle chips, and his Doritos, and when she was settled in her chair, he thanked her again.

"You can say the blessing," he stated, his gaze fixed on a group of guys outside another trailer who were just setting up camp for the night. They had a grill going and were filling a cooler with a couple cases of beer. They were loud and a bit punchy, and Justice was glad she and Brandon would be moving on shortly. When three women showed up with grocery bags, great big smiles, and even bigger hair, Justice tried not to pass judgment. Instead, she bowed her head and said a quick prayer for their food and for safe travels, and for speedy healing for Brandon.

"Thanks," he muttered, sounding angry again, almost as if the sight of the food had made him forget, just for a moment, about his arm.

They ate in silence as they continued to watch the festivities unfold before them. One of the women hollered over at them, having recognized Brandon, with an invitation to join them. He just waved politely and said, "Another time, maybe."

Justice squelched the flicker of jealousy that rose up inside her and turned in her seat a little so she could tuck one leg up under her. "I can drive tonight," she said. "I promise I won't fall asleep at the wheel."

Brandon snorted, a derisive sound, but she thought it was more out of disgust for his own condition than disbelief of her claim that she'd stay awake. She was notorious about falling asleep the minute they got on the open road. But that was only when she was a passenger. It was like a flip that got switched—responsibility off, sleep on. Behind the wheel, however, she was all systems go, unbending, unwavering, fully charged and in control. Jesus didn't need to take the wheel, because she could handle it just fine.

And how has that worked out for you? The little voice in her head sounded a whole lot more like her own than her father's this time.

Brandon said nothing else, so having finished her sandwich, she picked up her bag of chips. She loved the extra crunch of the kettle style, and the tang of the salt and vinegar flavor made her mouth water, her lips pucker, and her taste buds holler for more. She chewed loudly in the silence between them, but she didn't care. Doritos weren't any quieter, and oh, so cliché.

"Those chips suit you," Brandon said, a little too offhandedly.

Justice lifted her brow, not sure whether to be offended or not. Was he making another joke? Or poking fun of her. Or insulting her. "How so?" she asked when he didn't expound.

After a beat, he said, "They're obnoxiously loud and intense. I can smell them from here."

An insult, then. She'd do her best to blow it off. "You can smell me from there? I should have taken a longer shower."

He snorted again, but this time, he actually grinned, too. Finally, he said, "I can smell you a mile away, Justice Goodacre." He still didn't look at her, but there was a husky quality to his words that made her cheeks warm.

Flustered, she said, "Well, if I'm loud and obnoxious, then you can probably hear me a mile away, too."

"I didn't say you were obnoxious," he corrected. "I said you were loud and intense. Obnoxiously so."

"I see." She nodded slowly, trying to figure out where this conversation was headed. "And those chips suit you," she countered, waving a hand at his red Doritos bag. "Super cheesy and triangular."

Brandon chuckled and the sound warmed her heart.

"And you're pretty much everyone's favorite," she said, waving the same hand in the general direction of the party across the way. She wanted to bite back the words the moment they were out. She sounded petty, she thought, and prayed he wouldn't take it that way. She had meant it as a joke, but she could imagine how easy it would be to read jealousy into a statement like that.

Were they both making spiteful, petty jabs at each other, disguising their barbs as teasing?

He frowned slightly, his gaze settling on the group again, then shook his head. "Not everyone's favorite." The sullen note was back in his voice. He pushed up out of his seat, his injured arm held against his chest, then took his plate over to the hose that hung down from the water tank in the hay rack. Releasing the valve, he ran some into the rubber washtub they used to wash their dishes in.

Justice squeezed her eyes shut in frustration, then stood, too. "I'll wash up if you want to put the chairs away." They kept them, along with his hammock, just inside the escape door, which also happened to open into the third stall that Brandon was using as his locker. She hated seeing his stuff back there, the intentional distance he was putting between them. He could do the honor of stowing the chairs so she didn't have to.

"Fine." He turned quickly and almost ran right into her. He instinctively grabbed her shoulders with both hands to steady her, then grunted in pain.

"Oh, Brandon, I'm sorry," she gasped, reaching up to touch his brace. "Sorry," she murmured again when he pulled back, clutching his wrist to his chest. It was as if even the thought of her touching him was repulsive.

He shook his head and swallowed, his face having gone slightly green. "My fault," he muttered, then turned away from her and disappeared around the back of the rig.

Should she go after him? Make sure he was okay?

A loud thunk resounded through the trailer, making both horses whinny in response. It sounded like he'd punched the paneling, hard, and she fought the urge to go check things out. He'd better not have left a mark on her pretty Exiss. She heard the escape door open and Brandon's grouchy voice speaking soothing words to the beasts inside—and maybe even to the beast inside of him—before he finally came back around to pack up the chairs. "Sorry about that," he practically snarled. "Didn't mean to scare the horses."

She just nodded, finished drying the dishes, then went about packing up the rest of the odds and ends that always ended up outside the trailer at every stop. When she stepped back out to close everything up, Brandon was gone. She capped the water tank and stuffed the hose into one of the outside compartments, rolled up the awning, and stowed everything away.

She was just beginning to worry when Brandon came into sight over by the party group. He smiled and made a few comments that garnered a lifted beer, but didn't stop to visit. When he approached, she realized his hair, tied back in the long braid that hung down his back, was damp, and he had on a different shirt. He'd gone off to use one of the open air shower stalls set up near the porta-potties.

Well, good. They had three hours of driving ahead of them. He wouldn't stink up the truck.

Without another word, Justice climbed in behind the wheel, Brandon got into the passenger seat, and they made their way out of the campground. By the time they pulled onto the highway, Brandon had turned *All Creatures Great and Small* back on. Fortunately, James Herriot wrote long books, and the narrator had the perfect voice to tell his stories. There were three more audiobooks in the series, and a couple of short story collections to boot. They might be able to get through this whole season without speaking a word to each other.

Except that now they had Brandon's arm to consider. She didn't want to ask what he intended to do, but she knew he had no desire to sit around on his keester for the next two weeks. Or longer. Whatever he decided would definitely affect her plans.

EIGHT

He usually teased her about being a granny driver—both hands on the wheel at ten and two, never going more than two or three miles over the speed limit, keeping the rig in the slower lanes, and never, ever cutting anyone off. But as the road disappeared under the hood of the truck, Brandon was glad he didn't have to worry about her driving skills. He was tired and in more pain than he wanted to admit, and he was frustrated beyond measure over his broken wrist. He'd barely listened to what the doctor had said about rest and non-activity, not because he didn't understand, but because he knew, all too well, what this meant for his run this season. It was over.

He'd played down the diagnosis to Justice, telling her he'd have it assessed in two weeks. There'd be no reason to do so. With his paramedic training, he knew exactly what he was dealing with. He'd seen the X-ray and the angled line around his ulna. He'd tried to twist away under the weight of the steers hoof, and the torque he put on his arm in doing so was most likely what caused the fracture. He'd done it to himself, and he knew full well that it would be four weeks minimum before he could get rid of the brace. Even then, he probably wouldn't be given the go ahead to get back in the arena.

Nope, this season was pretty much shot for Brandon.

Sure, he could continue on as a medic, but it would likely be in a volunteer position. In other words, no paycheck. And Cowboy Christmas Week was just around the corner, the week he and the twins usually made a good three-quarters of their rodeo income. The week he'd make zero. Zilch. Nada.

Laws, he just wanted to go home and bury his head in work at Whispering Hills Ranch.

But he wouldn't be of any use there, either, not with the brace. This injury would keep him useless for weeks on all counts. His replacement on his First Responder crew wouldn't appreciate being cut out of a job for the summer.

And then there was the pain. It only added to his agitation, the way it throbbed in waves that radiated up his arm every time he so much as moved. But he refused to take the mind-numbing meds they offered him. He was of the mind that he'd rather feel the pain so he could gage his limitations than to have his neurotransmitters shut down and not be aware of what was going on.

Besides, the pain in his wrist kept his mind off the pain in his heart.

Justice, he had to admit, was being a trooper. No matter how hard he was on her, she kept going forward, staying steady. He'd battled with himself at every stop, knowing he should stick around and help her get ready for her show, hating himself for not being there for her, hating himself for feeling guilty about leaving her to her own devices. She didn't deserve his help, not after what she'd done.

Yet as a paramedic, often the first person on a scene, Brandon made it his job to never pass judgment on a patient, whether they be victim, perpetrator, or bystander. It was his job to offer aid, whether a person deserved it or not.

He could do so with complete strangers... but he couldn't bring himself to offer the same courtesy to Justice?

"Thanks for driving," he said, reaching over to turn off the audiobook. He winced as he did so, the motion sending sharp jabs through his arm. "I want to listen to this—it's good. But I think we need to talk." He didn't turn toward her, but he watched her from the corner of his eye.

"Okay," she said, her tone steady, her gaze darting over at him momentarily before going back to the road in front of them. But he didn't miss how her grip on the steering wheel tightened, how her shoulders went up the tiniest bit. Like she was gearing up for a hit.

Shoot. Did she think he wanted to talk about her and Ogden? "About my arm," he said quickly, holding it up and then biting back the groan that nearly escaped.

"Right." Her shoulders stayed up but her grip on the wheel loosened.

Neither of them spoke for several moments, and as the silence in the cab grew thick, Brandon considered turning the audiobook back on. Or the radio. Or rolling down the window to get some fresh air. It was Justice who spoke first.

"I've thought about what you said. About your arm, I mean." She looked over at him now, her expression serious. "Two weeks? It's broken, right? Fractured, I know, but it's still a break. Isn't two weeks... I don't know. Unrealistic?"

He should have known he couldn't pull one over on her so easy. Both the twins had suffered their share of fractures and sprains, of braces, casts, slings, and crutches. But he was reticent to admit it outright. "I was planning on getting a second opinion when we get to Greeley."

She nodded, facing forward again. "Good idea."

"But you're right," he conceded. "A fracture would prevent me from competing for at least a month, if not longer."

Justice chewed on her bottom lip, mulling over his words. He could tell she had something she wanted to say, so he waited. Once again, the silence elongated, so he focused on the not so dull ache in his wrist.

Finally, she spoke. Quietly, hesitantly, but he could tell she'd thought things through carefully. "I miss Courage," she began. "The Twisted Sisters show isn't the same without her. Obviously." She made a sound that might have been a rueful chuckle. "I'm amazed at how much she did to prep for our show while I ran around doing paperwork and checking in. By the time I'd get back from all of that, she'd have both horses painted, geared up, warmed up and ready to go. All I had to do was put on my costume, and do my hair and makeup, and half the time, she'd help me with that, too." She shook her head. "I never realized, Brandon. I thought I was doing the important stuff, you know?"

He was taken aback by her forthrightness, by how humbled she sounded, and he didn't know quite what to say.

"I owe her a debt of gratitude. I thought I'd come out here and show the world that I didn't need anyone, that I could get the job done just fine on my own." Her eyes glistened in the faint glow of the dashboard lights and he thought she was fighting back tears. "I—I think—no, I know." She clenched her jaw and shook her head again. "I'm a crap sister, Brandon. I *know* that in this big head of mine, I've always thought of Courage as my sidekick. Tonto to my Zorro. Robin to my Batman." She opened her mouth to say more, but closed it again and swallowed hard, her hands clenched tightly again.

Before—everything was now before or after in Brandon's mind—before, he would have peeled one of her hands off the wheel and held it gently while she poured her heart out to him. Or he would have reached over and cupped the back of her neck, his strong fingers massaging the base of her skull to help her unwind. Before, he would have told her everything was going to be okay.

But that was before.

Now, *after*, Brandon felt helpless. Physically, because it was his left hand that was injured and it would feel super contrived to twist in his seat so he could reach over with his right hand. Mentally, because this was a side of Justice he wasn't accustomed to. And emotionally, because what she was saying was stirring up the deep well of love he had for her, and his goal was to stay angry at her. Or at least distant and reserved. Right now, though, all he wanted to do was order her to stop the truck and get out so he could wrap her in his arms and comfort her.

"I keep meaning to call her and tell her so, to apologize for being so smug and self-important, but I feel like I need to say these things to her face to face. That they'll carry more weight when she can see my expression, when we're sitting across from each other." She spread the fingers of one hand wide, then curled it back around the steering wheel loosely. "When we're touching," she added in a whisper.

"I can understand that," Brandon said, his desire for the same thing—to touch her—making his throat tight.

Her next words stunned him back into silence. "I'm ready to go home if you are, Brandon." She still wasn't looking at him, but her jaw was set, her shoulders back and her chin high. "Just say the word, and I'll turn this thing around." Then she did smile, albeit just a small one. "I know Fire misses Flash like crazy, too."

"Justice," he began when he could speak again. "No. Just because I'm incapacitated doesn't mean you are. Sure, things are different for you without Courage, and you've had some major adjusting to do, but you're getting it. You're doing it. Yesterday's show was great."

"It wasn't great, Brandon," she countered. "It was technically spot on, but I'm not the same performer without Courage."

"Then be a different performer than the one you were with her. Be yourself. Be your own you." He shifted a little, this time cradling his arm to minimize the jostling of it. "You're a great performer. You're just trying to do a show that's intended for two people."

"No, I've changed it up a lot. I've taken out the two-people parts and replaced them with solo stuff," she began, but he cut her off.

"Exactly. You're taking a two-person show and trying to make it a one-person show. You have the skills you need, Justice. You need to build a new show—your show—from the ground up. Not a two-person-turned-one-person show, but a solo act designed just for you and Fire." He found it impossible to not let the "before" version of himself into this conversation. He tried, he really did, but he couldn't sit back and let Justice talk herself out of doing what she loved. What she was so good at. "Right now, you're dealing with expectations that you can't meet. Not your own expectations," he said when she started to open her mouth. He suddenly needed to get this out. It was as if it had been building up inside him without his knowledge, and now that he'd opened it up, there was no containing it. "Everyone else's. They come to see you and Courage performing The Twisted Sisters routine. From the moment you charge through the starting gate alone, you are unable to meet those expectations. Even when they're told you'll be performing alone, that Courage is injured, they still will automatically feel like they aren't getting their money's worth because they came to see two riders, not one. You can't please them, Justice. Not like this. Not with The Twisted Sisters act. You're set up to let your fans down, no matter how spectacularly you perform."

She turned to look at him for a moment before her eyes were back on the road, her brow furrowed, her expression vulnerable and contemplative. "I—I never thought of it that way."

"I'll help you." He held up his left arm with his right. "I can't braid hair, but I can still paint on glitter and use a curry comb." Crap, crap, crap! What was he saying? "I can help you come up with a new routine, tell you what works and what doesn't."

She shook her head slowly. "Brandon, we're two weeks into the season. I can't shift gears so dramatically. Where would we go? Where would we practice?"

"Let's skip a few stops. The next few on our route aren't big purses. Let's find a place along the way where we can board the horses and work out a new routine."

"I can't learn a new routine that quickly," she said, frowning now. "I can't. It's too much." She thumped the steering wheel with the heel of one hand. "Let's just go home, Brandon. Let's call this what it is—all of this. A lost cause. Over. Finished."

Her words were paralyzing. Did she mean the season? Did she mean The Twisted Sisters? Or did she mean the two of them?

"I—I can't do this anymore," she murmured, her voice cracking on the last word. "I'll do Greeley—I can't not show up for that, not without a dang good reason, and missing my sister and her horse won't cut it." She sniffed and continued. "But then I'm done, Brandon. I can't keep pretending things are great." She snorted and gave a rueful chuckle. "I can't even pretend things are just okay." She shook her head and pressed her lips together, swallowing back any other words that might slip out.

After yet another heavy silence, Brandon said, "So you're going to quit. Give up." It came out far crueler than he'd intended, and he saw her flinch. In fact, he hadn't intended it to be cruel at all. He'd meant to spur her on, to remind her who she was. Justice. Black and white. Right and wrong. All in. Go for the gold or go...

Or go home.

He squeezed his eyes shut. "Sorry. That didn't come out right."

"No," she shook her head, squaring her shoulders, blinking rapidly as she stared out the windshield. "No, you're right. I'm quitting. I'm quitting all of this." She swept a hand in front of her in a brusque slashing motion. "You are welcome to the trailer if you want to stay on the road. I'll call Daddy and have him pick Fire and me up. He hasn't been to Greeley for years, and I think he'd enjoy a day or two there. Reconnect with some of his old cronies." It had been years since Jed traveled with the girls for every show, but his face was as familiar as theirs' to the folks behind the scenes.

Brandon frowned and cocked his head at her. "And why on earth would I keep going with this bum hand?" He lifted it without thinking, grunted at the rush of pain, then turned to look out his passenger side window, lest she see his acute discomfort. "I'm pretty much along for the ride, now." And dang it, now he was getting all worked up again, too. "Tonto to your Zorro, is that what you called Courage? Except that I'm a pretty useless sidekick. I can't even cinch your saddle for you."

Justice turned and glared at him, her eyes blazing. "How dare you throw my words in my face like that? It's not my fault that stupid cow stepped on your wrist. It's not my fault you couldn't keep him down. And I haven't once—not *once!*—asked you for a lick of help."

"Steer," Brandon shot back, cringing at his childish response. "And my wrist may not be your fault, but the rest of this is." Now it was his turn to gesture wildly... with his right hand, he remembered, although the jerking motion still hurt like the dickens. "Your decision to try to carry the weight of The Twisted Sisters show on your own and its subsequent failure? That's your fault. Us—Ha! I mean, the nonexistence of us? Your fault." *Shut up, man,* a voice in his head screamed at him. But he blocked it out and let the atomic bomb drop. "Courage? Her absence here in this truck? Her fall?" Every word was cruelly poisoned with the pain of her betrayal. "You got it. Your fault. Your sister has been killing herself to make you happy. For years now, and you've been too focused on yourself to even notice. Well, guess what. You're the sidekick, Justice, but you're the only one who doesn't know it. She's the heart of your show, not you."

"Stop it!" Justice yelled, her voice wretched. "Why are you—"

But once unleashed, he couldn't seem to rein it in. "And believe me, I know from personal experience that nothing can survive without a heart. It's no wonder you and me didn't—"

Justice slammed on the brakes and everything seemed to slow down, just like it did in the movies. The sound of squealing tires, the fishtailing trailer, the creak and groan of the weight of the Exiss shoving the truck forward, momentum an unstoppable force. The screech of metal against metal... the surreal image—one that would be forever imprinted on his brain—of the eight-pronged antlers illuminated in the headlights, the buck's eyes glowing orange as he stared them down.

The cacophonous silence when everything finally—*finally*—came to skidding halt.

NINE

"Are you hurt?" Justice asked, her panicked voice high, her hand reaching across the console to grab his arm. "Oh, Brandon, I'm so sorry. Are you okay? I didn't see him. He was just there, and—and..."

"I'm okay," he said, his voice breathy, his hand covering hers. "What about you?"

Then she stiffened and began scrambling for her door handle. "The horses! Oh, please, God, please, God, let them be okay."

She practically fell in her mad rush to get out.

"Wait!" Brandon called, his voice ragged and harsh. "Watch for traffic!"

But she didn't stop, not even bothering to close the door before dashing to the escape door on her side of the trailer. The Exiss had stopped at an angle across the lane, so unless someone came along and plowed into it, she wasn't going to get hit.

She could already hear them, the harsh screams of the outraged horses. Her heart pounded so loud in her ears, she could hardly hold onto the thoughts racing through her mind. Which was probably good, considering that she was imaging all the worst-case scenarios.

By the time she flung open the door, she realized something was wrong with her right ankle. It hurt worse with every passing moment, and taking the single step up into the trailer made her want to cry out, except she couldn't seem to catch her breath. Not until she knew how the horses had fared. "Fire!" she called out, hitting the light switch just inside the door. "I'm here. Tank? I'm so sorry. Are you okay?"

Stomping and kicking, both horses were in a full blown panic, tossing their heads and making all kinds of ruckus. She couldn't tell anything, not with them enclosed in their partitioned stalls, but at least both of them seemed more afraid than in pain. At least they were upright. The more they kicked and screamed, however, the more panicked they became as the sound echoed around the small space. They had to get them out and let them calm down before they hurt themselves or each other. She prayed there was enough room on the side of the road to accommodate them. It was too dark to tell if there were fences, but the fact that the buck had made it across and disappeared gave her hope.

The back of the trailer flew open, and Brandon was there, tugging open the tack closet and yanking out lead ropes. "I'll get Tank," he called to her over the madness within. "You okay with Fire or do you want me to get him out, too?"

"No, no. You worry about Tank. As soon as you're clear, I'll get Fire out," she hollered back, reaching over the stall divider, palm out toward her horse, who batted her hand away with his nose. She waited there, trying to distract him from what was happening with Tank, talking softly, soothingly, hoping her horse could hear her voice over the chaos. Hoping he didn't hear the panic, or smell the adrenaline coursing through her system. "It's okay, Fire. You're okay, boy. I got you, baby. I got you."

He let her stroke his neck once, then kicked hard against the wall, eliciting an angry whinny from Tank. Justice could hear Brandon's voice, loud and firm, but calm, as he talked his big bay through what he was doing. "Opening the side rail, now, Tank, my man. Don't freak out. You're doing just fine. Come on, now. You gotta follow my lead, boy. Let me lead. This way. Whoa." Tank side-stepped and jostled beside Brandon, but he managed to direct the horse out of the back of the trailer without any major mishap.

Once Tank was out, the noise diminished radically, and Fire calmed quickly. He dipped his head toward her, nuzzling against her shoulder, then stepped back and kicked the wall again. "Whoa, boy. It's okay," she murmured, not reacting to his temper tantrum. At least that's what it looked like to her. He really did seem more put out than hurt, but she wouldn't know until she got him out and walking around.

Her mind raced ahead to the small town they were hoping to reach in an hour. Was there a place they could give the horses a full examination? Were the horses going to be willing to get back into the trailer? Could they manage another hour of driving?

Could she? In spite of her heart rate settling a bit, her hands shook visibly, and her ankle throbbed, and she wasn't sure she was in any condition to get behind the wheel again. At least not tonight. She wondered if Brandon would be okay to drive.

When she was certain Brandon and Tank were clear of the trailer and off the side of the road, Justice clambered down the side door step and hurried around to the back, her ankle aching menacingly with each hobble. Back inside the trailer, she reached for Fire's halter and deftly clipped the lead rope to it, then let go as he tossed his head again. She kept talking, telling him everything was okay. As her own pulse began to slow, Fire grew calmer as well.

Tank called to Fire once, and her horse responded with a nicker, but the frantic pitch was no longer there. Justice swung open the divider and led him carefully out the back. On the asphalt, Fire tugged against the lead and tossed his head a bit, but Justice held tight, giving him his head, but not letting him take over. "Let's walk it off, boy. Come on."

She'd just gotten him off the side of the road when headlights came around the bend a couple miles back. Brandon and Tank were up ahead of their rig, Brandon studying his horse's gait in the headlights as he walked him back and forth in short laps. Justice brought Fire up to join them. He stopped as Justice and Fire drew close.

"There's a car coming. Do you think we need to move the trailer now that the horses are out?"

He shook his head. "There's enough room for them to get by," he told her, running his hand down Tank's legs, pressing gently for any signs of tenderness.

"How are you guys?" Justice asked, leading Fire to walk back and forth the same way Brandon had with Tank. "Both of you? I'm so sorry, Brandon," she said again, her voice catching.

"He seems fine," Brandon assured her, but his focus was intent as he made his way around his horse, turning the animal as he went so he could use the bright beam of the headlights to check for bumps and scratches, any sign of bruising or injury. "What about Fire?" He finally looked up, then his eyes narrowed as he watched them. "You're hurt."

"No," she contradicted. "It's nothing. Just twisted my ankle a little. But I can already tell it's nothing." She'd been worried at first, but having walked around on it now, she sensed it was the kind of injury that would require her to be careful, but wouldn't prevent her from riding. She might have to alter her routine to coddle the ankle for a couple of days, but if she wrapped it well, she'd be fine. She'd had more than her fair share of twisted ankles in her career. She knew what she was dealing with, just by the feel of it. "But what about you? Your arm?" He had it cradled against his chest again, trying to do everything with one hand.

"I'm fine. It's fine," he said, his voice gruff. Was he angry at her? She looked away just as a beefy Dodge pickup pulled up behind the trailer and off to the side of the road, the headlights illuminating the four of them.

The cab lights went on as the driver's side door opened, and a tall woman in a White Stetson stepped out, then reached back inside and pulled a rifle down from a gun rack mounted behind the seat. She said something to the barking dog in the front passenger seat, and the animal sat back on its haunches and eyed the scene out the front window, his tongue lolling out of one side of his mouth. She closed the door and strode toward them, calling out a greeting. "Hey, there, folks? Everything all right?"

"Yeah," Brandon called back. "Almost took out a deer."

The closer she got, the taller she became. Justice's eyes widened as the woman approached, gun hanging loosely at her side, barrel down, her other hand holding an enormous flashlight, the beam of it pointed at the ground, too. Behind her in the truck cab, the dog stood, then sat, then stood again, placing his two front paws on the dashboard, his breath making a film of moisture on the windshield.

"Run-in with mule deer," the woman said, sizing up the situation. "They're out and about these days. Building up stamina and scoping out the competition," she added with a chuckle. "Rutting season is just around the bend."

Brandon stepped forward, awkwardly shifting the lead rope to his braced wrist so he could shake the woman's hand.

"Here," Justice said, reaching out to take it from him. "Let me hold it. Come on, Tank. Let's keep walking." Both horses were responding to the dog, and nickering with agitation. She led them in a slow lap, then came back to stand a few yards behind Brandon.

"I'm Brandon Stillwater. This is Justice," he said to the woman. "A buck. Thankfully, we didn't hit him, but we've had a scare. Just happened, so we're still trying to size up the damage, and hoping there isn't any. Haven't even looked at the truck and trailer yet." He glanced over at the rig. "Suppose we need to get this thing out of the road."

"Charlotte Rawlings," the woman said as she gave Brandon's hand a firm shake. Then she waved at Justice. "You rodeo folks?" she asked, eying the two horses. "Beautiful boys, you got there."

"Thanks. Yes. We were shooting for Truskee tonight," Brandon said, running his good hand over the top of his head. Justice could see he was frazzled and trying to keep it together. He was usually so calm in emergency situations, but he seemed to almost vibrate with nerves.

"I see." Charlotte nodded slowly, her brow furrowed. "That's a good hour or so away, especially hauling a load."

"Right." Brandon nodded, but said nothing more.

"What can I do to help?" Charlotte asked, shining the flashlight over the body of the trailer, then at the goose neck hitch mounted in the back of Brandon's truck. "Think she's drivable?"

Brandon took a deep breath and let it out slowly. "I'm not sure." He turned back to look at Justice. "You turned the engine off, right? It didn't die?"

Justice shook her head. "I shut it down."

"You were driving?" Charlotte cocked her head at Justice, her chin lifted a little as she gave her a measuring look. What was she thinking, her eyes narrowed like that? "You all right? You're limping."

"I'm fine. Just tweaked my ankle, but nothing serious," Justice assured her.

"Well, why don't you hop in, then," she said to Justice. "Brandon's right. We need to get this thing off the road before some idiot comes hauling through here all lit up." Charlotte headed back to her own truck, returned the gun to its rack, tousled the dog's head a few times, then rejoined them, flashlight still in hand. She gave it to Brandon. "Here you go. Use this if you need it." Then she turned to Justice and the horses. "Hello, boys."

Biting back a surge of fear so overwhelming she felt sick to her stomach, Justice handed over the leads to Charlotte, then climbed back into the truck and turned the key in the ignition. It started up without a complaint. She rolled both windows down so she could hear Brandon's instructions. She eased the truck into gear, then clutching the steering wheel tightly with both hands, she pushed down on the gas as gingerly as she could.

While Brandon watched, she pulled the truck forward several feet until the trailer lined up straight behind it, then stopped. "How's it look?" she called out the window. She could see him in her passenger side mirror, but Charlotte was closer.

"So far, so good," the woman said reassuringly. The horses, Justice was glad to see, were dipping their heads to graze.

"Pull forward a bit more," Brandon called out.

A few yards down the road, she stepped on the brakes when she saw his arm go up in a gesture for her to stop. He approached her driver's side and rested a hand on the frame of the open window. "Are you comfortable hanging out here with Charlotte and the horses for a few minutes? I'd like to take this for a short spin up the road and back to make sure it feels okay. I don't see anything, but in the dark, it's going to be hard to tell. And I don't want to load the horses up until we know we're going to be safe."

Justice nodded, darting another look in the side mirror at the woman standing with their horses. "Of course. She seems okay. Other than that big gun she's toting."

"She thought she might have to put an animal out of its misery," Brandon explained with a chuckle.

"Gotcha." Justice smiled at him, then tentatively covered his hand with her own. "I'm so sorry, Brandon. I'm sorry—"

"No!" He reached in through the window and cupped the back of her head, pulling her closer, his eyes suddenly bright. "Justice, no. This wasn't your fault." He closed his eyes briefly, then opened them again. He looked ready to cry. "My head—" He broke off, swallowed, then tried again. "My head won't stop spinning. My mind, I mean. What could have happened... I'm the one who should be apologizing. Justice—" This time it took several moments before he could speak again. "I'm so sorry."

"Stop," she murmured, reaching up to touch his cheek. "Stop." This time is wasn't much more than a whisper. "We're okay. The horses are okay. Even the stupid buck is okay." She leaned forward and rested her forehead against his. "But I wouldn't be sad if he had a heart attack out there in that field and keeled over dead."

Brandon chuckled, a shaky sound, his hand settling around the back of her neck, his fingers warm and a little clammy against her skin. "I was so afraid. Talk about a heart attack."

"Me, too," she whispered. She could smell coffee on his breath, and for once, instead of teasing him about it, she was glad for it. Breathing. Alive. Uninjured.

They stayed that way for a moment, then he pulled back and opened the door for her. "Come on out. Let's do this. I'll walk you back to Charlotte."

"No, I'm fine. You go ahead. I'll fill her in on what's going on."

By the time she'd hobbled over to stand with the other woman, she knew she needed ice. Sooner than later. The lace-up work boots she wore were a godsend for the support they provided, but she was dreading the moment she slipped them off. It wasn't broken, she was certain of that. It wasn't the right kind of pain for a break. No, she could feel the strain up the inside of her ankle and calf; she'd probably twisted it against the slope of the floorboard in her frantic efforts to stop the truck.

"That bum ankle," Charlotte began without preamble as she handed Fire's lead to Justice. "Not really fine, is it?"

For a moment, Justice was tempted to lie. Then she shook her head and grimaced. "I was hoping. But it hurts." She let out a forlorn sigh. "This has been the road trip from hell," she said with a rueful snort. "Brandon is going to take the rig for a short spin, then come back. He wants to see how it rides before we load up the horses," she explained to the tall woman. "Thank you for your help. I'm fine to wait for him with the horses if you need to get going. You've been very kind."

"Nonsense," Charlotte scoffed good-naturedly. "I'm not going anywhere until we get this sorted. You folks are out in the middle of nowhere, and I'm certainly not going to leave you and your boys alone on the side of the road. What if he gets down the way a bit and discovers there's a problem?"

Justice hadn't thought about that. "Right. Well, thank you. I hope you aren't going to be late to where it is you were going."

"I was heading home," Charlotte assured her. "The only ones who might notice my absence are my sheep, and they should all be settled in for the night anyway. We're all good."

"Sheep?"

Charlotte nodded. "Shetland sheep for their colorful wool. I'm a weaver and I do it all myself: shearing, cleaning, dyeing, carding, and spinning my own wool." She said it all so casually, it took Justice a moment to catch up. She had imagined the statuesque Colorado wild woman out on the range astride an elegant Arabian or an enormous Morgan, her hat pulled low over her eyes, the sun setting golden in the distance. No, Charlotte Rawlings raised colorful fluffy sheep. And she sat at a spinning wheel? Talk about reading a person wrong.

"Anyway, here's what I'm thinking." Charlotte continued as though nothing she'd said was anything extraordinary. Her eyes tracked the taillights of the trailer as Brandon took a bend in the road about a mile up. "Truskee's a long way to go on an iffy ride at night. There are some long stretches of empty road just like this one, and the next town is a good thirty miles down the way. They do have a Motel 8, I believe, and you can probably park the trailer with the horses out behind it, although you might have to pay a little extra. But you'll be lucky if the ice machine is functioning. Heck, you'll be lucky if they even have an ice machine."

"We've already got a campsite reserved near the rodeo there, so we'll probably try to make it that far tonight."

"Right, yes," Charlotte said with a nod. "Brandon said as much. But I'm thinking maybe you two should consider coming on out to my place for the night. It's about a mile up ahead, just around that bend, and you can stable the horses in my barn, or in the pasture, if you—or they—prefer. Get yourself a good night's sleep, some ice on that ankle, and see how things are in the morning. I saw Brandon had a brace on his arm. He might could do with a little extra rest, too. Wouldn't have to set up camp at my place. Pull in, unload the horses, and take advantage of my little guest house out back. It's essentially a detached master bedroom and bathroom—no kitchen, so you'd have to come inside for breakfast—but the bed's comfy and the room is clean, and the water in the shower is hot and plentiful." She chuckled softly. "If I know trailers, that last bit should convince you."

She was right. The idea of a long, hot shower just about made Justice swoon. Her shoulders were knotted and tight even before the accident, and she knew she'd be stiff come morning. The trailer shower would offer no such accommodations. "I—I don't know. I'll have to talk to Brandon."

"Of course." Charlotte nodded and smiled down at her from her towering height. The woman had to be over six feet tall.

"But thank you. I appreciate the offer. It's very kind." It was also a little surreal. This woman didn't know them from Adam and Eve, but here she was, opening her home to strangers she'd pulled over to help on the side of the road. Didn't she read the news? "I mean it." Justice felt a telltale tingle at the bridge of her nose. She would not cry. "Woman to woman, your offer sounds so good it hurts."

Charlotte chuckled. "Then we'll have to convince that handsome young man of yours that it's the best thing for everyone. Including these fellas," she added, turning to run a hand down Tank's mane. "I think the light of day will give us all a better perspective on things, don't you?"

Justice didn't respond; she was pretty sure Charlotte was talking to the horse, not her.

TEN

THE TRUCK SEEMED TO ride steady, no pull on the steering wheel to indicate any alignment issues, and the trailer cruised along behind it without any more than its usual swagger. He turned around when he came to a small cleared area a couple miles up the road, then headed back the way he came, getting the rig up to highway speed. Still there was no unfamiliar shimmy, no odd sounds. He waved when he whizzed past the little group on the other side of the road, sending them a thumbs up, but kept going. It felt just the way it always did without the added weight of the horses. He finally slowed, tested the brakes a few times, watched in the side view mirrors for any smoke or sparks, but everything seemed to be working just fine. His relief was profound, but he still hated the idea of driving another seventy or eighty miles without having a good look at things in the daylight.

They'd have to take it slow. Make several stops along the way to assess their condition. Which meant getting into Truskee a whole lot later than they'd planned. They were both already lagging, tired physically and emotionally. Not just from haul of the rodeo days, either, but from the prolonged tension that stretched like a tightly wound rubber band between them. He sighed loudly, the wind rushing the open windows sweeping the sound away, and pulled over just far enough off the road to get the rig turned around, then headed back the way he'd come. It was going to be a long night. "Okay, God. Let's do this."

He parked a few yards ahead of the little group on the side of the road, hit his flashers, and climbed out of the truck. He flinched when he landed on the pavement, the jolt sending sharp pains up his arm; he'd have to be more careful, or he'd set his healing back by days, if not weeks.

The women stood near Charlotte's truck, still holding the lead ropes of both horses, and chatting while they waited for him. Charlotte's dog, what looked like a mix between a shepherd and a lab, lay on his belly at their feet, his nose directed toward the horses grazing calmly at the ends of their tethers. They seemed unconcerned about the furry animal now.

Justice stepped over the dog and hobbled toward him. "How is it?" she asked, surprisingly calm in light of all that had happened. He saw the concern shadowing her eyes, though, and he nodded.

"It feels okay. No weird noises or shimmies. I wish I could take a look at it in the light of day, but if we can get to Truskee tonight, I'll give it a good going over tomorrow before we head out again. Think the horses are going to be able to stomach getting back in the trailer tonight?" He lifted his chin toward Tank, who'd raised his head and nickered in greeting before going back to nibbling the short grass just off the road.

"Actually, Charlotte had a suggestion," Justice began, glancing back over her shoulder at the woman who still leaned casually against her truck grill. "She's offered to let us stay at her place about a mile up the road—you probably passed the driveway if you went much beyond the turn up there. She's got a barn where we can put up the horses, and a guest house where we can stay."

Her words rushed out of her as if she thought he might reject the idea before he'd even heard it.

"A hot shower and plenty of water," Justice added. "Her words, not mine. She knows trailers." She smiled up at him, eyes beseeching.

"Seriously?" He looked past Justice to the older woman who was stroking her dog's belly with a booted foot. She smiled and lifted a brow, not having heard his response to Justice. "Are you sure?" Brandon asked a little louder. Talk about an answer to prayer. "I mean, you're okay with us crashing at your place tonight?"

"I'm sure, and I'm okay with it," Charlotte drawled, her smile growing wider. "You kids look like you could use a break. I'd be happy to have your company."

"Wow," he said, brushing his hand over the top of his head, then cupping the back of his neck and squeezing. The muscles there screamed in response. Crap. He hoped he wouldn't wake up with a stiff neck. He needed to be able to drive tomorrow. He certainly wasn't going to make Justice get behind the wheel right away. Not with that ankle. He'd seen her in his rear view mirror hobbling all the way back to Charlotte. "I won't say no to that offer, Charlotte. We won't say no," he corrected, putting his hand on Justice's low back as they stood together facing the woman. Fire bumped his nose against Brandon's shoulder, but he ignored the horse. "I'd feel so much better about getting back on the road with this thing if I can check it out in the daylight."

"Then it's a deal," Charlotte said with a brusque nod, straightening up and holding out the lead toward Brandon. "I'm close, a little more than a mile away, so if you can't convince these boys to hop back up into that trailer, I'd be happy to ride ahead and open up the barn for you. You can walk them up the road to my place, then I can bring one of you back for the truck and trailer."

The woman was going above and beyond, but Brandon was so relieved that he didn't second guess her motives. If he'd been in her shoes, he'd have made the same offer, truth be told. "You're very kind," he told her with a nod. "Let's see if they'll cooperate first. Then we'll go from there."

It took both him and Justice working together to get Fire into the trailer, but once the Irish Sport was locked into his stall, Tank didn't put up nearly as big a fuss.

"You're good with them," Charlotte called to Brandon as he closed up the back of the trailer. She and her dog had climbed back into her truck to wait so as not to be a distraction.

"Thanks. They're good horses." Justice rounded the end of the trailer to join him and he added with a grin, "Fire can be a little unpredictable, but then, so can his rider."

She flicked him in the bicep. "Hey, now. We're not unpredictable. We're mysterious. Enigmas."

Charlotte laughed and called out, "Follow me. It's not far." Then she rolled up her window and turned to say something to her dog.

Brandon stopped Justice as she started around to the driver's side. "Nope. I'm not blind. You're not driving."

"I'm fine," she insisted. "It's just a little sore, that's all." She didn't even try to pretend she didn't know what he was talking about.

"Neither of us are fine," he said, giving her a stern look. "But I'm driving." Then he made a rotating gesture with his hand and ushered her back toward the passenger side where he held the door open for her. "Up you go."

She didn't argue, which told him he was right. He frowned as he made his way around the hood of the truck. What would this mean for her upcoming shows? She often powered through minor injuries, but a twisted ankle wasn't something she could take lightly, not with all the crazy tricks she performed.

They followed Charlotte's truck until she pulled up in front of a big barn at the end of a long gravel drive. She hopped out, the dog bounding out behind her, then directed them to pull over to the side of the barn where there was more room to maneuver the trailer. By the time they were out of the truck, she had the barn doors open and was clearing out a stall inside. "I keep a bunch of extra junk in this one," she explained as she shoved a bin of grooming supplies and an extra saddle out into the main aisle. "But one of them can go in here, and the other in the stall straight across from it. Will that work?"

Charlotte had two horses of her own in the six stall barn. She'd converted one of the empty stalls into a work space, complete with a desk, an ancient wooden chair, and a floor lamp. Another stall was piled high with stacked bales of hay, and the last one was the one she was aggressively emptying. "Let me help," Brandon said, stepping forward to take a second large tote from her. She straightened, eyed him censoriously, then pointed one of her elbows at his left hand.

"I've got this," she said. "You get the boys out of the trailer. By the time you get the first one inside, I'll be ready here." She shoved the tote into the stall with the hay bales, then turned to Justice, who was hurrying over to help, too. "And you, missy." She pointed toward the stall with the desk and chair. "If you're going to insist on being in the middle of things, you're going to have to do it from there. On your butt, with your foot up on the desk. Brandon can unload the horses by himself."

Justice looked so surprised that someone was ordering her around, that she simply nodded and complied. Brandon grinned as he got busy, and in no time at all, the horses were stabled, fed and watered, and calling out greetings to their new neighbors at the other end of the barn.

"I'll show you your room," Charlotte said, waving her long arm in a sweeping motion to indicate they follow her. "Then we'll grab a bite to eat. It's late for dinner, but I have stew in a slow cooker, and I wasn't going to ruin my appetite by grabbing fast food on my way home this evening. If you're hungry, you're welcome to join me; there's plenty. If you've already eaten, you're still welcome to join me for a cup of coffee or something stronger, if you prefer. I've got a bottle of whiskey and a few lemons if you're needing a hot toddy—you both may be needing a dose or two come time to lay your heads down and sleep." She grinned over her shoulder at them, then led them to the door of a small building that looked like it had once been connected to the rest of the house but was now separated by a wide breezeway. "I had my niece living with me for several years," she told them. "When Natalie turned eighteen, I promised her we'd give her a space of her own. She had the master suite already, and this breezeway was once just an extra hallway and mudroom. So once we made certain we weren't going to do any structural damage to my home," she explained, waving a hand casually around the space. "Well, I think the remodel turned out something special, don't you?"

"You put in the breezeway yourself?" Justice asked, wincing a little as she took the single step up into the space. Brandon frowned and placed a hand at her back again, ready to assist her if she needed it.

"Sure did," Charlotte said with a cheeky grin. "I'm a git 'er done kinda girl. Once I get a notion in my head, I have a hard time waiting for anyone else to do it."

"You sound like me," Justice said, rolling her eyes. "I'm terrible about asking for help, aren't I, Brandon?" She turned to look up at him, a careful smile on her lips, her gaze hopeful.

"Terrible," he agreed, slipping his arm around her waist and pulling her carefully against his side. "But I'm always there offering anyway."

Justice blushed, but she nodded. "He is," she declared, turning back to Charlotte. "Always."

"I wish I had one of him," Charlotte chuckled. "Not that I'm objectifying you, Brandon. I just think it would be nice to have a helping hand around whenever I needed one. It's just me out here, along with Nutter," she said, reaching down to scratch the dog's ears. He ambled along beside her, clearly aware of where his bread was buttered. "The horses, of course, and my sheep."

She pushed open the door of the guest room and stepped back. "There you go. You can bring your stuff in while I go grab some linens from the house to make up the bed."

The bed. *The* bed. One. Single. Bed. And a diminutive purple suede loveseat, and two bright green armchairs in front of a small coffee table. A television was mounted on the wall across from the bed so that anyone sitting on the sofa or chairs could also see it, a dresser beneath it, and a bulky armoire took up a large section of another wall.

"This is lovely," Justice was saying to Charlotte, and although she sounded genuine in her gratitude, Brandon was pretty sure the high color in her cheeks had something to do with the same thoughts he was having. One bed.

"I'll be right back. You two get acquainted with the room. Towels are under the bathroom sink, and I presume you have your own bath products. That said, if you need anything, just holler. Because I live so far from a Wal-Mart, I stock up whenever I'm out that way, so I've got months' worth of supplies at hand." Charlotte chuckled and headed out the door, closing it gently behind her.

Brandon hesitated before turning to look at Justice. What he saw on her face had him crossing the room to her in three quick strides.

ELEVEN

"I NEED TO SIT down," Justice murmured, her voice tight with obvious discomfort. "Not because of my foot, though." She shook her head when he reached for her.

Not her foot? "What's wrong?" She looked like she might be on the verge of passing out. He ignored her refusal, or whatever that shaking head thing was, put an arm around her and led her to the loveseat. She was trembling all over, and when they lowered to the cushions, she brought both hands up to cover her face. "Hey," he said, reaching up to pull them away. "Hey," he said again, this time with far more concern. "What's going on, Justice?"

"I—I think—" she broke off, then moved one hand to her chest. "My heart's racing, Brandon. I'm having a hard time getting a good breath," she said, lifting her chin and elongated her neck in an exaggerated attempt to open her airway. "Like something's squeezing my chest. I think I'm having some kind of—I don't know. A heart attack? I—I don't know." The words were coming out in short bursts and squeaks. "I can't—"

"Whoa," Brandon spun around, shoved the coffee table out of the way, knocking it on its side. He ignored it and knelt in front of her. "Justice, look at me." She lifted wide eyes filled with genuine fear. Acute stress, most likely due to the emotional trauma of the last hour, in full onset. Her pupils were dilated, her breathing shallow, and he could see the pulse at the base of her throat fluttering like a hummingbird's wing.

"Brandon," she whimpered his name.

"I'm here. I've got you." He stood and scooped her up in his arms, and threaded his way through the furniture to the bed. She wrapped an arm around his neck and pressed her face into his shoulder. Her breath was warm against the skin above the neck of his shirt, but it was the rapid breathing that he focused on. Laying her gently on the bed, he turned her on her side and had her bring her legs up toward her chest so she was half-curled in on herself. He brought the edge of the comforter up and over her. "Listen to me," he said, crouching down in front of her again so she could look him in the eyes. "I want you to concentrate on my breathing and do it with me. You need to slow your breathing down; we're hyperventilating, okay? Ready?" He took her hand and pressed her palm flat against his chest. "In." He breathed in through his nose and held it, waiting for her to do the same before letting it out again. "Out. Good. In."

"I can't," she gasped after a few breaths. "Too slow. It's not enough air."

"Watch me. Feel me," he told her, pressing her hand more firmly over his heart. "Feel my chest rise as my lungs fill with air. That's right. In." He waited until she drew in a breath, her mouth open with the effort. "No, no. Don't close your eyes. Stay focused on me, okay? Good girl." She nodded, and they started the breathing process again. She seemed to be following along a little better.

Keeping her hand on his chest, he slid his fingers down to wrap around her wrist until he found her pulse. It was still rapid, but steady and strong. "Let's get your breathing under control so you don't pass out, okay? Then I'll get you some water and a cool washcloth."

"I'm—am I going to be okay?" she choked out.

"Yes," he assured her with a smile. He reached out with his injured arm and with a brush of his fingers, smoothed back the hair from her forehead. Even that small amount of pressure hurt like the dickens, but he masked his pain with what he hoped was an encouraging smile. "It may take you awhile, but the worst of it will be over in a few minutes. You'll be okay. Keep breathing slowly, in and out. That's right."

It took her several minutes, in fact, to get to the point where he felt he could leave her for a moment, then he rose and hurried into the adjoining bathroom. He found a washcloth under the sink, just as Charlotte had said, and in no time, he was back at Justice's side, pressing the cool cloth to her neck, then her temples, then to the insides of her wrists. "You doing okay?"

he asked, keeping his voice calm and reassuring. "I'll need to go out and grab one of our water bottles."

"Or I could just suck on the washcloth," she muttered, closing her eyes as he dabbed at her cheeks, then her forehead again. "I'm suddenly super thirsty."

"Yeah, no surprise there. You want to hold this while I go get some water?" At least she was joking around; that was a good sign.

Just then, a knock sounded at the door.

"Come in," Brandon called out, but barely turned to glance over his shoulder at Charlotte as she came in. "Charlotte," he said in his First Responder voice. "How about a glass of water? I didn't find a cup in the bathroom, but there are water bottles in the front console of my truck."

"Looks like you both could use one. I'll be right back with a couple of glasses," the older woman said without hesitating. She set a stack of linens on one of the armchairs, righted the coffee table without a word, then dashed back out into the night.

"I'm sorry," Justice muttered, her words muffled as she turned her face into the pillow and draped an arm over her head. "I don't know what's wrong with me. I feel like my head is going to just fly off my body right now. And I might barf. Just a heads up." She opened her eyes and met his again. "Oh. That's better."

"What's better?" he asked with a smile.

"Keeping my eyes open. Not so wobbly." She held out her hand toward him and he took it, bringing her knuckles to his lips without thinking.

"Good girl," he told her. "Just focus on me. I'm not going anywhere." And he meant it. In every way. He didn't know how he'd do it, but he knew he had to find a way back to her. "Just rest, okay?"

"Maybe you could talk Charlotte into letting us eat in here. I hate to turn a nose up at her hospitality, but—" Justice broke off and gave him a wobbly smile. "I'm probably not the best company right now."

"I'm sure she'll be fine with that," he agreed.

"She's pretty wild, isn't she?" Justice asked, her words a little sluggish as everything in her system started to revert back to homeostasis. "I mean, independent and capable. She's so strong and sure of herself. And, I don't know. Fierce, you know?"

"She is," Brandon agreed. "Wild."

"And tall," Justice added with a giggle. "I feel like a child standing beside her."

"Six-two," said Charlotte as she pushed through the door she'd left cracked open. "I hit this height in eighth grade. It took me another ten years to fully embrace it, but now I wear every single inch with pride." She tapped the heel of one boot against the other and added, "Six four with these puppies on." She winked at Brandon as she circled the bed to the far side. "You ready to sit up and have a drink or do you need a few more minutes?" She set a full water glass on the nightstand by the bed and straightened, her hands on her hips.

Justice rolled to her back and started to push herself up, but Brandon slipped his arm behind her to support her while Charlotte stuffed a few pillows at her back. "Thanks," she said, then took the glass of water Charlotte handed her.

"One for you, too," the woman said, handing him a second one across the bed. "How about I bring a tray of food over here?" she asked, and Brandon wondered how much of their conversation she'd overheard. "That way you can eat when you're feeling ready and able."

"That might be a good idea," he said, nodding. "I think she might need a little time to get her land legs." Turning to Justice, he added, "You should be fine by morning. Some food in your belly and a good night's rest will do you wonders."

"What was all that about?" Justice asked, her eyes still a little glassy, her cheeks pale. "I mean, you don't seem too concerned, so I'm guessing it's not a heart attack?"

"Nah." He lowered himself to sit on the bed beside her and pressed the back of his hand against her cheek, then her neck. Cool and no longer clammy. She instinctively leaned into his touch, making his pulse quicken a little. "Psychological or emotional shock, like a post traumatic stress panic attack. A serious thing, but not life-threatening. You kept it together there in the middle of things out of necessity, but now that you're in a safe place, your body's decided it's time to react."

"But," Justice started, then hesitated, a frown creasing her forehead. "I wasn't stressed about it. Not anymore. I mean, everyone is fine. We're safe. Why on earth would I panic now?"

Brandon didn't answer for a few moments, not because he didn't know what to say, but because he wanted to choose his words carefully. The last thing she needed to do right now was get defensive and worked up.

"I'm going to go get dinner sorted," Charlotte interjected before he could respond. "Stew's perfect, if I do say so myself, and I have some great crusty bread my neighbor makes, if you folks do carbs." She said it with a straight face, but there was a twinge of something in her tone he couldn't quite pin down. Not sarcasm, exactly, but maybe more like disbelief that anyone would purposely choose to live without carbs.

"Carbs are good," Justice assured her. "We like crusty bread, don't we?" She reached over and squeezed Brandon's hand.

"Then stew and bread it is. I'll be back shortly, and if you're up to it, we'll get that bed made up so you can get back in it when you need to."

After Charlotte had slipped out again, Justice turned to Brandon. "Am I going to be okay?"

He nodded. "Yeah. But sometimes it's people like you, Justice, who end up dealing with traumatic events this way. You're so strong and capable, you know? And you think you can handle anything, because 99.9% of the time, you can. But sometimes, *sometimes*, it's even too much for you. Except you don't realize it because you're just bearing up under it as usual. Your body, though..." He paused and studied her face for a moment, wanting her to see that he wasn't trying to be unkind or hurtful. "Sometimes you have to give yourself permission to feel the emotional reaction to a traumatic situation. And when you don't, your body will take you there anyway."

Justice kept her gaze locked with his, but nodded slowly. "Okay. So... is it over? I mean, is this a onetime dealio?" She tried to keep her voice light, but he heard the anxiety in her voice. "This is pretty rough, Brandon. My fingertips and toes are still kinda tingly, and my head feels super heavy, like my neck might not be able to hold it upright much longer."

He chuckled and squeezed her hand. "The worst of this one is over. It might take you several minutes, a couple hours, even, maybe the rest of the night to get over the after affects of it. You just released a lot of fight or flight chemicals into your system, and now your body needs some time to regain its balance. But you'll feel fine by morning."

"Okay," she said weakly, lowering her gaze to the near-empty glass in her hand, but he thought she didn't sound quite convinced.

"Hey." He waited for her to look back up at him. "I'm here. You'll be fine. I won't let anything happen to you."

"What if it happens again?" she asked, sounding like a little girl afraid of a monster under her bed.

"Then I'll be here for that one, too." He leaned forward and planted a kiss on her forehead. "I'm not going anywhere."

"But—"

"Justice."

"Sorry."

"You can't always be in control over everything, you know. Not even you get to schedule your own panic attacks."

"Ha ha. You're a funny guy," she harrumphed, nudging him with her foot. "Ouch."

The foot. In all the commotion, he'd forgotten about her twisted ankle. "How about I take a look at your foot now?" he asked.

TWELVE

THE STEW CHARLOTTE BROUGHT them in enormous white ceramic bowls was thick and chunky, heavy on the beef cuts and vegetables. The sourdough bread was just as she promised, delicious and crusty and perfect for dunking in the soup. Justice eyed the tray of food on the coffee table. She was ravenous by the time it arrived, and it was all she could do not to dig in while she sat in one of the armchairs, her foot propped on a thick towel on the other chair under a bag of crushed ice, and waited for Charlotte and Brandon to put the linens on the bed.

She was chilled, almost like she had a fever, but she knew it was just part of the aftermath of the anxiety attack she'd just had. The ice didn't help, but she had a blanket wrapped around her shoulders. It was terrible, and for a few minutes there, she'd actually thought she might die, that her heart would keep squeezing tighter and tighter until the blood couldn't flow through it, and then quit altogether. It hadn't been painful, not the way they said heart attacks felt, but she couldn't recall ever having experienced anything quite so acutely intense and overwhelming.

Other than how she felt when Courage fell off Flash.

Or those long, endless moments as the truck and trailer fishtailed wildly on the road, the buck staring her down as their rig hurtled toward it while she could do nothing but hold on... hold on.... What if they'd hit him? What if she'd rolled the truck, the trailer? What if—what if something had happened to the horses? To—to Brandon? To Charlotte? "Oh, God," she whispered, squeezing her eyes shut as visions of what might have been flashed before her eyes. "Please—"

"Justice?" Brandon was there in front of her in a flash. "Hey."

"I'm okay," she whimpered, gripping his shoulder tightly. "I just have to not think about it. Crap. Dang it. This sucks. My brain. My head. Geez. Is it going to be like this from now on?" She pressed her other hand to her chest over her heart and rubbed with the heel of her hand. Her heart was pounding—she could hear it inside her head—and she felt flushed and chilled at the same time.

"Come here," Brandon said, pushing the bag of ice aside and hauling her gently to her feet. "Let's dance." He pulled her close and pressed her head to his shoulder. "Put your arms around me and hold on. I got you."

She did as she was told, slipping her arms around his waist and gripping them tightly at his back. She balanced most of her weight on her good food, just resting the other on the carpeted floor, and let him lead, let him rock her back and forth, swaying in time to the old Johnny Cash number he sang close to her ear. She kept her eyes open, watching Charlotte deftly make the rest of the bed in her sure, intentional movements, and soon began to relax a little bit at a time. "I'm sorry," she whispered.

"I need you to stop apologizing," he whispered back.

"I'm sorry," she said again, then giggled. "For saying I'm sorry, I mean. I'll try not to do it again."

"Good."

Charlotte fluffed the pillows and smoothed the end of the comforter, then circled the grouping of furniture to stand by the door. "I'm going to leave you to it for now," she said, nodding at Brandon. He'd assured their host that Justice was in good hands, explaining that he was a paramedic and saw this kind of reaction on a regular basis, and that he'd let her know if he felt Justice needed medical attention. "If you want for anything, just come knocking. I'm a good sleeper, but a light one, so I'll hear you if you do. And of course, Nutter will let me know if I don't." She opened the door and the dog got up from the welcome mat to greet her. "Otherwise, I'll see you kids in the morning. I'm an early riser, but don't feel you have to do so yourselves. You get some rest, and we'll have breakfast when you're ready."

"Thank you," Brandon said.

"You've been more than kind," Justice added, straightening and stepping out of Brandon's embrace, although she stayed close enough to grab hold if she got wobbly. Any other time, she might have been embarrassed to be so intimate with him in front of a stranger, but her need for him far outweighed any lingering reservation she might have.

"Nah. Just being neighborly."

"We're strangers, though," Justice continued, shaking her head. "And clearly mad ones at that," she added with a wave at her own head. "How do you know we're not trouble? Bad guys? I mean, we're not, so you don't have to worry," she assured her quickly. "But still, you're awfully trusting."

Charlotte chuckled. "I'm a good judge of character," she said, then turned to head out, shooing the dog in front of her. At the last minute, she poked her head back in the door. "Besides, I've got a few guns, a good dog, and your horses locked in my barn. I don't suppose you're going anywhere without them." And with that, she pulled the door closed behind her for the last time that night.

"Did that sound slightly ominous to you?" Justice asked after a moment.

Brandon grinned. "I have a feeling she intended it that way. Setting things straight right up front," he added. "Hungry?" He gestured to the food.

"Starving."

"Want to eat sitting up or in bed?"

"I need a shower before I get between those clean sheets," Justice said, wrinkling her nose. "I feel like I've been through the gauntlet." She moved gingerly toward one of the chairs, propped her foot up again, and sat back while Brandon returned the bag of ice to the top of her foot.

"I'll say grace," she stated, then waited until he was seated. She bowed her head and said a quick prayer of gratitude for God's hand in keeping them safe, and for bringing someone as wild and amazing as Charlotte by at just the right moment. "And for this amazing little guest room," she added, glancing around the small space, knowing they'd have to address the sleeping arrangements shortly. But for now, she was just glad for all of it.

"This is delicious," Justice gushed after a few bites. They'd both been quiet as they finally, *finally* got some food in their bellies, but she could sense the rising tension the longer the silence lingered. She took a large gulp of water and settled a little more comfortably in the chair.

The ice was beginning to melt in the bag, and after a few attempts to reposition it where it could do the most good, she gave up and nudged it to the side and lowered her foot to the floor. "We need to talk about tomorrow," she said, deciding the bed could wait. "What's our plan? I think my foot will be much better by then." She flexed her ankle, cringed a little at the painful pull up the side of her leg, but it definitely felt solid. "I maybe shouldn't do the show for another day or two, but I think by the weekend, I'll be good to go. I want to spend some time with the horses out in the pasture, if it's okay with Charlotte. See how they're doing in the morning, too. I didn't see any indication of injuries, but I think we'll know more tomorrow."

"Right. Sure." Brandon nodded slowly, his eyes on the bowl of stew in his hand. "I need to give the trailer a good going over, but if it's all good, and if the horses are, too, then I don't see why we can't plan to be out of here by noon. We won't make it to Truskee in time for the opening act, but since you're thinking you won't be able to perform anyway, maybe we'll skip it altogether and make an early start to the next stop."

"That sounds good." The conversation died again and she was just taking the last few bites when Brandon cleared his throat. She looked up to see him setting his empty bowl on the tray.

"So do you want to shower first?" She always did when they were sharing the trailer. Brandon let the girls have the hot water and took whatever was leftover. Military showers, they were. Quick and efficient and without an ounce of wasted water or a second of wasted time.

"You go ahead," she told him. "Since you're finished eating already." Besides, while he was in the shower, she could try lying on the loveseat to see if she could make it work. She was a back-sleeper, and a sprawler to boot, but she'd be willing to give it a go. There was no way Brandon could sleep there.

After a long, hot shower that made her both drowsy and refreshed, she came out to find Brandon laying out a blanket and pillow on the floor next to the bed. "What are you doing?" she asked. "I can sleep on the sofa, Brandon. You don't have to sleep on the hard floor."

"You won't fit on that thing. Not with the way you spread eagle in your sleep," he said, grinning up at her. He wore a pair of sports shorts and a white tee-shirt that stretched taut across his shoulders, and Justice found it difficult to look away from the way his muscles moved underneath it. "I have a feeling it's called a loveseat for a reason. It'd be a cozy squeeze for two people just to sit on it together." He looked up at her. "I can sleep in the trailer, of course, but I'm not—"

"You can't leave me alone," she practically yelped. "What if that—what if...." She trailed off, not wanting to inadvertently conjure up another panic attack.

"I won't leave you alone. That's what I was getting at," he assured her. "I'll sleep here, right beside you. If you need me, just reach down and poke me."

He finished up and turned around to sit on the floor with his back to the bed, his legs drawn up a little, and rested his forearms on his knees. "How was your shower? Feeling a little more human?"

Justice nodded, recognizing that his change of subject meant the decision was made, the topic settled. She knew Brandon too well to even bother arguing. He'd decided he'd sleep on the floor, and that's where he'd sleep. Stubborn man. "I am feeling almost human again," she said, running a hand down over her wet, clean hair. She should probably wait for it to dry before going to bed, but she knew that wasn't going to happen. "I think I might fall over if I try to stay upright much longer, though. I'm going to brush my teeth, then go to bed. Is that okay with you? You can watch TV or whatever. I doubt anything will keep me up once I put my head on the pillow."

"I'm ready when you are. I brushed my teeth after my shower." He pushed up to his feet, then went to the tray of food. "I'm going to rinse these dishes once you're out of the bathroom, though. Otherwise, they'll be impossible to get clean in the morning."

"Thank you. I didn't even think about that. You're a good guest, Brandon," she teased, then held up her toothbrush. "I'll hurry."

While Brandon washed out their dishes, Justice slipped in between the cool sheets on the bed, then pulled the fluffy comforter up under her chin and closed her eyes, sighed with pleasure. When she opened them, Brandon was standing in the doorway of the bathroom, tray in hand, a strange look on his face. "What?" she asked, concern furrowing her brow. Was something wrong?

He shook his head. "I'm just glad you're all right," he said, his voice serious and quiet. "I'm—I'm just grateful, that's all." Then he crossed the room and set the tray back on the coffee table. He switched off the main lights. "You done for the night?" he asked as he made his way through the dark room to his spot on the floor. He'd left a light on in the bathroom and pulled the door half-closed so they could see if either one of them had to get up in the middle of the night, but otherwise, the room was cast in long shadows.

"I'm good," she whispered in the sudden stillness. "Goodnight, Brandon."

"Goodnight," came his reply, followed by the rustle of bed clothes and the gentle whumping sound of him plumping his pillow under his head as he got comfortable.

An hour later, she was still awake. As weary as she was, she found that she couldn't close her eyes for more than a few moments before images started flashing through her mind. The buck's glowing eyes, his antlers like evil prongs piercing the air, the brakes squealing as the enormous truck skidded along on the asphalt, being shoved forward by the weight of the trailer. The horses kicking and screaming... and then there was Courage, lying prone on the ground, Justice's exhausted mind piecing the two incidents together, and her eyes would spring open in a desperate attempt to shut down the spiraling thoughts. She tried to keep her breathing even, but it got harder and harder to do as the minutes ticked by.

On the floor beside her, Brandon didn't sound like he was getting any more sleep than she was. He tossed and turned, his movements indicating that he wasn't comfortable for one reason or another.

Finally, anxious for a reprieve, she whispered, "Brandon?"

"Hm?" He stilled instantly.

"You all right?" Justice asked.

"I'm good." His voice was gruff, ragged around the edges like she'd disturbed his sleep. Maybe she'd just imagined his restlessness. "How about you?"

"I'm fine," she said, feeling bad for disturbing him. "Sorry if I woke you."

After a moment, he said, "You didn't. And you're apologizing again."

At a loss, she turned onto her side and peered over the edge of the bed at him. He was on his back, one braced arm crooked up over the top of his head, the other resting on his chest, his fingers drumming a soft rhythm against his sternum. Justice reached a hand over the edge of the bed before she gave it much thought.

He tipped his head up to meet her gaze in the low light from the bathroom. Then he took her hand and brought it to his chest the way he'd done earlier, pressing her palm over his heart. "Justice," he said, his voice harsh.

"Yes?" She lifted her head off the pillow and looked down at him. He sounded terribly upset.

"I'm sorry." He didn't move, but the pressure on her hand grew stronger. "For the terrible things I said to you. For the way I spoke to you. I'm sorry for the way things are going with us. This isn't how it's supposed to be with you and me. I've been hateful and unforgiving." The words tumbled out of him, a geyser of misery pouring out into the night. "Tonight, when I thought I might lose you, that my terrible behavior distracted you so your eyes weren't on the road—" He swallowed hard, but he kept going. His thumb rubbed hard over the back of her fingers, almost painfully, but she didn't pull away. "When I think of what might have happened, what I could have caused...." His words faded, and the room fell silent again.

"Oh, Brandon, now you're the one apologizing. Stop, please," she murmured. "We're alive. We're okay. And we've got our own guardian angel just across the breezeway."

"I know, but—"

"Stop," she said again, this time more adamantly. She pulled her hand free of his grip and pushed up on her elbow so she could see him better.

"This is no time to point fingers. The things you said?" She made a dismissive noise in the back of her throat. "It's all true. All of it."

"No, Justice. No, it's not. It was my anger talking," he insisted, coming up to a sitting position. He brought his knees up under the blanket and rested his forearms on them. She couldn't make out his features with the light from the bathroom behind him, throwing his face into shadows, but she knew he was looking at her. "It was my anger eating me up from the inside out, and I'm sorry."

"Regardless, there is still truth in what you were saying."

He cut her off. "Why are you being so gracious about this?" came his harsh reply. Was he crying? "I was yelling at you, raging at you in the truck. It was inexcusable."

"But I am responsible for so many of the things that have happened lately. I have been selfish and self-focused for so long, thinking I was special or unique. Like I was somehow better than everyone else. I treated you and Courage, my whole family, even our fans, as if you all owed me your love. Like the rules didn't apply to me. What I did to Courage, forcing my will on her until she felt like she couldn't say no? What I did to —to you?" She had to push the words out, and still they hurt to say them. "It was unforgivable, Brandon, and I can't blame you for your anger, for your rage, or for your words."

Justice flopped back on her pillow and took a deep breath. "But oh, how I miss you, Brandon. I miss us. I won't apologize again, not for today, not for this month, and not for last summer and Tanner, because you've made it clear you don't want another apology." She forced herself to swallow back the tears that wanted out. "I just want you to forgive me, so we can move on from this terrible place where everything feels so stuck and broken. There are pieces of us worth salvaging, Brandon."

She turned her head on her pillow so she was facing him again, but his features remained completely in the dark. When he didn't say anything, she continued. "I have to believe that," she said, her voice breaking. "And I hope you can find it in your heart to believe that, too. That our pieces are worth putting back together. We may not end up in the same shape we were before, but I'll take whatever I can have from you." A small sob slipped out in spite of her best efforts to hold it back. "I miss you so much," she whispered.

Brandon reached over and took her hand, holding it gently in his good one. He still didn't speak, but he didn't let go of her, either.

Justice lay there in the dark, wondering what tomorrow would bring. Surely, after tonight, they wouldn't go back to the barbed tension of the last few weeks, would they? But if he still couldn't find it in his heart to forgive her, then how could they ever find a better way between them? She ached for him to say something, to tell her he forgave her, that he still loved her, that he still wanted her, but the longer he remained silent, the more she believed those words were lost to her forever.

"There's something I need to tell you," Brandon finally said, his voice suddenly loud in the quiet room. He hesitated, but she didn't speak, her breath held. She already knew she didn't want to hear what he had to say. She had no idea what it was, but she knew it couldn't be good.

"I started putting out resumes a few weeks ago. I—I didn't think I could stay in the hollow. Not with you, not with what's happened."

"Oh, Brandon," she murmured, wanting him to stop, to hold back whatever was coming next.

"I've been offered a job in Bowling Green." He let out a short huff that might have been a laugh. "I'll be moving down there the end of August."

Right after they were scheduled to be back in Plumwood Hollow.

The news hit her like a sledge hammer in the center of her chest. For the second time tonight, Justice wasn't sure she'd ever be able to breathe again. When she could finally get a few words out, she managed to say, "Congratulations, Brandon. I know you'll be the best thing that ever happened to Bowling Green. I mean it." Then she withdrew her hand from his, rolled onto her side away from him, and closed her eyes against the pain that washed over her. She tucked both hands under the comforter so he wouldn't try to reach for her again.

THIRTEEN

Brandon let his eyes follow the curves of her body, evident even under the bulky comforter. His Justice. His beautiful, broken girl.

But not his. Not anymore. Not completely. There would always be a piece of her that belonged to Tanner Ogden. Brandon wanted all of her or nothing.

Make up your mind, man. He loved her, there was no doubt about that in his mind. But he no longer knew if that was enough. Hearing Tanner's name on her lips had been like being doused with a bucket of ice cold water, knocking him for a loop and shocking him into stepping back to look at the big picture.

Nothing had changed. Not really. He could forgive her, sure, but that wouldn't fix things between them. That wouldn't erase what she'd done. He wasn't God—he could forgive, but forgetting wasn't something mere mortals were capable of doing.

He loved her and she loved him, he was sure of it. So why hadn't that been enough for her? Why hadn't *he* been enough for her? What was he lacking that she had to go searching for elsewhere?

He sat there in the dark, staring at her back, wishing someone could come alongside him and tell him how to manage these treacherous waters. He wanted to kill her, he wanted to hold her. He wanted to rage at her, he wanted to weep over her. He wanted her underneath him, murmuring his name as she gave herself to him, and he wanted to toss her aside in disgust at the very thought of it.

Nothing had changed. Tonight had just reminded him of how much he loved her, and in so doing, had also reminded him how much she'd hurt him.

He finally slid back down under his blanket, shoved his pillow under his head, and turned on his side with his back to the bed. He prayed for sleep to come.

He awoke out of a sound sleep to Justice's harsh cries of fright. Shoving his blanket aside, he lurched to his feet and crawled across the bed to get to her. "Justice," he said, trying to be gentle, even though his voice was raspy with sleep. His heart pounded erratically in his chest. "Justice, baby. Wake up."

She rolled onto her back, her eyes wide and unfocused, tears streaming down her cheeks. "Brandon? Oh, Brandon?" She gasped his name, her voice high and breathy, then she reached up and wrapped her arms around his neck. "You're alive," she whimpered. "Oh, God, thank you, thank you. You're alive." She clung to him tightly until he reached up and pried her arms loose.

"It was just a bad dream," he said, holding one of her hands against his chest. He was still crouched over her. "I'm fine. I'm here." He rested his braced hand on the pillow above the top of her head and brushed his fingers against her hair.

She turned onto her side toward him and curled in on herself. Her body shook with quiet sobs. "I thought—I thought you were—"

"Shh," he soothed. "I'm fine. It's okay." Then he lowered himself to the mattress beside her and let her scoot closer to him, pressing her forehead against his chest. "I'm here." He released her hand and wrapped his arm around her, holding her against him, while she cried.

When her hand moved slowly up over the planes of his chest and she pressed her palm against the column of his neck, he froze. Her fingers slipped into the tangle of hair at the back of his head and then she lifted her face and pressed her warm lips to the sensitive hollow under his jaw. Surely, she could feel his pulse pounding beneath the tender skin. What was she doing?

"Brandon," she whispered, her voice soft as silk, her breath warm over his collar bones. "I don't know how I'll bear it when you move away. I need you. I love you." Like honey, her words flowed soft and sweet from her mouth, a mouth he wanted to ravage. Her hands were in his hair and on his skin, the curve of her strong body pressed against his, and even with the comforter between them, ripples of pleasure coursed through him. "Please, Brandon," she murmured against his neck, one hand sliding up under the hem of his shirt, her fingers brushing over the bare skin of his belly. "Please."

Nothing has changed, a voice in his head whispered. *This is what she offered Tanner Ogden, too.*

He reached down and roughly jerked her hand out from under his shirt. "No. No, no, no, Justice." He pushed away from her, putting space between them. "What are you doing?" he demanded harshly, his breath coming in ragged gulps. "You think sex is going to solve this? That's what got us here in the first place." What was *he* doing? Up, down, this way, that way, yes, no. He was as unstable as she was. His stomach churned with incompatible feelings of passion and self-loathing.

"I—I don't—" She broke off and reached up to cover her face with her hands. "Oh, Brandon, I'm such a wretched person. I'm so—I feel so desperate. You don't deserve my chaos." She rolled away from him and pushed up to sit on the other side of the bed, then rose and headed into the bathroom. When she closed the door, she took all the light with her, leaving Brandon alone in the dark.

Her absence felt like a fresh wound, even as his body tingled with the memory of her wandering hands, her feminine curves, and her warm lips on his skin. He breathed slowly, almost afraid to move. Could this night possibly get any worse?

When Justice came out of the bathroom, she skirted the end of the bed to sit on the far side, picking up her pillow and holding it tightly to her chest. Her shoulders slumped forward and she didn't look back at him. "I know I said I wouldn't apologize anymore but Brandon, I really am sorry about—about—" She waved a hand in a vague gesture, then dropped it back to her lap. "About all that. I don't know what I was thinking. Please forgive me," she said through a stuffy nose.

What a mess. What a stinking-pile-of-rotting-carcasses mess. He lay there on top of the covers, his nostrils filled with the scent of Justice, his body aflame with desire for her, yet his mind telling him it was up to him to make the best of what remained. Finally, he took a deep breath and said, "Stop apologizing and come here." He held the blanket back for her. "Get in and lay down. You need to get some sleep." It took a little convincing, but when she was settled, he slid his arm under her head. "Put your head on my shoulder," he ordered. "But no funny business," he added, then smiled at her derisive snort.

She did as she was told, and a few minutes later, her breathing slowed and he felt the tiny twitching of her body as she drifted off to sleep. He gingerly pulled his arm out from under her head, but he rolled away only far enough to reach down and grab up his blanket and pillow from the floor. He tucked the pillow under his head, pulled the blanket over him, then turned on his side toward her and wrapped his good arm around her sleeping form under the thick comforter.

She slept the sleep of the exhausted the rest of the night.

He slept a little more fitfully, but then, he held the woman he loved—and kind of hated—in his arms, and couldn't imagine a better—or worse—way to spend a night.

FOURTEEN

At some point, Brandon finally did fall asleep, but he awoke before Justice anyway. He studied her in the low light of morning, her features soft, her mouth relaxed and half-open. Her eyes were puffy from both sleep and tears, and she snored quietly, but he couldn't imagine waking up to a more beautiful sight.

Her words came back to him, what she said about there being pieces of their relationship worth salvaging. He knew she was right. And after last night's very real face to face with death, the flame of anger and betrayal that burned hot inside him every time he was near her seemed to be less intense this morning. They needed to find a way through this—he needed to find a way to get them both through this—so they could get to the other side. It would never be the same, she was right about that, too, but they'd been a part of each others' lives, a part of each others' past, present, and future, for too long to simply give up and walk away.

Then what are you doing taking that job in Bowling Green?

He sighed and rolled carefully away from her, then rose and headed to the bathroom, scooping up the pair of jeans and shirt he'd brought in last night.

In the mirror over the sink, he studied his reflection. His long, black hair was a tangled mess, and although he usually wore it loose to sleep in, this morning, he looked like he'd wrestled with a mountain lion all night. He grunted; perhaps that's exactly what he'd done. Dark circles under his eyes were evidence of his lack of sleep, and even after washing his face with cold water, he looked like a haggard old man. "Get over yourself," he muttered, then took a brush to his hair and slipped back out into the room.

Brandon sat on one of the armchairs facing the bed as he pulled on his socks and boots, then he sat back and just watched the girl in the bed for a few more minutes. He loved her more than life itself, he thought, and maybe that's why he felt so cheated by what she'd done. She'd taken his love for granted. Didn't grasp the enormity of it. Didn't put the same value on his love for her as he did on her love for him. He would never break her heart the way she did his, but that clearly wasn't the same for her.

Which is how she treated everyone in her life, it seemed. Like she thought she was entitled to their love. She'd even admitted it.

Ironically, Justice wasn't a very lovable person. Brandon made a quiet rueful sound at the back of his throat. A prickly pear, she was. A juicy, sweet, prickly pear. It took strength and determination to love Justice Goodacre, the kind that Courage had, the kind that Jed Goodacre had, the kind that Brandon had. People willing to get past the barbed outside to the soft, tender flesh underneath.

The thought of soft, tender flesh had him lurching to his feet. He could do with a cup of strong, black coffee and a brisk walk in the chilly morning air.

Brandon paused in the breezeway just outside the guest room door and dragged in a few deep, head-clearing breaths. Even in the middle of summer, Colorado mornings were usually brisk and clarifying. Holding the tray with their dirty dishes from last night in one arm, he was just about to knock on the kitchen back door, when he heard his name.

Charlotte was coming out of the barn, Nutty at her heels, carrying what looked like a medical bag with her. "Love your hair." She reached up to touch her own long hair that was streaked with silver strands. "Mine used to be that color at one time. It was straight like yours at one time, too. The older I get, the wilder it gets. Just the opposite of me," she added with a chuckle.

"Wild looks good on you," Brandon said, returning the compliment.

"Why thank you, Brandon Stillwater. That's high praise coming from a young buck like you." She peered over at him, then smiled sympathetically. "I was going to ask how you two slept." She gestured toward the kitchen. "I've got coffee brewed inside. Hot water, too, if you're tea drinkers."

"Coffee sounds great. Justice is still passed out, but I'll take her a cup, if that's all right."

"Rough night for you both." It was a statement, not a question. She pushed open the door ahead of him, then held it wide as he passed. "Let me take that," she said, depositing the bag she was holding on the floor under a coat rack and reaching for the tray. "Coffee's next to the fridge, mugs in the cupboard above it, and there's real cream in the fridge. Sugar's by the mugs."

Justice would be thrilled—she liked her coffee with all the fixings, heavy on the cream and sugar.

While Charlotte made quick work of washing up their things and leaving them to drip dry on a sideboard, Brandon filled a mug, and blew on it just long enough to be able to take a sip of the steaming brew. It was scalding hot, almost burning his tongue, but it was good. "Thanks for this. Great coffee."

"Thanks. I like it strong, so if you need to water it down, feel free," she said with a grin over her shoulder.

"Nope. This is perfect." He watched her move around the large kitchen, fixing her own cup of coffee. It wasn't her first, he was sure. Which meant the full pot on the counter wasn't her first pot, either. How long had she been up and about? She added a generous dollop of milk to hers, then turned and leaned her back against the counter so she could study him.

"I hope you don't mind," she began, then waved a hand at the bag she'd been carrying. "I was a vet tech for a large animal doctor in my other life." So it was a medical bag. "I took a look at your horses this morning. They both seem in pretty good shape. No signs of trauma, at least not that I can find without X-rays or blood work. I know you'll want to check them out for yourself, but I figured an extra set of eyes wouldn't be a bad thing."

"Thank you. No, I really appreciate it. You've done so much for us already." He took another swig of the strong black brew. "Is there anything I can do for you while we're here? I'm good with engines, I'm strong if you need any lifting—"

"You're my guests, Brandon."

"Guests who were thrust upon you unexpectedly. Not quite the same thing. I—we'd—like to repay your kindness somehow."

She cocked her head and narrowed her eyes as though pondering his request. Finally, she said, "Let me think about it. You go look after that woman of yours, then see how your vehicles are doing. Then if there's still time, I might just be able to come up with something for you to do." She set her mug on the counter and turned toward the refrigerator. "In the meantime, I'm going to whip us up some scrambled eggs and bacon. I've got some good fruit I'll set out, too. Apples, blueberries, and cantaloupe."

Brandon pushed open the guest room door to find Justice still in bed, but just waking up, looking rumpled and grumpy. She scowled over at him, the light from the open door making her squint in the room still shrouded in shadows with the window blinds closed. She didn't respond to his "Good morning, sunshine," but when he handed her the doctored up coffee, she emitted a grateful grunt.

He settled onto the little loveseat to enjoy his second cup—to enjoy watching her enjoy her first cup, knowing he'd made it just the way she liked it—and after a few minutes of almost comfortable silence, he asked, "How are you feeling?"

Justice sighed and moved her shoulders up and down, her grumpy expression turning to one of discomfort. "I feel like I've been lifting weights. I'm sore all over. Probably from tensing up during the—" She broke off and took another sip of her hot drink.

"Need a one-handed shoulder rub?" he offered, regretting it instantly. He didn't need to be touching her right now, not with his emotions still in such turmoil.

"Would you?" she asked, already shifting over under the covers. Did she want him to join her on the bed? He couldn't do that. But then she slid her legs out from under the blankets and crossed the room to drop cross-legged on the floor at his feet. "You give the best back rubs," she said, sweeping her long hair out of the way in front of her and hunching her shoulders up in anticipation.

Not only had he given her a thousand shoulder rubs in the past—and she'd returned the favor—but she wore a long sleeve t-shirt with a sports bra underneath, so there was no reason for him to feel like this was some intimate act between them. But his hands trembled a little after he set down his coffee cup and leaned forward. His fingers were warm from holding the mug, and the moment he rested them against the column of her neck, she sighed, a sound that made his blood grow hot.

He soon found a semblance of ease in the familiar sweep of his good hand over her shoulders and down the long curve of her spine. Justice was petite, but she wasn't fragile. It took incredible strength to perform the tricks she and Courage did, and both girls had solid, muscular frames. He closed his eyes and visualized the fibrous tissue under her skin resisting, then finally giving way under his probing fingers as he followed the lines of the deltoid muscles from spine to shoulder blade, then back up to the occipital protuberances, the knobs at the base of her skull, his thumb pressing hard on those pressure points. Justice groaned under his manipulation, but she didn't pull away from his aggressive treatment.

Finally, as he felt her body starting to uncoil, he slid his hand down to her ribcage and tickled her softly. She yelped, sloshed a little of what was left of her coffee on her baggy sweatpants and shot to her feet, her arms outstretched. He laughed out loud at her look of surprise, then ducked when she snatched a throw pillow from one of the chairs and threw it at him. He was on his feet, too, then, when he saw her grabbing another cushion from the other chair. He scooped the one she'd thrown off the floor and held it in front of him when she came toward him, hers raised in attack. She'd set her cup on the coffee table, so she meant business.

"I was just starting to relax, you big bonehead," she grouched, then swung her cushion at his head. He lifted his to deflect the hit, but too late realized it was just a distraction. She went in for the kill, diving under his upraised arms and digging her fingers into his ribs.

Both pillows went flying as he tried to grab her wrists to stop her. He was far more ticklish than she was, and she knew it. She also knew that he had a bum wrist, and she took advantage of it. While he wrenched one of her hands away from his vulnerable ribs, he could do nothing about her other one, his braced arm held up and out of harm's way. So he hooked his foot around the back of her legs, making her knees buckle, and she fell against him, laughing and grunting with the effort to stay upright. He dropped her hand and caught her around the waist so she wouldn't fall backward, but held her too tightly for her to be able to lobby another jab at his ribcage.

She finally stopped trying to wriggle free of him and rested her forehead on his shoulder. "Uncle," she muttered in defeat, her breathing heavy. "You're squeezing me too tight. I can't breathe."

Immediately, Brandon's arm loosened around her, afraid he'd trigger another anxiety attack. But when she tipped her head back to look up at him, she was smiling, her still puffy eyes bright with exertion. "You don't play fair, you know," she admonished him. But as he watched her, the smile faded, and those velvet brown eyes darkened in response to what she surely saw in his.

She didn't pull away, but he felt the shift in her posture, the sudden stillness of her body against him. Her eyes widened as her mouth fell open with a faint 'pop', and that was his undoing. He slid his palm up her spine to cup the back of her neck, his fingers threading through her hair as he turned her head so their mouths met at a perfect, oh, so familiar angle. Her lips were soft and warm, and when she sighed and melted into him, tiny lights flickered behind his eyelids and he thought surely his heart would burst right out of his chest.

He could taste the strong sweet coffee in her mouth, smell the woodsy smell of the shampoo they both used while on the road, the tremble in her fingers when she touched the sensitive skin of his neck just below his ear. She arched into him, rising up on tiptoes, moving her lips against his, as hungry for this kiss as he was.

Familiar, and oh, so simple, this connection between them...

Brandon summoned every ounce of his evaporating self-control and lifted his head. Justice made a small noise, the sound a drowsy child might make when startled, and her eyes opened slowly, almost as if she had to force them to do so. Carefully, Brandon slid his hurt arm around her waist to hold her steady, then caressed her cheek with his good hand. "I miss you, too," he murmured, then pressed a slow kiss to her forehead. "I miss this." He gently pressed her head to his shoulder and swayed ever so slightly. "But I think we have a lot farther to go before—" He didn't know how to finish the sentence. Before what? Before they could kiss again? Before they could ease each other's aching muscles with back rubs? Before they could trust enough to fall into each others' arms?

She nodded against his chest. "Okay." The word was so small, her voice trembling, and Brandon wondered how many more times his heart would break before things started getting easier again.

"Charlotte is making breakfast for us," he finally said, stepping away from her. "Are you up to eating over at the big house or do you want me to bring it to you here?"

FIFTEEN

Mouth-watering aromas met Justice as she stepped through the back kitchen door in front of Brandon. He'd waited for her while she freshened up in the bathroom, although if she'd had her way, the earth would have opened up and swallowed her whole while she stood in front of the vanity mirror. Her skin was blotchy, both from the array of emotions coursing through her and the rub from Brandon's morning stubble.

That kiss. What were they thinking? What was *she* thinking? He was leaving her in a little over a month, leaving all of them. Whispering Hills Ranch would lose one of their finest horsemen and the Plumwood Hollow First Responder team would lose their leader. And she, well, she would lose the only man who had ever seen past the tough exterior she presented to the world, the only man she wanted to let in, other than her father.

When her mother died, all seven of the Goodacre sisters had stumbled around in the dark long after the tragedy, their father unable to cope with his own loss for the first few years, and therefore, unable to help his girls cope with theirs. Inevitably, they'd paired off out of desperation. Not even a full-fledged teenager, Faith had taken over mothering the whole lot of them, something she was good at, having helped their mom for years over the course of her decline. But no one should have to be in charge of a family of eight—including a tiny baby—at that age. So in some unspoken agreement, the rest of them did what they could to look after each other. Faith finished the last half of her high school years on an independent study program so she could stay home to care for Baby Abby. Charity and Hope were inseparable, and they helped out with Prudence, who was just starting school. Justice and Courage were already attached at the hip, as most twins invariably were, but for the next few years, their attachment was even more physical than usual. They were never out of arm's reach of each other, took turns sleeping in each other's beds, and held hands whenever they left the house. Even inside their home, they remained within sight of each other at all times, even in the bathroom.

That terrible grieving period played a big part in determining their roles in their relationship. Justice stepped into the foreground, dragging Courage along with her, lest they both get lost in the shadows that hovered around Seven Virtues Ranch. Courage found solace in Justice's strength and protection. Over the years, those roles became characteristics, and those characteristics became identities. Courage was "the sweet, gentle twin," while Justice was "the tough cookie." How many times had she heard them referred to in variations of those labels?

Brandon knew better. He was the first boy to ever see her cry. She could still remember how afraid she'd been that he would laugh, or mock her, or tell someone that she was a baby. When they'd first started school together, he'd seemed like the kind of kid who would do just that. He'd shadowed the girls as they walked home, taunting and teasing, and although they did their best to ignore him, it rankled Justice something fierce. She'd wanted to turn around and run him off, or throw rocks at him, but Courage had said something that stopped her. *I think his mommy is sick like ours,* she'd whispered one afternoon after school. They'd pushed out through the heavy front doors of the school to find the scrawny, black-haired Brandon Stillwater loitering on the sidewalk, waiting to follow them home. Faith had called his bluff, but in the best way possible, asking him to protect and defend the twins from the classroom bully who wouldn't leave them alone. She'd known it was him, but she'd given him the opportunity to be a better version of himself, and Brandon had picked up the gauntlet thrown at his feet.

The day he found Justice crying wasn't back then, though. It had nothing to do with her mother's illness or subsequent death. No, it was because their teacher, Mrs. Falsted, had gotten angry at her for speaking for Courage. In front of the whole class, she'd said, "Your sister won't always have you around, Justice. She needs to learn to do things for herself, to think for herself, and to answer for herself."

It was bad enough that all her peers had heard the woman say such a harsh thing to the girls, but it was the first time anyone had so plainly said that they would not always be together forever. For Whatever reason, it had blindsided her. She'd gotten to her feet, stumbled out of the classroom, ignoring Mrs. Falsted's demands that she take her seat, and ran from the school. She'd hidden under the weeping willow tree about a block away.

Even worse than Mrs. Falsted's attack, Courage didn't come for her, which only proved their teacher right. Her sister, she later learned, had sat there in that classroom at Mrs. Falsted's orders, tears streaming down her face, afraid to make a decision without Justice's direction, proving the teacher right, in spite of the wretched woman's cruelty.

Brandon, under no such compulsion, had asked to use the restroom, and had come after her. He found her there, her back to the tree, her knees drawn up to her chest, head down, silent sobs making her whole body quake. She'd looked up when he parted the branches and told him to go away. He'd kept his eyes downcast, not because he was afraid, but to allow her to keep a semblance of dignity, and dropped to his backside beside her. He didn't touch her, he didn't say a word. He just sat there with her so that she wouldn't have to cry alone.

They'd never spoken of it since, not even when Jed and Brandon's grandmother got called in to the school the following day to discuss the kids' behavior. Mrs. Falsted figured out pretty quickly that Brandon hadn't left the classroom to use the facilities, and between Justice's defiance, Brandon's deception, and Courage's disobedience—she'd stayed in the classroom, but Mrs. Falsted's commands to stop crying had gone unheeded—the teacher had insisted the principal get involved.

Jed had been livid, not at the kids, but at the teacher. Even he could see that there were bits and pieces of the story missing. Anyone who didn't know him might not have realized just how angry he was, but after listening to Mrs. Falsted's version of the incident, he'd turned to Justice, Brandon, and Courage, who sat between them, and asked if that was how it happened.

Justice, still feeling the aftershocks of Mrs. Falsted's painful words, asked Courage if she wanted to tell them. She'd nodded, opened her mouth to speak, closed it, then took Justice's hand on one side, Brandon's on the other. It wasn't until their fingers were locked tight that Courage was able to speak. She repeated the teacher's words, including the woman's orders that Courage was not allowed to go see what was wrong with her sister, as well as the unkind racial slur she tossed out about Brandon when she realized he'd lied to her.

And then Courage had burst into tears.

Mrs. Falsted had been absent the next day. And the next. And then the next.

Fired. It wasn't because of her unkindness toward Justice and Courage specifically, although if Jed had had his way, the woman would have been drawn and quartered on that basis alone. It was the things she'd said about Brandon to a classroom of impressionable, malleable students that made it abundantly clear to everyone the woman was not fit to be educating young minds.

About two weeks later, after they'd had a chance to get accustomed to their new teacher, Principal Hazlett had come to the classroom and spoken openly about racial prejudice, about kindness, and about being sensitive to the needs of others. She hadn't mentioned any names or pointed any fingers, but she'd made it clear that she would not tolerate hatred or cruelty in her school.

The very thought of losing Brandon now made Justice feel as lost as she'd been that day under the willow tree, weeping alone, waiting for someone to rescue her.

He had rescued her back then, just by being there. But if he was leaving, who would come for her? Who would rescue her now?

Once again, Courage had stayed behind, not because she was afraid this time, but because she no longer needed Justice in order to be brave. And now, Brandon wouldn't be there, either, and she didn't have a willow tree to hide under. Her hands tingled with the need to hold onto him, to cling to him, to restrain him, but just like with Courage, Justice had to let him go. If this job was what he wanted, if he thought he'd be better off without her—and who could blame him, really—then she had to let him go.

And she had to start letting him go now.

"It smells amazing in here," she said, hoping no one else would hear the tremor in her voice. "You didn't have to do all this for us, Charlotte."

"It's my pleasure," the older woman said. In the bright morning sunshine, Charlotte was even more stunning than Justice had realized the night before. The golden light of day revealed skin that glowed with good health, large green eyes accented by laugh lines, deep grooves around her wide mouth bearing witness to someone who found great joy in life, and a crooked nose that looked suspiciously like it had been broken once or twice. Charlotte's hair—she must have been wearing it up last night, because Justice didn't remember it—reached almost to her waist, thick glossy strands in at least fifty shades of gray. This morning, she wore a pair of snug jeans that sat low on her hips, a peacock blue peasant blouse with embroidered trim around the neckline and cuffs, and a pair of chili pepper red cowboy boots that had seen better days.

Stunning. Wild. Fierce. Justice was just the tiniest bit in love with her.

"I wish you could meet my dad," she said without preamble. The thought had arisen out of nowhere, but she suddenly knew that Jed, too, would find Charlotte fascinating.

Brandon looked over at her with a curious expression, obviously wondering where she was going with the comment, but she just shrugged. "I've been thinking about home, about my family," she said, not quite sure how to explain her train of thought. "Missing them. My dad, especially." She smiled brightly, then turned toward the coffee pot to hide her glistening eyes. "Can I get a refill?" she asked, holding her empty cup up.

"Of course. Brandon, how about you?" Charlotte said, waving a spatula at him. "You know where everything is. Cream, sugar. Have at it, then why don't you kids take a seat. This is pretty much ready to go."

When Justice finished doctoring her coffee, Brandon held a chair for her at the big, square kitchen table. Charlotte set the iron skillet down on a trivet at the center, then Brandon held a chair for her, too.

"Thank you, kind sir," Charlotte said with a cheeky grin. She was obviously enjoying having a gentleman around.

Justice thought she might start drooling at the sight of the fluffy scrambled eggs confettied with sun dried tomatoes, chives, basil, and capers. Already on the table was a heaping plate of bacon strips, a platter of fresh fruit, and a small cutting board with a block of Parmesan on it. A fancy little hand-crank cheese grater sat beside it. Between Charlotte and Brandon's plates were gathered an assortment of condiments, including three different hot sauces.

"I like a little spice in my life," Charlotte said, tapping the top of one of them. "I usually douse things pretty heavily when I'm only cooking for myself, but I'll let you determine your own heat level this morning." Holding out her hands toward each of them, she said, "In this house, we thank the good Lord for our daily bread." It wasn't a command, but it wasn't an option, either.

"How's that foot of yours?" Charlotte asked after the blessing. She took Justice's plate and started dishing it up with eggs. "Tell me when," she ordered with a nod at the plate.

"It feels pretty good this morning," Justice assured her. "I think keeping my boot on as long as I did last night was the best thing for it. By the time I iced it and showered, I could tell it wasn't going to be nearly as bad as it could have been. I don't know how I twisted it, but I must have been stomping on the floorboard with both feet in my zeal to stop us. Oh! Whoa. That's plenty." She put up a hand to stop Charlotte from adding yet another generous helping to her plate.

After tasting the delicious fare, though, she thought she probably could have eaten the whole skillet of eggs herself. The bacon was perfection, not chewy and not so crisp it might break a tooth, and the fruit—the blueberries, especially—was ripe and tangy and sweet. There was nothing like a good meal to start a day.

The three of them made short work of cleaning up after breakfast, then they headed out to the truck and trailer to give the vehicles a thorough going over. It didn't take them long; miraculously, there seemed to be no evidence that anything untoward had happened the night before. Other than the new minor dents to the inside paneling at the backs of the stalls where Tank and Fire had made their opinions about the mule deer known.

"You certainly kept our guardian angel on his toes last night," Charlotte said, resting a hand briefly on her shoulder as they waited for Brandon who was repacking one of his bags in the empty stall inside the trailer. He hadn't closed things up before they left their last stop, and some of his stuff had gotten tossed around.

Justice nodded. "I did. I always do, in fact. As a trick rider, I keep mine pretty busy," she said with a little laugh.

"I have a feeling our guardian angels are a lot busier than we give them credit for," Charlotte said. "Who knows what we've avoided in our lives because of them? I heard my pastor say that we're indestructible until God determines it's our time to go."

"That's one of my dad's favorite quotes, too," Justice told her. "I think you'd like him."

"Who? My pastor or your father?"

Justice smiled, enjoying the woman's wit and wisdom. "Both, I'm sure, but since I've not met your pastor, I can only speak for Daddy."

"Then maybe one day I will. And if you're ever with him in my neck of the woods, you bring him by."

"Maybe one day I will," Justice echoed with a smile, then turned to watch Brandon as he approached. His relief was evident in the relaxed expression on his face. "Everything okay?" she asked anyway.

"All is well and locked down tight, just in case you decide to do pull some more of your stunt driving before our next stop," he teased.

Together, they headed into the barn, then lead Fire and Tank out to a corral behind the barn. "Let them loose for a while," she told them, then pointed across the small field to a tall willow with a group of Adirondack chairs underneath its waterfall branches. "We can sit in the shade over there and watch them for a bit."

A willow tree. Justice hoped no one would ask why she was grinning. She wasn't sure she'd know how to explain.

SIXTEEN

Under the shade of the willow, the three of them sat for almost an hour, watching Tank and Fire rub shoulders with Charlotte's two geldings. Fire, the only stallion among them, was also the smallest of the horses by far, and he seemed to know it, because he trotted around trying to prove himself the whole time.

"Sheep," Charlotte said, dry humor lacing her words, "might be dumber than rocks, but they sure are a lot easier to tend than horses. Those two Quarter horses might be the last I own—they're expensive to feed, expensive to treat, and cantankerous as all get out when they're not comfortable with the way things are being done. Johnson over there," she pointed at one with a black mane and tail. "He just recently decided that he no longer cares for wearing a saddle. Oh, I can walk right up to him with it, I can bring it right up to his nose, and he doesn't bat an eyelash. But the moment I go to set the thing on his back, he sidesteps and shimmies, fighting me the whole way. Once it's strapped on, he seems to relent, but getting it there is a battle I've never had to fight with him in all the years I've had him. Crazy horse." She waved a hand toward the sheep. "Those creatures out there? They don't care what I do to them as long as I tell them they're pretty."

"How did you get into weaving?" Justice asked, curious about the woman who'd opened her home so generously to them. Charlotte had walked them through the house before heading out to the barn, showing them her artwork hung in almost every room other than the cozy farmhouse kitchen. There were weaving looms scattered about, too, all in various sizes, some as small as a man's hand, others designed for making horse blankets and ponchos. One enormous loom with the beginning of a new design already started on it, stood bathed in morning sunlight in front of a large bay window that looked out over the backyard, the barns, and beyond toward the pastures.

There were baskets and bins of weaving implements, too, such as hand-carved forks, picks, and shuttles, and skeins of wool ready for her to work her magic with in shades of charcoal, russet, chocolate, and cream, colors natural to the Shetland sheep she raised for that reason, she'd explained. The Shetlands weren't a large breed, and some of the sweetest natured sheep in the business, making it easier to manhandle them—"woman-handle them" as Charlotte put it—and the fleece was some of the easiest she'd found to work with.

"I do dye some," she'd added, holding up a twisted braid of sunflower yellow. "But I only use natural dyes. This color comes from turmeric, and that one there," she said, pointing at a forest green bundle, "is made using spring greens like spinach and basil. That's a tough color to set, but I love it, so it's worth the hassle to me."

"I grew up among the Navajo," she told them. "My father was the pastor of a small church in Arizona until I was almost sixteen. I spent hours sitting among the women as they wove, their conversations rising and falling like music as their nimble fingers moved in and out on their looms. At first, I couldn't understand a thing they said, but it didn't matter. I felt like I was a part of something bigger than myself, something meaningful. I didn't even realize it was happening until suddenly, one day, I was making music right along with them, understanding, and conversing, and working my own fingers in and out of a belt loom—or a backstrap loom—one of the older women, Haseya, had gifted to me."

"That's like the one hanging above your mantle, right?" Justice asked, recalling the simple contraption made up of a few hand-carved dowels, rings, and a well-worn wide leather strap that wrapped around the weaver's low back when in use. The loom still held that last piece of art Charlotte had constructed on it, only about eighteen inches wide, depicting a white bird with its wings spread against a smoky gray sky sprinkled with stars.

"Not just like it; that *is* the exact one." Charlotte's eyes softened as she said, "Dedicated to Haseya, who has long since passed away. Her name means 'she rises' and I made that blanket right after I bought this property. It was the first piece of my art I hung in this home."

"It's a beautiful tribute," Brandon said quietly, and Justice wondered if he was thinking of his mother and the intricate beaded jewelry he used to help her make.

Charlotte's expression grew nostalgic as she continued. "I really struggled to master the Navajo style—Haseya explained to me that it was because I didn't have Navajo blood, and that I was aiming for the impossible. She encouraged me, instead, to find my own way, that God had made my fingers to create designs of my own."

She lifted both hands in front of her, turning them this way and that, studying them as she spoke. They were sprinkled with age spots, crisscrossed by tracks of blue veins, and her nails were kept short and unpainted. Beautiful, nonetheless, in an earthy way, they were the hands of a woman who wasn't afraid to let hard work leave its mark on her. She wore several silver rings on her fingers, despite knobby knuckles that likely made getting the jewelry on and off difficult, a few with chunks of colored stones—Justice recognized turquoise and jade, and some red stone she couldn't name.

Charlotte lowered her hands and folded them on her lap. "So I started experimenting with my own colors and styles and patterns. Once I broke out of the mold I was never intended to fit into, it suddenly came naturally, and it's never left, that desire to create something beautiful out of the humble wool yarn."

Brandon made an agreeable sound, but when Justice glanced over at him, his eyes were closed, his head resting against the back of his chair. She wondered how much sleep he'd gotten the night before, and a wash of shame flooded through her at the reminder of her behavior.

"It wasn't until I discovered these Shetland sheep and their luscious wool, that I knew I wanted to incorporate them into my trademark style, my brand of art." Charlotte continued, unaware of Justice's inner turmoil. "I love the natural colors they produce, the way that particular wool feels in my hands, between my fingers. Just enough oil to make the fibers malleable and easy to work with." She tipped her head back and gazed up into the lacy branches overhead, the sunshine filtering through to cast shifting patches of light and shadow over her features.

"When I sold my first piece, I thought I'd died and gone to heaven. I was sure I was going to be a gazillionaire." She laughed softly, the long lines of her throat rippling as she did. She straightened and looked over at them, her gaze moving slowly from one to the other. "It took me almost five more years to actually start making enough off my art to live on, but in the meantime, I worked hard every day, never giving up. I did everything I could in order to keep doing what I loved—I hired out as a cowgirl every summer, I gave piano lessons, I cleaned houses and barns and offices and churches. I wasn't too good to do anything—other than stripping or setting myself up on a street corner, that is—and every penny that didn't pay for gas in my truck, a roof over my head, and food on my table, went back into my business."

"And now, look where you are," Justice said, a little in awe of the woman.

"Yes, look where I am," Charlotte agreed, gazing out toward the pasture beyond the corral to where her flock of colorful sheep dotted the fading grasses, their spring shorn coats beginning to fill in again. "This place is as close to Eden as I can imagine."

There was a 'but' in there, and Justice wondered if she should ask about it. She didn't have to.

"Although, if this is Eden, and I'm Eve?" She chuckled softly. "I sometimes feel the absence of Adam around here."

SEVENTEEN

Goodbyes to Charlotte were surprisingly difficult. The woman and her home had been an oasis to them, a place of rest and rejuvenation after the near-catastrophic encounter with the buck, and a reprieve from the painful tension between Justice and him over the last several weeks.

On the road again, this time with Brandon at the wheel, it seemed the two of them had forged a small piece of middle ground of sorts. He could look at her, at least, without his stomach knotting quite so tightly. Whether it was because of those kisses—that shared, familiar intimacy—or because he'd finally let Justice speak her mind, and he'd actually listened to her rather than shutting her out, he wasn't sure.

Regardless, the silence between them was definitely more comfortable now. Which was good, because he had a lot to think about. So when Justice suggested they turn the audiobook back on, he shook his head. "I think I need the silence for now, but if you want to listen ahead, that's fine with me if you don't mind using your headphones."

Justice nodded slowly, then pulled out her phone and slid open her audiobook app. "I have a different one already loaded on my phone. I'll listen to that so you don't miss anything." She plugged in her earbuds, and after grabbing a neck pillow from the back seat, she slipped it on and leaned her head against the passenger window, her eyes closed. She'd be asleep in a few minutes, he was certain.

Which was fine with him, because the more he thought about what was between them, the more unsettled he became. Not in a bad way, but because he knew things had to change. And not just on her part.

The memory of their kiss—those gut-wrenchingly sweet moments that felt like coming home—wouldn't leave his thoughts, and he kept circling back on it, to the way she felt in his arms, the way her mouth moved and opened under his, her sigh against his lips that said far more than any words ever could.

And yet, what had once been to him a sure thing, an absolute, between them, had shifted inexorably. Sure, in the heat of the moment, the kiss had felt like coming home, but when his eyes were open and his arms empty, he could see that the home they'd once made together had been broken into and ravaged by looters.

Caught up in the tug-o-war between his head and his heart, he felt simultaneously hot and cold, strong and weak. Both sides of the battle were motivated by passion; a passionate heat driven by his carnal desire for her, but also a passionate determination to set aside his physical need to examine what was left of his love for her.

Because he did love her still, no matter that she'd hurt him in ways he'd never thought her capable of. The last twenty-four hours at Charlotte's place had made that abundantly clear. Justice's suffering had presented him with an opportunity to set aside his anger and betrayal to be what she desperately needed, and he hadn't thought twice before jumping in.

What he felt now, he realized, was the rising up of the man he knew he was. He needed to prove to himself, if not to Justice, that he was strong enough to handle the life he'd been given, including the life he shared with her, no matter what that ended up looking like. Even if they wound up settling as just friends, he wouldn't run away like his father had when being a dad to Brandon got too difficult. He wouldn't abandon her like his mother had abandoned him when living with psychological illness got too hard.

However, nor would he accept less than one hundred percent from her. If he was going to give one hundred percent, then he would expect the same from Justice.

And what did that mean for his job in Bowling Green? He hadn't been exactly honest with Justice last night when he'd told her about it. Yes, they'd offered him a position, and they did, indeed, want him there as soon as possible. He'd told them up front that he wouldn't be available before August, and they'd been fine with that.

But he hadn't officially accepted the offer.

Oh, he'd had every intention of doing so. In fact, the only reason he hadn't sent his reply was because he wanted to talk to Cord at Whispering Hills in person, to offer to assist in finding his replacement since he'd only just taken the job and moved onto the ranch less than a year ago.

At least, that's what he'd told himself when he'd hit "save" and not "send" on the acceptance email he'd drafted two weeks ago.

Now he acknowledged that maybe he'd hesitated because he still hoped that somehow, some way, against all odds, he and Justice could find their way back to each other. The bridge between them, or what was left of it, was choked with all kinds of perils, ugliness he didn't want to face, but deep in his gut, he knew he was strong enough to cut through it all to find her heart again.

It was up to him. It was on his shoulders now. Did he have what it took to fight for her?

And then there was Tanner. *God, how will I handle that—that—.* He left the thought unfinished. God knew what he felt about Tanner Ogden. *What am I going to do about him? How am I going to face him?* Because they would see each other, if not in the next few days at the smaller stops along the way, they'd eventually cross paths in Greeley at the end of the month. It was inevitable.

Everything in Brandon wanted to hunt the guy down and pound him senseless, but he knew real strength wasn't found in fighting, in exacting revenge, but in knowing when to fight, and when to walk away.

He glanced over at Justice, who, by all appearances, had indeed fallen asleep. "Give me the strength to walk away," he muttered under his breath, knowing she wouldn't hear him.

"Did you way something?" Justice asked, lifting her head and tugging an earbud out.

Brandon winced, but shook his head. "Just talking to myself." He smiled over at her. "I thought you were asleep; didn't mean to wake you."

Justice sighed and straightened in her seat, pulling the neck pillow free and setting it on her lap. "You didn't wake me," she said. "I'm trying to concentrate on my book, but you're thinking too loud and I can't."

"I'm thinking too loud?" he asked with a chuckle.

"Yep. Sound waves are radiating off of you at ear-piercing decibels, and I can't focus."

"So what am I thinking?"

"About me," she said, almost flippantly, darting a sideways glance over at him. "About whether or not I'm worth your effort."

Brandon felt his eyebrows rise at her blunt intuition, but he shouldn't have been surprised. This was Justice, after all. He kept his gaze focused out at the road ahead of them. "About you, maybe, but not about your worth."

Justice made a derisive sound. "Liar."

"Actually," he countered, "I was thinking about my own worth, if you must know. About what kind of man I am."

"Oh." It was a small sound, that single word, and when he glanced over at her, she was facing straight ahead, too.

They fell silent for several minutes, but before long, he noticed her fidgeting, her fingers toying with the seams of the pillow in her lap, the way she crossed and un-crossed her ankles. She caught her bottom lip between her teeth and frowned, a sure giveaway that there was something weighing heavy on her mind.

"What's going on in that mind of yours?"

She hesitated, then shook her head. "Nothing," she muttered. "It's nothing."

"Liar," he shot back, echoing her.

She rolled her eyes. "You really want to know?"

The way she asked made him think that maybe he didn't. But he nodded anyway. "Tell me. I can handle it."

She made the same noise as she had a minute ago, but then sighed. "I'm afraid of... of seeing Tanner again."

Hearing her speak that name in the cab of his truck was like the sound of nails on a chalkboard. Brandon wanted to demand she take it back, to hose down the space with a powerful antiseptic, to rid the air between them of the toxins the words evoked. But it struck him that he'd not once considered how Justice must be feeling as they closed in on Greeley.

Brandon knew what people—what guys—said about the Goodacre twins. The fact that the sisters 'held out' was common knowledge among the rodeo regulars. It wasn't as if everyone fooled around all the time, but between shows and performances, rodeos could become quite a party, and the regulars knew who played and who didn't. The Goodacre girls didn't.

At least not until last summer.

And now Justice was going back to face the music.

Up until that moment, Brandon had assumed her growing agitation and subsequent withdrawal with each stop they made had been due to Courage's absence. But now, he realized there was much more to it. Justice was facing her peers, her cohorts and competition alike, knowing that they knew she'd compromised. Because Tanner Ogden wasn't quiet about his conquests.

Justice wasn't just facing them, she was facing them alone. Without Courage, and from her perspective, possibly without Brandon at her side, either. Soon enough, she'd be facing Tanner, himself.

She must be terrified, he realized, shame over his own selfishness washing over him.

"I'll stand by you," he said, then cleared his throat. The words were almost painful coming out of him, but he was glad to hear they were strong and sure.

She swiped at her eyes and shook her head. "It's my battle, Brandon. I'm going to have to face him sooner or later. It's my own doing, not yours."

"Wait a minute," he said, resisting the urge to reach across the console to take her hand. He wasn't quite ready to touch her just yet, not with Tanner the subject of their conversation. A gentle handhold might quickly turn into a bone-crushing squeeze. "Didn't you just tell me last night that you had to learn to accept help when it was offered? That you aren't an island?" He frowned and tapped his chin, as though trying to recall her words. "That you can't do everything on your own and in your own way?"

"Yes, but—"

"Yes, but," he echoed, cutting her off. "You know, I wasn't lying when I said I was thinking about the kind of man I am. The kind of man I want to be." He could feel her watching him as he spoke. "I want to help you. I want to be here for you. I'm offering because that's who I am."

"But I don't want trouble, Brandon," she said, her voice flat. "I want to avoid him as much as possible. I want to do what we came to do, then go home. He and I don't run in the same circles, you know? At least not outside the arena. The only reason I even bumped into him that night was because I was stupid and bratty and went out with—" She broke off suddenly and took a deep breath. "I don't ever want to relive that night again, not even in my thoughts," she muttered, almost too quietly for him to hear.

He didn't want to either, but he knew that Tanner Ogden wasn't going to pretend nothing had happened. Justice Goodacre wasn't a rodeo wallflower. Popular, self-confident, and competitive, she'd made it her mission to stand out wherever she went, often dragging Courage along behind in her wake. Now, without her sister to back her up, Justice would be easy pickings for the likes of Tanner and his pals.

"I'm not going to let you fight this one alone," Brandon stated, not bothering to give her the option. There would be trouble, whether she wanted it or not. *God, give me the strength and wisdom to know when to fight and when to walk away.*

EIGHTEEN

Justice wasn't sure how to feel about Brandon's assertions, but she didn't want to argue about it, either. The tentative peace that had settled between them was like a balm to her bruised soul, and she wanted to stay in that place of solace as long as she could.

They'd driven right past Truskee, and would be in Benton within the hour in plenty of time to stake out their site and settle in for a couple of days. It was considered a small town rodeo, but the place swelled to bursting right before Greeley, making for a decent purse size. Definitely worth the stop if Justice could perform. Getting there a day early would give her plenty of time rest and work out some of the kinks in her routine.

She'd done a few practice runs out at Charlotte's to test the stability of her foot, and now she was to actually perform under pressure. Her ankle hurt, especially during stunts like the Hippodrome and reverse one-leg stands, but as long as she wrapped it well under her tightly-laced wrestling shoes—the most ideal footgear for trick riding—she was confident it was stable enough to perform on. Tomorrow morning's ride would be a good practice run before the big competition at Greeley.

Besides, folks at Benton loved The Twisted Sisters, and although Justice wasn't looking forward to explaining Courage's absence to yet another disappointed crowd of fans, she was still expecting their typical warm welcome. Another balm; she'd take all the comfort she could get.

That evening, they warmed up a pan of some of Charlotte's beef stew she'd packaged up for them, and stayed close to the trailer. The site was full to bursting with others who'd arrived early, but although crowded, there was a sense of hushed anticipation for the next day's events among the folks gathered. No one seemed to want to be the first to get rowdy, at least not in their section.

Which suited Justice just fine. She'd been fighting off a tickle of panic all day. Every time she closed her eyes, she saw that stupid deer in the road, saw the flash of headlights across his angular head, his glowing eyes. Time and time again, she'd had to force herself to take slow, controlled breaths just to feel like she was getting enough oxygen. How long would this go on, she wanted to ask Brandon, but she didn't want him to worry.

A good night's rest in the comfortable familiarity of her camper bed would surely help, wouldn't it?

They'd both turned in early, Justice inside the Exiss, Brandon settled into his hammock hung across the trailer's door. She wasn't sure about him, but sleep had come quickly; she had worn herself out trying to pretend everything was okay during the long hours they'd spent on the road that day.

The next morning, with Brandon's help, Justice and Fire were ready in plenty of time. He wouldn't be volunteering his first aid services just yet, and true to his word, he was staying close to her side. He'd even offered to braid her hair for her before he remembered the injury that was keeping him out of the arena. But he took over painting glitter tornadoes on Fire's haunches, and safety-checked all the straps and loops on the custom trick saddle.

"Thank you, Brandon," Justice said, making a point to acknowledge him, to not take his assistance and his presence for granted. She started to take Fire's turquoise lead rope from him, expecting him to stay behind and keep Tank company, but Brandon hung onto it and fell into step beside her, leading Fire for her.

"You're not losing me that easily," he told her. "I always watch your show; you know that."

She tried not to look surprised. Up until this season, sure, but she'd only seen him at one of her performances since leaving the Hollow, and she was pretty sure he was only there under duress, since he'd been with a few of his rodeo buddies he hadn't seen since the year before.

"Hey, Justice!" The shout came from a trio of girls hurrying across the parking lot toward them. One of them, Tara, was an up-and-coming barrel racer, a nice enough girl who had a whole lot of talent and skill but lacked the competitive edge she'd need to rise to the top. Complacency usually frustrated Justice, but she liked Tara well enough—always cheerful, always helpful, and always optimistic about both her wins and losses. The two girls flanking her were her younger sisters, and the three of them were dressed in identical dark blue jeans, pink pearl button shirts with tassels across the chests, stunning white cowboy hats with wide pink bands, and pink leather belts with enormous silver buckles. Their boots, however, were all different, and for some reason, that made Justice like them even more.

"So," Tara said as she stepped close and looped an arm through Justice's. Even though Justice wasn't exactly comfortable with the familiarity of the gesture, she recognized it as part of the physical language of sisters and large families. Tara had three brothers as well.

"I heard about you and Tanner," Tara gushed. "You are so lucky. He is so amazing." She drew the syllables of the last word out, closing her eyes as she did so.

Justice stumbled—she actually stumbled—at the girl's declaration, and she might have even gone down if Brandon hadn't reached out and gripped her elbow to steady her. His fingers around her arm weren't gentle, telling her he wasn't immune to Tara's words, either. He was just a little better at keeping it together than she was, apparently. She didn't pull away from him, though, the pain from his grip giving her something to focus on.

Justice had no clue what to say to Tara, how to even react. What on earth was Tanner telling people? What exactly had Tara heard? Who besides Tara knew... knew what? Her stomach clenched in anxiety, the scrambled eggs and toast they'd had for breakfast threatening to rebel. A faint buzzing sounded in her ears and her pulse quickened. She could feel her heart pounding against her ribcage, but she couldn't tell if she was livid or terrified.

"Not sure what you heard, Tara." Brandon's voice rose above the clamor in Justice's head. "But there is no Justice and Tanner."

Casual, calm, together. He'd slipped into his First Responder role, it seemed. But his grip on her elbow hadn't let up. She didn't think he even realized how tightly he was holding on, but she was pretty sure she'd have his fingerprints in shades of black and blue imprinted there by nightfall.

Justice looked up at him, hoping he could see the gratitude in her eyes, but he was smiling past her at the three sisters on her other side.

"Oh." Tara faltered, her brow furrowing as she kept in step with them. "But I heard—" She broke off and started again. "My brother said— Um, he was hanging out with Tanner, and Tanner said that...." She didn't finish the sentence, and her cheeks went pink. "Sorry. Probably just a rumor."

"Does that mean he's single?" one of the younger sisters asked, completely oblivious to the growing tension in the air.

"Couldn't answer that," Brandon responded, his tone still deceptively nonchalant. "Maybe you should go ask him."

Tara, clearly embarrassed and confused, unhooked her arm from Justice's, but then grabbed her hand and squeezed it. "I shouldn't have said anything. Me and my big mouth," she said, the look in her eyes one of sincere remorse. "Stupid gossip, that's all." Then she shooed her sisters ahead of her and the three of them veered away.

"You're hurting me," Justice murmured, straightening her arm to loosen his grip.

"Sorry. Oh, man. Sorry," he said again, pulling his hand free and opening and closing his fingers. "I didn't mean to..."

"I know. It's okay," she assured him.

The composed expression he'd worn only moments before in front of Tara and her sisters was gone, and in its place was something of a mixture between misery and anger. It was a look that had become all too familiar to Justice over the last several weeks, and her heart sank. She felt like she needed to apologize for what had just happened, but doing so, she was certain, would only make things worse. She dropped her gaze and focused on the lingering buzz in her ears, the tingling of sensation on the inside of her arm where she could still feel his fingers gripping her.

By the time they arrived at the arena and she found her place in the lineup, one more bright-eyed woman had approached Justice to congratulate her on snagging Tanner. Once again, Brandon set the record straight, and even though Justice didn't stumble in surprise that time, and although he didn't put a strangle hold on her arm, Justice had no doubt that Brandon wasn't getting any happier about the rumors.

Justice, too, was pretty badly shaken by the way things were unfolding. She had to find out what Tanner was saying about her. So far, it sounded like he'd spun it in what he seemed to consider a positive light, touting them as something of a couple, but no one had come right out and said what details they knew. She had to know what everyone around her had heard.

Didn't she?

"I need to focus," she muttered under her breath, keeping her head low and her hat lower. She was all but hiding behind Fire as she waited with him in the holding pen before her show started. Brandon had slipped away to greet one of the medics team members he'd worked with before, but Justice was pretty sure it was an excuse to get away from her. If it was hard for her to hear the rumors, she could only imagine how difficult it must be for him.

And yet, he'd defended her twice now, standing by her, just like he said he would.

Greeley, however, was just a few days away, and with Greeley, came Tanner in the flesh and blood.

Would Brandon stand by her then?

"Tanner Ogden, hm?" The voice was sticky sweet molasses and big Texas twang. "I hear you gave as good as you got." Sandy Hayward stood just outside the stall, her jeans riding low on her hips, her western shirt tied in a knot just below her full breasts, her smooth, tanned stomach bare. She didn't wear a hat—it would mess up her glorious blonde curls that cascaded down her back, almost to her waist.

Justice chose to ignore her, acting like she hadn't heard the woman, but something ugly and bitter, rose up in her. Who was Sandy to judge Justice? Sandy was a rodeo groupie. Not there to perform or compete, at least not in the arena. She performed and competed for other things, and it was all Justice could do not to cut the beauty down a notch or two. But she held her tongue and moved around Fire to stand as far from Sandy as she could get.

"Got tired of flying your V-card high, hm?"

Justice cringed as Sandy's voice grew louder. Not the response she was hoping for. Pretty soon she'd be drawing a crowd.

"So how does your boyfriend feel about you giving it up to someone else? Or is he officially single now?" From the corner of her eye, Justice could see Sandy making a show of looking around. "Good news for the rest of us—that Brandon is hot stuff."

Justice wanted to cover her ears with her hands like a child. She hated what Sandy was saying, but then, weren't they the same things she taunted her own reflection with?

What time was it? Wasn't it her turn yet? And where was Brandon? Had he found a seat somewhere? Or had he left the arena to go back to the trailer? To get as far away from her as possible?

"And where is your little Bobbsey twin?" Sandy jeered, propping a shiny black boot on the lowest bar of the fence. "Did she drop you like a hot potato, too?"

"She died."

At the sound of that voice, relief washed over Justice like a cold shower on a hot summer day. Brandon. He hadn't abandoned her after all.

"Oh." The word came out stilted, unsure. "Oh," Sandy said again. "Wow. Seriously?"

"Back off, Sandy. And you're not supposed to be back here; this area is for performers only." Cool, casual... No. Chilled. Frosty. Hard as steel. That's what Brandon's voice sounded like as he spoke to Sandy.

"I'm here with Josie Tucker," Sandy shot back, straightening her shoulders and lifting her chin.

"Oh yeah?" Brandon challenged. "Except, I don't see Josie Tucker anywhere."

"I'm waiting for her."

"Wait for her somewhere else."

Sandy opened her mouth to argue, but when Brandon took a step toward her, she thought better of it. She huffed loudly, flipped her hair over her shoulder as she spun on her heels, then sashayed angrily away from them.

Justice dipped her head to hide a small smile. Brandon could come across as intimidating with his six-foot-two frame and his austere features, but Justice knew he wouldn't hurt a flea. He was in the business of patching up wounded and broken bodies, not inflicting injury. Granted, she didn't see him angry very often—well, up until this last year—so she didn't blame Sandy for turning tail and running. If Justice didn't know Brandon the way she did, he might have scared her, too.

Besides, it was nice—really nice—to have him stand up for her, especially to someone who was obviously out to hurt her.

"Starting rumors of my own," Brandon muttered as he slipped between the railing bars to stand near Fire's head. "Sorry. I shouldn't have thrown Courage under the bus that way."

"Well, it got her to stop talking," Justice said with a good-natured shrug. "And I'm sure Courage will find it funny."

"You okay?" He studied her over Fire's back, and she nodded.

"I'm fine." She wasn't fine. Between Sandy's cruel attack, her still-jangly nerves, and the buzzing, tingling sensation that seemed to be building inside her the longer she waited, she wasn't fine. "Just ready to get out there. What's the holdup?"

"A minor injury," Brandon said, his eyes narrowing at her response. He could see right through her false pretenses. "Someone came off a horse a little early. A sprain, possibly a break, but no head trauma, so you'll be up soon."

Less than three minutes later, a young man in a very large black cowboy hat dropped by to let her know she could head for the chute. Brandon gave her a leg up, then patted Fire's neck before holding open the pen gate for her. As she passed, he put a hand on her knee, making her pause to look down at him.

"You've got this. I believe in you."

She wiped her sweating palms on her jeans, offered up a quick prayer for safety and a good run, then made her way toward the start gate as the MC began his introduction.

And of course, he hadn't gotten the word that Courage wouldn't be riding today. Justice groaned inwardly as she heard him announce them. "And here they are, folks, Justice and Courage Goodacre! The daring duo, the twin tornadoes, the sibling cyclones, The Twisted Sisters!"

The music started and she listened for the beat above the roar of the crowd. There it was. Beneath her, Fire heard it, too, and he tensed, coiled, ready to spring into action with the tiniest nudge of her heels.

NINETEEN

IT WAS A DISASTER. The whole ride. The whole performance. The whole shebang, as her father would have called it. Rather than waiting for her heel nudge, at a slight shift of Justice's weight in the saddle, Fire shot out of the chute before Justice was ready. By the time they were halfway around the arena, she'd only managed to perform two of the five quick stunts she usually started the show with, and not with any finesse, either. They were dramatic and daring, flipping and spinning from one side of the horse to the other in a quick succession of moves that made the crowd gasp and cheer. Usually, Courage on Flash raced alongside her, and when the two of them performed the tricks in perfect synchrony, the crowd had a hard time staying in their seats.

That wasn't the response she got today.

The second time around the arena had her dropped into a shoulder stand, her long braid tips brushing the earth as she hung head down over Fire's side. She found herself listening for Courage's command, for Flash's hoof beats pounding out a matching rhythm with Fire's. When Justice rose up into the Hippodrome, her arms high above her head, the colorful Sweetwater sponsor banner unfurling behind her, she could tell the effect simply wasn't the same without Courage standing tall and proud beside her, their twin stallions churning up the earth as they charged around the arena at a breakneck speed.

And when the final notes of their "Made in the USA" soundtrack rang out over the sound system, Justice was sure the applause was polite, perhaps even a little confused, and it held nowhere near the thunderous appreciation it usually did.

All in all, the performance was technically sound, she kept reminding herself, but she knew it had none of the flair The Twisted Sisters were known for. Justice wasn't sure she'd felt Courage's absence more acutely than she did at that moment.

Back in the holding pen, she slid from Fire's back and circled around to his head to fidget with his bridle. There was nothing wrong with it, of course, but she had to look busy, to give her hands something to do, give her mind something to focus on. If Courage were here, the two of them would lead their horses out to one of the large corrals where the public could gather around. Then Justice would take over tending the horses while her sister did the meet and greet with all their fans.

"Hey." It was Brandon. "Let me take Fire while you go out and talk to your groupies." He slipped through the fence rails and reached for the horse's lead, but instead of letting him take it, Justice pulled away.

"I—I don't want to see anyone right now."

Brandon frowned, but he didn't play dumb. "Okay." He nodded slowly. "I understand. Ten minutes, though. Give them that much."

Justice leaned her forehead against Fire's steaming neck. The horse's coat was damp with sweat and he was still breathing heavily, but Justice knew that if she climbed back into the saddle, he'd be ready to go in a heartbeat. Maybe that's what she should do. Get back on her horse and ride away from all of this; the fans, the crowds, the Sandys, and the Tanners.

Finally, she took a deep breath and let it out in a loud whoosh, startling Fire, who turned and knocked the side of his head against hers. "Ouch," she muttered, then peered over at Brandon who stood on Fire's other side. "I'll go. I just don't want to. Me and kids, you know?" She shrugged self-deprecatingly. "Not the most winning combination."

She didn't really hate kids. In fact, she kind of liked them, especially her nieces and nephew. But she was never quite comfortable around children she didn't know. It made her a little afraid of what kind of mother she'd be, if, indeed, she ever became one. That aside, the majority of their fans who gathered after the show were young girls and some boys, in awe of the acrobatics on horseback she and Courage performed.

"We got this, Fire and I," she assured Brandon, putting on a brave face. "We are not afraid. You don't have to hold my hand. Or my horse's hand. Or lead."

She knew that Brandon knew she wasn't afraid of kids. He also knew full well that it wasn't children she didn't want to see. "I'm going with you," he said, his voice low and serious.

She frowned at him, holding his gaze, but said nothing, suddenly afraid to hear what he might say next.

"Tanner's here." He didn't look away, and Justice could see the array of emotions wreaking havoc behind his eyes. It matched the swarm of emotions churning in her gut at his words.

"Here? But—but why? This isn't his usual—"

"I don't know and I don't care. But I'm going with you," he repeated, and this time, she heard the tightness in his throat, like a steel band of self-control holding back the words he really wanted to say.

A sudden wave of heat washed over Justice and she looked away, her palms sweating, her pulse racing. *Breathe,* she commanded herself silently, but the more she thought about it, the more difficult it became to take in enough oxygen. She closed her eyes and pressed into Fire's neck again, and for whatever reason—maybe he sensed her disquiet—he rested his head over her shoulder and let her lean into him without fidgeting. They stood that way for what seemed like hours before she finally felt somewhat back in control of her mental capacities.

This rush of anxiety, or whatever it was, was getting old. She wasn't a nervous person. She wasn't accustomed to her feelings and emotions having such sway over her. Why did it matter if Tanner was here or not? In fact, wasn't it better to face him now at this smaller venue than to have to do so in Greeley where he was surrounded by all his pals?

When she finally opened her eyes and lifted her head, Brandon was still standing close by, but he wasn't looking at her. Could he simply not bear the sight of her? The terrible thought sent a quick jab of pain through her chest.

"You don't have to do that, Brandon. This is my problem, not yours." She spoke softly, not wanting him to get the wrong idea. She wanted him with her—oh, how she wanted him at her side, always—but this wasn't his burden to carry. This was her sin, her mess, her bad choices, and he shouldn't have to clean it up for her, or even *with* her.

Brandon made a sound that might have been a growl, then turned to glare at her. His expression made her flinch. "When are you going to get it through your thick skull that this absolutely *is* my problem." He jabbed a finger in her direction. "*You* are my problem, and that makes *Tanner* my problem, especially if he intends to make problems for you. Got it?" His volume increased as he spoke, and Justice felt her eyes widening with every word. "I am going with you, like it or not. You will not face him alone."

"Well, what if he doesn't show—"

"He'll show, I guarantee it." He snapped his mouth shut, his lips pressed together in a firm line. The muscles at his jaw bunched visibly as he reached under Fire's head and plucked the lead line out of Justice's hand. "Stop being a big chicken. Let's go," he snarled.

Something inside her snapped to attention, and she stepped back, her chin up. "I am not afraid of him," she declared, her own jaw tight with emotion. "He can't hurt me anymore than he already has."

"Oh, yes, he can," Brandon shot back, a rueful laugh under his words. He pushed open the pen gate and guided Fire out into the corridor that led to the public areas. "And when he figures out that you actually mean 'no' this time, he'll do everything in his power to change your mind. He succeeded once, didn't he? Surely, he'll be able to get another yes out of you before everyone goes home, right?" And with those parting words, he marched off, practically dragging her horse behind him, and leaving her standing alone in the middle of the pen.

Anger warred with fear. Anger at Brandon for his cruel words, fear because she had more than just a suspicion that every one of them was true. Tanner might be talking nice about her now, but he wasn't one to take rejection lying down. She'd heard the stories about his treatment of women he'd cast off, women who didn't live up to his expectations, or women who didn't find him quite as irresistible as he thought he was. Most of it was just ugly words, but words had a way of setting seed wherever they fell, and like weeds, gossip and rumors that took root could choke the truth to death.

Fear had her hurrying after Brandon and her horse. Anger had her walking stiffly on Fire's other side, refusing to look over at the man who knew exactly how to push her buttons. Or punch her in the gut.

To her great relief, Tanner didn't show his face during her little after-show gathering. She explained time and again where Courage was, skirting the question about whether or not she'd be returning, and although she was loathe to acknowledge it, she was exceedingly grateful to Brandon repeatedly steering the conversation back to trick riding, costumes, and horses.

Fifteen minutes later, she told the few stragglers that she had to get Fire cleaned up and fed. Just as she and Brandon started back toward their trailer, she caught a glimpse of Tanner heading their way, surrounded by a small posse of people, including, she noticed, Sandy Hayward, and a few other women who likely weren't too happy about Tanner's interest in Justice. She turned her back on the group, hoping against hope that he hadn't seen her notice him, and picked up her speed. Her ankle was beginning to throb inside her boot, but she made every effort not to hobble, unwilling to show any signs of weakness.

Thankfully, Brandon kept pace with her, and although she didn't dare look back over her shoulder to check on Tanner and the gang, she didn't slow down, either, until they'd reached their trailer. Only then did she allow herself to look back the way they'd come, and to her relief, Tanner was nowhere in sight.

"Better get some ice on that," Brandon said as he led Fire around toward the back of the trailer where he started removing the horse's tackle. "The cooler is in the shower stall," he added, his voice raised to be heard above Tank's welcoming stomps and snorts. He'd been cooped up in the trailer during Justice's performance, and he was none too happy about it. Once Fire's tack was put away, they planned to set up the portable corral they always carried with them—the collapsible panels were lashed to brackets on one side of the trailer strapped to the side of the trailer—then let the horses chill and stretch for a bit before brushing them down and loading them back up for the night.

Justice couldn't help but feel sorry for Tank. The horse wasn't accustomed to doing nothing. Neither was his owner, for that matter, but right now, she wasn't feeling quite so sorry for him. He'd been a jerk, and the things he'd said still rang in her ears. On top of that, Tanner hadn't made trouble for her, at least not face to face, so Brandon could take his guarantees and stick them in his ear.

"And I'll ice my foot when I'm good and ready, and not a moment before," she muttered to herself as she began to unhook the straps around the panels of the mini corral. In a voice loud enough for him to hear, she hollered, "I'll set up the corral so you can let your poor horse out. I don't need him tearing up my trailer."

In slow motion, Brandon's head and shoulders appeared from around the back of the trailer. He glared at her, but didn't say a word, then disappeared again.

His response, or non-response, only added fuel to the fire, and with a careless jerk, she tugged hard on the last of the straps, and several of the lightweight aluminum panels toppled off the brackets and landed in jangling heap at her feet. One of them knocked against her shin and had her stepping back, an ugly word catching on the tip of her tongue. When Brandon's floating head once again made an appearance, she was standing straight and tall, one hand on her hip as if she'd done it all on purpose.

"Need help?"

She narrowed her eyes at him, imagining his head was detached from his body. "Nope."

"'Course not," he muttered, and disappeared once more.

She allowed herself to consider exactly *how* Brandon's head had become detached from his body... then stooped to pick up the fence panels and began setting up the corral.

TWENTY

He knew he'd made her mad. That was his intent. He didn't like goading her like that, but he had seen that she was unraveling, and quickly. The only thing he could think of was to get her riled up, to put her on the defensive so she'd fight back. So he'd poked at the wound they both shared, and she'd risen to the occasion just like he knew she would.

But Lord, have mercy, how it hurt him, too. He pressed the heel of his hand to his chest just over his heart, then lifted it to look for traces of blood.

There was nothing there, of course, so he turned his attention back to the small tack closet at the back of the trailer. They'd rearranged things because of the extra room they had without Courage's gear, but after the near run-in with the deer, things were a bit jumbled. He took his time reorganizing stuff, even though he knew the horses were antsy, especially Tank who just wanted out of his stall. He'd wait until he was sure Justice had the corral set up first; he really didn't want to engage with her right now. As much as he hurt *for* her, he was also reeling from his own pain.

And confusion. Or was it frustration?

Despite his certainty of Tanner's intentions where Justice was concerned, the guy hadn't made an appearance. Brandon had heard that Tanner was looking for her, that he planned to pick up where they'd left off. The worst of the rumors had been the ones Sandy Hayward had tossed his way, but he was pretty sure Sandy's version of things was seasoned with a large helping of spite, both toward Justice, and in some backhanded way, toward him for rejecting her so soundly last year.

Even so, there was a measure of truth to what was being said. So far, it seemed to be public knowledge among certain circles that Justice had slept with Tanner, that she'd fallen off her high-falutin' virgin throne. And from what he could tell, Tanner planned on proving to the world that it wasn't just a one time, drunken lapse in judgement.

Even though Brandon knew Justice had no intention of picking up with Tanner again, even though he knew she regretted all that had happened, even though he knew she hated the pain she'd caused everyone, it still sat like a lead ball in his gut that they were in this predicament at all. If only she'd—

A shrill yelp sent a tremor up his spine. He dropped the harness he'd been untangling and dashed around Fire to find Tanner holding Justice up against him, his arms wrapped around her from behind, clearly having caught her completely unawares.

"Let go!" she demanded, twisting and flailing in his hold.

Tanner nuzzled her neck with his chin and said something too quiet for Brandon to make out. Then again, it might have been blocked out by the noise the hive of angry bees inside his skull was making. Or the molten lava bubbling and hissing to the boiling point in his chest.

Justice elbowed Tanner hard in the stomach, making his grip loosen, but not enough for her to get free. "Let me go," she ground out, pushing against his locked arms.

"What? Not a warm welcome for your favorite cowboy?" Tanner asked, his words a little choppy from Justice's well-placed elbow thrust. His grin, however, made it crystal clear that he was getting a certain kind of thrill from the encounter. "Whoa-ho-ho! I don't remember you being quite so feisty the last time—"

The word turned into a startled yelp as Brandon grabbed him by the shoulders and hauled him off, practically throwing him to the ground.

Tanner stumbled, but kept his feet under him. Pain shot up Brandon's arm from the wrenching his wrist took, but he raised both fists and started toward the guy.

"Brandon, no!" Justice cried out, lurching forward to try to step in front of him, but he skirted her easily, seeing red. By the time he reached Tanner, he was already swinging.

Tanner, however, was a rodeo champion for a reason. He was an athlete; quick on his feet, agile and responsive, and he ducked out of the way of Brandon's flying fist so that the punch glanced off his shoulder instead.

"Whoa there, pony boy! So she didn't tell you?" Tanner taunted, backing up and bouncing a little in his crocodile skin boots, his own hands curled into fists, but hanging loose and limber at his sides rather than raised to fight.

Brandon had heard the nickname before. It wasn't his Shawnee bloodline folks were mocking when they called him by it, but his refusal to cut his hair, which, in the end, made it all about his Shawnee bloodline, after all. And because of that, it never bothered him.

Until now.

Ignoring Justice's pleas to stop, Brandon lunged forward again, this time going in low with an uppercut, but Tanner managed to deflect it with a raised forearm before dancing out of reach again.

It was obvious the guy wasn't interested in duking it out. No, Tanner was all about preserving his pretty boy image, and a fist to the face might mess up his model features. But he certainly wasn't above tossing out a few verbal punches, the kind that went straight to the gut and knocked the breath right out of a man.

"That's right," Tanner said, bouncing around like he thought he was Muhammad Ali. "Justice Goodacre finally met a man she couldn't say no to." He dodged another swing from Brandon, backing up a few more steps.

Like a raging bull, Brandon lurched after him, feeling what little self-control he had left in his tank slipping away. If he got his hands on the guy, he might just kill him.

"Enough!" Justice screeched, throwing herself hard against Brandon's side, knocking him off balance just enough to step between the two men. She got right up in his face and shoved him in the chest with both hands, hard. "Stop it, Brandon Stillwater. Stop now."

"Get. Out. Of. My. Way," Brandon snarled, each word coming out a complete sentence. A fleck of his spittle landed on her cheek and she barely flinched.

She didn't so much as step back. Instead, she wrapped her arms around his waist and held on. "Don't do this, Brandon," she ordered, her voice low and throaty now, her eyes never leaving his face, even as he glared past her at Tanner who still danced around at a safe distance. "He's not worth it."

"That's not what you said last summer," Tanner crooned. "How about we get together and talk about old times. You and me, Ms. Goodacre." He might have been speaking to Justice, but his taunting gaze never left Brandon's face. "Tonight at Bucky's Bar and Grill. I'll wine and dine you and treat you real nice." He didn't need to say more; his lurid expression made his meaning explicit: Then it would be her turn to treat him real nice.

Tanner's words weren't any less barbed now, but Justice's arms around Brandon gave him something else to focus his attention on. The smell of her hair in his nostrils, the weight of her body against his, solid and warm and reassuring. Steadying.

"He's not worth it," she said again, and her voice, sure and familiar, was like a glass of cool water to his burning insides.

"There'll be fireworks tonight," Tanner cajoled. "We can watch them from Bucky's patio."

"Not happening, Tanner. Go away," she told him, voice raised, but not taking her eyes off Brandon.

Apparently, the idiot wasn't ready to give up. "We can set off some fireworks of our own."

Brandon still wanted to kill the guy, but with Justices' eyes locked on his, he found it less and less important to pay attention to anything Tanner said.

"Get out of here, Tanner," Justice ordered, her voice no longer raised, but no less steely. "I mean it."

"Aw, come on, Justice." He was whining now, wheedling. "I thought you'd finally loosened up last summer, were ready to live a little."

Justice did turn around then, but kept her arm around Brandon's waist, her body tight against his side. "If spending even one more nanosecond with you is what you call living a little, then I'd rather die. Now, I'm going to say this nicely one more time. Leave me alone."

"I know you don't mean that, Justice. You and me, we—"

Justice cut him off. "You know, I thought you were smarter than this. But maybe you just have an extra thick skull, so let me make this explicitly clear to you." She spoke slowly and deliberately. "I don't want your attention, your affection, or any of your advances, inappropriate or otherwise."

"Hey, now," Tanner said, raising both hands in the air. "Chill out, okay? I mean, I'm just playing around with you. Teasing you because I like you, Justice Goodacre. I want to spend time with you. That's not a crime, is it?"

Just as Brandon had predicted, Tanner wasn't the kind of guy to handle rejection well. But then, not many people were. He, himself, hadn't handled it very well, had he? Brandon opened his mouth to speak, but Justice jumped in first.

"Tanner Ogden, I'm serious as a heart attack. Leave me alone. Be polite to me when our paths cross, and I'll pay you the same courtesy, but don't go out of your way to run into me." She jutted her chin a little higher and her arm tightened around Brandon. He widened his stance, more than happy to be the man she chose to lean on. "And this is the last time I want to hear about that night in Greeley."

"I can't help it if people talk," Tanner shot back, his voice thick with petulance.

"You can help it if *you* talk."

"You threw yourself at me, not the other way around. I just took what was being offered me," he taunted, doing his best to get one last hit in. It was pretty obvious he knew he'd lost.

"And you're still talking," Justice said, shaking her head in exaggerated disbelief.

But she was done. She stepped away from Brandon's side, took his good hand, and all but pulled him with her to the back of the trailer where Fire still stood patiently waiting for someone to finish tending to his needs, his lead loosely draped over the back bumper.

"Let your horse out," she ordered, then led Fire into the corral she'd set up. She'd already hung two half full feedbags for the horses to munch on.

Brandon stepped up into the trailer, unhooked the latch that locked the stall divider in place, and led his impatient gelding out into the open to join Fire. Tanner was nowhere to be seen.

"I'll take care of the water," he started to say, then saw that Justice had already attached the hose to the topside water tank, and was in the process of filling two buckets latched to the side of the trailer.

"I've got this," she said, not looking at him. "But if you want to get an ice pack ready for me, that would be great. I still have to get out of this costume." She flapped an arm like a wing, shaking the tassels hanging from her sleeve.

Feeling suddenly and thoroughly emasculated, Brandon straightened his shoulders and stepped toward her, reaching for the hose. "I'll finish this and get the ice pack ready while you change."

Justice glanced over her shoulder in the direction Tanner went.

"I won't engage with him if he comes back," Brandon assured her. Sometimes it was so easy to read her mind.

Justice cocked her head up at him, clearly not believing him.

"I give you my word," he said, a wave of affection washing over him as he gazed down at her face, the shape of it, the lines and curves, the shadows and planes of it so familiar and precious to him. "Unless he forces me to, and then I will do my best not to hurt him," he teased. He inwardly cringed as he thought about how his rage had made him practically ineffective in the fight with Tanner. If his sore knuckles were any indication, the two hits he'd landed would leave their marks on the other guy's shoulder and forearm, but Brandon had been aiming for Tanner's jaw and solar plexus.

He didn't know which bothered him more, that he'd let his anger reduce him to throwing punches at the likes of Tanner Ogden, or that the punches he'd thrown had missed their marks.

Brandon was pretty sure God was looking down at him with the same expression Justice wore at that very moment.

He took a deep breath and let it out slowly when she handed him the hose and headed inside the trailer.

TWENTY-ONE

Justice took the cooler out of the shower stall and set it on the floor in the tiny kitchenette so Brandon could get to the ice. She hung her clean clothes on a hook on the back of the bathroom door, pinned her braids up on top of her head, and took a military shower. When she didn't wash her hair, she could get it done in under three minutes.

Dried off and dressed in a pair of shorts and a gray baseball tee with red sleeves, Justice slipped her feet into a pair of flip-flops, grimacing at the ache in her ankle. She needed to get it up and on ice soon. She scooped up her costume from where she'd stepped out of it, hung it carefully on its padded hanger, ran her fingers through the fringes to untangle them, then stepped out of the tiny bathroom.

Brandon stood with his back to the counter, a plastic bag of ice in one hand, a glass of water in his other. He dwarfed the already tiny living quarters, and when she made to get past him to hang her costume in the narrow closet at the end of the bed, he didn't move. So she stopped and peered up at him, one eyebrow arched.

He returned the look and still didn't move.

"Do you mind?" She flapped her costume in front of her.

"Be my guest," he replied with a shrug. "I've got your ice," he added, holding the bag up, further blocking her way.

A standoff, then.

"Why are you angry at me now?" Was it because she'd stopped the fight? Because she'd pulled him away from engaging with Tanner? Or was this how it was always going to be between them now; one minute, they were good, the next minute they wanted to rip each others' throats out?

Justice sighed and turned away from him. Fine. She'd go out the escape door through the bathroom and circle around the trailer to come in the other way. She wasn't going to try to push him out of the way, and she certainly wasn't going to force her way past him.

"Hey."

She stopped, but didn't turn back to face him. "What?"

"Sorry."

"For what?" she asked, wondering if he was saying it just to get her to apologize, too.

Brandon didn't respond, so she shook her head and said, "I forgive you," then bee-lined through the bathroom and out into the horses' end of the trailer. She hoped Brandon wouldn't follow as she pushed open the escape door and stepped out into the afternoon sunshine. She took a deep breath, then another, willing her nerves to uncoil.

Something sinister hovered at the edge of her awareness, a sense of foreboding, but she couldn't quite zone in on it. The sensation was so foreign to her, that inability to grab life by the tail and manhandle it into submission, and it left her feeling unstable and vulnerable.

It also made her miss Brandon that much more, ache for what they'd once shared, something it seemed they'd never have again.

She made her way slowly around the end of the trailer, took her time checking on the horses, promised Fire she'd be out soon to give him a little TLC, and complimented Tank on his muscular chest. The big guy tried to nibble at the sequined collar of her costume, and she laughed and pushed his head away.

A noise brought her head up and she turned toward the main door of the trailer to find Brandon standing there, watching her. Great. Was he going to block her entrance there, too?

"I meant it," he said, dropping to the ground and holding the door open. He gestured inside. "I was being a jerk. Come in and let's get some ice on that ankle."

She hesitated, then crossed the distance between them.

"I can hang that up for you," he said as she drew near. He reached to take the hanger from her, but when she didn't relinquish it, he flashed his boyish, lopsided grin at her. "I'm offering to help you," he said, his hand still out.

Justice rolled her eyes, but handed him the costume, then climbed the steps into the trailer. The air conditioner had kicked on—Brandon must have turned it on while she was in the shower—and it was significantly cooler inside than out.

She snatched the bag of ice from the sink where Brandon had left it, dropped to the sofa seat, kicked off her flip-flops, and brought both bare feet up onto the cushion beside her. She gasped at the chill of the bag as she formed it around her ankle, but by the time Brandon had followed her inside, hung her costume, and lowered himself into the only other chair in the tiny space, she was beginning to relax and enjoy the therapeutic effects of the ice.

He didn't meet her eyes, so she studied him openly. He sat hunched forward, his elbows on his knees, fingers laced together in front of him, his gaze fixed on her foot. "Brandon?" she finally said, more to break the impasse than because she was afraid he might not know she was talking to him.

"Hm?" He did look at her then, lifting his eyes to hers.

"Are you going to be able to compete this season?"

By his expression, it was evident that had been the last thing he'd expected her to say. "Um... this season? What?"

She didn't raise her voice or speak slowly like he was an idiot; she just pointed at his hands and repeated her question. "Are you going to be able to compete this season? Tell me the truth."

He was silent for so long, she thought he might not answer her, but then he straightened in his seat and shook his head. "Nope."

It was as she'd suspected. "So you're just along for the ride, then? To be my driver? My hairdresser?" She touched one of the braids that she still had in.

He narrowed his eyes at her, but only said, "I'd planned to check in with Blake Saddle Medics at Greeley, see if they needed help, then hook up with them again at Frontier Days in Cheyenne."

Justice nodded slowly, her spinning thoughts slowing as she made up her mind. She shifted the ice bag on her ankle, took a steadying breath, then said, "Let's go home."

Brandon stiffened, like he'd been blindsided. "No," he said firmly after a moment, shaking his head. "That's not an option."

"For whom?" she shot back. "For you? And this is? Spending the next six weeks on the road with someone you can hardly stand to share breathing room with, hoping to find enough to keep you busy, spending money all along the way, money you have no chance of making back? And what about Tank? It's hardly fair to him to haul him along for no reason, is it? Seems like this here," she said, waving her hand in a broad gesture around the trailer, "isn't an option, either. Not for you."

"But it's not just me we're talking about," he argued, sitting forward again. "You've got performances booked across the country, Justice. I'm not going to cut and run because I made a stupid mistake in the arena."

"I'm not talking about cutting and running, Brandon. I'm talking about calling it a day. Look at us," she said, shaking her head slightly. "We're a mess. You with your wrist, me with this ankle. These panic attacks or anxiety attacks or post traumatic stress things I've been having? Whatever they are, they're starting to interfere with my ability to perform, and I don't think pushing through to the next show and the next is going to make them magically resolve themselves. Courage gone—and you're right, you know. She really *is* the heart of The Twisted Sisters, and I'm—"

"No, don't," Brandon cut in. "I was wrong to say that, Justice. It's not true."

"But it is true," she insisted. "I may be blind to some things, to a lot of things," she corrected, "but I know a good performance when I see it, when I give it, and I know a great performance, too. I'm good," she stated with a frown. "And I could probably keep earning a little money doing this if I really set my mind to it, but that's all it would be. My mind, not my heart. If I've learned anything over these last several weeks, Brandon, it's this: It takes heart and soul to be great, at least for The Twisted Sisters."

Brandon was shaking his head the whole time she spoke, but when she fell silent, he said nothing. It was as clear a confirmation as she could have asked from him.

"I'm not the only one," she added, her brow furrowing. Brandon gave her a questioning look, and she continued. "I lost another sponsor today," she said, jutting her chin toward her cell phone where it was plugged into a charger on the end table. "That's two of my major money makers, and one of the new ones we picked up just last year. I can't blame them; they want to invest in a sure thing, and without Courage, The Twisted Sisters are no longer a thing at all, sure or not."

"Justice, I can't let you just quit. This isn't like you. I don't—I don't get it," he grumbled, more frustrated than adamant.

"Hear me out, okay?" She waited for him to nod. "Before we left home, Courage and I had a long conversation about the future," she began, her voice quiet, but firm. She went on to tell him about her sister's idea of a trick riding academy at Seven Virtues Ranch. The more she talked, the more it made sense.

"I've been thinking about it this whole time we've been on the road. And today? My crappy performance? This thing with Tanner? This isn't me, Brandon. None of this is. I don't fit in with this crowd, not anymore. Maybe not ever. Not without Courage. I have a competitive nature, believe me, I know that," she said with a self-deprecating snort. "But I'm my own competition. I love riding with Courage; it's working together that makes us great. I honestly don't want to do a solo gig anymore, Brandon. I thought I did, I thought I could pull it off, you know?" She shot him a rueful grimace. "But every time I charge out into that arena, I feel more and more detached from it. Fire senses it, my uncertainty, my less than a hundred percent commitment, and now he's acting uncertain, too. I can feel it in the way he's constantly looking to me for guidance in areas he's always just taken the lead on. Or followed Flash on, I suppose."

"Justice," Brandon said, his voice low, his tone earnest. His eyes were intent on her. "This isn't you, either. You don't just walk away. You don't quit just because—"

"I'm not quitting anything, Brandon. I'm not walking away, either. I'm moving on. And I'm calling Courage right now and telling her I'm in." She'd never been surer of anything in her life, and no matter what Brandon said, she was certain it was the right thing to do.

Justice started to rise, then dropped back to her seat. "Oh, Brandon," she murmured, horrified by a new thought. "You can't go back, can you? I mean, your paramedic job, right? Did you already give your notice? And what about Whispering Hills? Does Cord know you're leaving? Have you already moved out of the cabin over there?" The questions flew out of her mouth as fast as they entered her mind, but she couldn't seem to curb them. "Does Faith know? Charity? Did you tell them already?" Did everyone know about his plans to move to Bowling Green but her? "I didn't even think about the possibility that you might not want to go back to Plumwood Hollow right now."

Brandon pushed to his feet, his long braid swinging like a rope over his shoulder. He shook his head. "No, you didn't. But then, that's nothing new, is it?"

His words hit her like a slap, and it was all she could do not to flinch. Even worse, he didn't seem angry, just weary, almost like he was succumbing to the inevitable. Like he simply didn't have it in him to argue with her anymore. "I'm sorry," she whispered.

"For what?" he asked, but he wasn't looking at her anymore. He crossed to the couch, gently moved the ice bag aside and picked up her foot, cupping her heel in his palm as he examined her ankle. He was so close, she could smell a hint of the aftershave he used, even though he'd put it on the night before. Brandon shaved at night before he went to bed; his facial hair didn't grow in thick, and he got a closer shave when he did it at the end of the day instead of in the morning when he first woke up. She also caught a whiff of dust and leather, telltale signs of a working cowboy, and she instinctively reached out to brush at a spring of hay that clung to the back of his shirt. He twitched when she touched him, and she jerked her hand back.

"You should stay off that the rest of the night," he told her, returning her foot to the cushion and setting the ice pack back in place. "I'll take care of dinner."

"Okay," she conceded, although she hadn't planned on doing much of anything the rest of the evening anyway. They'd planned to spend the night there, then hit the road for one more overnight stop before Greeley first thing in the morning.

At least, that had been the plan before her grand epiphany.

Now, she had no clue what the next twenty-four hours held.

Brandon started toward the door, but stopped with his hand on the edge of the counter. For a few seconds, he just stood there, his back to her. Then he turned and said, "I think you're making a mistake, Justice. I think you need to stick around and face the music. Tanner isn't finished with this; you know that, right? If you walk away now, you're taking your reputation with you."

Justice set her shoulders and lifted her chin. "My reputation is shot already, and you know it. I've already faced Tanner and I've told him how it's going to be—"

"And the only way you'll be able to hold him to that is if you're there, showing your face, letting folks know he didn't run you off."

"But he didn't run me off, Brandon," she insisted, shoving the ice aside and lowering her foot to the floor. She wasn't going to stay sitting while he loomed over her, even from four feet away. "I'm leaving of my own accord, and I never cared what people thought of me before, so why should I start caring now?" She pushed to her feet, winced when she put her weight on her sore ankle, but stood tall and straight nonetheless. "I don't have half my team, Brandon. It would be like you trying to team rope without a header," she offered, frustrated that he obviously didn't believe her reasons for leaving.

"If I don't have a header, then I do a different event," he shot back. "I don't just quit and go home."

"Wow," she said, her hackles raised now. "Once again, I'm not quitting. I'm moving on to the next thing. And home just happens to be where my next thing lies. I'm not tucking tail and running, like you seem to think I am."

He made a quiet hissing sound, pushed open the trailer door and took one step down before turning back to face her once again. "And what about me, hm? What if I don't feel like bailing on this season? Did you even think to ask me first?"

"I'm asking you now," she retorted, cocking her head slightly.

He laughed, but it wasn't a pleasant sound. "No, you're not. You're telling me what you've decided and you're expecting me to just nod and tag along. What if there are people I actually want to see at Greeley? Or Frontier Days? Or any of the stops along the way? What if I have connections I need to make for next year?"

With Brandon standing on the lower step, they were now closer to the same height. Justice narrowed her eyes at him. "You just told me you had nothing going on except to see if the medics needed help."

"No," he corrected her, smacking a palm on the counter beside him. "I did not say I had nothing going on. I told you I was going to volunteer, but that didn't mean I had no other plans."

"Fine." She planted her hands on her hips. "If you have somewhere to be, someone you have to meet up with, then we can go do that first, then we'll go home." It sounded shady to her, like he might have just made it up, so she called his bluff. "So where do we need to go? And why wait until tomorrow morning? Let's pack up and get on the road now."

Brandon clenched his jaws in frustration. "You can't just quit," he said again, barely getting the words past his teeth.

"I just did," she said, her own jaw tight. She reached over and snatched her cell phone off the console table. "I've got phone calls to make, so if you can give me your itinerary, I'd like to be able to let my sister know what's going on."

Brandon stepped back into the trailer, pulling the door closed behind him, once again looming over her. They were a lot closer now with both of them standing in the narrow space, and she hated that she had to lean her head back to maintain eye contact with him.

TWENTY-TWO

BRANDON WASN'T EXACTLY SURE why he was so upset by Justice's decision. Maybe she wasn't exactly running away, but she certainly wasn't facing the consequences of her actions. She was the one who caused this mess in the first place, so why did she get to just wash her hands of it and walk away?

He didn't have any connections he absolutely had to make, but what about next year? If she quit, did that mean if he wanted to keep riding the rodeo circuit that he'd be on his own? How on earth was he going to be able to cover the expenses the three of them always shared? It was already a stretch with only two of them this year, especially since neither of them would be going home with much money in their pockets.

Then again, had he really expected her to want to continue partnering with him once he moved to Bowling Green? For that matter, had he really thought he'd be able to just run the rodeo with the twins next year after... well, after running away?

The thought made him grimace. Wasn't he considering doing the exact same thing he was accusing her of doing? Cutting and running?

The questions whirled around and around in his head like a tornado, and the notion made him grunt. Like a Twisted Sister. Justice Goodacre.

Justice Goodacre. Except in his mind, she'd always been Justice Goodacre Stillwater. And now, when he thought about it, standing there, towering over her in the tiny living quarters of her trailer, that was how he still thought of her. As his. In spite of everything, in spite of his broken heart, his wounded pride, his anger and resentment, the desire to rip

Tanner Ogden's heart out of his chest and throw it into the path of a herd of stampeding cattle, in spite of it all, in his heart, she still belonged to him.

No, *with* him. Justice belonged with him, and he belonged with her.

But she hasn't paid her penance for what she did to you. She hasn't fixed it yet. The voice in his head practically shouted the words at him. *How do you know she won't grow bored of you again?*

He stared down at her, wondering if she could read his thoughts. Justice held his gaze, her eyes wide, but guarded. Surely, she could see the turmoil inside of him.

How do you know she's truly sorry? After what she's done, does she really deserve your forgiveness? Does she deserve the kind of selfless, faithful love you've always given her? What if—

No! He swung a fist backward against the closed door behind him, hitting it hard enough to jostle the trailer. Justice flinched, but her expression didn't change. No, he would not give in to that ugly spirit of doubt and resentment that still wanted to take root in his heart. He had to pluck it free and toss *it* into the path of the stampeding cattle, not Tanner's heart.

Things had changed for Justice and him back at Charlotte's ranch. The walls of anger and pain between them; hadn't they started chipping away at those? He'd believed Justice in the quiet sanctuary of that place. And the willow tree? Although they hadn't acknowledged it openly, he'd seen the look on Justice's face when Charlotte led them out to sit under the umbrella branches of that willow. He'd sensed the peace that came from acknowledging God's hand in things. It was there, in the dappled light under that tree, that he'd felt his heart turning toward home. Not toward Plumwood Hollow, but toward Justice.

Lord, what do we do now?

The moment the thought—the prayer—formed in his mind, that same peace washed over him, the same desire to surrender and let go that he'd felt... was it only this yesterday?

"Listen," he said, trying to keep his voice steady. He still wasn't sure he agreed with her decision to walk away. Or move on, as she put it. He needed time to process the idea of pulling out of the rodeo scene, of at least cutting back on their involvement, of Justice and Courage taking their trick riding in a complete different direction. Of what that meant for him and his future. If he'd need to figure out how to do the circuit on his own for the very first time... if he even wanted to continue without the twins. Sure, with his skills, it could be good money when all went well, but all it took was an injury like his, especially when it happened early on, and his season was shot.

But was he ready to throw in the towel?

Tanner is going to think you're—

No. He wasn't going there. He would not let himself worry about what Tanner Ogden thought. He needed to worry about what Justice thought. About what God thought.

Brandon took a deep breath and sidestepped so that he was leaning a hip against the counter again, putting another foot or two of space between them. He wasn't exactly relaxed, but he knew his posture was far less intimidating in the confines of the trailer, and it didn't escape his attention that Justice's shoulders lowered a little.

"First of all, please sit." He dropped his gaze to her ankle. She was standing with all her weight on one foot. "Get that foot up and the ice back on it."

She hesitated just long enough he thought she might refuse—*Lord, did you have to give me such a stubborn woman?*—but then she slowly lowered herself back onto the sofa and brought her leg up beside her. The relief on her face spoke volumes to him. Maybe her lack of flair in the saddle today had more to do with her twisted foot than she let on. He waited until she had the ice repositioned over her ankle before he continued.

"I'm not a hundred percent sure I agree with your decision."

"You're not changing my mind, Brandon." Her statement wasn't belligerent or defiant, just a matter of fact. "Every single thing that's happened over the last few weeks, over the last few months, has been like flashing red lights, signs pointing me back home, back to Seven Virtues Ranch. It's not just Tanner. He's nothing in the grand scheme of things."

Brandon closed his eyes at her words. The guy wasn't "nothing" to him.

"I don't mean what happened with Tanner and—and me means nothing," she amended, intuitively sensing the emotions behind his silent response. "I just mean that if it were just that, I'd be gearing up right now to go have it out with him. What I meant is that he's nothing because he doesn't really play a part in my decision to move on." She paused, then said, "But combined with everything else? The buck, your wrist, my lousy shows these past few weeks, even before I twisted my stupid foot. My stupid foot," she said with an impatient gesture. "Meeting Charlotte, our angel in disguise—I mean, Brandon, have you thought about it? She showed up on that deserted road exactly when we needed her, with exactly what we needed. A place to rest and recover. She gave us sanctuary, a much needed one."

Justice's choice of words—a sanctuary—settled over him like a comforting blanket.

"This—" Justice waved a hand between them as she searched for the right words. "This—wedge between us? I can't go on like this, Brandon, pretending that we can just keep doing what we were doing, hoping that it will just resolve itself. What Charlotte offered us? That sanctuary? That safe place? That's home. I need to go home where I can sort through some of this stuff, surrounded by people who love me in spite of myself." She smiled up at him, but her eyes were glistening with unshed tears. "Where people will pray for me, *are* praying for me, even as we speak. My dad—" She broke off, her smile wobbling a little. "You know what? I miss my dad. I want to go home and sit in his big, lumpy chair and smell his Barbasol shaving cream and listen for his boots on the back porch." A single tear slipped from the corner of her eye, and she swiped it away quickly. "I want to hear him tell me that everything's going to be okay, Brandon, that I haven't screwed things up beyond repair. I know I'm making it all about what I want, but—" She broke off, unable to continue, and turned her face away from him to stare out the window behind the couch. The blinds were down but open, and beyond her head, he could see the first hints of what promised to be a spectacular Colorado summer sunset.

While she'd been talking, an idea had formed in his head, and as he listened to her words, he realized it might be exactly what they both needed.

"I'm not going to try to convince you to change your mind," he said, then added with a soft chuckle, "I know better than to try that." When she didn't respond, he went on. "But what if we take our time, Justice? What if we don't rush back to the Hollow just yet?"

"I'm not going to Greeley." She spoke quietly, but firmly.

"I'm not talking about Greeley." He waited, hoping she'd turn to look at him, but when he saw more tears falling, he knew she wouldn't. She hated anyone seeing her cry. "What if we call Charlotte and ask her if we can stay there for a few days, maybe a week? Before we left, I asked her how we could repay her for her help, and she might have been half-joking when she said it, but she told me there was always something that needed done around the place. Fencing, repairs, the usual. Maybe we can offer a few days of manual labor in exchange for room and board while we deal with this—" He drew a line on the floor with the toe of his boot. What had she called it? "This wedge between us. I don't really want to go on like this, either, you know."

For several moments, Justice didn't speak. She kept her face averted, not even acknowledging his suggestion. But he knew her well enough to understand that she wasn't ignoring him, so he remained quiet, not wanting to push her.

"She did say that thing about Adam." Her words were so quiet, he had to lean forward to hear them. "I mean, about sometimes feeling the absence of a man, or a partner, in her life. I think she might be lonely," Justice said, then finally turned to look up at him.

Those eyes, like strong coffee, the deep brown turned amber by the glisten of tears... he could lose himself in those eyes. What had she just said? He nodded, knowing he agreed with whatever it was.

"I have to make a few phone calls if we're going to do this," Justice went on. "I'm going to be leaving a few folks high and dry by pulling out now, so I'd like to see if I can find another team or solo act who'd be willing to fill in for me at the places I've already committed to."

Brandon nodded, his attention back on what she was saying. "I can help with that." Had she agreed about going to Charlotte's or was she still making plans to go straight back to the Hollow?

"No, I'll make those calls. I think it'll be better coming straight from me; I think it's the right thing to do. But if you want to call Charlotte and talk to her?"

Relief flooded through him and he nodded slowly, unable to speak around the lump that rose in his throat.

"Okay." Justice lowered her gaze to her ankle. "Stupid foot."

Brandon shrugged, even though she wasn't looking at him. "I don't know about that. Seems your foot might be the smartest one here."

Justice snorted. "My left foot."

Brandon knew the movie she referenced. She'd made him watch it with her for a paper she'd written in high school, and as difficult a movie as it was to watch, her point was made. A left foot with a mind of its own could make a big difference in a person's life.

TWENTY-THREE

Charlotte insisted they return that night. "She said she hasn't changed the sheets on the bed yet, so we might as well make use of it," Brandon told Justice as he stepped into the trailer just as she was finishing up a phone call of her own. Then he turned away quickly, mortified by the way that sounded.

Justice stifled a giggle with a hand over her mouth, but not before he heard it.

He rolled his eyes. "Get your mind out of the gutter," he muttered, half-teasing, half-serious. They would not be sharing that bed again, of that, he was certain. As many years as they'd known each other, as many times as they'd traveled together, shared tiny, cramped spaces together, they'd never shared a bed like they had at Charlotte's. What on earth had he been thinking?

Justice held her phone up. "I got a lot done, too," she said. "Not everyone is happy, but I did get a few folks telling me they were considering replacing me anyway, since it was only going to be me and not both of The Twisted Sisters." Now it was her turn to roll her eyes. "I don't know what I was thinking, presuming I could pull this off."

Brandon chuckled softly as she echoed the words he'd just asked himself, albeit about another topic altogether. "Did you talk to your sister?" he asked. Surely, there hadn't been enough time. He'd expected her to be on the phone with Courage when he came back in.

Justice gave him a wry look. "She's too busy to talk to me right now. Farmer Joe and his mother are taking her out dancing tonight."

"Dancing?" Courage's fall hadn't happened that long ago, and Brandon couldn't imagine her being anywhere near ready to dance. "Is she—"

Justice laughed and shook her head. "No, no. She's going out with Joe and his mother. Sarah insisted she needed a male dance partner, and when she asked Joe, Courage was so anxious to see him dance—can you imagine? Farmer Joe two-stepping?—that she insisted they all three go so she could watch."

Brandon shrugged. "I can see it," he said with a smile. "I've seen Sarah Lynxwilder dance. That woman's got moves, and if Joe inherited even half her skill?"

Justice giggled again. "That's what Courage says. In fact, Sarah informed my sister that she'd taught Joe to dance from the time he was tall enough to be her partner, and that since her husband died, Joe had been her practice partner all these years. So yeah, I guess he knows his way around the floor." She reached down and picked up the bag of half-melted ice she'd set on the floor sometime while he was outside talking to Charlotte. "Anyway, I told her to call me in the morning, but I didn't tell her why."

"I'll take that," Brandon said, putting a hand out to take the bag from her.

Instead of handing it to him, she put her other hand in his. "Thank you," she said, her smile gone now. "For—well, for all of this. I know it's not what you would have done."

He waited, knowing there was a 'but' coming—"But I had to do this my way," or "But it's what's best for all of us," or any number of other justifications she might throw at him.

Nothing else came, though, and at a loss, he squeezed her hand, then let go. Why was this so hard? Why was change so difficult? Was he really so inflexible?

"You're welcome," he finally said into the awkward silence, then pushed open the trailer door to dump the ice water out onto the dusty ground outside.

"What do you think?" Justice asked once his back was to her. "Should we pull up camp and head back to Charlotte's tonight?"

"I'm not sure," he said over his shoulder. "Even if we hurry with the horses, it will get us there well past midnight."

Charlotte had insisted it wouldn't matter to her. "Nutter will let me know when you arrive," she assured him. "But you two know your way around the place, so I won't even bother getting up to greet you, if you're all right with that. I'll leave the lanai door unlocked for you."

"Right," Justice said. He could see her nodding slowly from the corner of his eye. She looked a little troubled, and it occurred to him that she might want to get out of here before Tanner decided to make another appearance. Who knew what the guy would do after he got a couple of drinks in him later tonight.

"Charlotte said she'd leave the lights on for us," he added quickly. "That she didn't care what time we got in."

She pushed to her feet and took a step toward him. "Then let's go," she said, her tone bordering on urgent. "Let's ditch this joint and get the heck out of here, okay?" She straightened her shoulders. "And I love my bed in here," she added, gesturing at the loft bed at the head of the trailer. "I'll sleep in here and you can have the guest—"

"Right." He shook his head, raised one eyebrow in a sardonic expression. "You'll take the guest room, period." He wouldn't even entertain an argument on that subject. He might opt to use his hammock rather than the bed Justice had been using, though. A rush of heat enveloped him at the thought of laying his head on her pillow, the fragrance of her filling his senses as he drifted off to sleep.

They spent some extra time rearranging and reorganizing the trailer so that Brandon would have everything he needed inside, instead of stashed in the extra stall. He used the shower stall as his temporary closet; he'd use the bathroom facilities in Charlotte's barn or in the guest room. The horses weren't exactly thrilled about getting loaded up again so soon, but they were both fed, watered, and carefully groomed, and with a little coaxing with a cut-up apple, they clambered into their stalls and hunkered down for another drive.

They slipped away from the campsite just as the sun was disappearing over the horizon, and sure enough, the sky overhead was draped in streaks of orange and gold, fluffy clouds lined with silver and gold drifting across the glorious backdrop. Another sign, Brandon thought to himself as they drove off into the sunset together.

They reached Charlotte's ranch just after midnight, having stopped for gas and something to eat along the way, and sure enough, the gate was open, the lights were on outside the barn where they'd parked their rig before, and the porch light at the guest room was lit up, too, shedding a welcoming glow in the otherwise velvety blackness of the prairie lands. There were stars overhead, scattered like tossed jewels across the sky, but there was no moon.

From somewhere inside the big house, they heard Nutter bark a few times, then a light flickered on, but Charlotte didn't make an appearance. With as little noise as possible, Brandon and Justice unloaded the horses and led them into the same stalls they'd used before. Charlotte had feedbags and water troughs already filled and ready for them.

Once the horses were settled, while Justice packed up her things into a duffel bag and collected her toiletries and other sundries in a separate bag, Brandon made use of the gues bathroom for a quick shower. By the time he was finished, Justice was in the room and getting settled for the night.

He stood just outside the bathroom door and watched her for a few moments, more than a little tired after the long day and what little sleep he'd gotten the last few nights. "You good?" he finally asked when she looked over at him with a careful smile.

"I think I got everything," she assured him, gesturing at the duffel bag that was now spilling out onto the bed. "And if I forgot anything, it can wait until tomorrow. How about you?"

Why did things have to be so awkward between them? "I needed that shower," he said, nodding. "I have a feeling I'll sleep like the dead tonight. Thanks for letting me use your bed," he added.

"Oh!" Justice glanced toward the door. "Do you want to trade pillows? I can bring mine in and you can take these. I haven't washed the sheets out there since we left."

Brandon was already shaking his head before she finished speaking. "Nope. Go to bed. You look ready to drop, too. I'll see you in the morning, okay? Want me to wake you up at any certain time?” As much of a control freak as Justice was, she was also notorious for hitting her snooze on her alarm clock a few too many times, or worse, turning the alarm off altogether. It usually fell to his lot to make sure the girls got up and going when they were on the road.

Justice took a deep breath and pursed her lips in thought. “I guess if I’m not up by nine? Do you think that’s rude of me to sleep that late?” She darted another look toward the door. “What time are you getting up?”

“You know me. The sun comes up and I’m awake.” It had always been that way. Didn’t matter what time he fell into bed, Brandon was up with the dawn. “And no, Charlotte won’t think you’re being rude for getting a good night’s sleep. She knows what time we pulled in.” He started across the room, his dirty clothes in a roll tucked under his arm.

“You can leave those here.” Justice’s words stopped him, and she dipped her head toward the bundle he carried. “I’ll do a load of laundry tomorrow if Charlotte doesn’t mind us using her washer and dryer. And in the morning, you can bring in anything else in that needs washing, too.” She rested a hand on a small jumbled heap of clothes on the bed. “I’ve got a pile of dirties started already.”

“Okay, then,” he said, crossing to the bed to add his things to hers. “Thanks.” He started to turn away, but stopped when he felt her hand on his arm.

“Brandon?” Her voice was tentative, almost shy, and so unlike her.

He was so tired, so weary of the war of emotions inside of him. He lifted a hand and cupped her face, then closed his eyes briefly when she pressed her cheek into his palm, bringing her own hand up to cover his. He wanted to hold her, to pull her against him, to tuck her face into his neck, to feel her breath against his skin. He wanted her to wrap her arms around his waist and press her ear to his chest, to tease him about how fast his heart was beating with her up against him like that.

But he did none of that. Instead, he brushed the pad of his thumb over her lips, dipped his head, and kissed her softly, every ounce of his will holding him in check. She made a tiny sound, or maybe he just imagined it, and he straightened, waiting for her to open her eyes and look up at him. "Goodnight, Justice. Sleep well, and I'll check on you in the morning."

"Goodnight," she whispered back, even though there was no one around they might disturb.

Then, before he gave in to the promise in her eyes, he pulled his hand from her cheek, curled his fingers into a fist at his side as if he might hold onto the warmth of her skin a little bit longer, and crossed the room to the door. He didn't look back at her, certain that if he did, he wouldn't have the strength to leave before daylight.

TWENTY-FOUR

To her surprise, Justice was awake before eight the next morning. Groggy and a little stiff, she got up to use the bathroom, then crossed to the window to open the blinds, hoping for a glimpse of Brandon. Was he up yet?

The day looked gorgeous outside; was Brandon already up and about, tending to the animals, or elbow deep in some project inside the barn? In the light of a new day, Justice wasn't feeling quite as certain about everything as she had been last night. She opened the window to let in the cool morning air, then stepped closer to the window to breathe it in.

She wasn't quite ready to face Charlotte, yet, either—there'd be a lot of explaining to do, she supposed.

Colorado in the summer was remarkably different from Plumwood Hollow. The air here was so dry and crisp that it made her lungs feel a little papery, while back at home, between the summer squalls and almost daily cloudbursts, the high humidity of the Midwest kept everything just this side of soggy. "I don't mind soggy," she murmured to herself, toying with the tip of one of the messy braids she still wore in her hair. Brandon's braids. She must look a fright right now, and she was glad he was nowhere to be seen. If he noticed she was up, he'd be at her door in a flash to check on her, offer her coffee, or to bring her breakfast.

He was so good to her. And she'd taken him for granted. No, she'd thrown his goodness in his face. Why?

"Morning, Brandon. You two slept out here?" The question startled Justice and she stiffened before she realized it wasn't meant for her. It was

Charlotte, just stepping out of the barn and looking toward the trailer, presumably at Brandon.

"Good morning," she heard Brandon respond, his voice raspy from sleep. It made her smile. Not only had the sun been up for at least two hours already, but she kind of liked the sound of his voice, all gruff and manly, first thing in the morning. So Mister Awake-With-the-Dawn had slept in.

"I told you kids you could sleep in the lanai," Charlotte began again, her tone just the slightest bit admonishing.

"I know," Brandon assured her. "And we took you up on your offer. Justice took the guest room last night." He cleared his throat, a nervous tell that Justice recognized. "Um, we're—well, we're not together. A couple. Not—we're just friends." He stumbled over the words, and Justice couldn't help feeling sorry for him.

"Right," came Charlotte's response, seemingly taking it all in stride. Justice couldn't see her anymore; she'd disappeared behind the trailer. "Well, this still is unacceptable. You take the lanai and Justice can take my guest room inside the house."

"That's all right," Brandon began, but their hostess cut him off, her words friendly, but firm.

"Not with me. You two are my guests, and I have two guest rooms available to you. You take the lanai, and I'll go get my second room ready for Justice when she wakes up. She'll adore the bed in there—it's an antique four-poster with a mattress so tall you have to strap on climbing gear to get up onto it." She let out a good-natured laugh, then appeared strolling around the front of the trailer. "Come on inside when you're ready for a cup of coffee. I'm putting on a fresh pot."

When she heard the kitchen screen door swing shut, Justice pulled on a lightweight zip up hoodie over her knit pajamas and headed outside. She didn't bother wearing shoes, and although her ankle felt a little better this morning, she was careful where she stepped so as not to turn it again. "Brandon?" she called out softly as she started around to the other side of the trailer. She thought it only fair to give him a heads up that she was on her way out to see him.

"Justice?" Even with his early morning groggy voice, she could hear his surprise. "You're up already?" He was sitting on the ledge of the escape door, tying up his work boots. He flashed a grin up at her, his dark eyes a little puffy from sleep, his hair, although brushed, still hung loose around his shoulders. He wore an open flannel shirt over a plain white tee, and a pair of worn jeans, gone threadbare at the knees the old-fashioned way. As he bent forward to settle his pant legs over the tops of his boots, the shirt pulled tight across his broad shoulders.

"My goodness," she said before she thought to stop herself. "You are a beautiful man, Brandon Stillwater."

He stilled, just for a moment, but his smile didn't falter and he didn't look away. Finally, he straightened up, then pushed to his feet. "Well, thank you, Justice Goodacre. Coming from a beauty like yourself, that's high praise."

She reached up to touch one of her braids again, knowing he was just flattering her, and felt herself blush. "I'm a mess," she said with a snort. "I actually didn't come out here to compliment you, you know. I just got distracted by—" She broke off, shaking her head. "Never mind."

"By all this man beauty?" Brandon teased, striking a Herculean pose, hands on hips, his head turned to offer her his profile, his long hair spilling down his back in a thick curtain.

Justice laughed and nodded. "Yeah. All that man beauty. No." She shoved her hands in the pockets of her hoodie.

He crossed the distance between them and pulled her into a quick, platonic hug. "Good morning to you, too," he said, then kissed the top of her head and stepped back before she could pull her hands free of her pockets and return his hug.

The action left her feeling a bit bereft, a little unsteady on her feet, and she heard his words to Charlotte in her head. *We're just friends.* A tightness formed in her chest and she dropped her gaze to their feet, the worn tips of his work boots facing her bare, teal-polished toes. The sight made her feel exposed. "I'm heading inside for some coffee," Brandon continued, apparently not sensing her disquiet. "Want me to bring you a cup or do you want to come in with me?"

"Would you mind?" Did he sense her reticence to face her hostess with the decisions they'd made last night? What had Brandon told Charlotte? Had he explained the reasons behind their abrupt return? "I need to freshen up—"

"I don't know. I kind of like this rumpled look you're sporting," Brandon said, reaching out to tug on one of her braids.

Justice playfully slapped his hand away. "Yes, it's very me. Seriously, though, I feel like I need to put on some armor before I face the day," she said, even though it was Charlotte she was worried about facing.

"She won't bite, you know," Brandon said, apparently reading her thoughts. He knew her too well.

"I know." She frowned up at him, her hands back in her pockets, her fingers nervously toying with the hidden seams inside. "I guess I'm just feeling a little vulnerable right now, and you know how I get when I feel this way. I don't want to talk to anyone, to deal with—well, she's practically a stranger, you know? And we're asking a lot from her, and it makes me feel—I don't know. Indebted to her, I guess?" It came out a question, because she wasn't sure that was the right word. "I feel like I owe her an explanation for all of this, but I'm not sure I can even explain it all to myself yet."

Brandon nodded. "I know. I understand." He looked past her toward the house. "I have a feeling she would, too."

Justice just nodded. Although she agreed that yes, Charlotte was probably going to be pretty sensitive to them right now—there was no way she couldn't have figured out that there'd been trouble of some kind to bring them back so soon—but that didn't make it any easier for Justice.

"You go get ready for the day," Brandon finally said. "I'll bring you coffee in about fifteen minutes, then we can both head inside together for breakfast, okay?"

Justice nodded, a part of her wanting to refuse his help, his offer to take on the role of her defender, her protector. She didn't need him to do that for her. She didn't *need* anyone, not really. But although it was a little scary to let someone else take the lead, take charge, there was something kind of nice about stepping back.

But just for the time being. She couldn't always be this way, that was for sure, this delicate, fragile, exposed little creature. It wasn't who she was. "Thanks," she said, then turned to hurry back to the guest room. "I'll try to be ready when you get back with my coffee," she called over her shoulder.

She pushed inside the room, closed the door behind her, and leaned against it.

We're just friends.

That's how he was behaving this morning. Like they were just friends. She'd thought that kiss last night... But no, it had just been a sweet, goodnight kiss, like a thousand other sweet, goodnight kisses they'd shared before. Granted, that was when they actually were dating, when they considered themselves a couple. But more often than not, especially in the last few years, those sweet kisses had turned to something more, to promises of things to come, to burst of passion and desperate exercises in self-control.

Last night, for just a moment, she'd sensed that familiar fire in him, the magnetic bond between them, the way they could just melt into each other. But then he'd pulled away and left her standing there, certain only of her own need for him, of how much she loved him, missed him, ached for him.

Today, her ache remained, while he seemed to have put whatever he'd let out last night back under wraps. She didn't know whether to be hurt, relieved, or offended.

"Relieved," she said aloud. Because it was the only way she could hold her head up right now.

She rubbed her eyes, still itchy from not quite enough sleep, and fought the desire to crawl back under the covers on the bed and go back to sleep for a little longer. She had a slight headache, too, but that would probably go away once she got some food in her.

Fifteen minutes later, she was dressed in a pair of jeans possibly as old as the ones Brandon wore, and she wore a long-sleeved snap up shirt, open at the front and knotted at the waist, with a cheery yellow tank top underneath. She studied her reflection in the bathroom mirror. The bright color contrasted nicely with her skin, although today, she looked kind of pale. She felt a little flushed, and it showed in the pink spots on her cheeks, but surely, once she got the next hour out of the way, once she saw for herself that Charlotte wasn't judging her, surely, then she'd feel a little more like herself.

Just as she stepped out of the bathroom, a knock sounded on the door. "Room service," Brandon called through the screen before coming in. She'd opened the main door to let the fresh air into the room, and she grinned at him as he entered, carefully carrying a tray that held two steaming mugs. He had a tea towel draped over his braced wrist.

"Look at you," she teased. He hadn't bothered braiding his hair yet, but it was pulled back into a man bun at the back of his head, something most men couldn't pull off, she'd be the first to say. But somehow, with his bold, elegant features, and his devil-may-care carriage, Brandon Stillwater could. Heck, he could probably pull off pigtails if he tried.

She smiled to herself at the silly notion and crossed the room to clear a space on the little coffee table. "Set it here," she said, standing back to let him.

Brandon set the tray down, handed her the obviously doctored up cup of pale, creamy coffee, then sat down on the edge of one of the armchairs with his own. "Sit," he ordered her, not unkindly. "I should tell you what I told Charlotte."

Justice dropped onto the sofa in relief, nearly spilling her drink. "Please," she said, then covered her show of emotions by lifting the mug to her lips.

It was good. Bold and creamy, sweet and thick, just the way she liked her coffee. Brandon did, indeed, know her well.

TWENTY-FIVE

"So basically, between our two injuries and your sister's absence, there are enough reasons for our decision to call the season a wrap without having to come up with any others," Brandon told her. "I didn't mention Courage's riding academy idea, either; I figured you could bring that up in conversation with Charlotte if you wanted to."

Justice nodded. "Right." She peered at him over the rim of her cup. "Do you think she'll sense there's more?"

"I know she senses there's more, Justice, but she's not pushing me for answers. Of course, I don't know how she'll interact with you, but for now, she seems to be taking things at face value. And she's very appreciative of our offer to help around here. She cleared a pasture this spring and wants to start using it, but the old fencing needs to be repaired in several places before that happens. She's hoping we'll help her get the job done."

"You told her we would, right?" Justice lowered her cup, then shifted in her seat so she could bring her injured leg up onto the love seat beside her. "This stupid foot might slow me down, but I'm more than willing to do everything I can. I may not be able to dig fence post holes, but there's nothing wrong with my arms." She held her free hand up and made a bicep curl, although there wasn't much to see beneath the loose sleeve of her shirt.

"I did." He held up his wrist and smirked. "You can be my left arm; I'll be your left foot. Once again, the smartest body part in the room."

"Ha ha," she said with a derisive snort. "You're so clever."

"And smart." Brandon lifted his mug in a salute, then studied her as she sipped her coffee. She looked tired, he thought. Beautiful, but tired. She'd been up before he was; maybe she hadn't slept well.

He, on the other hand, had buried his face in her pillow, breathed her in about five times that he could remember, and that was it. The next thing he knew, he awoke saying her name into the quiet, intimate space where she usually slept, the morning sunlight slipping between the closed blinds to whisper that it was morning. He'd slept like the dead, and the dreams he did remember were actually worth remembering. They were all of Justice.

A few minutes later, they headed across the breezeway to Charlotte's kitchen from which delicious smells once again emanated. Justice lifted her nose as she stepped into the room ahead of Brandon.

"You're going to spoil us, Charlotte," she said, then added, "Good morning."

"Good morning to you, too, pretty lady," the older woman said, turning to glance over her shoulder at them. She stood at the counter slicing a pineapple into thin half-circles. "How did you sleep?" she asked. "And how's that ankle of yours?"

"That bed out there is as comfortable as they get," Justice told her. "And the ankle is all right. Could be better, could be worse."

"I can imagine," Charlotte returned, then went back to fanning the yellow fruit slices onto a pretty blue platter.

Brandon watched in silence as the two women exchanged small talk, Justice offering to help, Charlotte assuring her there was little to do except to refill her coffee and have a seat.

"Maybe Brandon and I can cook for you tonight," Justice suggested, turning to him with a question in her eyes. "Well, Brandon can cook and I'll help. Or watch. I'm a bit unpredictable in the kitchen."

Brandon chuckled and nodded. "Especially with big knives. But sure. I make a killer hamburger. I always carry my special blend of spices with us when we're on the road, and I make my own barbecue sauce, too. I'm pretty sure we have some of the sauce left out in the trailer fridge, but if you have the ingredients I need, I can always make some fresh."

"Take a look through my cupboards and fridge. Whatever you find is yours to use," Charlotte said agreeably. "I love making breakfast, but I have to admit that at the end of a day, especially if I'm still in the middle of a project, it's tough to garner the energy to actually get in here and cook." She skirted the table with the plate of fruit, then sat down in a chair across from Brandon. "I certainly won't say no to having you two make yourselves at home in here, and I do love a good burger. I think I even have some sesame buns in the cupboard." She waved a hand at the olive green vintage metal bread box on the counter beside the fridge. "Pickles I canned just last month, too. I had so many cucumbers this year; you be sure to take a couple jars home with you when you leave."

The woman was beyond generous, and Brandon made a note to do above and beyond everything she asked of them. He had a feeling the three or four days they would be on this ranch would be worth every drop of sweat, every aching muscle, and every minute spent in this comfortable, homey kitchen with the two women sitting around the table with him.

Not more than an hour later, they were crammed into the front bench seat of Charlotte's truck, Nutter running alongside them, the bed loaded with split rails. "I love the look of them," Charlotte said when Brandon asked why she chose to use the old-fashioned fencing, especially with sheep. "And this pasture isn't for sheep. I'm looking to raise a beef cow or two out here. I have a rancher friend on the other side of town who will do all my butchering for me in exchange for letting him put a few cows of his own out with mine. I figure it's a fair trade, and I'll know exactly what my meat's been fed on." She glanced at Justice who sat between them as they bounced along the rutted dirt road that skirted the fields already being used by her sheep. "You're a rancher's daughter. Beef cows, right? Maybe I'll pick your brain a little while you're here. I've never raised beef before, and although I'm game to try anything, I don't like making mistakes."

Justice made an inscrutable expression, but nodded. "Yes, the daughter of a rancher, the sister of a rancher, the girlfr—the friend of a rancher, the cousin of a rancher, and so on," she said, stumbling only momentarily on the girlfriend part, but it was enough to make Brandon's stomach clench.

He looked out the passenger window, trying not to let his emotions show, lest one of the women happen to glance over at him.

"Pretty much makes you a rancher, too, then, doesn't it?" Charlotte said with a chuckle. "You just might have the answers to questions I don't even know to ask," she said. "Talk about providential."

By noon, all three of them were ready to take a break. Even Nutter was camped out under the shade cast by Charlotte's truck, and when his mistress pulled the lunch cooler from the floorboard—sandwiches, sliced vegetables, tortilla chips and a homemade chunky salsa—the dog barely lifted his head. Until she brought out the little container of dog treats she kept under her front seat.

Nutter, with his one blue eye and one brown, was clearly madly in love with and deeply devoted to Charlotte. Even when Justice offered him one of the little round meat treats, he wouldn't take it from her until Charlotte gave him permission.

"He reminds me of my sister's dog, Jack, doesn't he, Brandon?" Justice had dropped to the blanket they'd spread under the shade of the only tree in the pasture, and leaned back on her hands, her ankles crossed in front of her. "There's nothing like a good dog."

"Do you have one?" Charlotte asked, her long fingers stroking Nutter's head between his ears. Nutter rested his chin on her lap and gazed up adoringly at her.

"No," Justice said, eyeing the dog, a soft smile on her lips. "I always wanted one of my own, but I figured it wouldn't be fair of me to have one since I'd have to leave him or her behind every time I went on the road. I know some people take their dogs with them, but I just never thought I could swing it." She glanced over at Brandon. "But who knows? I may decide to get a Nutter or a Jack of my own one day."

"They're good company," Charlotte said, more to the dog than to the two of them. "They may bark at ridiculous things just for the heck of it, but they eat what you feed them, they come when they're called, and they're always happy to see you." She cupped the dog's chin and tipped it up. "Besides, how could anyone resist this face?" she cooed.

Brandon grinned and ducked his head. He could imagine Justice with a dog like Charlotte's. She'd need one who adored her, one who looked to her like she was queen of everything.

"I have to ask," Justice said, giving Charlotte a goofy grin. "Nutter? Surely, there's an explanation behind that name."

"Nutter Butter," Charlotte replied with a laugh. "Those peanut shaped peanut butter sandwich cookies. When I first got him, he'd sleep on his stomach with his legs curled up underneath him. He looked like a little peanut with a cute face. He used to have a lot more brown in his coat when he was a puppy, and the name just fit."

Nutter sighed and flopped onto his side, almost as if to say he'd heard that story a thousand times already.

"I'm thinking we should wrap things up out here for the day," Charlotte said after a few minutes of comfortable silence. A gentle breeze drifted around them, lulling them all into a full-bellied, hot sunshine inducing trance. She studied Justice for a moment. "We can come back in the morning when it's cooler, okay? You look a little wrung out, Justice. Probably time to get off that foot for the day."

Brandon agreed. Justice did look a little peaked. He, on the other hand, wasn't quite ready to take a load off. He still had a lot of processing over how best to move forward from where he and Justice were, and he did his best thinking when his hands were busy. "I noticed the tarp you've got tacked up on the roof of the small barn behind the house. There was also a case of shingles inside," he said. "I can get up there this afternoon and take care of that for you."

Charlotte cocked her head at him and grinned. "Why thank you, Brandon. That would be lovely. I hate to admit it, but I've been putting that off for several weeks now." She chuckled ruefully. "I have this thing with heights, you see, and although I wouldn't say I'm afraid of them, I readily admit that I just don't like them very much."

Brandon grinned and nudged Justice's leg with the toe of his boot. "Sounds like someone else I know," he said. "Never admits to being afraid, but you should see her in tight spaces. Scared to death."

"I'm not scared," Justice shot back, but she was grinning unabashedly. "I just don't like them very much," she said, echoing Charlotte's words.

The women laughed in mutual understanding. The two of them, Brandon realized, were more alike than he'd first thought. He could picture far more than Justice with a dog like Charlotte's; he could picture her with a life like Charlotte's. A strong, independent woman, self-sufficient and self-reliant, not needing a man, nor anyone one else to take care of her.

Yet hadn't Charlotte said that she sometimes wished for companionship? Hadn't she welcomed Justice and him back to her ranch with something akin to exuberance? They were practically strangers to her, yet she'd jumped at the chance to have them visit again so soon. They were company. They brought help and two-way conversations, and warm bodies to sit in the empty chairs around her kitchen table.

He stood and stretched out his shoulders, then moved to stand a few feet away, peering back across the open space to where the house and barns sat. He gave half an ear to the conversation between the women, Charlotte asking questions about raising cows, Justice asking questions about sheep and living alone. He wondered what she saw when she looked at Charlotte. Did she see herself in the woman the way he did? Would she look at Charlotte's life, her bold, solitary, wild existence, and find that it resonated with her?

Perhaps the bigger question was this: Was there a place for him in her life? Not just now, but in ten years from now? Twenty years? Fifty?

Maybe they should reconsider staying with Charlotte. Maybe they should get on the road for home as quickly as possible; not give Justice any ideas about a life without him.

He made a fist with his injured hand, measuring the pain to see how much more he could manage today before he made things worse. Another couple of hours would be okay, he decided, then pushed to his feet and headed to the truck to load up the leftover lumber and their tools.

TWENTY-SIX

Back at the barn that afternoon, they let the horses out to exercise under the watchful eyes of Justice and Charlotte, and Brandon dragged out the extension ladder he'd found in the barn. He made short work of the roof repair, doing as much of the task as he could with his good hand, using his left one just to hold each shingle steady while he hammered in the roofing nails.

But during the two hours it took him to do the job, he'd let his mind run amok, and by the time he came down the ladder, he was agitated and irritable, and not just because the sun was high in the sky and burning a brand between his shoulder blades.

He put the ladder and tools away, stored the few leftover shingles on a high shelf inside the small barn, then headed for the trailer to get a cold drink. He could use a shower, but he didn't feel like going inside the guest room, especially if Justice was inside with her foot up.

"While I slave away out in the hot sun," he muttered to himself.

Unless she'd already moved over to the house. Charlotte had made it clear she wouldn't take no for an answer on that matter.

Maybe the guest room was his now.

In fact, even if she hadn't moved, Justice could just clear out. He deserved a shower if he wanted one, to wash the grime of manual labor off of him, especially if the women expected him to cook for them tonight. Because Justice hadn't been kidding; she could burn water.

Brandon marched to the little shower stall at the back of the trailer, rifled through his things until he dug out a clean pair of old chinos—it wasn't his problem that they were one of Justice's favorites on him—a t-shirt, underwear, and socks, then shoved open the trailer door with a little more force than necessary, making it bounce back at him. He uttered a word he didn't use very often, then glanced around to make sure no one had heard him.

Actually, he didn't care if Justice heard him or not. It was her fault he felt the way he did. But he didn't want to offend their hostess. Regardless of his riotous feelings toward Justice right now, he appreciated Charlotte for everything she was doing for them.

The coast was clear, and he strode purposefully across the drive toward the front door of the guest room, pausing momentarily on the step before lifting his hand to deliver two short, hard knocks on the door.

There was no response, but he didn't hear voices through the screen door of the kitchen behind him, either. Justice had to be in there.

He knocked again.

This time, he thought he heard a faint, muffled reply. "Justice?" he called out, his frustration still getting the best of him. When he was met with only silence, he pulled open the screen and tried the handle of the main door. It opened to a dark room, but he knew the moment he stepped in that Justice hadn't moved out.

In fact, she was in bed, the covers pulled up under her chin, her head burrowed deep between two pillows. She made an incoherent sound when he said her name again, but that was it.

A shaft of alarm shot through Brandon, and he hurried across the room, dropping his clothes in a heap on one of the armchairs as he passed by. Without thinking, he turned on the lamp near her head, then quickly switched it off again when she let out a pitiful moan.

"Justice?" Brandon said softly, touching her cheek with his fingers, his alarm ratcheting up at the heat emanating off of her. "What's wrong?"

"I don't know," she whispered, her voice cracking with the effort. "I feel terrible."

So the flush in her cheeks this morning, the fatigue on her face, he hadn't imagined it after all. "Did you tell Charlotte?" he asked, not sure why it mattered. Except that surely, if Charlotte had known Justice was sick, she'd have told him, wouldn't she?

"Nnnmph," Justice muttered unintelligibly. She tried again. "I just need sleep," she managed to get out.

Brandon straightened, putting on his First Responder cap so he could consider the situation and his options objectively. If it was just a fever, if her body was fighting off some virus, then plenty of fluids and plenty of sleep were exactly what she needed. And between all the stops they'd made over the last few weeks, and all the people they'd been exposed to at every stop, that was probably exactly what it was. A virus she'd just have to wrestle with for a few days.

"So much for getting out of here early," he grumbled under his breath.

"Hm?" She squinted up at him, even in the shadowy room. "What?"

"Nothing," he told her, smoothing her hair from her forehead with gentle hand. "Tell me what your symptoms are, Justice. Headache? Stomach? Are you feeling nauseated?"

"No barfing," she grunted. "Thank God. Just feel like I've been hit in the head with an iron skillet, and I'm achy all over." She hunched her shoulders higher up around her ears, pulling the thick comforter with them. "I'm so cold," she added, her voice trembling a little. "A fever, too, I guess." She sounded like she wanted to cry.

"When did it start?" he asked. "While we were working?" It might be heat stroke. It had gotten hot out in the pasture that morning and they'd worked hard for several hours.

"I think before then. Maybe when I woke up? I felt weird, but not like this. My cheeks were hot," she explained, one of her hands sliding out from under the blanket to touch her face. "But I thought it was because I was nervous about seeing Charlotte." She closed her eyes again and her hand disappeared. "I'm thirsty, too," she added.

"Have you had anything to drink since we got back this afternoon?" he asked, noticing there was no water near at hand. "How long have you been in bed?"

"I don't know," she groaned, then started to push back the blankets like she intended to get up.

"What are you doing?" he asked, grabbing the comforter and pulling it back over her shoulders.

"I need a drink." She pushed his hand away, although none too forcefully.

"I can get it for you."

"But you're not, are you?" she grumbled. "You're standing there talking while I'm dying of thirst. Besides, I need to use the bathroom." She pushed the covers away again, this time sliding her legs out from under them.

Brandon's brows rose in surprise at the sight of her, but he didn't allow himself to smile. He could tell by the bulk of her clothing that she wore several layers, both top and bottom. Poor thing was shivering even as she pushed herself up to sitting. "Do you need help?" he asked, offering her his hand.

"No," she snipped, turning her face away. "Please get out of my way." Then she lurched to her feet and stood there for a moment, steadying herself before starting for the bathroom. "And there's a glass in the bathroom, so I'll get my own water, too."

"Really?" he asked, waffling between feeling pity for her and being irritated by her. He reached for her when she stumbled, but she knocked his hand away and kept going.

"Leave me alone, Brandon. I don't need your help. I just need to pee, drink, and sleep, okay?"

He did laugh at that; he couldn't help himself.

Justice slammed the bathroom door behind her, but not before he heard her muttered, "Jerk."

He wasn't offended by her behavior, not really. Justice hated being sick, and even more, she hated being around anyone when she was sick. Some people craved extra attention when they were under the weather, but not Justice. She preferred to shut herself up in her room like a hibernating bear, sleeping straight through as much as possible while her white blood cells waged war against whatever was attacking her, and woe to any who might wake the proverbial sleeping bear.

That included Brandon, and although he braved it more often than most might, he knew better than to take her brusqueness personally.

I don't need your help.

That didn't mean it didn't rankle him something fierce to hear those words from her, especially when he was already struggling with the notion—no, the knowledge—that she might be right.

That maybe, just maybe, she didn't need him at all.

So she loved him. At least she said she did. But was that enough?

Because it hadn't been enough last summer, had it?

TWENTY SEVEN

"Well, maybe its better that she stays isolated out there," Charlotte said in response to Brandon's news about Justice. "She was definitely flagging this morning, but I'd hoped it was just general fatigue. The rodeo circuit can take its toll on folks, that's for sure."

He walked with her as she moved among her sheep, her eyes darting over each one, checking for any signs of injury or distress, making sure they were all well and accounted for before rounding them up and bringing them into the enclosed pen for the night.

"We have a real problem with coyotes around here," Charlotte explained as she swung the heavy gate open then stepped inside, the sheep dutifully following along behind her. "So the flock comes in at night."

Brandon stood off to the side and watched the operation, the song, "Mary Had a Little Lamb" traipsing through his mind at the sight.

"This pen was once an indoor arena—the folks I bought the place from raised and trained miniature horses." She didn't expound, and although she spoke almost offhandedly, Brandon got the sense that she wasn't a fan of the miniature horse. "It's a small one, to be sure, but once I pulled out the bleachers along one wall and redesigned it to hold the sheep, it's been perfect for our needs. My flock won't ever be much larger than it is now, and there's plenty of room in here for them." She pointed to one end of the arena that had been sectioned off into a few small enclosures. "I've got birthing pens at that end, but I don't use them very often. In fact, they tend to get used more often as sick bays than anything else. Or for storing stuff," she admitted with a chuckle.

Brandon helped rally the last of the sheep into the modified arena, then closed the gate behind them. "It's remarkable what you've done with this place. It runs like clockwork around here."

"It has to," Charlotte replied as she patiently weeded her way through the sheep pressing in around her, all of them vying for her attention. "It's just me and Nutter, and if something goes sideways, it can get overwhelming pretty quick." She unlatched the gate and stepped out to stand beside him, then turned and leaned on the rails, her eyes on her flock. Nutter sprawled at her feet and started gnawing on a stick held between his front paws.

After several moments, Brandon spoke into the comfortable silence that had settled between them. "How do you do it?" he asked. "This is a lot for one person."

"You mean for one little old lady?" she prodded. Even though she wasn't looking at him, she was smiling, and he didn't think she was offended by his question.

"No, actually, it's a lot for anyone. You're clearly far more capable than most people, Charlotte. You're strong and independent, a force of nature. And I'd never call you old. Or little." He held up a hand to indicate her height.

Charlotte chuckled. "No, folks don't usually accuse me of that."

"Look at what you've built here," Brandon continued. "You've made this place into a self-sustaining operation. You raise the sheep that produce the wool that you need for the art you create that in turn pays for the feed and land you need to raise the sheep." He wasn't telling her anything she didn't already know. Putting it into words was more for his benefit than hers. "It's pretty amazing."

"Well, if you're asking what I think you're asking," Charlotte said after a long pause, "then yes, I get overwhelmed. Every day in some seasons. Other times, I can convince myself that I can handle it all, that I'm just fine with things the way they are. I have my dog, my horses, my sheep for company." She dipped her head in the direction of the other barn. "There's a barn cat, too, but you wouldn't know it. Kat Miss Neverseen, I call her, because the only time she shows herself is when I bribe her with fish guts."

"Nice," Brandon said with an appreciative grin. Who would have thought his hostess would be a *Hunger Games* fan? "Haven't seen her myself, but now that I know how to draw her out, I might just have to give it a shot. I like cats."

"You do that," she said, sending him a sideways look. "Let me know if she shows herself. I'll start calling you Peta if she does." Then she pushed off the rail. "Walk with me; we'll lock up the horses for the night and check on your Justice before we head inside. I don't know about you, but I'm getting hungry and you promised me burgers."

Brandon nodded, followed her out, then slid the sheep barn door closed behind them, flipping the sliding bolt arm into place to keep the flock safe inside. "Sounds like a plan," he agreed, still pondering the things she'd admitted to him about her solitary life.

"And yes, Brandon," Charlotte said, nudging his arm with her elbow as he fell into step beside her. "I get lonely. All the time. This ranch feels like it gets bigger and emptier every year, no matter how many animals I bring in. That's why I offered you and Justice a place to crash when I came upon you two out there on the highway. I could tell you needed a respite, and I was in need of some company. I'd gotten sad news while I was in town that evening, and I wasn't looking forward to coming home alone to my empty house." She shrugged and said, "I might have needed you more than you needed me that night. The good Lord knew it, and He practically dropped you in my lap, didn't He?"

"Goes both ways," Brandon acknowledged with a nod. "We definitely needed a sanctuary that night." He made a rueful sound at the back of his throat. "Right now, too, and not just because Justice is sick."

"Well, like I said, the good Lord knows what his children need even more than we do. I'm glad you came along when you did, and the fact that you didn't hit that big old mule deer just goes to show that He doesn't do things by mistake or coincidence. He just stopped you in your tracks which happened to be right in my tracks."

"Well, that's one way of putting it," Brandon agreed.

"I'm alone, Brandon," Charlotte said as they ducked into the cool interior of the horse barn. "Not by choice, but because of some of the choices I've made in my life. This strong, independent force of nature, as you say? Well, I've kind of backed myself into a corner. I don't have any choices left as far as I can tell. I have to be independent. I have to be strong and sure of myself."

They tended the horses while they talked. Actually, Brandon didn't say much. He found himself wanting to tell Charlotte all about Justice and him, to open the story of their lives to her and to ask her for some advice, some counsel. But he didn't feel right doing so without Justice's knowledge. So he just listened, hoping to glean words of wisdom from the words Charlotte shared with him.

"Just because a person is capable of doing things well and by themselves, doesn't mean it's the way it should be done. If I've learned nothing in all the years I've been a lone wolf, Brandon, it's that. When I was young, I was fierce about my independence and fearless in my efforts to prove to the world that nothing could stand in my way when I set my mind on something."

"Sounds like someone else I know," Brandon murmured before he could stop himself, then grimaced, feeling guilty for saying even that much. He did not want to sound disloyal to Justice, and he didn't want to talk about her behind her back, at least not in a negative light.

Charlotte nodded knowingly. "Oh, I see it," she said gently. "I see me in her, your Justice."

"She's not mine," he said softly.

Charlotte let out an acknowledging snort. "She belongs to no one but herself, right?"

Brandon didn't say anything, but he didn't have to. The woman didn't need confirmation.

"The thing is, you know the world I worked so hard to prove myself to?" she continued. "That world doesn't care. No one else cares if I have a crew of a hundred or if it's just me, as long as I get them my art. That's all they care about—what's in it for them. So I'm the one who lost out." She pressed a hand to her chest. "I am the only one who cared about what I had to prove. And in the end?" She pulled a hay rake from a rack and handed it to him, then grabbed one for herself. They ducked into neighboring stalls to muck out the day's manure while they continued the almost one-sided conversation. "In the end, this is what I'm left with, this solitary life I lead."

Brandon backed out of the stall and dumped his scoop into the wheelbarrow he'd parked in the passageway. "You seem happy, though," he said. "Or at least content."

Charlotte lifted her head and pointed a long be-ringed finger at him. "Exactly. You hit the nail on the head. I seem happy and content, and most of the time, I pretty much am. My life is good, Brandon, don't get me wrong, because I've made the best of what I have. I love my ranch. I love my sheep, and I love working with the wool and doing my art. I love my home and the freedom I have to do as I please with it. To invite who and what I want into it, and to not have to answer to anyone. All those are good things, things I appreciate."

She paused to maneuver her rake around the back legs of one of her horses. Brandon moved the wheelbarrow a little further down the way to the stall where Tank was contentedly pulling small clumps of hay from his feedbag.

"Hey boy," he said as he moved around him.

Charlotte leaned against the half-wall between them. "But I'm living in a trap of my own devise," she said. "My desire to be self-sufficient comes wrapped in a package of isolation and loneliness, you see?" She watched him work for a few moments before she smiled sadly and waved a hand in his direction. "One other person around here would be lovely, that's for certain."

"Could you hire someone to help around here? You've got the guest quarters. Maybe include room and board?"

"I've thought about it," Charlotte said, turning back to her own work. "I'm kind of out here in the boonies, so that would make it quite a drive for someone if they lived in town."

"What about men?" Brandon asked, then felt his face grow warm at how invasive the question sounded. Charlotte must have thought the same thing because she practically hooted out a laugh, startling both him and Tank. "That didn't come out right," he said, mortification making his voice tight. "I meant—well, look at you. A guy would have to blind to not notice you." He closed his eyes and ducked his head. He wasn't making it any better. "What about love?" he asked. In for a penny, in for a pound, he told himself.

"Ah, love," Charlotte said, drawing the word out. He could still hear the laughter in her voice, but he didn't dare look at her. "I've thought about that, too," she told him. "In fact, there's been a time or three when I've done a lot more than think about it. Unfortunately, love in my life has tended to be more of a temporary respite than a long-term commitment." She didn't explain and he didn't press for more. He was already embarrassed enough.

"I see," he said.

But Charlotte wasn't finished. "Honestly, I'm ridiculously set in my ways. I could never ask a person I love to sacrifice their normal life to come live in my solitary, isolated world. It worked too well, my well-laid plan," she concluded, a note of resignation ringing in her words and dragging its feet through the silence that followed.

Brandon didn't know what to say to that, so he worked quietly, talking softly to Tank, and then to Fire when he moved to the stall with Justice's horse.

"What about you, Brandon? You and Justice?"

He responded slowly, carefully. "What do you mean?"

Charlotte was peering at him from where she worked on the other side of the barn. "That girl isn't just sick. She's hurting; I can see it in the way she holds herself, in the way she watches you, the way she hesitates before she speaks. I'm not telling you something you don't already know, Brandon, but I recognize those symptoms for what they are."

Brandon sighed and shook his head, then pushed out of Fire's stall just as Charlotte finished up what she was doing, too. "I don't feel right talking about her behind her back," he said, hoping he didn't sound uppity or standoffish. He pushed the wheelbarrow toward the back door of the barn and she followed, directing him to the manure compost behind the building. In the distance, the willow tree swayed its languorous branches in greeting, and he felt a pang of longing for home cut through him.

"Good for you," Charlotte said as she locked up the barn doors behind them. They started back toward the house and approached the door into the lanai where Justice presumably still slept. "Want to poke your head in on her while I go wash up?" Charlotte asked. "I can get things started if you want to shower before you come over."

Was that a hint? Brandon resisted the urge to sniff down the collar of his shirt. He hadn't showered after finding Justice sick in bed, but now, more than ever, he was ready to do so. "Sounds like a plan."

"In fact, I'll whip up a batch of chicken soup for her. You ask if she's hungry, okay?"

"You don't need to do that," he started to protest, but she waved his words away with a grin.

"By whipping up, I mean I'll unscrew the lid on a jar of homemade soup my neighbor put up last month. I buy several jars off her every time she does, because the woman knows how to cook."

"Sounds like a plan," Brandon said again, then ducked inside the quiet guest room.

He'd waited around to make sure Justice made it back to bed before he'd gone to find Charlotte, and now, at least an hour later, she'd hardly moved. The blankets were mounded up around her, making him feel overheated and claustrophobic just looking at her.

"Justice?" he said in a voice barely above a whisper.

She didn't respond, so he moved to the edge of the bed and laid the back of his fingers against her temple. The hair there was damp with perspiration and her skin felt much cooler. Good. The fever was beginning to break. She'd probably go through a couple cycles of this, but so far, her body seemed to be doing what it was supposed to.

He scooped up his clean clothes he'd left on the chair and headed for the bathroom to shower quickly, praying he wouldn't disturb her. It would do her good to get some soup down her—in retrospect, she hadn't eaten much at breakfast or lunch. Homemade chicken soup sounded like just the medicine she needed.

When he came out of the bathroom, the light behind him spilled out into the room enough for him to see that she was awake, her head a little higher on the pillow, one of the blankets pulled back. "Hey," he said softly. "Did I wake you?"

"Hey," she said back, and shook her head slightly. "No. I woke up sweating like a race horse and all tangled up in my blankets. Had a mini panic attack," she added with a grimace.

"You hungry? Charlotte has some homemade chicken soup she's warming up for you. I can bring it over—"

"No, no. I'm fine," she said, lifting her hand to flutter it at him, like she was waving away an irritating bug. "I don't need—"

"You don't need anything," he said, cutting her off the way she'd just done to him. "I know."

"Sorry," she said after a moment. She shot him a sheepish grimace. "You know how I get when I'm sick."

Brandon nodded, but didn't say anything. It suddenly seemed like just an excuse to him, like justification for her bad behavior.

"Sorry," she said again, then closed her eyes.

"I'm going over to the house to make burgers," he said, still not acknowledging her apology. He wasn't sure what she was sorry for, and he honestly wasn't sure if she knew, either. "Do you want me to make one for you? Save it for you for tomorrow?"

"No, no," she said, shaking her head. She didn't bother opening her eyes. "You guys enjoy your dinner. I'll be fine,"

"Right." And he was nodding again, his head bobbing up and down like one of those dashboard bobble head figures. "Got it. Okay." He glanced around the room, his eyes landing on a pile of clothes near the front door. The legs of his jeans poked out from the bottom of the pile; the dirty clothes she'd planned to wash today. He crossed the room and scooped the pile onto a towel, bunching the four corners together into a makeshift bag. He'd get them started tonight, then finish the load in the morning. Laundry was the last thing Justice needed to worry about right now. "I'll be back to check on you after dinner, then," he said, and pulled open the door.

"Thank you, Brandon." Behind him, the bedside lamp came on. When he turned around, he found her watching him through eyes squinted against the soft glow. "I'm sorry I'm such a terrible patient."

"You're not—" he started to say, then stopped. "No, you are a terrible patient, Justice Goodacre."

"I know," she said wryly. "I need to work on that. I might be the patient, but you're the one with all the patience."

He waited, but when she said nothing more, he nodded in acknowledgement. "I'll bring you a bowl of soup when I come back. Maybe you'll be hungry by then."

"Okay," she said meekly. "Thank you."

He pulled the door closed behind him and headed across the breezeway to Charlotte's kitchen where he was greeted by a joyful Nutter and the dog's smiling mistress.

"How is she?"

"Doesn't need anything," he told his hostess, then held his bundle of laundry aloft. "I have a huge favor," he began.

"The washer and dryer are in the utility room through that door." Charlotte pointed toward a short hall with only two doors off of it. "The other door is a bathroom so you can't miss it. Detergent is on the shelf above the washer, wool dryer balls in a basket next to it."

Back in the kitchen, Brandon worked quickly to season the hamburger meat Charlotte had pulled out of her freezer to defrost that morning. While he prepped and cooked the patties, she put together a huge tossed salad with crisp leafy lettuce, diced tomatoes, slivered onions, Greek olives, and a little crumbled feta cheese.

"Want to take this meal outside?" she asked him when it was time to dish up their plates. "It's a beautiful evening and I'm sensing you're feeling a little cooped up in here."

He started to tell her he was fine, then stopped himself the same way he'd done with Justice just a short while ago. "Actually, that sounds good. You're right. I'm not the best company tonight, but maybe eating outdoors will help me chill out a little."

TWENTY EIGHT

Justice hated being sick.

She hated being fussed over even worse.

Especially when she was sick.

But she also knew that Brandon didn't realize he fussed over her. He thought he was taking care of her.

Which, to her way of seeing things, felt a whole lot like fussing.

She let out a miserable groan and slid down in the bed a little, ducking her face under the blanket to shield her eyes from the warm glow of the bedside lamp. She didn't even have the energy to reach out and turn it off again. Getting up just to go to the bathroom had completely sapped her.

Granted, she'd stayed in there longer than necessary. But the moment she'd stepped into the small room that was still a little steamy from the hot shower Brandon had just taken, she'd been enveloped in the scent of him. It was a smell so familiar to her that she would have recognized it as his anywhere. Thank goodness her nose wasn't plugged.

She'd gotten a little lightheaded just breathing him in.

Standing there, leaning over the counter, supporting herself on her elbows as she splashed her face with tap water, she'd known in her heart that she'd hurt his feelings. Sure, he'd hovered, even knowing how much it bugged her, but he'd only done so because he was worried about her. Because he still cared about her.

Maybe he even loved her still.

But had he forgiven her?

Her head hurt too much to ponder on that for very long. She filled the glass she'd left by the sink, downed the whole thing, then topped it off again. Her hand shook as she carried it back to the bed with her, and by the time she eased under the blankets, she was shivering again.

"Stupid fever," she muttered. The thought of a hot bowl of chicken soup was starting to sound really good. If nothing else, it might warm her up on the inside.

Charlotte had offered Justice her guest bedroom in the house earlier while they were sitting out under the willow tree watching the horses. They'd come in from working on the fence and had ended up out there with a couple of Mason jars full of ice cold sun tea. They'd talked of cows and sheep, of trick riding and wool weaving.

Charlotte's business, her artwork, fascinated Justice, not because it was something Justice could ever imagine herself doing, but because of the woman's ingenuity, her ability to take the bristly wool fibers she sheared from the sheep she raised, and through the magic of time and patience and hard-won skill, convert those rough natural resources into the woven masterpieces that sold for more money than Justice ever saw in a single rodeo season. It was a little mind boggling.

"When you get settled," Charlotte had told her, "I'll walk you through my process of carding and spinning. It's really quite relaxing. I usually put on a movie or listen to an audiobook or podcast while I work."

Justice had nodded as she'd listened, but she'd been distracted by the way the sunlight flickered over Charlotte's face as she spoke. At one point, it even seemed that the woman had a bit of a halo hovering behind her head, but when Justice blinked, it was gone.

"You look worn out," Charlotte had finally said, sitting forward and bracing her hands on the arms of the Adirondack she'd been lounging in. "Look like you could do with an afternoon nap."

Justice had felt her cheeks warm with embarrassment; it must have been obvious she'd been struggling to pay attention. "I'm sorry," she'd said. "I think you're right. I'm not usually a nap person, but if I don't get up and move, I might just fall asleep right here."

"That wouldn't be such a bad thing," Charlotte had chuckled. "But you'd probably wind up with a crick in your neck. Head on back to your room, catch a little shuteye, and when you get up, you can move your things inside so Brandon doesn't have to sleep in the trailer again."

"I hate to intrude even more than we already are," Justice had started to say, but Charlotte had waved her off.

"I'm happy for the company, child." And although the older woman's smile was still wide and warm, there was a hint of sadness lurking behind her eyes. It was enough to make Justice bite back anymore resistance.

Well, she wouldn't be moving into the house any time soon, Justice thought, pulling a soft pillow toward her so she could wrap her arms around it. She rolled onto her side, her back to the lamp, and prayed for sleep to take her away again. Maybe by the time Brandon returned later that evening, she'd feel more human. Another hour or two of sleep surely had to help, anyway.

Just as she was drifting off to sleep, her phone rang, the theme for The Lone Ranger filling the quiet room. It was Courage. Fortunately, she'd left her cell close by on the night stand, but even so, she barely got to it before it went to voice mail.

"Hey," she said, tying to school her voice to sound normal, but Courage wasn't fooled even for a moment.

"Hey yourself," her twin responded, concern evident in her tone. "What's wrong? Are you crying?"

"No, no," Justice assured her, touching her face to make sure she wasn't lying. She'd shed a lot of tears the last several weeks. "At least I don't think I am. But I'm sick as a dog."

"You sound awful. Where's Brandon?" Just the sound of her sister's voice stirred up a well of emotions inside Justice, making her miss her terribly. If Courage were there, she'd be either in bed next to her, lying close enough to share her warmth, or she'd be sitting in a chair close by, reading or scrolling through her phone, keeping watch over Justice.

"He's making dinner," she finally said.

"Okay," Courage replied, worry still coloring her words. "Where are you? In the trailer? Sorry I didn't call you this morning, especially now that I know you're sick. I got called in to do a morning shift at Schooners. Someone called off sick."

It occurred to Justice that since they hadn't talked that morning, Courage still had no clue about all that was going on.

"Well, that's kind of what I wanted to talk to you about."

"Um... Schooners?"

"No," Justice said, a smile tugging at her lips. "About where I am right now."

"Oh." The single word held a mountain of unspoken questions.

How did she even begin to explain everything to Courage? Where did she begin? Having her head all muddled and foggy didn't help, that was for sure.

"Is... everything okay with you and Brandon?" The question was hesitant, but direct.

"I'm—we're coming home," Justice finally said, then turned onto her side again, drawing her knees up under the covers so that she was curled in on herself, her face away from the light. "I'm done for the season, Courage. So is Brandon. We... well, it hasn't been easy, that's for sure, but we're both a little beat up. Emotionally because of all this stupid stuff with stupid Tanner and stupid Greeley—"

"Tell me how you really feel about it," Courage teased gently.

"Ha ha. But now we're physically beat up, too. He sprained his wrist pretty badly and won't be able to compete anymore this season, and I twisted my ankle. I could probably keep going, but I'm not even close to performing at a hundred percent."

"Oh Justice," Courage murmured softly on her end of the line.

"I wouldn't be a hundred percent even without any physical injuries, though, Courage," she continued, doing her best not to let her voice break, not to falter. "The Twisted Sisters is a team act. I can't fill both of our shoes. I don't know what I was thinking."

"Sissy," Courage crooned, sympathy and sadness drawing the endearment out.

"I thought—" Justice broke off, then started again. "I miss you, Courage. It's not the same without you. It's not what I thought it would be, this whole going solo thing. I—I don't want to do it anymore."

And there were those dang tears again. Justice sniffled softly, and used a corner of the sheet to dab at her face. She'd gotten some sun that morning, and her cheeks were sensitive. Or maybe that was just the fever again. She couldn't tell. All she knew was that she was miserable inside and out, body, heart, and soul.

"Do you want me to come?" Courage asked, not an ounce of hesitation in her voice. "Tell me where you are. I'll drive all night if I have to."

"No," Justice whispered around the ball of tears in her throat. "No, I'm in good hands." Over the next several minutes, she filled her twin in on all that had happened to them since leaving Plumwood Hollow, starting with her first awful performances, the sponsors pulling out, Brandon's injury, the encounter with the buck, being rescued by Charlotte, the altercation with Tanner, and her decision to go home.

"I've been thinking and praying about your riding academy idea," Justice said as she came to the end of her tale. "And every time I do, it resonates with me more and more. It just makes sense, Courage. You and me, we're best when we're together. Ask our patrons at Schooners. Ask our Twisted Sisters fans." She huffed softly. "Ask Brandon. He'll tell you."

"Wow." And that was why Justice loved her sister so much. She listened. Not to Justice's words, but to Justice's heart. "So you're back at Charlotte's now. How long do you plan to stay there?"

Justice took a deep breath and let it out slowly, holding the phone away from her mouth so she wouldn't exhale a hurricane into her sister's ear. "Two or three, I think. Brandon told her we'd stop back by here on our way home to do some work around the place to repay her for taking us in that first night. She's got this place running pretty smoothly, but you know how it is. There's always something that needs doing on a ranch."

"Right. And Brandon has an eye for that stuff. He sees the things that need attention and gets right on them."

"Even with his bad arm," Justice concurred. "He worked circles around both of us women this morning, then climbed up on one of the barns to repair a section of roofing."

"A good guy to have around," Courage said, and if Justice didn't know her sister so well, she might have thought the comment was made in passing. But she heard the underlying message in the sentence. A good guy to *keep* around if only Justice could manage to figure out how to do so.

"A good guy to have around," she echoed, her voice rough with the emotions she was trying in vain to swallow. "He—he's leaving, Courage," she said, the words coming out on a trembling sob. "He got offered a job in Bowling Green, and—and he said yes."

"Oh, Justice, no." Now it sounded like Courage might be crying, too. "I can't believe he'd do that."

"He told me about it when we were here before," Justice whispered, pressing the sheet against her eyes again. "He said he couldn't stay in the Hollow, not with me there and all this stuff between us."

Courage made an odd sound. "He said that? To you?" she asked, disbelief making her questions come out loud and a little shrill.

"Yes. I told him—I told him that I loved him and I missed him and I begged him to forgive me." She gulped back a sob. "He's leaving in August," she added.

After a pregnant pause, Courage said, "Then you have time. You have until August, Justice, to convince him that he needs to stay in Plumwood Hollow. That this town is his home. It's where he belongs. That you, sister, are his home, and that he belongs with you."

Justice was shaking her head slowly, even though Courage couldn't see her. "No," she whispered. "No, I can't do that. I'm not going to stand in his way. If this is what he wants to do, then I need to encourage him. I need to let him go without making him feel guilty or obligated to do otherwise. I've toyed with his life too long. I need to let go of him."

"But Justy—"

"Stop, Courage, please." Her voice was firmer now, her tears slowing. She swallowed hard and made a concerted effort to get her emotions in check. "You know Brandon. We both know he'd do anything for me. If I asked him to stay, he'd stay."

"But you wouldn't know if it was because he wanted to stay or because you asked him to," her sister finished for her.

"Yep." Her one word response sounded almost flippant, but she had to steel herself for the inevitable. Might as well start now.

Courage sighed deeply on the other end of the line. Finally, she said, "Okay." Justice could picture her nodding slowly. "Okay, then," her twin said again. "Text me Charlotte's number, all right? Just in case. Get some rest. Get better, then come home. We'll talk more about the future when you get here."

"I miss you, sissy," Justice told her, trying not to give in to the tears again. "I love you."

"I love you, too. I'll see you soon."

TWENTY NINE

You know Brandon. We both know he'd do anything for me. If I asked him to stay, he'd stay.

Her words throbbed through him like an angry drum beat, reverberating inside his skull. Did she think he was so weak? So malleable, so—so needy?

Brandon stared down at the tray in his hands, the steaming bowl of chicken soup, the mug of sleep-inducing herbal tea sweetened with local honey Charlotte bought from a beekeeper in town, the plate of fresh, buttered bread ready to dip into the stew. It was all for Justice. For Justice, whose last words to him not more than an hour ago were *Leave me alone.*

Yet, here he was, doing just the opposite. He was fussing over her. Like a coddling housewife. A helicopter mom.

"Like a needy boyfriend," he muttered, frozen on the step outside the screen door of the guest room. The porch light he stood under was a spotlight on his head. *Look here, everyone. Look at the fool. The last one to know. The only one to not get it.*

He wanted to hurl the tray out into the yard, to shatter the dishes against the side of the room where he'd thought Justice was peacefully sleeping. What a fool he'd been.

He could tell it had been Courage she was speaking to. She got this tone in her voice when she conversed with her twin—they both did. Even before he heard her words, he'd known who was on the other end of the conversation in the room. He'd left the main door of the lanai open just an inch or two when he'd slipped out earlier, not because he worried that the sound of the latch would disturb Justice if he came and went from the room, but because he'd planned to return, just like he was doing, his arms laden with tokens of his adoration for her.

Tokens of his addiction, more likely.

"I'm addicted to her," he muttered, half-snarling the words as he turned in a slow half-circle, uncertain of what to do next. "Even while she destroys me, I keep going back for more."

He couldn't take the tray back into the kitchen. Not yet, anyway. Charlotte was in there doing the dishes and prepping something to put in the slow cooker in the morning. And he couldn't—he *wouldn't*—go inside the room with Justice, not in a million years.

He'd only prove her right.

The contents of the tray rattled and he realized he was shaking with the effort to contain his frustration. He had to get out of there now, before he did something stupid.

Before he shoved open the door and told Justice where she could go.

Before he let himself see her, weak and vulnerable, curled up under her blankets, needing him to take care of her, even though she would never admit it in a thousand lifetimes.

He practically launched himself off the step and out into the yard, making a beeline for the trailer. Inside, it was closed up and a little musty—he hadn't bothered opening the windows all day since he'd expected to sleep in the guest room that night.

He slammed the tray down on the little kitchenette counter, sloshing the soup, splattering the bread and silverware, soaking the paper napkin he'd carefully folded around her spoon. Miraculously, he hadn't spilled a drop of the tea. He didn't bother cleaning it up; maybe he'd take it out to the barn and see if he could woo Kat Miss Neverseen out of hiding with it.

Brandon made quick work of opening every window in the living quarters of the trailer, grateful for the cool night breeze that swept across the prairie to help soothe his temper. He didn't bother turning on any lights, but instead, dropped onto the couch and reached up to switch on the stereo mounted on the wall behind his head. He didn't turn it up, although he really wanted to—he needed something to beat out the hammering of her words in his head—but instead, tuned the dial to a station that played popular country music. He preferred indie Americana folk music with lots of acoustic strings and raw vocals, but the songs were familiar and the best he without digging through his playlists for something to better suit his mood.

Fifteen minutes. He'd give himself that long to calm down, then he'd take the bowl of soup—what was left of it, at any rate—out to the barn. If the cat wasn't interested, he'd take it as a sign to swear off all females from this day forth.

And if Charlotte discovered him out there, he'd make up some lame excuse about hearing a ruckus in the barn. Perhaps he'd make a ruckus himself just so he wouldn't have to lie about it. Surely there was a bucket to kick or a loose board that needed hammering back into place.

When Shania Twain started crooning her old hit, "You're Still the One," over the airwaves, Brandon shoved to his feet, downed the still scalding mug of tea intended for Justice—hey, maybe it would help *him* sleep better—snatched up the bowl of soup, and shoved out of the trailer door, leaving the dark-haired songstress rambling on and on about beating the odds, holding on, and going strong.

Ha. What did Shania know about love? What husband was she on now?

Inside the barn, the horses nickered and stomped in greeting, but he could tell he'd disturbed them from their rest; the feedbags hung half-full but still. Long early evening shadows vied for space against the lingering shafts of fading sunlight that still streamed in through a few gaps in the wood siding and around hatch doors and windows. Even the dust motes seemed to wake up just long enough to question his presence in the peaceful place before settling back to the ground for the night.

"Here, kitty, kitty, kitty," he called out softly, waving his braced hand over the soup bowl as though that would help the cat get a better whiff of the tempting meal. He stilled, cocking his head to listen, but there was no responding meow. "It's yummy soup, Kat. And you deserve it a whole lot more than *she*—"

What was he saying? Brandon shook his head, headed toward the last stall that was empty, except for several bales of hay, and set it down. "Come and get it if you want it," he said. "I don't care. No skin off my back."

Then he dropped onto a bale of hay.

In the half-open barn door, silhouetted against the deepening shades of the sunset, Charlotte stood with one shoulder propped against the frame, her arms crossed. Brandon couldn't see her face, but he knew she was studying him. How long had she been there? How had he not heard her? He was usually so in tune to his surroundings.

"I heard your music," she said as if reading his mind. "When I looked out the kitchen window, I saw the barn door was open. I was hoping it was you."

"Sorry," he said, running a hand over his head, then gripping the back of his neck.

"For what?" Charlotte asked, straightening up and glancing over her shoulder at the guest room before looking back at him again. "Or am I just standing between you and the intended recipient of that apology?"

Brandon frowned at her. "That's not it at all."

"Hm." The sound came out short, amused.

"I'm not the one who needs to apologize." He wanted to smack himself in the forehead. He sounded like a little kid.

"I see," Charlotte said, dipping her head as if attempting to hide her expression. She needn't have worried. He couldn't see her features anyway.

With the woman blocking his only exit, Brandon felt trapped, antsy to get outside under the big Colorado sky. He stood, shoved his hands in his pockets, and started toward her and the barn door, then remembered the bowl of soup. Should he leave it and come back for it later? What if Charlotte found it before he got to it? What would she think about him feeding the barn cat her precious chicken soup? Brandon felt a wave of shame wash over him. He stopped in front of Tank's stall and reached out a cupped hand for his horse to nuzzle, the big sleek head bobbing slowly as he looked for some kind of treat.

"I got nothing tonight, buddy. Tomorrow, okay?" Brandon murmured, hoping if he talked low and quiet, maybe Charlotte would get the hint and back off. Give him some badly needed space. Leave him alone.

"Are you sure it's an apology you're after?" the woman asked. Even though she spoke gently, the question carried through the air like a fog horn, making him wince.

"I'm not after anything," he insisted, not looking at her. Tank lifted his head and bumped Brandon's shoulder with his nose.

"Then why are you here, Brandon Stillwater?" Charlotte asked after several long moments of silence.

Brandon wanted to tell her to mind her own business, to go away, but he couldn't. He and Justice had come to her, asked her for sanctuary. Maybe not the first time, but definitely this go around. They'd come here looking for answers, hadn't they? Did he really think Charlotte wouldn't have questions of her own?

"And please don't tell me it's because of your injuries. I've seen that girl ride. A mild sprain isn't going to keep her out of the arena."

Brandon's head snapped up and he turned to look at her. She'd stepped inside the barn and now stood with her back to the wall, her long legs crossed at the ankles, her thumbs hooked in the pockets of her jeans. He could see her face now, and her expression was one of authentic concern.

"You've seen Justice ride?" he asked, buying himself some time.

"I have, indeed," Charlotte said with a nod. "The Twisted Sisters. Those two girls put on quite a show. I live in rodeo country, Brandon," she said with a brief smile. "I've seen you wrestle a steer or two as well. That's one of the reasons I wasn't too worried about inviting you to my home. Figured I had an inkling about the sort of people you were. Figured you had a story, too, seeing as how Justice was riding without her sister and you with your arm in that brace. I wasn't going to get nosy, though; not until you asked to come back. I think you two are in the kind of mess you're not sure how to get out of."

Brandon snorted, startling Tank, who jerked his head back in surprise. "Sorry, boy." To Charlotte, he said, "You're right about that, but I'm not sure talking about it like this is going to help matters." He hadn't meant for the statement to come out so brusquely, but his hostess didn't seem to take offense.

She shrugged and cocked her head to one side. "I don't know. Seems to me you came looking for something from me or my place, or maybe both. I don't have much to offer you other than a bed to sleep in, food to eat, and a whole lot of manual labor to help you work off some of that bottled up steam."

"Exactly what I'd hoped for," Brandon said, then started toward her again, this time determined to get outside before he started crawling out of his skin.

"I also have some free advice I'd like to offer you," she began, then laughed when he stopped in his tracks and narrowed his eyes at her. She held up a hand to stay his response. "I'm not asking you to share your troubles with me, Brandon. I'm offering to share mine with you so that hopefully, you'll learn from them before you get to my age."

Brandon dropped his gaze to the ground in front of him, clenching his jaw in frustration.

"I've got an apple pie coming out of the oven in about ten minutes," Charlotte said, shifting gears. "Some vanilla ice cream in the freezer, too. Why don't you take a few minutes while I check on Justice, then come on inside and we'll have us some dessert. You worked hard today; you deserve it."

He wanted to refuse, but he had the sinking sensation that it would only be putting off the inevitable. He nodded, then lifted his gaze to meet hers.

"Just so you know," he told her. "I think I already got the answers I came here to find. At least the main one." Once again, he heard Justice's phone conversation in his head.

We both know he'd do anything for me.

Oh, really? He had some calls of his own to make in the morning. Bowling Green was looking pretty good to him right about now.

THIRTY

THE CINNAMON SPICE OF the fresh-baked apple pie met Brandon as he approached the door to the kitchen. Through the screen, he could see Charlotte standing at the counter, a well-used cookbook open in front of her, running her fingertip down the page as though checking to make sure she had everything right. She snapped it shut and pulled open the freezer just as he stepped into the room.

"You want me to soften the ice cream a little first? The pie is still warm, so it should melt pretty quickly, but my daddy used to leave his bowl sitting out on the counter until it was practically milkshake consistency. By the time he got through his pie, he could have used a straw."

"No need to let it sit on my account," Brandon told her. He stood awkwardly just inside the door, uncomfortable in the inviting room for the first time since setting foot on Charlotte's property. It had taken all his willpower to haul his backside over there. He'd seriously considered pretending he'd fallen asleep in the trailer, but had finally pulled up his bootstraps and forced himself to make the short walk across the yard.

"Have a seat, then," she told him, waving at the table. The pie sat on a wooden trivet in the center of the table, two plates, a pie-server, and a couple of forks and spoons beside it. Charlotte pulled the lid off the ice cream carton, stuck a serving spoon in it, and set it down next to Brandon. "Would you like some coffee? I don't usually drink it in the evenings, but it's not possible for me to fully enjoy apple pie without a cup of coffee."

"Sure," Brandon nodded, seeing as she'd already brewed a pot.

"Cut yourself a slice," Charlotte ordered. "Then load me up a slice, too, will you? And no scrimping on mine. I don't make pie often, but when I do, I make a point to enjoy it."

Brandon felt the reluctant smile pull at his lips. He really did like this woman who had decided to take them under her wing. He wasn't thrilled about the pending lecture, if that's what it was going to be, but he couldn't help picturing Charlotte as an older version of Justice; t was a little like seeing her in one of those time-lapse videos. They certainly both had the same appreciation of good food.

"Justice was sleeping soundly when I went in there," Charlotte said, almost as if she was simply adding on to the end of his train of thought. "I thought she might want a piece of pie, but she hardly stirred, even when I called her name."

"She might have been faking it," Brandon said without really considering how it might sound.

"Doesn't like folks fussing over her when she's sick, does she?" Charlotte set a steaming mug beside his plate, then sat down in front of the piece of pie he'd served for her.

"Not so much," he said, not bothering to apologize for Justice. He watched his hostess as she pulled the carton of ice cream close and scooped an enormous spoonful onto her plate.

"She's still running a fever," she continued. "I didn't wake her, but I felt her forehead. Seems low-grade to me though, almost more like she's just worn herself out. These competitions can take it out of folks."

Brandon only nodded, not wanting to add his current opinion of Justice to the conversation.

They ate in silence for a few minutes. "This is really good," Brandon finally said. Should he ask what she wanted to say to him? Prompt her somehow to begin? He took a swig of the scalding coffee, grimacing a little at the heat on his tongue, then quickly scooped a spoonful of ice cream into his mouth to take the edge off.

Across the table from him, Charlotte polished off her own piece of pie before pushing her plate away. She sat back in her chair, and wrapped both hands around her mug. "She's hurting, that young lady next door," she suddenly began.

"So you said earlier," Brandon muttered under his breath. Wow, was he ever feeling surly tonight.

Charlotte didn't quite acknowledge his comment, but she narrowed her eyes as she gazed into her coffee. "I get the feeling you're the only one who really knows how badly."

Brandon scoffed quietly. "A month ago, I might have agreed with you," he said. "But now? I kinda think her pain isn't nearly as deep as she'd like everyone to believe."

Charlotte frowned and cocked her head to study him. "Justice doesn't seem the disingenuous type," she rebutted, even though it was said so gently that it took him a moment to parcel out that she was disagreeing with him. "From what I can tell, she's walking around with a hole the size of the Atlantic through her chest. Seems like it'd be hard to fake, Brandon."

He shook his head. "I thought so, too, but I'm apparently wrong. As usual," he added ruefully.

"I don't get it," Charlotte said, a tiny thread of frustration in her voice. "I mean, it's no secret that you two love each other." She circled her face with a finger. "It's plain as the nose on your face when you're looking at each other."

"Ah." Brandon held up his fork and shook it casually in her direction. "See, there's where you're only half right. It's not each other we love, it's her we both love. I love her. *She* loves her. Common interests, yes, but not conducive to a healthy, two-sided relationship."

Charlotte's brows furrowed. "I think you're trying awfully hard to convince yourself of that," she finally said. "But you know it's not true."

Brandon grinned, his eyebrows rising as he let out a humorless chuckle. "You're wrong there, Charlotte. And I don't mean to be rude, but you've only just met us. You really don't understand how things are between us."

"Then help me understand," she countered. "I thought I did, at least when we first crossed paths. The way you were looking after each other right on the heels of your near miss with the buck. Explain to me why you're so sure it's only one-sided, because from where I'm sitting, what you're feeling for her goes both ways."

He clamped his teeth shut and shook his head slowly. He wasn't going to talk about Justice behind her back.

But then, why on earth was he being so reticent? Why shouldn't he unload everything on this woman who clearly just wanted to help? She was basically a stranger, after all, so what did it matter if she knew what had happened between them? In fact, it kind of made her the perfect person to talk to. Objective, not invested in their past or future, and loaded with a few more years under her belt than he and Justice combined.

Besides, Justice didn't seem to have a problem talking about him to Courage. Justice had her sister to unload on, someone to be her sounding board, someone to talk to. Brandon needed someone on his side, someone on the other end of his phone call, and what was stopping him from opening this can of worms up with Charlotte?

"Maybe instead of apologizing to her about something you can't quite nail down—or waiting for one from her," she added when he opened his mouth and then shut it once again. "Why don't you tell her you love her, tell her you're going to fight to hold on to her." She pointed at him across the table for impact. "For better or worse."

"Oh no," Brandon countered, shaking his head fiercely. "No, no, no. Not going there."

"What exactly are you running from?" she shot back, waving an index finger at him. "What are these lines you're drawing between you two?"

Brandon pushed his chair back from the table, stopping himself just before shooting to his feet. He lifted both hands in self-defense and said, "I'm not drawing lines, Charlotte, okay? At least not any new ones. Nor am I the one who crossed the lines, so you can stop pointing fingers at me." He planted his palms on his thighs and gave her a steely-eyed glare. "Literally."

She was like a dog with a bone. "What line did Justice cross? Does she even know she crossed it? Or are you waiting for an apology that she doesn't know she's supposed to give?"

"Not that it's any of your business," Brandon ground out, then pressed his lips together. She was making it harder and harder to be polite, no less remain calm, something he prided himself on being able to master, even in the most harrowing circumstances. As a First Responder and the head of his crew, it was his job to remain in control of a situation, and that started with himself.

"I beg to differ," Charlotte countered, crossing her arms over her chest and holding his gaze in spite of his angry glare. "You made it my business the moment you picked up that phone and asked if you could bring your troubles onto my property."

Brandon planted his hands on the table again. "Right. Then we'll take our troubles and leave." His voice was tight as he started to stand, but she held up a hand to stay him.

"Hold up, there, cowboy. I accepted them when I said yes to your request," she continued. "Because I can see you two are in a bad place, yes, but I can also see that you also have something worth fighting for, and I love a good fight for the right reasons."

A half-growl of frustration worked its way out between Brandon's clenched teeth. The woman was nosy, intrusive... and right.

"Believe me, Brandon," she added, speaking gently now, "when I say that I know what I'm talking about. I know what it means to give up the fight way too soon."

He slumped back in his chair, his head lolling forward under the weight of defeat. "Justice already gave up the fight, Charlotte. She's quit. And not just us. She's quit trick riding, she's quit the rodeo, and she's been talking about quitting her law school plans, too. Instead, she wants to open a riding academy with her sister back at home."

Charlotte considered his words for a few moments, then shrugged. "Sounds like someone who knows what she wants. A riding academy isn't such a bad prospect. With their name and reputation?"

"Maybe not for her sister, but for Justice? She's no homebody, Charlotte. Plumwood Hollow is the last place she wants to end up, or at least it was up until now."

"So she changed her mind. She isn't allowed to do that?"

"Justice doesn't just change her mind," he ground out. At least she didn't used to. When Justice made up her mind about something, there was no deterring her. Which was one of the reasons her apparently unplanned impulsive decision to be with Tanner had shaken him so badly.

He squeezed his eyes shut and clenched his teeth, waging war with the words scrabbling up the back of his throat. He didn't want to talk about this anymore. Not with Justice, not with God, and certainly not with Charlotte.

Did he?

What difference would it make? If anything, maybe getting it off his chest once and for all might help him clear his head a little. Might help him actually get a good night's rest, something he hadn't experienced in far too long. Every time he closed his eyes these day, all he could see was Justice and Tanner. Tanner and Justice. Justice kissing Tanner the way she'd kissed—

Charlotte tipped her head to one side, her brow furrowed as she studied him. "Did she cheat on you or something?"

THIRTY ONE

"So let me ask you a question," Charlotte said, the words coming out slowly, thoughtfully. Brandon could tell she was choosing her words carefully.

"Hit me." He was sitting forward, his forearms braced on the table, both hands gripped tightly around his empty mug as he stared down into it. He'd downed the last drop several minutes ago in the midst of unloading his burden into the space between them. Once the floodgates had opened, there'd been no holding back. He could almost picture it sitting in the middle of the table, a great big glob of his guts, ripped out and laid bare for Charlotte to see. *Go ahead,* he wanted to tell her. *I'm already bleeding all over the place.*

"You say you're saving yourself for marriage, right? And that's not my question. I just need confirmation." She, too, tipped her cup to peer inside, frowning down into it.

"Yep." He thought about getting up to grab the carafe from the counter, but he felt like a deflated balloon, like all his bones had turned to rubber. His legs might not support him if he tried to stand.

"Marriage to Justice? Again, confirmation."

"Yep." He lifted a narrowed look at her. *Make your point already, lady.*

Charlotte rose and crossed to the coffee maker, returning with the carafe. She proffered it to him and he slid his cup forward, accepting what felt like her peace offering.

"Thanks."

She filled her own cup, then studied him again, brow furrowed. "Have you and Justice slept together? And don't play stupid with me. Have you had carnal knowledge of each other, even the kind that can't get you pregnant?"

"Wow." Brandon wasn't expecting such a blunt question. He sat back and shifted his long legs into a more comfortable position under the table, accidentally nudging Nutter, who was napping at Charlotte's feet, with the toe of his boot. The dog lifted baleful eyes to him. "Sorry, boy," Brandon apologized, not sure if he was relieved by the interruption or not.

The dog put his head back on his paws and sighed. Charlotte said nothing, just waited.

"No. We made a commitment to each other that we would wait." He'd already told her so, told her about their promise under the willow tree back home.

"Right. Okay, then hear me out. I'm not trying to be facetious. If you are saving your first time together until after you're married, then won't it still be your first time together?"

Brandon scowled at her. "Mine, yes. Hers, no."

Charlotte shook her head. "If you haven't slept together, then it will be her first time, too."

"Haven't you been listening to a thing I've said?" Was she serious? "She's not a virgin anymore. She gave herself away to someone else!" His voice was starting to rise, and he clenched a hand into a fist under the table. Forcing himself to calm down, he added, "And not to someone she loved, either. She threw it away like pearls before swine. I almost think I might have been able to accept it if she'd fallen in love with someone else."

Charlotte made a noncommittal sound and nodded, but he could see in her eyes that she didn't believe that anymore than he did.

"What?" he finally snipped when she remained quiet. "What's your point?"

"She says she sorry, right? And you believe her?"

Brandon nodded. "I do believe her. I know she's sorry. I had to tell her to stop apologizing because it was getting old. She's sorry, sorry, sorry, sorry." He rotated his shoulders, trying to loosen the knot that had taken up residence between them. "But being sorry after the fact is easy, isn't it? Trust is gone, Charlotte. She threw that away, too. I mean, come on. How can I ever trust her again? What if she has another 'moment of weakness'?" He held up to fingers to form air quotes around the last three words.

"I see," Charlotte said, nodding slowly. "Are you more upset that she slept with someone else or that she's no longer a virgin?"

"Both!" he shot back, the sound of that word making his blood boil. "We made a commitment to each other before God," he reminded her.

"I see," she said again, remaining perfectly calm, which only served to infuriate him. "Well, the way I see it," she continued, holding his gaze. "And excuse me if this sounds vulgar, but man—that's you and me, Brandon, *and* Justice, too—puts far too much value on the condition of a woman's hymen, while God—that Holy Being you made your commitment before—would much rather have us focus on the condition of a woman's heart."

Her frank—and yes, some would say vulgar—statement hit him like a slap in the face and he actually reeled back a little.

"You say she's sorry. She's repented. She's made it very clear to both you and this Tanner fellow that she made a mistake."

It was spoken as a statement, but Brandon felt the challenge in her words. He wanted to argue, but everything she was saying hit home.

"You *can't* trust her? Or you won't trust her?"

"I—I can't trust her," he replied, sounding defensive even to his own ears. "She's not trustworthy."

"Right," Charlotte frowned and took a sip of her coffee. "Worthy." She spoke the word softly, more to herself than to Brandon, as if mulling it over, unwrapping it and studying it. "Not many of us are, you know."

"When it comes to promises, I am," he retorted. "I don't break my word. If I make a promise, I hold up my end of the bargain, come hell or high water."

"I see," she said, yet again. Then she locked eyes with him. There was a deep sadness in her gaze that made his stomach hurt to look at her. She thought he was delusional; it was written all over her face. Her next words were measured, deceptively casual. "With a few exceptions, though, right? Like, if she breaks her word, or drops her end of the bargain, as you put it, then you're off the hook?"

"What's that supposed to mean?" But he had a feeling he knew exactly what she meant. "I'm here, aren't I? I'm still showing up every day. Still here for her, still helping her, still making sure all her needs are met." He guffawed coarsely. "Well, except for one. Tanner met that need, because apparently, I wasn't worth waiting for."

"Okay," she said, her eyes narrowing as she watched him. "So you're still here with her, but you're not together. Your words, remember? Just friends?"

"My words, her choice. Yep."

"Why? Why are you still here?"

"Because I said would be. I don't cut and run. I don't leave. I don't abandon. I don't—" He broke off as an image of his mother flashed through his mind. The absence of his father in his childhood, the all but nonexistent connection they now had. "I don't break my promises."

"So you didn't promise to love her?"

Until death do us part. The thought came unbidden, clanging like church bells in his mind. How many times had he thought of the words they'd one day speak to each other before God and all their loved ones? *In sickness and health. For richer or poorer. In good times and bad.* "I never promised I'd always love her."

"So why don't you leave?" She spoke slowly, driving the point home with her words. "It sounds like it would be easier on both of you."

"I don't leave," he repeated, ignoring the little voice in the back of his mind that kept saying, *'Bowling Green'* on repeat like a broken record. "I don't leave, Charlotte." He spoke slowly, too, repeating himself like she was hard of hearing or slow to comprehend his words.

"Right. Got it. Instead, you stick around and make sure she knows—make sure everyone knows—that she screwed up. Make sure she knows that she's not worthy." Her tone was gentle, ringing with kindness, but her words cut him to the quick. "How long are you going to punish her, Brandon? When do you think she'll be worthy of your trust, of your love, again?" She waved a hand toward the guest room where the woman they were discussing was holed up. "I think after all these years, you owe her that much. A time frame. A list of tasks she can complete to reinstate her worth in your eyes."

Ah. That was sarcasm if he'd ever heard it. Brandon shook his head. "Oh, no. You are not going to do this. I'm not going to do this. She made this bed, now she can lie in it. I don't owe her anything, Charlotte. Not a list, not a time frame, and not my trust."

Love? He wished he could blow that out of the water, too, but there was nothing he could do about loving her. It was part of who he was.

"Not even forgiveness?"

"I've forgiven her, okay? I know she's sorry. I know she hates what she did and she says she'll never do it again. I just don't trust her. *Can't* trust her." He pushed his chair back and rose, reaching for the dirty dishes still in the middle of the table. "I need to be done talking about this," he said, wishing now that he'd kept it all to himself. He took a shaky breath in an effort to collect himself. "Thank you for the pie and coffee, for listening, but I need to call it a night. I feel like I'm on the losing end of the twelfth round."

Charlotte rose, too, and picked up the pie dish. She said nothing while they cleaned up, but when he hung the dishtowel on the stove handle and turned toward the door, she stopped him.

"Brandon, people make terrible mistakes. They do the wrong thing, sometimes over and over again. But God is a God of second chances. He's a God who heals and restores. You involved him in this relationship early on when you made that commitment before him." She leaned her backside against the counter and loosely crossed her arms. Her expression turned beseeching. "Don't leave him out of things now, okay? Get on your knees, my friend. Ask for wisdom; it's free for the asking when you're a child of God, and he doesn't wait until we're worthy to receive it. He also promises to never leave us or turn his back on us, not because *we* are faithful, Brandon, but because *he* is faithful. And he's the only one who never breaks his promises."

THIRTY TWO

The next two days passed in a continuous cycle of fever and chills, coupled with hallucination-like encounters with Charlotte bringing hot liquids and cold cloths, followed by drenching sweats and longer and longer periods of lucidity. By morning of the third day, Justice awoke in a near panic to get outside, to breathe in fresh air. "And to eat something solid," she muttered into the stillness around her. The wide slats of the wooden blinds were closed so only tiny lines of daylight filtered into the room, but they made her think of the silver lining around the clouds at the end of the day, a sign of rest to come and a new day to follow.

In spite of the weight of her blankets—she was so weak!—she got herself up to the side of the bed and sat there, her hands braced on either side of her, until the room steadied itself. What was that smell? She pulled the front of her nightshirt open and bent her head forward to take a whiff, then wrinkled her nose. "Ew." She needed a shower, clean clothes, and clean sheets.

She had her work cut out for her.

By the time she stepped out of the shower, her legs were shaking, not from fever, but due to weakness from prolonged bed rest, and hunger so bad, she thought she might faint. She draped a towel over the closed lid of the toilet and sat down to dry herself off—her ankle wasn't bothering her too badly, but between that and her wobbliness, she wasn't going to risk falling in the bathroom. She dressed slowly and carefully, swept her wet hair into a spider clip at the back of her head, and brushed her teeth.

"Ready as I'll ever be," she said to her reflection, then pushed open the bathroom door. "I need coffee."

The bedroom was awash with light from the open windows, the bed freshly made—clean sheets!—and on the little table in front of the sofa was a tray laden with toast, scrambled eggs, and, blessed be, a mug of hot coffee, a matching cream and sugar set beside it.

Justice sat down and eyed the tray, wondering if she should wait for whoever had brought it to return, or if she could dig in. *Dig in*, her stomach growled loudly. She had just doctored her coffee when Charlotte's figure appeared at the screen door. She tapped twice, then came in without waiting for an invitation.

"I heard the shower and figured you must be feeling better," she said by way of greeting. "I changed your sheets and opened things up." She pointed at one of the windows.

"It was getting a little close in here, wasn't it?" Justice asked with a little laugh. "I do feel better, thank you. Shaky, but a little food and fresh air should help with that." She held up her mug. "And a lot of this magic elixir."

"Got you covered," Charlotte assured her, dropping into one of the chairs opposite her. "There's a whole lot more where that came from. Please," she added, nodding her chin toward the tray. "Eat up. I'm just hiding from that slave driver you brought with you. That guy can work circles around me and it's not making me feel any younger."

"Brandon? Yeah, he's a workhorse, that's for sure. He has an eye for seeing things everyone else just passes over, but rest assured, whatever he sets his hand to will be done the right way, the best way, the *only* way, according to him." She made air quotes around the word *only*.

"Ah, yes. I've gathered as much," Charlotte said with a nod.

"Yep. He's a lot like my dad that way. There's only one to do a job, and that's the right way the first time." Justice smiled softly, a tiny burn starting at the bridge of her nose. She suddenly missed her father and her sisters fiercely. "But then, as a single father raising seven daughters, he really couldn't afford to take more than one shot at things. It's amazing we're all still alive and kicking, all things considered, and we really have him to thank for it."

"Seven daughters!" Charlotte exclaimed, her eyes growing wide with equal parts surprise and admiration. "He sounds like an amazing man, your father."

"He is. As I said before, you'd like him." Justice eyed her hostess over the rim of her mug. In fact, Daddy would like Charlotte, too. "If you're ever out our way, you must pay us a visit. I'd love to show you the Hollow, and our little cattle ranch, Seven Virtues. You could learn everything you need to know from my sister, Faith. She's the one who took over after my father had a near-fatal accident with a rogue tractor. She practically turned the place around."

"I'd like that," Charlotte said with a nod. "I've often thought of heading toward the Midwest with my sheep. They handle the cold out here really well, but it's the arid climate that's hard on them. And my hands," she said, holding her palms out toward Justice. "I make my own salve just to try to keep my hands soft, but sometimes they get so dry and rough that working with the wool can be problematic."

"You should try some of the stuff my sister, Prudence, makes. It's miracle goo. Of course, that's not what she calls it," Justice clarified with a shrug. "I've got some in one of my bags. I'll leave you a jar."

Brandon moved into view out the window that overlooked the barn, catching Justice's eye. He had a roll of rope looped over one shoulder and a shovel in the other hand. His hair hung in a thick braid down the middle of his back, and his hat was pulled low in the front to shield his eyes from the morning sunlight so she couldn't see his face. She frowned and sighed deeply, the thought of his eminent move never far from her mind. How she would miss him.

"He's a good man to have around," Charlotte said quietly. When Justice turned toward her, her cheeks burning, the older woman was studying her, not Brandon.

Justice heard Courage saying almost those exact words—what was it? Two days ago? Three? "He is," she agreed, scooping a pile of the scrambled eggs on a piece of toast.

"Well, he's tackling projects that have been on my To Do list for far too long. I'll certainly miss him when he's gone."

"I will, too," Justice said without thinking. She glanced over at Charlotte who cocked her head slightly, one eyebrow up. "He's been offered a job," she explained. "He's moving sometime in August."

Now both of Charlotte's brows rose. "Moving?" That single-word question carried a hefty punch.

"He's a First Responder, a paramedic. He's really good at what he does; keeps a cool head in some pretty bad situations." She couldn't help recalling watching him in action with Courage after her fall. "He's been offered a job in Bowling Green. Kentucky. It's a good job from what he's told me. They're going to get their money's worth out of him."

"How far away is Bowling Green from where you live?"

The question seemed to be leading the conversation into uncertain waters, and Justice took a large bite and chewed carefully before responding. "About an hour away, depending on the weather and who's driving."

"I see." Charlotte nodded slowly, her gaze drifting to the window that looked out toward the barn.

It was obvious her thoughts were elsewhere, so Justice took a few more bites of the delicious breakfast, remembering to pause between each one to make sure her stomach could handle solids after three days without. "This is really good," she commented after a few minutes. "Thank you. You've been very kind."

"Well, your Brandon out there is certainly working off both of your room and board," she said with a chuckle. The smile didn't quite reach her eyes, though, and Justice was rather curious what was going on in the older woman's mind.

She didn't have long to wonder.

"Listen, Justice. I need to talk to you," Charlotte said. Her tone was casual, but her expression had grown quite serious. "I had a long and somewhat uncomfortable conversation with Brandon the other night. I think it's only fair that you should know. I don't like talking about folks behind their backs, and if his reticence to share was any indication, neither does Brandon. But, we did, indeed, talk about you."

"Oh." The eggs in her belly did a little floppy shuffle. "Okay." Charlotte was right about one thing; Brandon didn't gossip about people. He didn't complain about them. In fact, he didn't discuss his problems unless he was looking for solutions to them. Not even with her. So what on earth had he shared with Charlotte?

"He told me about you and that Tanner boy."

Okay. I'm going to kill you, Brandon. Justice turned to look out the window toward the barn, her eyes narrowed as if she could hunt him down with a tractor beam and burn the skin off him with her laser eyes.

"He also told me about your commitment to each other." She'd left out the word *broken*. The broken commitment. The one Justice had split in two.

"He told you a lot," Justice said, then took a sip of her coffee, trying to wash down the lump that had risen in her throat. Not tears. Nope. Not today. Anger. Resentment. "So now you know. I'm a scarlet woman. Shamed. Rejected. Dirty. An untouchable."

When Charlotte didn't respond, Justice lifted her chin and turned her gaze on her hostess. "I guess I'm not surprised," she said, even though she was. "I mean, it's not like he's keeping his anger toward me a secret, is he?"

"No, he's not," Charlotte concurred. "Neither of you are very good at keeping your emotions to yourselves, that's for sure."

Justice didn't look away, but she lowered her chin a notch. "I'm tired of secrets," she said, deciding not to expound. Apparently, she didn't need to as it appeared that Brandon had already shared her secrets with the older woman lounging in the chair across from her.

"You hurt him pretty badly, didn't you?" Charlotte asked, her voice tender, but her words pronged.

Justice bit back the retort she wanted to spew at the woman, that it was none of her business, but she reminded herself that secrets weren't the only thing that hadn't worked out for her. Pushing people away, especially those who only wanted to help, hadn't worked out very well for her either.

"I did," she admitted, forcing the words out past the resistance in her throat. "Unforgivably."

"There's no such thing."

"Actually, there is," Justice countered. "I speak from experience on this." She met Charlotte's gaze straight on and continued. "I have loved him my whole life, but it wasn't until I realized I'd lost him that I woke up to the fact. I'm a slow learner," she said with a rough shake of her head. "Brandon, my sister. I have to face losing them before I realize how much I need them." She ached over the rifts she'd caused in so many lives. "All I want is his forgiveness," she acknowledged. "I'd apologize a million more times if he'd let me, if it would do any good, because I don't know what else to do."

"Sounds like you're having a hard time forgiving yourself," Charlotte said.

"Well, yes, of course." She let out a harsh sound meant to be a laugh, but it came out more of a groan.

"Want some advice from a lonely old woman?" Charlotte was hardly old—she'd be young even if she lived past a hundred—but Justice had caught glimpses of the woman's loneliness.

"Will it help?"

Charlotte grinned back at her. "Depends on if you take it or not."

"Then yes." Why not? If she didn't like what she heard, it was only advice.

"Stop apologizing and don't stop telling him you love him."

"I've tried." It wasn't that simple. Love was never that simple. "I really have."

"I don't mean with words."

"Ha!" Justice let out another rough sound. "Tried that, too. The first night we were here. Went over like a wet blanket."

Charlotte's eyes grew wide and a tiny grin tugged at the corners of her mouth.

"Yep. Tried to seduce him. Right here in this room, no less. Got a little desperate," Justice admitted, although her tone dripped with sarcasm.

Charlotte laughed out loud, no longer able to hold it in. "So that's why he's sleeping in the trailer."

"Thought maybe if I slept with him, then he'd stop thinking about me sleeping with Tanner. Maybe I could show him that I wanted him and not Tanner." Justice snorted derisively. "Like I'm some goddess in the bedroom or something. How stupid could I be?"

"Oh, honey," Charlotte said, settling back into her chair. "Love is lovely until one of you makes a mistake. It's like riding in an air balloon that bursts, only to discover that it's a water balloon. It douses everyone with a cold, cold mess, and before you can come up spluttering for air and gasping with shock, you hit the ground hard. If everyone survives the fall, you're left with a huge wreck that needs to be rebuilt the right way from the ground up. Guess where you are right now." She chuckled softly. "Throw sex into the mix and things are just going to get messier."

"I figured that out," Justice interjected wryly. "Thank goodness he said no."

"Because he loves you."

"Or hates me."

Charlotte studied her for a few moments, then said, "I'd like you two to stick around a few more days, if you think that's possible with your schedules."

She'd changed the subject so abruptly, Justice had to replay her words in her mind to make sense of them. "Um...."

"I have a mower tractor that needs some attention, the kind I don't know enough about. Brandon thinks he can get it running for me, if I can get him the right part. If I order it today, it can be delivered to the parts store in town on Monday. What do you think? That would give you another couple of days to get back on your feet before you have to hit the road again."

Couple of days? Until Monday? "What's today?"

"Thursday. Once your fever broke yesterday morning, you passed out." She glanced at the large watch she wore. "You slept for well over eighteen hours."

So she'd lost more than three days lying in that bed. "Wow."

"Yeah, whatever bug that was hit you hard. Fortunately, I've got the fortitude of a prairie woman, and I don't get sick. Can't afford to," Charlotte added with a rueful chuckle. "So what do you say? I wanted you to know what I know before I offered, just in case it makes things too awkward for you. If you're good to stay a little longer, I'll extend the invitation to Brandon, too."

Justice shrugged, not sure how to respond. She was stuck between a rock and a hard place with this situation. She wasn't quite ready to go home and face the music that accompanied a rodeo season cut short. People would ask at church, at Schooners, anywhere and everywhere she went, and she still wasn't sure how she would explain her decision to go home early. But knowing that Brandon had spilled his guts to Charlotte—behind Justice's back, no less—was a tough pill to swallow, too. She wanted to ask Charlotte what he'd said, how he'd said it, what the older woman thought of their situation, but she couldn't get the questions out, not and save what little dignity she had left, too. "I guess if Brandon is fine with it, so am I. I don't really have to be back in Plumwood Hollow until sometime in August for work."

Charlotte braced both hands on her knees and leaned forward in the chair. "Perfect. I'll go see him about it now." She pushed to her feet and gestured toward the tray. "You finished with that?"

"I am," Justice said with a nod. "Thank you. It hit the spot."

Once she was alone, Justice rose to her feet and crossed to the window. Where was he? What had made him open up to Charlotte that way? And what had he said? The more she thought about it, the more desperate she became to know everything about the conversation. It wasn't like she could change anything, but at least she wouldn't be going into the next few days completely blind while the two of them exchanged knowing glances behind her back.

Except Charlotte didn't seem to be the kind of person to do something as petty as that. And hadn't she been forthright just now? Hadn't she made it a point to let Justice know about it?

"So why didn't *you* tell me, Brandon Stillwater?" she asked under her breath, still searching for his form out the window.

Then suddenly, there he was, striding out of the huge barn door, brushing his hands together to knock dust and debris from them. He headed toward the kitchen, then disappeared around the corner of her room, reappearing briefly through the screen at her door as he passed by. He didn't even glance her way.

When had he last been in to see her? Was it before or after his conversation with Charlotte?

Justice moved back to drop into one of the chairs and thought back over the last few days. Brandon had brought her food twice? Three times, maybe? He'd showered in the bathroom at least once, but she was pretty sure that had been the first day she'd fallen sick. Had he moved into the guest room inside? The one Charlotte had offered to her?

Now that she thought about it, Justice hadn't seen Brandon yesterday morning. It had been her hostess who'd brought her herbal tea, bone broth, and applesauce and told her she looked like she'd been through the wringer a few times too many. It had been Charlotte who'd brought her a cold washcloth and something hot to drink the night before, who'd told her to rest and to stop apologizing for being sick. It had been Charlotte who'd come and gone for at least the last two days.

Did Brandon just not want to get sick? Or was he purposefully avoiding her?

"Do I really want to know the answer to that?" she whispered to herself.

THIRTY THREE

"It looks amazing in here," Charlotte called out as she came out of the tack room at the end of the barn. Brandon had spent the day putting up a new shelving unit and several racks and pegs, then had proceeded to organize the space for her.

"Everything has a designated spot now," he said, proud of his handiwork. He loved the sight of a neatly organized tack room, and got a great sense of accomplishment from putting things to right. He pointed to the wheelbarrow he'd left out in the corridor. It was half full of assorted items. "Those are things you should probably throw away or have repaired if you really need them."

Charlotte peered into the pile, then crossed her arms and shook her head. She made her way toward him to where he was busy stacking hay bales in the extra stall at the other end of the barn. "I'm not even going to look through it. Otherwise, I'll find reasons to keep it all. You just get rid of it for me, okay?"

Brandon grinned at her over the pony wall. "You sound like Justice. She keeps everything, just in case she has need of it someday."

Charlotte nodded. "That girl is a lot like me, I think," she said thoughtfully. "She seems a lot better today. She ate well."

The older woman had just come from Justice's room; he knew because he'd paid attention. He'd been in and out of the barn since waking up with the sun, and his eyes never strayed far from the guest room door. After Charlotte had disappeared inside with the breakfast tray, only to reappear with an armful of bedding, he'd half expected Justice to follow on her heels. He'd ducked back inside the barn, not quite prepared to see her.

Except that he was also desperate to see her, too. He'd kicked at the frame around the barn door and had gone back to work, making every effort, futile though it was, to *not* think about Justice.

"That's good to hear," he said in response to Charlotte's update. "As soon as she's well enough, we'll get out of your hair."

"You're not in my hair," the woman said with a laugh. "I'm certainly not complaining; look at all you've done while you've been here. My barn roof, the tack room, the pasture fence, my oil change. I'm running out of things for you to do."

"Wish I had access to that part," he said, jutting his chin in the general direction of where the tractor was parked beside the smaller barn. "I'd love to get that thing up and running before we leave."

"About that." She propped her arms on top of the gate and hitched a booted foot on the bottom rung. "I don't know that Justice is all that anxious to rush out the door. She's still a little wobbly on her feet from what I could tell."

"She hasn't eaten much in almost a week," Brandon said with a nod. "I'm not surprised."

"Well, I asked her how she'd feel about staying for a few more days."

Brandon buried the hay hook into a new bale and hoisted it up on top of the stack he was working on. "What did she say? I'm sure she's anxious to get home."

"She was open to it. Said it was up to you."

"Right. Okay. I'm good to stay. You're sure you're okay with it? We can chip in for food and stuff."

"You're already chipping in plenty," she said, but something in the way she was watching him had him pausing in his work.

"What is it?" he asked. They'd spent plenty of time together over the last couple of days, but they hadn't done much talking since that first night. Charlotte seemed to be giving him space, time to think on the things she'd said to him, the things he'd shared with her. He was glad for it, and glad for the work that needed to be done.

He wasn't looking forward to going home early, truth be told. He could keep busy over at Whispering Hills until the summer was over, until he figured out the whole Bowling Green job thing, so it wasn't the work. No, somewhere in the back of his mind, he was afraid. Afraid to go home with things still so fraught between him and Justice. Afraid that if they left this sanctuary without some kind of resolution, that they might never find their way back to each other.

If that's what they even wanted to do. He leaned a hip against a stack of hay and unstrapped the brace from around his wrist to let his arm breathe. It was hot in the barn, and he was sweating something fierce, but it wasn't anything he wasn't accustomed to.

"I've been thinking these last couple days."

"Mm-hm." He eyed her, not sure he liked the sound of that.

"I think Justice needs to be rescued."

For a moment, Brandon stared at her, not sure he'd heard her right. Then he guffawed. "Rescued? Are we talking about the same person here? Justice doesn't need anyone or anything. Ask her. She'll tell you."

"Yes. You've said so before," Charlotte said with a nod. "But I don't believe it. I don't believe her, and I don't believe you do, either."

Brandon shrugged, then strapped the brace back in place. He'd pay for the heavy lifting by the end of the day, but he had to keep busy.

"Remind her of what she has to lose. Her sister is already slipping away—"

"Courage isn't going anywhere, Charlotte. That girl is as entrenched in life at Plumwood Hollow as anyone could possibly be."

"She may not be going anywhere physically," the woman countered, "but her heart belongs to someone other than Justice now. That's another form of separation."

"Okay, sure," he conceded.

"And if she doesn't take Courage up on this academy plan—which I think is a brilliant idea, by the way. If they don't take on this project together, their paths will fork, and life will come between them. Not necessarily in a bad way, but in a permanent way."

"That will be Justice's choice," he said, hating how bitter he sounded. "It's about what Justice wants, not what she needs."

"Again, I don't think you really believe that. If you stay here for a few more days, Brandon, then I am going to charge you, to challenge you to remind her shy she doesn't *want* to lose the people and places that are precious to her. Her sister. Her riding. Her hometown. You. She may not want to need you, but she does."

"No," he shook his head and thrust the hay hook into another bale. Over his shoulder, he said. "She doesn't. She's made that clear."

Charlotte pushed back from the gate and smacked her palms on the top rail, startling him enough to make him straighten and look back at her. "You know, Brandon Stillwater, for a man who pays such close attention to details, you seem to be missing some pretty important ones where Justice is concerned. And I have to say, that surprises me."

"Oh really?" he retorted. "So you think you know her better than I do after a few days?" Argh! Why did he have to get all belligerent every time the topic shifted to Justice? He'd been thrilled to hand over her care to Charlotte when the woman asked to take over.

"She might be more polite to a stranger," she'd said, and she was right, of course.

He'd taken Charlotte up on it because it hurt his heart to see Justice so miserable, and he really didn't want to feel sorry for her right now. He needed to clear his head of her and the sympathy she stirred up in him, and putting physical distance between them had seemed like a good idea.

All it had really done, though, was made him think about her even more, made him worry about how she was feeling. Made him wonder if she needed him, or if she was perfectly content with the care Charlotte was providing her.

Charlotte sent him a teasing smirk. "Don't bite my head off," she said, lifting her hands in surrender. "I'm just pointing out facts here."

"And what facts are those?" Why was he taking her bait? He didn't want to hear what she had to say. "What's your point?"

She hesitated briefly, then instead of answering his question, she said, "If you had told me when I was your age that I needed help from anyone, that one day I would regret doing things for myself, I would have run in the opposite direction." She made a self-deprecating sound at the back of her throat. "What's my point? That's exactly what I did. And look where it got me." She held her arms out at her side and did a slow twirl just outside the stall. "Not needing anyone, sure, but not having anyone either."

Brandon hefted the bale up, using his knee to give leverage for his injured wrist. "Maybe she might take it better coming from you."

"You know, that girl is head over heels in love with you, but she's terrified you'll reject her." She hooked her thumbs in her belt loops. "I can't say I blame her for it, either. The fear of rejection part, not the loving you part," she clarified caustically.

"She's the one who rejected me, Charlotte. Over and over and over again," he ground out, emphasizing he words by driving the hook into another hay bale.

"You know, maybe she's not the needy one here," she said after a few moments' consideration.

"I'm not needy."

"Because from this angle," she continued as if he hadn't spoken, "you seem to need her to be needy before you'll forgive her."

Brandon threw the hay hook into the corner of the stall where it bounced off the wall and landed with a muffled flump on the loose hay scattered about. It was a completely unsatisfying sound for someone on the verge of throwing a temper tantrum. How about a crash and a bang or two? "I can't win, can I?"

"That's a cop out. Sure you can. Want to know how?" She laughed and held up a hand before he could speak. "Don't answer that. I'm going to tell you how. You work on you. You know, there's a reason that saying still exists after all this time. You know the one I'm talking about, right? If you love something, let it go?"

"It it was meant to be, it'll come back to you. Yeah, yeah. Believe me, I've worked that one over so much it's threadbare. And it's idealistic and meaningless."

"That's because in this case, in your case, if you love something, you have to let it go *and* stop beating it with a big stick."

"Oh, for crying out loud," he snapped, once more leaning against the hay. "How about letting a guy get some work done around here, hm?" If anyone was getting beat with a proverbial stick, it was him, and Charlotte was doing the beating.

"She's taken enough abuse, Brandon," the woman said, ignoring his question. Her eyes had grown steely as she held his gaze. "And most of it is self-inflicted. Believe me, the whacks you're getting in are nothing compared to what she's doing to herself. You should have heard the things she called herself today. Things she thinks *you* are calling her, if not out loud, then in your heart."

"I'm not—"

Charlotte held up a hand to stop him. "Like I said, Brandon, self-inflicted." She took a few steps closer and once more leaned on the gate. "She needs a soft place to fall right now. I'm pretty sure she's sick because her immune system is shot. She's so worn down and discouraged that her body is having a hard time holding up under the strain she's put on herself."

That didn't sound like Justice. "She's not a weak woman," he muttered.

"I didn't call her weak. She's taken more on her shoulders than she can manage on her own, and we all know what happens when too much is heaped on top of us. We crumble." She pointed toward the house. "She crumbled, Brandon, and if you can't be there for her to fall on, then for the love of all that is holy, find it in you somewhere, somehow to be there to help her back up. And yes, even if she tries to refuse you."

"But I—"

"Oh, and one more thing. You don't abandon? You don't cut and run? Is that right?"

Brandon frowned at her, his shoulders tensing. He did not like the challenge in her voice. "That's right."

Charlotte tapped the toe of her work boot against the bottom rail of the gate, the dull metallic clunk sounding ominous. "But you're leaving town when you all get home, right? You're leaving your job." She wasn't asking him for clarification. "And you're leaving Justice behind."

"No, I'm not," he said, rising to his feet. "I'm not taking the job." The moment the words were out, he realized the decision had been made long ago. Maybe even before he'd applied for the position. He didn't want to go. He didn't want to walk away. He just didn't know how to stay.

His mother hadn't known how to stay.

His father hadn't, either.

But he was not his parents. *I am not my parents.*

"You're not?" Charlotte sent him a sharp look, and for a moment, he thought she'd read his mind. "Then why does she think you're cutting your losses come August?"

He dropped his gaze for just a moment, then took a steadying breath. "I was considering it for awhile. Well," he amended, "I was thinking about considering it. I applied for the position without really giving it a lot of thought."

"But that doesn't answer my question. Why does she think you're leaving in August?"

"You know, you might just be the nosiest person I know."

"Are you avoiding the question now?"

Exasperated by the woman's sheer tenacity, he still couldn't help smiling at how much she reminded him of Justice. "I'm not avoiding the question," he told her. "I'm just acknowledging how out of line you are."

"Yeah, well, you're only upset because I'm acknowledging how out of line *you* are," she shot back.

They both stared hard at each other, the air crackling between them. Brandon broke first. A low chuckle rolled out of him, then Charlotte followed suit, both of them laughing at the absurdity of their exchange.

"Oh my lands," Charlotte said when she could catch her breath. "I was going to say that you bring out the worst in me, but I have to be honest with you. I haven't been this fired up by a conversation in a very long time. You kids make me feel young again." She crossed the small space to one of the hay bales and dropped down on it, then removed her hat and fanned her face.

Brandon sat, too, a few feet away. "I told her I was leaving," he finally said, still smiling. "I guess I wanted her to beg me not to go."

Charlotte chortled softly. "How did that work out for you?"

"She congratulated me and told me I'd be the best thing that ever happened to Bowling Green."

"No begging you to stay, then?"

He ducked his head as he recalled just exactly what she'd begged of him that night, not wanting Charlotte to see the flash of heat in his eyes. "No," he murmured. "She didn't beg me to stay."

"Do either of you have to be back home right away?" she asked him after a few moments. "You haven't turned in any resignation letters, right?"

"No on both accounts. We both have summer replacements at our jobs, although I shouldn't speak for Justice."

"Then I think you should consider staying on an extra week or so, not just a few more days. Take a break from the work you're doing around here and soak up some of the solace and peace this place has to offer in abundance. You deserve it after all the work you've put in around here, especially with that wrist of yours."

Brandon frowned, but didn't say anything. Had she already suggested as much to Justice?

"Stay here and sort things out where you're away from the stress of real life, from people who know you and have expectations about you. And for heaven's sake, start by telling that poor girl that you aren't going to take that job."

"I know," he said with a humbled dip of his head. "I need to clear the air on that. I led her to believe it was a done deal."

Charlotte's brow furrowed and she held up a hand. "Actually, before you do that, answer me this. Do you plan on sticking around for the long haul? Is that why you're not taking the job? Because you want to be a part of her future?"

He took a deep breath and let it out slowly, puffing out his cheeks. "I do," he finally said, not missing the weight of those two powerful words. "I do," he repeated.

"Then you're going to have to stop dragging her back to the past. She's not a quitter, you know, and you need to stop calling her that."

"I know."

"She's going through a soul awakening. An identity crisis, I think folks call it these days. Changing her mind, her direction, making stupid mistakes? That's part of the process, I'm afraid." Charlotte shoved her hat on her head and tipped the brim back. "I'm not trivializing what she's done, but you shouldn't trivialize how much she wants to make things right. She knows what—and who—she wants and where she wants to be, Brandon. It's how to get there that's got her in knots." She pointed at him. "That's where you come in. Your role is to help her untangle the lines, especially the ones between you. You want her to trust you with her heart?"

Could he trust her with his? "I do."

Charlotte chuckled. "You're very good at those words. Have you been practicing in front of the mirror?"

Brandon rolled his eyes, but didn't deny it.

"If you want her to trust you with her heart, then you have to trust her with yours. Don't wait for her to offer it to you again, Brandon. She won't risk more rejection from you."

But she's the one who—He cleared his throat to drown out the petulant voice that kept trying to convince him he was the victim here.

Charlotte was right. He hadn't proved himself to be very trustworthy, either. He hated what Justice had done, her betrayal of his trust, but in the end, that didn't justify him rejecting her. Two wrongs don't make a right. Although he'd heard the adage a zillion times over the years, it had never meant more to him than it did right now.

"She thinks I'm a pushover," he finally said, still clinging to the last vestiges of his resentment, flinching at the memory of Justice's words to Courage. *We both know he'd do anything for me. If I asked him to stay, he'd stay.*

"I don't know about that," Charlotte said with a frown. "She seems pretty unsure of everything where you're concerned, except, of course, for how she feels about you."

"I heard the words straight from the horse's mouth, Charlotte." Brandon held a hand up to his ear to mime a phone call. "On the phone with her sister. She thinks all she has to do is ask, and I'll lie down and go belly up. Do whatever she wants."

"If she's anything like me," Charlotte, still frowning, continued, her gaze shifting toward the barn door and the house beyond, "she'd rather be alone then wonder if you just said yes so you could keep her."

"You'd think," he muttered

"It takes a strong man, a strong woman, to forgive an indiscretion like unfaithfulness, Brandon. For all parties involved. You aren't weak for choosing to stay and love her. You're weak if you choose to run away, knowing your heart wants to stay and fight for her. For a future together." She rose to her feet and brushed her hands against her backside, sending bits of hay floating to the ground. "You know, if she and Courage do go through with this riding academy, they're going to need someone like you to help them. The way Justice talks about you, she already knows that. Maybe you should let her know you're interested in the job."

Brandon shook his head, even though the same thought had been circling for days inside his mind. "I have a job."

Charlotte ignored him. "I don't usually spout Scripture, but this one won't dislodge itself, and I'm pretty sure it's not stuck in this brain of mine for my sake." She tapped her temple, then said, "The second book of Timothy, first chapter, seventh verse. 'For God has not given us a spirit of fear, but of power and love and self-control.' You heard it?" She didn't wait for a response. "Time to put all that stuff the Good Lord gave you to use, my friend. Power, love, and self-control? Pretty awesome weapons he's armed you with. You just have to find it in you to pick them up and use them the right way."

He took a deep breath, then let it out slowly. "I'm at a loss, Charlotte."

"Think big." She spread her arms wide. "Grand gesture big, Brandon. Surprise her. Surprise yourself."

Her words resonated with truth, but was he asking for future trouble, future heartache, if he took her back?

Wasn't he succumbing to future heartache if he didn't?

She turned to leave, but over her shoulder, she added, "I'm making sandwiches at noon. Heads up: I have a feeling Justice might join us for lunch. She's got a bad case of cabin fever."

THIRTY FOUR

It took another twenty-four hours before Justice worked up the courage to do more than stand at the open window in her room and soak up the sunshine. After the breakfast Charlotte had brought her the morning before, she'd promptly fallen asleep on the sofa. About half an hour later, she'd awakened with a crick in her neck and feeling too irritable for polite company.

So she'd gone back to bed and pulled the covers over her head to shut out the midday sun streaming in her windows.

Later that afternoon, she'd finally checked her phone, and was shocked to see all the messages and well wishes she'd received from friends back home, along with the outpouring of love and support from fans leaving her messages through The Twisted Sisters website and social media platforms. Overwhelmed by it all, she'd returned her phone to the nightstand face down and burrowed back under the covers. She'd call Courage in the morning and ask her to help her respond to everyone. Her sister always knew the right thing to say.

It was Friday morning and Justice knew she needed to get up, get dressed, and face whatever the day would bring. "Coffee," she said into the quiet room. "That will help."

But first, she needed to talk to Courage. Oh, how Justice longed for her sister's comforting presence and reassuring words. She picked up her phone and texted her twin. *Can you talk?*

Just as she sent the message, her phone pinged with a text from Courage. Justice grinned at the uncanny connection they shared. Her sister's message was almost identical to what she'd just sent. *How you feeling - can you talk?*

After assuring Courage that she was feeling much better, Justice caught her sister up on her version of the last week's happenings. Courage had been keeping close tabs on her through Brandon and Charlotte, but neither of them were very forthcoming about anything besides Justice's physical condition, and Courage wanted to know what was going on in her sister's heart.

"Well, Brandon would have to be completely brain dead to not know how you feel about him," Courage said, her tone thoughtful.

"Right," Justice agreed. "Or not interested."

"Which we know isn't the case," Courage countered.

"Actually, we don't know that," Justice said quietly. "Not anymore."

"Sorry, sissy, but you can't convince me of that. He loves you. He's just a little gun shy right now. Skittish. Think horses. You spook them, they may still want to please you, but it can take awhile for them to find their footing with you up in the saddle again. We've been through it with Fire and Flame enough to know how it works."

"Brandon isn't a horse."

Courage giggled on the other end of the line. "I don't know. Sometimes I think he might be at least part horse with that luscious black mane and those long, muscular legs and—"

"Okay, okay," Justice interjected, cutting her off. "Stop drooling over my man."

"See?" Courage practically shrieked into the phone.

Justice held it away from her ear, then pressed the speaker icon. "See what?" she asked, sliding her legs out from under the covers. She was too restless to stay in bed, and her stomach was starting to growl.

"You aren't ready to give up on him yet. Otherwise, you wouldn't care if I drooled all over him."

"Whatever. But no, I'm not ready to give up on him. I just don't know what to do next. And he's been avoiding me, I think. I haven't seen him in days."

Courage was quiet for a moment, then in a tender voice, said, "You two need to find your way through this before you come home, Justice. How much longer are you going to be there?"

"I don't know. I think until early next week. Brandon is doing some work around the place for Charlotte." She explained the tractor repair and added, "But Charlotte agrees with you. She told me we should stick around and try to sort things out before we go back to normal life."

"You know, I really like that woman."

"I do, too. She's pretty amazing."

"I have an idea," Courage said in a tone that indicated she was choosing her words carefully. "It's risky, I know, but I think you're going to have to go all in, sissy. All or nothing. Don't hold back." She chortled mischievously and added, "I mean, don't stick your hand up his shirt or anything like that, mind you."

"Shut up," Justice retorted. "For that, you're coming in the bathroom with me. You'll have to listen to me—"

"Oh, come on," Courage groaned, interrupting her. "Call me back when you're done. I'm hanging up now."

"Fine."

Several minutes later, after Justice had finished her ablutions and changed into a pair of jeans and a pale blue tee, she and Courage picked up the conversation where they'd left off.

"What's this big risk you want me to take?" Justice asked, wincing as she dragged a brush through her tangled hair. She sat the little sofa again, her eyes glued to the window in hopes of getting a glimpse of Brandon.

"Ask him out. Like on a date."

"A date? Seriously, Courage? We can barely be in the same room together right now. Remember? He's avoiding me."

"Serious as a heart attack," she said, ignoring Justice's sarcasm. "A really nice one. Not fancy, but, you know, intimate. Cozy."

"We're out in the middle of nowhere," Justice said, drawing the her hair forward over one shoulder to braid it. "I doubt they have much more than a watering hole in town. A bar or two, but not a nice restaurant."

"Actually, we do."

Startled, Justice spun around to find Charlotte standing in the doorway with a hot cup of coffee in each hand. "You scared me!" she said, pressing her hand to her chest.

"Sorry about that," the older woman said with a grin. "I tried knocking with my elbow, but I couldn't manage it without sloshing. Then I realized you were on the phone, so I was just going to sneak in and leave yours here." She nodded her chin toward the phone on the cushion. "But I couldn't help overhearing your conversation. Hello, Courage," she called out, raising her voice a little.

"Hey, Charlotte," Courage returned the greeting, her own smile evident in her voice. "What do you think of my idea?"

"I think you're on to something," Charlotte replied as she settled into one of the armchairs. Justice glanced from her hostess to the phone and back again.

"Would you two like me to step out of the room so you can continue your discussion of my life?" She wasn't really upset, but the whole situation felt a little surreal to her.

Charlotte chuckled and shook her head. "No, no. You stay right here and drink your coffee. We'll work around you." Then she reached over and patted Justice's knee. "I'm just teasing you. I don't want to intrude, but I do think your sister has a great idea, and I know just the place. You can take my truck so you don't have to unhitch Brandon's. Rosita's has booths with high backs and they serve the best fish tacos. Casual, intimate, delicious."

"And safe," Courage added. "No one knows you there. You'll be totally out of your element."

"Other than the fish tacos, the whole thing sounds a little ridiculous," Justice said. "Why can't we just talk here?"

"A date, sissy," Courage stated. "Not two angry friends trying not to pick fights with each other."

Charlotte chortled at Courage's turn of phrase, but covered her mouth when Justice narrowed her eyes at her. "Act like you're just getting to know each other," she said. "Courage is right; no one knows you two have been friends since diapers."

"Exactly," Courage agreed. "Sometimes you two act like an old married couple who have forgotten to be intentional about love."

"We do not," Justice argued.

When Courage said nothing on the other end of the line, Charlotte spoke again, the teasing glint in her eye fading. "What have you got to lose, Justice?" she asked.

"Everything. I mean, he knows how I feel. I don't know how I could possibly make it any clearer than I have already. At least if I lie low, we may be able to be friends again, but if I ask him out? That could very well be the straw that breaks the camel's back. He may go running for the hills."

"Not a chance," Charlotte said, shaking her head.

"What if he says no? What if he doesn't want me anymore? What if he rejects me again?" The questions shot out in a rush of words, and she held her breath, almost afraid to hear their responses.

It was Courage who spoke first. "He wouldn't be so awful toward you if he didn't want you anymore."

"And there's a possibility that he might, indeed, say no," Charlotte added sagely. "But you'll have to be brave enough to ask anyway. Brave enough to risk everything on him. On the two of you."

"I—I don't know if I can." The words came out wobbly, uncertain.

"Sure, you can. You love him, right? Perfect love casts out fear; that's what the Good Book says." Charlotte said. "In fact, I'm already planning on attending your wedding, so you'd better send me an invite. It'll be a good excuse to come check out your neck of the woods."

"That would be awesome!" Courage hooted over the phone. "I'd love to meet you in person."

"It's a date, then. But first," the older woman said with a laugh, "we have to deal with this date. How about you come out of your cave sometime this morning, Miss Justice? Come help me in the kitchen for a bit—I'm making another apple pie to take to my neighbor tomorrow in exchange for a couple jars of her peaches. Then you can go round Brandon up for lunch, and while you're at it, ask him about the date."

"You make it sound so simple."

"It really is, sissy," Courage said. "All you can do is ask."

THIRTY FIVE

A COUPLE HOURS LATER, Justice ran her sweating palms under the cool water in the bathroom sink and stared at her reflection in the mirror in Charlotte's bathroom off the kitchen. She'd changed out her t-shirt for an emerald green camisole top that Brandon always complimented her on, and she'd let her hair out of the braid. It hung soft and wavy around her shoulders. Her cheeks were tinted a pretty pink as much from anticipation as from the work she'd been doing at the hot stove. The air was heavy with the aroma of cinnamon, pastry, vanilla extract, and apples sautéed in butter, and Justice hoped the fragrance would linger on her long enough to tickle Brandon's senses when she went to find him out in the barn.

She stepped out of the tiny wash room and stood with her arms out to her sides. "How do I look?" she asked Charlotte who was busy pulling out ingredients for Reuben sandwiches.

"You look lovely." Charlotte beamed at her.

"Thank you." Justice took a deep breath. "Okay. Here I go."

Charlotte crossed the room to her and gave her a quick squeeze. "You got this."

All was quiet in the barn when Justice stepped into the shadowed interior. The horses were out in the pasture enjoying the sunshine, and the sheep had been put out in the far pasture, the one they'd repaired the fences on, since there were no cows to graze out there yet. The sounds the little wooly creatures made were faint and far off.

"Brandon?" she called out, her voice echoing around the rafters. "You in here?"

There was no answer, so she slipped back outside and headed for the other barn. It, too, was empty. Nor was he working on Charlotte's disabled tractor. She even checked inside the Exiss. Where was he?

The willow tree, she thought. Maybe he was taking a break out under the willow. It's where she would go.

She circled the barn rather than going through it, relishing in the sunshine drenching her shoulders with heat. She picked up her pace, her pulse doing the same in anticipation. What better place to ask him if he'd go to Rosita's with her than under the willow tree?

But he wasn't there, either.

Deflated, her shoulders drooping now, she started back toward the house, when a movement out at the far edge of the pasture caught her eye. Brandon straightened from a crouched position and added a bright yellow stalk of wildflowers to the bouquet he held in his other hand.

He was picking flowers. For her?

The thought made her giddy and she quickly ducked back around the side of the barn, hoping he hadn't seen her. When he continued along the fence line, pausing now and again to reach down for more flowers, she knew she'd gone unnoticed. She waited until he had his back to her, then dashed on shaky legs back to the house.

She collapsed into a chair at the kitchen table just as Charlotte came in from the living room. "Is everything all right?" the older woman asked. But her look of concern changed to one of curiosity at the sight of Justice's grin. "What's going on?"

"Go look out the window," Justice told her, then unable to help herself, she crossed to the window first. "Look," she said, pointing out to where Brandon was making his way in from the pasture.

Charlotte gasped when she saw him, saw what he held in his hands. "Flowers," she murmured, placing a hand over her sternum. "Oh, Justice. You two make me long for my youth again. For a man who will bring wildflowers in from the field for me."

Justice lifted one shoulder in a futile attempt to look nonchalant and unaffected. "Maybe they're for you," she suggested, even though every cell in her body hoped the bouquet had her own name on it.

"Of course they are," Charlotte shot back with a gentle elbow jab to Justice's rib. "Because that man out there is head over heels in love with this old woman."

Justice laughed along with her, then sobered as Brandon drew near the house. She straightened her top and asked Charlotte again, "How do I look?"

Charlotte's expression was tender as she reached out to touch Justice's hair where it spilled over her shoulder. "Like a woman in love. A woman ready to risk everything for that love."

Justice bit her lip, then voiced the question racing through her mind. "Does he look like a man who might be willing to take a risk on me?"

Charlotte grinned and nodded, but only said, "I'm taking Nutter out to check on my sheep. You two be good and don't forget to eat." She started out the door, the dog at her heels, then pointed at the two pies cooling on racks on the counter. "And don't you let that boy touch my apple pies."

THIRTY SIX

Brandon tapped on the kitchen door the way he usually did before entering, but when he peered through the screen, he only saw Justice standing at the large bay window that overlooked the barns and pastures. She'd turned to face him when he knocked, and he froze, struck by how soft and feminine she looked, how vulnerable and, if he was reading her right, as unsure of herself as he was. He tucked the bouquet of flowers behind his back, even though she must have seen him from the window, crossing the yard with them. He pulled open the screen door and stepped inside.

"Hi," Justice said, the single word in her sweet familiar voice, one he hadn't heard in days, one he didn't know he could miss so badly, settling around him like home.

"Hey, Justice," he managed to get out, and was surprised to hear that he sounded normal. At least a lot more normal than he felt. "How are you feeling?"

"Much better today, thank you," she said, clasping her hands together in front of her, fingers laced tightly. "We made pie." Her eyes grew wide the moment the words were out.

Brandon grinned. So he wasn't the only nervous one in the room. "I see that. It smells great in here." They were still standing on opposite sides of the large room, he, just inside the door, and Justice with her back to the window, the big square kitchen table between them. He took a step forward. "Is Charlotte around?"

"Oh. No. She, um, went with Nutter. To check on—on the sheep." She closed her eyes briefly, like she was gathering her wits about her. "I guess I'm still a little addle-brained from being sick. I can't seem to form a coherent sentence." She sent him a rueful look.

She was blushing.

She was beautiful.

The sunlight streaming through the window picked up the traces of red in her auburn hair and heightened the pink in her cheeks. And he loved that top she was wearing; the tiny straps that skimmed her pale shoulders, the deep green making her skin practically glow. His fingers itched to touch her, to smooth the hair back from her face—

She chuckled self-consciously, interrupting his wandering thoughts. "I don't know why I said that about the pies. Nothing like stating the obvious for you."

"Sometimes a man needs the obvious spelled out for him." He'd intended it as a man-joke, but realized the truth of the words even as he said them. "At least this one does," he added, taking a few more steps into the room. He felt the need to put a little distance between himself and the door; he didn't want her to think he was poised to run. He had no intentions of cutting out on her, not today. And depending on how things went in the next few minutes, not ever. "You look very pretty. I like your top."

"Thank you." Her blush deepened and she ducked her head. Brandon had never seen Justice shy before, but that's exactly how she looked right now. He wasn't sure whether he liked it or not. Was it really shyness that had her dropping her gaze? Or was it fear of rejection? Fear of him? That thought didn't sit well with him.

"Were you outside a while ago? By the barn?" He'd caught a flash of movement from the corner of his eye, but when he'd turned to look, no one was there. Now he thought perhaps his eyes hadn't been playing tricks on him, after all.

She nodded, sending a spark of anticipation through him. "Yeah. I was looking for you, but... well, I couldn't find you."

Her words pierced him in a way she probably didn't intend them to. "I'm not surprised," he said, his smile gone. "I've had a hard time finding myself lately."

Justice didn't say anything, but she crossed her arms in a subconscious act of self-preservation. Something else he didn't like seeing. His headstrong, confident, bold as brass Justice protecting herself from him.

He took a deep breath and squared his shoulders, then circled the table to come stand in front of her. "But I'm here now."

Justice lifted her gaze to meet his, a beam of light turning her brown eyes into golden amber.

"These are for you." He drew the flowers out from behind his back.

Her hands came up slowly, almost as if she were afraid to believe him, then she lifted the bouquet to smell them. He quickly covered the tops of the flowers with his hand, chuckling at the startled look in her eyes.

"You don't want to smell them. That purple one is putrid. Pretty as a picture, but smells like old goat. Or a family of skunks." That garnered a laugh from Justice, but she brushed her fingertips over the delicate blossoms anyway, her appreciation for them evident in her smile.

"Thank you," she said softly. "They're—they're perfect."

Like you are. He didn't say the words out loud, but he hoped she read the message in his eyes. "They made me think of you," he said instead. "When I was out there in the field, I was struck by how resilient they are, how bright and colorful the purples and yellows are against the dull tones of the summer grasses. Beautiful, resilient, and bold. Spirited. Like you."

"Wow," she whispered, self-consciously bringing the bouquet close to her face again. Then she wrinkled her nose as she caught a whiff. "Oof. I sure hope I smell better." She giggled and looked up at him from under her lashes. "I did finally shower," she told him with a disgusted grimace. "After three—or four?—days."

"Yikes," he teased. "Why do you think I stayed away?"

As soon as the words left his mouth, her brows drew together and her smile faded. "Why did you?" she asked in a small voice. "Stay away, I mean."

He could tell by her tone that she'd been hurt by his disappearing act, but he'd needed the space between them. He'd needed time away from her to clear his head, to think about what life would be like without her, or what kind of life he wanted with her. He'd needed to miss her, to feel the pull of her, to remind himself of why he loved her, needed her, before he could figure out how to remind her that she loved and needed him.

"I mean, I know I was pretty sick. Maybe you were afraid to catch it, and I wouldn't blame you." She was giving him an out, and for a millisecond, just one, he almost opted to take it.

"It wasn't because you were sick," he said, reaching out to touch the curve of her shoulder. He skimmed his fingertips down her arm, a surge of warmth coursing through him when she trembled slightly under his touch. He pulled his hand away, afraid he might give in to the much stronger urge to move in closer. There would be time for that later, God willing.

"Oh." He heard the resignation in her voice and it kind of broke his heart.

"I needed to sort through a few things on my own, Justice." No, that was too vague, too cliché. It sounded too much like an 'it's me, not you' excuse. "I needed to get a good look at myself," he tried again. "Without wondering or worrying about how you looked at me."

"Oh," she said again, but he was pretty sure she still didn't understand.

"I thought about you every minute of every day, though." It wasn't much of a consolation, but he couldn't stand the misery on her face. "And I wanted to come see you," he admitted. "But I wanted to make sure my motives were right. I wanted to *want* to see you for the right reasons. For the best reasons, not just for good reasons."

Justice nodded, her brows still drawn, but her expression softened with his explanation. A silence fell between them as if they were both holding their breath, waiting to see what the other would do or say next.

Brandon glanced around the room, wondering if now was the right moment to broach his question to her. It had taken him no more than twenty-four hours of being away from her to know that it wasn't what he wanted. It had taken another twenty-four to realize that he needed to make it as clear to Justice as it was to him that he wanted her, that he chose her to be the one who held his heart. And he wanted her to know without a doubt that he could be trusted to hold her heart as well.

A grand gesture, Charlotte had charged him. He was here to surprise Justice with a grand gesture. He was thinking big. He was thinking forever.

But suddenly, a rush of insecurity swept through him. What if she said no?

"Why were you looking for me?" On the counter next to the pies was a plate of sandwiches; maybe she'd just come out to tell him it was lunch time. He hoped not.

Justice lowered the flowers and stood a little straighter. The blush hadn't left her cheeks, but now color crept up her chest and neck, too.

Brandon steeled himself for whatever she planned to say. Whatever it was would determine his next move.

"I, um, was looking for you because—" She faltered and looked away, biting her bottom lip. He watched the muscles in her throat work as she swallowed hard before turning back to meet his eyes. Her next words came out in a rush. "I wanted to ask you to go out to dinner with me. On a date."

What? No. No! This was not how this whole thing was supposed to go. He was shaking his head before he even realized it. "No," he said, his voice gruff with frustration.

"No?" Justice took a step back, the flowers trembling in her hand. Her eyes widened in surprise, then almost immediately began to fill with tears. She blinked fast, but not quickly enough. She turned on her heel and strode away from him, skirting the table in quick strides as she shot for the door.

"Wait," he called, his feet slow to take up pursuit of her. But she pushed through the screen door, and dashed out into the breezeway. By the time he stepped outside, the guest room door was closing behind her, and he heard the click of the deadbolt as she locked herself inside.

Away from him.

A stem of purple prairie verbena lay beside the woven doormat where it had fallen, unnoticed, from the bouquet he'd given her.

He'd blown it. Big time.

Talk about a grand gesture.

THIRTY SEVEN

HER WORST FEAR HAD come true. He'd said no.

With her back to the door, Justice slid slowly down until she was sitting on the floor, her body shaking with sobs. She flung the flowers away from her, the bouquet exploding across the floor, and she covered her face with her hands, unable to bear the sight of them. What a fool she'd been to put her heart out there that way.

Risk everything, Charlotte and Courage had told her. That's what she'd done.

Well, at least now she had her answer. And not just a 'no,' either. Brandon's 'no' had been adamant, forceful, appalled, even. And his attempt to stop her from leaving the kitchen had been lackadaisical at best. She was weak from being in bed for days, plus she had a bum leg. He could have caught up with her, stopped her, without much effort at all. But she'd been across the room and pushing the door open before he had even made a half-hearted effort.

She should have known better. She should have trusted her instincts, her fear. She should have listened to her gut and kept her mouth shut, her heart locked down, and her hope caged. She should have—

A knock on the door startled her and she let out a small squeak of surprise. "Justice?"

Brandon. What did he want? She couldn't let him see her crying like this. She held her breath, hoping he'd go away.

"Justice, open up," he said, and from the way his voice carried through the paneling, she could tell his face was close to the door, maybe with his ear pressed to it. Had he heard her sobs?

She eased herself onto all fours and crept across the floor a few feet away from the door, then stood and made a beeline for the bathroom. She'd close herself in there and pretend she hadn't heard him.

"Justice, please," he called out. "Let me explain."

She shook her head as more tears fell. Hadn't he explained himself already? *I needed to sort through a few things on my own*, he'd said. *Without worrying about how you look at me.*

In other words, without her.

She couldn't bear hearing him reject her again, no matter how many different ways he said it, no matter how hard he tried to soften the blow. She closed the bathroom door, turned on the ventilation fan to drown out the sound of his voice, his repeated knocking, then sank to the floor next to the tub. From the rack on the wall above her head, she pulled the wet washcloth she'd used just a half an hour earlier, and pressed the cool, damp fabric to her hot cheeks, to her burning eyes.

A good fifteen minutes later, certain Brandon would have given up by then, she pulled herself to her feet and bent over the sink to splash cold water on her face. Her reflection made it clear that she wouldn't be able to leave the room anytime soon, not unless she wanted to explain to Charlotte why her face was blotchy, her nose red and bulbous, and her eyes puffy and red-rimmed. She was a mess. If only Courage could see her now; her sister always complained that Justice could cry a river and no one would know.

"Now this, dear sister of mine," she muttered to herself, "is ugly crying like you've never seen before."

She switched the vent fan off, then listened for any sound of company before she slowly opened the bathroom door. For a moment, she wondered if Charlotte might be standing on the other side of it, hands on hips, keys in hand, having come in search of her. But the room was empty, and after listening for a few moments, all seemed quiet on the front stoop, too. Good. No Brandon, either.

She sighed heavily at the sight of the flowers strewn across the floor. What a confusing message they'd carried. She couldn't decide whether to sweep the lot into a pile and toss them out the window, or gather them up, hold them to her chest, and revel in the idea of Brandon thinking of her as he carefully plucked each one of the dozens of stems of Indian Paintbrush, false Golden Asters with their camphor-like scent, the stinky purple flowers he'd warned her about—cleomes, she thought, remembering Prudence talking about a flower she called Skunkweed—and brilliant tie-dyed Blanketflowers, spikes of silvery lavender Lupines, and hot pink Fireweed. She thought she'd seen some of the low-growing purple verbena in the mix, too, but maybe not.

Then again, it was probably a mercy bouquet. Trying to let her down easy. *Throw them away,* the bitter little voice in her head snipped.

The rest of the room wasn't exactly neat as a pin, either. Someone had washed the pile of dirty laundry she'd started when they first got here, and her clothes were now folded neatly in a stack on one end of the dresser. But the bags she'd brought in, the duffel with her clothes and the backpack with her toiletries and other miscellany, looked thoroughly rummaged through. "I think it's time to pack up," she muttered. "As soon as he gets that stupid truck fixed, we're outta here."

Indeed, it was time to go home.

Where she belonged.

To the people to whom she belonged.

As much as she liked Charlotte, as much as she loved Brandon, she clearly didn't belong with either one of them.

She made her way around the room and gathered up the flowers, recreating the bouquet as best she could. A few stems were bent or broken, but the majority of the bundle remained intact, in spite of her rough handling. She carefully arranged the flowers in a glass of water in a corner of the vanity counter where the bright colors lent a splash of cheer to the pale blue and white bathroom. She found a hand broom and dustpan under the sink and swept up the scattered bits of leaves and petals left behind.

When she was satisfied that there was no evidence left of her temper tantrum, Justice brought both the duffel bag and the backpack up onto the bed and upended the contents of each. In no time at all, she had everything reorganized and repacked, leaving only enough out to get her through the next two days. They'd likely attend church with Charlotte on Sunday morning, so she hung a floor-length ocher sundress on a hook on the back of the door for the occasion. Of the few dresses she owned, it was her favorite. The fabric didn't wrinkle and she could dress it up or down depending on what shoes and jewelry she wore with it. The color looked good on her, too, which helped her feel better about being in a dress, especially when she paired it her chili pepper red cowboy boots and chunky turquoise jewelry.

Once her bags were packed and as ready to go as possible, she set them on the floor, then kicked off her sandals and settled back onto the bed. She needed to call Courage to tell her how things had gone.

When her sister didn't pick up, Justice texted her, telling her to call when she could, and added a tearful emoticon at the end so Courage would have an inkling that things hadn't gone the way they'd hoped. She laid the phone on the bed beside her, crossed her ankles and laced her fingers over her stomach, then closed her eyes to wait for Courage to call her back.

She came out of a deep sleep suddenly; a noise, a sound, something had startled her awake, her heart pounding with the rush of adrenaline coursing through her system. The light from the window had shifted and softened, indicating that it was well into the afternoon, but at least she hadn't slept the whole day away.

She picked up her phone to see if Courage had called her back, if that's what had disrupted her nap, but there were no missed calls. She grimaced when she saw the time—it was almost four o'clock. She'd been asleep for nearly three hours.

What had awakened her, though? She lay still, listening, her eyes itchy and tender from the quantity of tears she'd shed.

There! A sound at the front door had her turning her head, her eyes honed in on the door knob, half-expecting to see it turn slowly. She held her breath, certain someone was out there on the front step.

Sure enough, she heard the screen door open, and she waited, not daring to breathe, but no knock came. A moment later, the screen door gently latched closed again.

Justice scrambled to her feet and hurried to the window, craning her neck to try to see who'd been out there—Brandon or Charlotte?—but no one came into view. Had Charlotte brought her one of the uneaten

Reuben sandwiches she'd made for lunch? Surely the woman would have knocked, though. Had Brandon come back to try to talk again, then changed his mind at the last minute?

She moved to the door, her hand hovering above the knob. What if it was Brandon and he was still standing right outside?

She pressed her ear to the wood, then said in a small voice, "Hello?"

There was no response.

Finally, unable to stand it a moment longer, she unlatched the deadbolt and cracked the door open half an inch.

No tray of food, no guy with a man bun. Or a braid.

She pulled the door open a little wider and started to reach for the screen door when she saw it. The cluster of purple verbena tied with a piece of dark brown wool to a small envelope with her name on it. It had been left on the narrow threshold between the two doors where Justice would have to be blind not to see it when she finally left the safety of her lair.

She glanced around one more time, but still saw no one. She bent and picked up the missive, then ducked back inside the room and closed the door again. She slowly crossed to the edge of the bed and sat, staring down at the black ink letters that spelled out her name under the lace of the verbena's purple petals.

So it had been Brandon at her door. Where had he disappeared to so quickly? Inside the big house? Or had he known she might be watching for him and purposely stayed out of view of her windows?

Setting the spray of flowers on the night stand next to the lamp, she turned the envelope over in her hands several times, debating on whether or not she should open it. Whether or not she could bear to risk her heart again, even alone and behind the closed door where no one could see her fall apart. "I can't," she whispered, laying the envelope on the comforter beside her. She folded her hands in her lap and bowed her head. "Oh Lord, what do I do?"

A verse from the Bible, one she'd claimed as her own years ago, suddenly popped into her head. *For God has not given us a spirit of fear, but of power and love and self-control.* The first time she'd read that passage, her pulse had raced as the words reached deep down into her very soul.

Power, love, and self-control. Fighting words, they were. And Justice Goodacre was a fighter. She didn't have to let fear dictate her life, her decisions, her choices, because fear did not come from God. Pain might—no, it would—come here on earth. Suffering and sorrow would show up, too; it was inevitable. But she didn't have to face them with fear in her heart. She could look boldly toward whatever came next because God had given her power, love, and self-control, and he expected her to use them.

Brandon may have rejected her, but that didn't mean she had to hide from him, from her love for him.

She picked up the envelope before she could talk herself out of it and carefully tore it open. "Power, love, and self-control," she murmured as she pulled out the single sheet of paper folded in half inside.

Please come look for me again. You'll find me this time, I promise. I'll be waiting for you under the willow tree.

He didn't sign his name. He didn't have to.

Justice stared at the three lines for what seemed like a life time. Could she do it? Could she risk everything one more time?

"Power. Love. Self-control. I can do this," she said aloud. "I can do this."

She got to her feet and crossed to the bathroom where she washed her face and brushed out her bedhead hair. It only took a quick glance in the mirror to determine that she needed a whole new face of makeup, a little extra, in fact, to hide the worst of the damage her crying jag had caused. Brandon wouldn't be fooled, of course, but she wasn't about to face him without her face on.

"This girl needs all the armor she can get," she muttered, validating her decision to pull out her makeup bag a second time that day.

She took her time getting ready, not because she needed it, but because she thought it might be good for Brandon to have to wait. "If he's still there when you finally show up, then you'll know he thinks you're worth waiting for," she told her reflection as she closed one eye to sweep a soft copper shadow into the crease of her upper lid. Maybe she was tempting fate, maybe it was an act of self-preservation. Maybe it was an avoidance tactic, or just a spark of her old obstinate self.

Standing in the middle of the room, she shook out her shoulders, took a couple of deep breaths, then started for the door. The dress she'd pulled out for church caught her eye. She turned and eyed the red boots standing at attention beside her duffel bag.

What had Brandon called her? Resilient. Bold. Spirited. That's right. Well, she'd show him spirited.

Justice stripped out of her blue jeans and green top—it was a little rumpled from her nap, anyway—and slipped the dress over her head, tugging the elastic waist into place and settling the fluttery skirt down over her legs. She dug a clean pair of socks out of her bag, pulled them on, then shoved her feet into the boots. She didn't bother with jewelry, other than the narrow rose gold pinky ring that matched the one Courage wore on her own little finger, rings the twins never removed.

Then, at the last minute, she rooted through her purse for the tiny leather pouch she'd brought with her—her good luck charm. She pried open the drawstring with shaking fingers, then slid the beaded band out into her palm. Without giving herself time to talk herself out of wearing it, she draped it around her wrist and latched it carefully in place.

Risk everything. There is no fear in love.

After one last look at her reflection, she decided she looked ready for whatever Brandon could throw at her. Then she stepped out into the late afternoon sunshine.

The barn cast long shadows over the pasture beyond it, and out in the field, she saw Charlotte wending her way toward the sheep fold on the other side of the barn, her flock scuttling along after her. Charlotte looked up just as Justice stepped out of the breezeway and lifted a hand in greeting. Justice waved back, suddenly nervous.

She peered down at her dress, at the shiny red tips of her boots sticking out from under the ruffled hem of her dress. "What am I doing?" she muttered, wishing Charlotte hadn't seen her. Then she could have ducked back inside and crawled under her covers to hide for the next three days. Now that she'd been seen, she had no choice but to go looking for Brandon. Surely, Charlotte knew about his invitation.

"Why did I put this stupid dress on?" she groused through gritted teeth. At least if she'd stayed in the same clothes she'd had on earlier, she could have feigned ignorance and gone about her business as though she'd never received the note. But no, it was pretty obvious that she'd dressed for the occasion, so there was no pretending she didn't know about it.

Her stomach gurgled loudly, but not purely from nerves. She hadn't eaten since breakfast, and now she was regretting skipping out on the sandwiches. "There'd better be food involved," Justice muttered, patting her belly in sympathy. "Since he's the reason I didn't eat any lunch."

She blew out a long breath, then started across the yard toward the barn. She'd check inside to see if the horses had already been brought inside for the night first, and if Fire was there, she'd exchange a little sweet talk with her favorite boy, giving her time to work up some more courage before facing Brandon.

The barn, however, was empty except for a pretty tabby cat with enormous golden eyes and white feet. "Hello, kitty," Justice said as she approached the animal and bent over to run her palm down the sleek back. The cat rose to her feet and arched up into the caress, then wound itself around Justice's legs a couple times, purring loudly.

"Aren't you a pretty little thing," Justice cooed, but the cat trotted off without letting her pet it again. Even so, the interaction with the creature seemed to help settle her nerves, and she straightened and made her way back out and around the barn.

Fire nickered when he caught sight of her, then cantered over, flinging his head to and fro in greeting as he sidled up to the fence line. "Hello, stud muffin." Justice wished she'd thought to bring a treat with her, but she reached over the fence to stroke the horse's neck and let him blow kisses against her hair. "You are my handsome boy, aren't you?" she gushed when he nudged her head with his nose.

She hadn't yet looked directly at the willow tree, so she wasn't a hundred percent certain Brandon was there, but she felt eyes on her nonetheless. She greeted Tank, then Charlotte's two geldings, then took one more fortifying breath and finally turned her gaze to the tree.

THIRTY EIGHT

It felt surreal, like a dream, Brandon thought, watching Justice make her way around the pasture toward him, the horses trailing her on their side of the fence. Her long dress, the color of sunflower fields, fluttering behind her as she moved, her hair loose and soft around her face. He couldn't take his eyes off her, partly because she was so breathtakingly beautiful, but also because he'd been so afraid she wouldn't show, and now he was afraid if he looked away, she'd disappear.

He'd been waiting for her under the willow tree for almost an hour. He'd seen her pick up the flowers and note he'd left at her door, so he knew how long it had taken her to make up her mind about whether or not she'd accept his invitation. Justice didn't need an hour to get ready for anything. In fact, knowing Justice, he wouldn't be surprised if she'd purposely kept him waiting.

He would have waited another hour, another day, another year, another lifetime, if that's what it took. He wasn't leaving this spot until he'd said what he needed to say.

Justice approached the tree, stopping just beyond the curtain of its branches.

"You came," Brandon said as he stepped forward.

"You're here," she replied, not coming any closer.

"Because I wanted you to find me." He reached out a hand toward her. "Come."

She hesitated just for a moment, then settled her hand in his. He drew her under the whispering leafy canopy to the blanket he'd spread out on the ground in the sun-dappled shade.

"Oh my," she whispered when she saw the picnic basket and the insulated wine carrier off to one side. "What's all this?"

"An early supper," he said, nudging the basket with the toe of his boot. "Or a late afternoon snack, depending on how hungry you are." He thought he saw a flash of relief on her face and he had to bite back a smile. She truly must be feeling better if she was thinking about food.

He stepped onto the blanket, then gave her hand a gentle tug when she once again hesitated to join him. "Come on," he coaxed. "Sit and have something to eat with me. You must be famished."

With a tiny nod, she let him lead her forward, then she sat down, folding her legs beneath the full skirt of her dress.

He waited until she was settled, then turned to the basket and lifted the lid. He'd scoured Charlotte's kitchen and put together a few of Justice's favorite treats: soft bagels with whipped cream cheese spread, a small bowl of firm, tart blueberries, a bag of sundried tomato and basil flavored wheat crackers—"I knew I liked that girl," Charlotte had said when Brandon asked if he could include them in his basket. "They're my favorite, too."—and a Mason jar filled with peanut butter M&Ms. Those he pulled out of his own stash since he and Justice both thought the morsels were pretty much manna from heaven.

"Wow," Justice said, the smile on her face growing wider with each item he pulled from the basket. "You really went all out."

Brandon set between them a mug stuffed with a meat bouquet of hickory smoked beef jerky on the blanket, and the sound that slipped past Justice's lips made his blood race.

"All out," he echoed, chuckling at her wide-eyed response. "Here you go," he said, handing her a pretty plastic plate with a floral design on it. "Dig in while I pour us some drinks."

From the wine cooler, he withdrew a bottle of fancy Italian lemonade, something he'd discovered at the back of Charlotte's pantry. She'd forgotten it was even there and had waved away his offer to pay her for all the stuff he was making off with. "I have a vested interest in this whole thing, too, young man. Everything I have is yours to use as you see fit in your quest to win the fair maiden's hand and heart. Take it with my blessing."

He couldn't keep from grinning as he watched her load up her plate. She spread a bagel that she spread with a thick layer of the cream cheese, spooned up a large helping of fruit, a fistful of crackers, and plucked several pieces of the jerky from the mug. She set her plate on the blanket in front of her, popped a few pieces of candy in her mouth, then took the tumbler of lemonade he handed her. "Thank you."

"There's also some of your apple pie in a container in there," he said, pointing at the basket. "But I figured we'd save that for dessert."

She snickered as she snagged a few more M&Ms from the jar between them. "I hope you cleared that with Charlotte. She was pretty adamant earlier about making sure you kept your hands off the pie."

Brandon pointed a piece of jerky at her. "It cost me," he told her with a laugh. "So don't make me regret it by getting too full to eat any."

"Not possible," Justice said, shaking her head. "Mmm. You did good, Brandon." There was still a cautious glint in her eyes, but her smile seemed genuine. She shifted a little so she could look out over the pasture while she ate. The horses seemed to have lost interest in what they were doing and had wandered off to graze contentedly.

Brandon stretched his legs out in front of him, crossing his ankles and leaning back on one elbow. "Tank and Fire have really enjoyed themselves here," he said, keeping his tone light and conversational. *Feed her first*, he kept telling himself. Then go for broke.

"They look good," she commented in between bites of her bagel. "Fire looks like he's put on a little weight."

Brandon had to admit that both the horses looked a little rounder than they usually did while on the road. "Tank, too. I haven't had much of a chance to exercise them, but I kinda figured with all this room, they'd get enough while we're here. We can get them back into their regular routine once we get home."

She darted a wary, sidelong glance at him, but didn't say anything.

"Have you talked to your sister today?" he asked after a long silence.

"This morning," she responded quietly, then took a long sip of her lemonade and didn't expound. Instead, she set her plate aside and brought her knees up in front of her under her long skirt, wrapping her arms around them. Finally, she said, "Man, I miss her."

"I know." He spoke gently, wishing he felt confident enough to reach over and touch her, to pull her against his side and let her rest her head on his shoulder. But he wasn't going to make any more mistakes today. This was his one shot, and he was going to aim carefully, because he had a feeling it might just be the only shot he had left.

She turned and gave him a sweet smile before resting her chin on her upraised knees and gazing back out at the horses.

"Ready for some pie?" he asked casually, noting that her plate wasn't empty. It was as if she'd suddenly lost her appetite.

She nodded, held out her plate to accept the piece he proffered, but took only two small bites before setting down her fork.

He wished he could see inside her head at that moment, to know what she was thinking. Was she thinking about him or was she thinking about how to get this little rendezvous over with so she could get away from him?

When she finally spoke, her words surprised him.

"I'm ready to go home." It was barely more than a whisper, but there was no uncertainty in her voice. "I know you've committed to staying to fix Charlotte's tractor when the part gets in on Monday, and I'm fine with that, but as soon as it's done, I want to get on the road." A breeze blew some of her hair across her face and she swept it back with one hand, tucking it behind her ear.

Brandon sat up, rehearsing in his mind exactly what he wanted to say. He felt like he was losing her; he had to act now, to speak his mind right here under this willow tree, but he also had to get the words right.

"If you want to stay longer, then I can have Courage or Daddy come pick me and Fire up," she said when he didn't respond right away. "They can be here in a couple of days. And of course, you're welcome to use the trailer as long as you need it," she added.

"No," he shook his head, realizing too late that he was responding to her exactly the way he had in the kitchen that morning. But the last thing he wanted was for them to go their separate ways. Not now.

Not ever.

"It's not up to you," Justice said, not looking at him. She plucked a blade of grass from the edge of the blanket and twirled it between her finger and thumb. "I'm going home on Monday or Tuesday next week. I just need to know if you will take me or if I need to call my family."

"That's not what I meant," he said, shaking his head. "Hold up." He pushed to his feet, then reached down to offer her a hand up, too. "I'm messing this up again."

The wary look was back on her face and Brandon wanted to rail with frustration. It had all been going so well until he'd brought up Courage and home. Why had he gone there? He knew how much Justice was feeling Courage's absence.

"It's all right," Justice told him. "I'm not upset with you, Brandon. I really do understand why this isn't working out anymore, and I'm fine with it. I want us—I want us to stay friends if that's possible, but I can't do that here. I need to go home."

"Please," he said, wishing he could stop the flow of words coming out of her. He took both her hands in his. "Hear me out, Justice, please."

Her fingers quivered in his and she closed her eyes briefly. When she opened them again, he saw the telltale sheen of the tears she was trying to hold at bay.

"What is it, Brandon?" she asked, trying to tug her hands free. He held on a little tighter, refusing to let her pull away. Not yet.

He had so many things he needed to say to her, so many things he needed to set right between them, but he felt it all slipping away from him. Where did he start? How could he make her understand in as few words as possible?

"I—I need to—you need to let go," Justice said, her voice cracking. "Please let go of me." She stepped back and jerked her hands out of his grasp, then crossed her arms over her chest, tucking her fingers against her sides. "Thank you for all of this," she said, her voice trembling, even as she did her best to keep her expression pleasant. "I really was famished." She looked down at the little smorgasbord of treats at their feet.

"What can I do to help clean up?" She didn't wait for an answer, but knelt and started stuffing things back into the basket. "I'll take all of this back to the house if you can get the cooler and the blanket."

"Stop." The word came out hard, and she stilled, but didn't look up at him.

"Justice, stop," he said again, this time more gently. When she didn't rise, he dropped down to one knee in front of her, then pushed the basket and its contents out of the way. She kept her gaze averted, so he reached out and curved his hand against her cheek, not surprised to find it damp with tears.

He moved a little closer. "Please look at me," he murmured, cupping her face with both hands now, tilting her head up. She resisted for a moment, but finally gave in, the raw misery in her soft brown eyes making the last of Brandon's words slip away.

He dipped his head and covered her mouth with his, capturing the surprised gasp that escaped her lips. He felt her jaw muscles clench beneath his palms, and for a moment, he thought she might pull away. He braced himself for the impact of her rejection, but then he felt it, the uncoiling of something wound tight between them, and she sighed, a soft sound of surrender, one he breathed in like a drowning man. Her hands slid up his biceps and over his shoulders until her arms were wrapped around his neck, and he pulled her hard up against him, almost knocking them both off balance.

Justice whimpered softly, but it was a sound of pleasure, not of pain, one he knew so well for having heard it a thousand times in the years she'd been his. He waited for it every time he kissed her, he ached to hear it when they weren't together, and he longed to know what came next, what other sounds she would make in his arms, even though he would wait until the time was right. Until she was truly his.

He broke their kiss just long enough to get to his feet, pulling her up with him, one of his arms wrapped tightly around her waist, the other cupping the back of her head, his fingers wound through her hair as he once again lowered his lips to hers.

This time, though, he held himself in check, and his kiss was gentle, searching, telling her that he recognized her vulnerability, that he knew both the bold and spirited Justice as well as the fragile, breakable parts of her, and that he wanted all of it. He loved all of it.

He loved all of her.

With his kisses, he tried to tell her all the things he couldn't find the words to say.

When the last of her resistance melted away and she sagged against him, he lifted his head and looked down into her eyes. They were soft and heavy-lidded and he had to resist the urge to kiss her again.

Instead, he smiled gently, then let her lay her head against his chest. They stood that way for several minutes, his cheek pressed to her hair, breathing in the fragrance that was so uniquely Justice.

Finally, he felt her draw in a deep breath and exhale it on a long, sweet sigh. He waited to make sure she was steady on her feet, then took a small step back before he spoke.

"Justice," he began, waiting for her to lift her gaze to his. What he saw in her eyes gave him all the courage he needed. Out of all the hundreds of words he'd rehearsed before this moment, he now knew exactly which ones he needed to use. "I love you. I have always loved you, and I will always love you."

That was it. That was all that mattered in the long run.

He slid his palms down her arms to clasp her hands in his. When he touched the bracelet around her wrist, his eyes grew wide and he glanced down at it, then back at her face.

"You kept it," he said gruffly, rubbing the pad of his thumb back and forth over the rows of tiny beads.

"Of course, I kept it," she said, smiling shyly up at him. "I don't wear it anymore because I don't want it to break, but it's always with me."

"Wow," he murmured, feeling his eyes burn with emotion. There was more promise in the fact that she wore the delicate piece of beaded jewelry than he could ever have hoped for.

He dropped to one knee in front of her, and when he reached into his shirt pocket, she covered her mouth in an attempt to catch a gasp.

Brandon smiled up at her before turning her hand over to place a kiss in her palm, never taking his eyes from her beautiful face. "Justice Goodacre, I want to be your home. I want to be the safe place for you to fall. I want to be the sanctuary you run to. I want to have your heart, and I want you to have mine."

Justice was beaming down at him, her eyes glistening with tears.

"Will you marry me, Justice? Will you share the rest of your life with me?"

She was nodding before he finished the last question. She swallowed hard, then whispered, "Are—are you sure?"

Brandon surged to his feet and crushed her to him, holding her tight against him until he could get his emotions in check. He didn't ever want to see that uncertainty on her face again, not when it came to how he felt about her.

He brought both hands up to cup her face, lifting it again so he could look her into eyes. "I have never been more sure of anything in my life."

She smiled up at him, her features lit up by the sunlight flickering through the leaves overhead, then she rose up on tiptoes, slid a hand up the back of his neck and drew him down to meet her kiss halfway. "Then yes," she said against his mouth in between the kisses she planted there. "Yes, yes, yes, to all of it. To all of you."

When she finally let him come up for air, he took her hand in his, the one adorned with the bracelet he'd given her so many years before, and lifted it between them.

"This is just a place holder," he said, then slipped a delicate band of tiny colorful beads on her ring finger. She let out a very feminine sound of delight that made him chuckle, and she pressed both her hands flat over her heart.

"I love it," she exclaimed, her voice breathless with happiness. "Did you make this for me?"

Brandon nodded, elated over her response. "I did. A while ago."

She cocked her head and looked up quizzically. "What's a while ago?"

"The moment I knew I wanted to marry you." He shrugged, and kissed the tip of her nose. "I think I was ten. I'm amazed it actually fits you."

"Oh, Brandon," Justice gushed. "You've been carrying it around all these years?" She pressed her hand to her chest and covered it with the other. "I love it. It's perfect, and I'll have you know this is no placeholder. This is my engagement ring."

Brandon chuckled, pulling her close again, dipping his head for one more heady kiss. "Whatever you want, woman," he said.

"This," she murmured softly, resting her cheek against his chest. "I want this. I want you. I love you, Brandon, with all my heart and soul."

EPILOGUE

Charlotte couldn't have been more pleased when she caught sight of Brandon and Justice meandering slowly across the back yard toward the house, arm in arm, both of them smiling like children on Christmas morning. Brandon carried the picnic basket in his free hand, the blanket flung over his shoulder, one corner dragging along the ground behind him unnoticed, the drink bag nowhere to be seen. They'd likely left it somewhere under the willow tree, too caught up in the sweet euphoria of making up and second chances to notice they didn't have it. They could get it later when they brought the horses in, although she might have to remind them to do that, too.

She had good news for them, too. Tony from the parts store had called to tell her that her order had arrived early, and she was heading into town to pick it up in a few minutes. While she was there, she was also going to stop by Rosita's to pick up a few orders of their famous fish tacos—Charlotte couldn't let the kids leave without trying them.

She'd send them on their way as soon as Brandon finished her tractor—she had no doubt he'd have it up and running by noon tomorrow—but she had every intention of seeing them again. She'd been serious about coming to their wedding, and if they took her advice, it would be sooner than later. In the few short days they'd spent together, Charlotte had experienced a kinship with the two young people—Justice, especially—that she hadn't felt with anyone in a very long time. If she'd had a daughter, surely, she'd have been just like the young woman out there.

Charlotte couldn't wait to meet the rest of the Goodacre family. Something about Justice gave Charlotte a sense of belonging, not just to some *place,* but to some*one.*

She liked the sound of that. She liked the way it resonated in her heart, in her very soul. She liked the idea of belonging to some*one* after all these years.

And who knew? While there, she might just discover some new *place* to belong to as well.

Prudence, the sixth Goodacre sister, believes in soulmates, in the kind of love that transcends time and space.
But what if her soulmate doesn't believe in her?

Are you ready to read the next book in the Seven Virtues Ranch Romance Series?
My Dear PRUDENCE
~ ~ ~

PRUDENCE HAS AN UNCANNY ability to read people. Some call it women's intuition, others say she's an old soul; her insight carries weight, and when she speaks, folks tend to listen. She knows better than most that sticks and stones may break bones, but words have the power to both heal and inflict immeasurable pain.

Although Prudence imparts wisdom and clarity into the lives of others, hers is hobbled by deferred hopes and shelved dreams.

Once upon a time, she thought she knew her own heart... and the heart of the man she offered it to. But his soul-crushing rejection made her question the idyllic truth she lived by: that love conquers all.

It's taken some time to accept the loss of her innocence, but she's found solace, if not exactly contentment, in the haven of Seven Virtues Ranch.

Collin Stewart remembers things differently. And now he just wants a chance to explain.

But Prudence isn't prepared to rearrange her memories, not even for him.

She has good reason to keep him at arm's length, lest he prove her fears right and run roughshod over what's left of her heart.

But love and fear cannot share the same ground, Prudence must choose which one she's willing to risk her hope and happiness on. And this time, she's not the only warrior wielding a weapon.

Collin is armed with words of his own, and every one of them is like a siren call to her battered heart.

~ ~ ~

Keep reading for your sneak peek from
My Dear PRUDENCE

A Note from Becky

An Excerpt: My Dear Prudence

Chapter 1

~ ~ ~

"IT'S BEAUTIFUL, ISN'T IT?" Prudence whispered, leaning her head on her father's shoulder. Her hand rested in the crook of his elbow as they stood in the foyer of the little church, peering through the open doors into the sanctuary. The room was hushed, anticipation heavy in the air. A champagne-hued satin runner covered the dated burgundy carpet of the aisle, and the pews were cordoned off with draped ribbon, each wooden bench festooned with bouquets of dried flowers, sprays of autumn leaves and curling willow branches. At the front of the church, up on the dais, an arched trellis made of woven birch saplings stood ready, decorated with similar autumnal foliage. On either side of it, matching waterfall candelabras were lit, the flames aglow in their elegant crystal globes.

"It makes my chest ache to look at it," Daddy murmured, more to himself than to her, she thought. Then he patted the back of her hand and turned to smile down at her.

Prudence's heart, too, felt enormous and tight in her chest. It overflowed with love for the family and friends gathered together for this momentous occasion, to celebrate the beginning of a life-long journey for her sisters, Courage and Justice, and for the men to whom they were, at that very moment, preparing to pledge themselves. How right that the twins should share this most precious day, and how noble that Joe Lynxwilder and Brandon Stillwater were only too happy to stand together before practically all of Plumwood Hollow in order to make their brides happy.

Even God seemed to be granting special favors today. There was a definite nip of pending winter in the air outside, but the sun was shining crisp and warm in a cerulean sky. The trees had burst into riotous color over the last two weeks, and the rain that typically fell sporadically all month long had taken an unexpected sabbatical a few days earlier. The local weather forecaster—and Daddy, who was usually more accurate than any old weather channel—wasn't calling for more precipitation for at least another three days.

"You've done a beautiful job, sweetheart," Jed said, leaning over to plant an affectionate kiss on Prudence's temple. "Your mother would be so proud. As am I."

"It wasn't only me," she corrected. "I just helped. Trilby and Alexia, they're the wedding planners."

Jed turned toward her and cupped her upper arms in his big, gnarled hands. "Pixie Cut, look at me." He'd started calling her that the day she discovered the pair of scissors in the bathroom cabinet, and chopped off the majority of her near-black curls. Her five older sisters had produced a variety of responses, all negative—Faith had actually cried—but her mother had smiled and hugged Prudence to her rounded belly; Mama had been well into her pregnancy with Abby at the time. Then with those same scissors, and with patient, gentle hands, she'd cleaned up the mess her daughter had made.

A pixie cut, Mama had said. *It suits you perfectly, my little fairy child.*

She'd been Pixie Cut to Daddy from that day on.

And Prudence had pretty much kept her hair the same style since. It was her clearest memory of her mother, and every time she cut it, a task she'd grown much better at over the years, she imagined her mother's sweet smile of approval, of acceptance.

"What?" She looked up into her father's face. His expression was equal parts stern and adoring as he studied her.

"You have worked hard to make this day special for your sisters, just as you worked hard to make Faith's wedding day special, and Hope's wedding day special, and even Charity's anniversary party last month special. I know how much of yourself you pour into these events, and I want you to *know* that I know. I look around and see your love for your sisters everywhere in this sanctuary." He pulled her into a sturdy hug, holding her a little longer than he usually did. She heard him swallow hard before he added, "I see you, Pixie Cut."

"Stop, Daddy," Prudence whispered against his bony shoulder. Age had whittled away at the thick layers of working-man muscles Jed had once sported, but he would always be a giant of a man to her. She sniffed his neck, breathing in the old-fashioned scent of his shaving soap, and willed herself to keep it together. "You'll make me cry and ruin my makeup."

He set her away from him, gave her shoulders one last squeeze, then bent forward and kissed her on the forehead. "You don't need any makeup."

Prudence rolled her eyes at him, but she knew he only said it to tease her. Back in her early high school years, they'd had it out about her creativity with hair products and cosmetics, and he'd come to terms with her blue and pink streaks, her false eyelashes, green nail polish and purple lipstick, accepting that it was just her way of expressing herself. By the time she graduated, she'd toned things down considerably, and although he still insisted that he preferred his girls 'without all that goop' on their faces, it was never really an issue with him. In fact, he got a kick out of the elaborate makeup and costumes Prudence donned when she did photo shoots for her Pixie Cut Botanicals website. She'd disappear into the woods for hours with her camera, a tripod, and an assortment of flowery, fluttery outfits, all made up to look like something straight out of a Tolkien book. She'd return after the sun had set with a whole new series of otherworldly images featuring her as part human, part forest creature.

"I love you, Daddy," Prudence said, reaching up to pat his cheek, appreciating the smoothness of his freshly shaved jaw under her palm. "You look quite debonair today, you know."

Jed stepped back, smoothed his jacket front and squared his shoulders. "You think?" he asked, arching one brow, an expression the eldest Goodacre sister, Faith, had down pat. It always made Prudence laugh when she saw it on either of them.

"Mama would fall head over heels for you all over again," she assured him. Then in a softer voice, she added, "I so wish she were here today."

"Well, now, I do believe she is, daughter of mine." Jed gestured out the large foyer windows to the glorious day outside. "Who do you think petitioned God for the weather this week?"

"Of course," Prudence agreed, but she didn't miss the telltale glisten in her father's eyes. She knew full well that he would prefer his sweet Caroline to be standing right there with them, too.

With all his daughters getting married and moving on, Prudence couldn't imagine how Daddy must be feeling, the house he built for his wife and girls emptying out around him. It had to be a little like saying goodbye to Mama all over again, but in bittersweet increments, one piece of his heart at a time. Was it any wonder he'd made the decision last year to buy the property across Carpenter Road where he planned to build something new for himself?

All his daughters except for her, that is. Abby wasn't getting married any time soon, at least not that anyone was aware of, but she was definitely moving on. She'd migrated to Nashville right after high school when some big country music hotshot had scooped her up after seeing her play at The Smokehouse last year.

Prudence, however, had no plans to marry or move on from Seven Virtues Ranch and Plumwood Hollow. If she had her way, she'd stay right where she was, plant her gardens, make her bath and body products in what Daddy called her Mad Hatter's Workshop, and only leave the ranch to go to work at Trilby's Flowers and Books. Part time. Except when she was helping Trilby and her wedding planner, Alexia, put together events like this one.

Now that Courage and Justice were moving forward with their trick riding school at Seven Virtues, however, would there still be a place for Prudence on the ranch? The only home she'd ever known?

Was she destined to become the old maid of the family, living off the good graces of her sisters?

Courage was moving in with Joe and his delightful mother, Sarah, but Justice and Brandon would make the ranch house their home. Like that wasn't going to be awkward, especially once Abby headed back to

Nashville in a few days. Just her and Daddy and the two newlyweds in the bedroom across from Prudence. And once Daddy moved out? Ugh.

Maybe she should talk to her father about her moving to the new place with him. Her heart wilted at the thought.

She didn't want to move. She might be floundering, unsure of what she wanted out of life—.

No, she knew what she wanted, but what she wanted, she couldn't have.

So until she could figure out where she belonged, she needed to stay in the safety and security of the ranch.

"Aunt Pru? Where are you?" Her niece's voice echoed down the corridor that led to the Sunday School classrooms the wedding parties had commandeered as dressing rooms. Faith's daughter, Jasmine, came darting around the corner, dragging along with her Yvette, her best friend turned cousin by marriage, thanks to Hope winning the great big heart of the great big town butcher and Yvette's father, Levi Valiente. The cousins were still young enough to relish the role of flower girls, and they looked lovely in matching garnet dresses, black patent leather Mary Janes, and twig and berry crowns—handmade by Prudence—in their hair. Their faces sparkled with a combination of sheer giddiness and a touch of glittery makeup, and they each touted delicate wicker baskets nearly overflowing with colorful autumn leaves they'd be scattering in the path of the brides and Grandpa Jed in less than an hour.

"We're here, you beautiful girlies," Prudence said, greeting the two with a wide smile. They looked like something right out of a bridal magazine, Jasmine with her sun-burnished chestnut curls, golden skin, and moss-green eyes, and Yvette, her exotic mocha coloring and straight blue-black hair swept away from her face, eyes the color of brown velvet set off by sooty lashes and slashing brows.

"Grandpa! You're here, too. Good." Jasmine gave him a quick squeeze around his waist then leaned back to look up at him. "Mommy wants to know if you've seen Abby. She still isn't here."

Jed hugged her back, then stretched a hand out to Yvette, who still waited to be invited into the affectionate relationship he offered her; Hope and Levi's marriage made Jed Yvette's grandfather, too. He didn't push her, though; he just kept making a point to include her, to involve her, in the hopes that one day, she'd feel just as comfortable with him as Jasmine did. "I haven't seen her yet," he told them.

Jasmine turned to Prudence. "And we've been waiting for you so we can take pictures of all of us dressing and doing each others hair and makeup and all that girlie stuff."

Jed chuckled and tugged on one of Jasmine's curls. "Why don't you three head back to the girlie stuff room and I'll see if I can hunt down Abby. She should have been here by now."

Abby had arrived in town late the night before, and had begged off going to the church with the rest of them first thing in the morning. She'd promised to get ready at home, and be there at least an hour before the wedding, in plenty of time for pictures. Unable to attend in person, she'd video chatted with them during the rehearsal the evening before, and assured Prudence she knew exactly what was expected of her.

"Thank you, Daddy," Prudence said, stepping forward to join the girls. "I hope you don't have to go home and drag her out of bed. She called half an hour ago and said she was almost ready, but you know how she can be."

Jed waved her and the girls off. "I'll deal with Abby. You scoot."

Chapter 2
~ ~ ~

When the wedding invitation first arrived, Collin was surprised by the unsettling wave of what felt like jealousy that surged through him. Jealousy toward his buddy, Joe Lynxwilder... but not because he coveted his friend's soon-to-be bride, Courage Goodacre. Actually, how that had all come about was still a bit of a puzzler to him. How on earth had the quiet farmer Joe won the heart of one of the fancy pants trick riding twins, The Twisted Sisters? Surely, that was a love story worth hearing.

No, the surge of jealousy, swift and unprecedented, was because he had once entertained illicit thoughts of having one of Jedediah Goodacre's lovely young daughters for himself. The second to last one, specifically.

Prudence, with her elfin features, those luminous eyes that seemed to see right into people's souls, her skin so pale it was almost translucent, her dark hair all choppy and messy, like she'd just rolled out of bed and hadn't even thought to run a comb through it. Knowing her—and he liked to think he had, at least at one time—he wasn't sure if she even owned a comb. Or a brush. Or whatever women used to fix their hair these days.

Well, he knew she owned a pair of scissors. She'd once told him she cut her hair herself.

Did she still dress in the chaotic mismatched outfits she'd once preferred? Tops she pieced together from scraps of fabric and other people's castoffs, skirts with jagged hemlines that looked like something out of Picasso's wardrobe. Boots in all colors and styles, or strappy gladiator sandals that looked like a chore to lace up?

And the flowers. She always had a sprig of something colorful tucked into her hair, in a pocket, or a small bouquet clutched in her hand.

He stared at the double wedding invitation from Joe and Courage and Brandon and Justice. Now that was no surprise. Brandon Stillwater had practically imprinted on Justice Goodacre when they were kids. Collin had heard that story more than once during his time in Plumwood Hollow.

No, his eyes weren't focused on the letters of the invitation, or the words they formed.

A wedding. He imagined, just for a moment, standing before his friends and family, watching Prudence and her father walking toward him, her crystalline gaze locked with his, her bow-shaped lips curved in a smile of anticipation, her snowdrop skin tinted pink with happiness...

Then he replayed the last moments he'd spent with her, the things he'd said—the things he'd left unsaid. How her enormous eyes glistened before she lowered her chin in shame, her mouth a thin line of repressed pain.

No, he'd done nothing to ever deserve a celebration like the one to which he'd been invited, and he'd be the first to acknowledge as much.

But it didn't change the fact that he still longed for it with every fiber of his being, a longing that hadn't lessened in the five years that had passed since he'd last set eyes on Prudence Goodacre.

~ ~ ~

Read the rest of Prudence's story today!

My Dear Prudence: Seven Virtues Ranch Romance Book 6